ALL
HEARTS COME
HOME
FOR
Christmas

ALL
HEARTS COME
HOME
FOR
Christmas

*A Regency
Christmas Collection*

SARAH M. EDEN
ANITA STANSFIELD
ESTHER HATCH
JOANNA BARKER

Covenant Communications, Inc.

Covenant

Cover image: *Woman in the Snow* © Sandra Cunningham / Trevillion Images

Cover design by Christina Marcano © 2019 by Covenant Communications, Inc.

Published by Covenant Communications, Inc.
American Fork, Utah

Printed in the United States of America
First Printing: September 2019

11 10 9 8 7 6 5 4 3 2

ISBN 978-1-52441-109-1

CHRISTMAS AT FALSTONE CASTLE

SARAH M. EDEN

KIELDER CHRISTMAS GUESTS
BY MARRIAGE

Kielder

Joseph Boyce,   Harriet,
Duke of Kielder   Dowager Duchess of Kielder

Lancaster

Adam Boyce, —❤— Persephone
Duke of Kielder

Harry Windover —❤— Athena

Evander

Arabella Hampton —❤— Linus

James Tilburn, —❤— Daphne
Earl of Techney

Artemis

CHAPTER ONE

Falstone Castle, Northumberland
1785

FALSTONE CASTLE HAD BEEN ADAM Boyce's haven for all his seven years of life, the place where he and his father had lived and been happy. But Father was gone now, snatched away without the tiniest warning. Everything that had been safe and warm was empty and cold without him.

The servants moved Adam's things from the nursery, lugging them by the armful. He swallowed back a lump emotion. Everything about this was wrong.

His nursemaid, Nurse Robbie, stood beside him, watching the efforts.

"I don't want to leave the nursery," he told her. "I like being here."

"The master's rooms are yours now by rights," she said.

"But I'm only seven," he said.

"Aye, but you're a wee duke now. Your father taught you to be a duke; I know he did."

He most certainly had. One of Father's many lessons was that dukes don't cry. Adam took a shaky breath. *Dukes don't cry.* Even when every crack in his heart ached. *Dukes don't cry.*

"Is Mama—is my mother staying?"

"Only until you leave for school, love." Nurse Robbie put an arm around his slight shoulders. "Then she's for Town."

Of course she was. Mother hadn't lived at Falstone Castle for years. Even before she'd moved away for good, Adam had few memories of her being present for more than a day or two at a time, always running off on an adventure. She'd written to Father, but never to say that she was coming home.

After a time, Father had stopped reading the letters and Adam had stopped hoping she would return. She'd come back for the funeral but was leaving again.

"I'm going to be all alone." Adam tried to hold back his tears like a good duke.

"You'll not be alone. I'll be here 'til you're grown. Jeb'll stay. We're not family to you, but we care about you, sweet bairn."

"Dukes aren't supposed to be sweet."

She chucked him under his chin. "Dukes also aren't supposed to be seven years old. But I suspect you'll manage."

"I don't want to be the duke." He couldn't entirely hold back his emotions. "I want Father to be the duke again."

Nurse Robbie pulled him into a full-armed embrace. "We'd all like that. He was a good man, your father. Took good care of the castle and all who live here. A good man and a good duke."

"And a good father," Adam added, breathing through the pain searing his chest.

"The best of fathers," she answered.

"And he never called me 'My poor boy' like Mother does just because my face is scarred and ugly."

"Scarred, aye, but not ugly."

He tossed her a dry look of disbelief. "I know what I am."

With a smile she asked, "And what are you, my wee Adam?"

He pushed out a breath. "I'm a duke."

A footman placed a traveling trunk in the corridor.

"That isn't mine," Adam said.

"It's Her Grace's," the man answered, sketching a bow.

Mother was already packing, already preparing to leave, just as she had done again and again all his life. She was never there when he wanted her to be. When she did come, she didn't stay. Now he didn't even have Father to care about him and help fill that Mother-shaped void.

His eyes filled with tears as he stared at that trunk, willing it to unpack, to be put away for good.

Don't go, Mother, he silently pleaded. *Don't leave me here alone.*

Another trunk was placed beside the first, and he had his answer. His next breath shuddered. He sniffled and hiccupped. *I am a duke now,* he reminded himself.

Father had taught him to be a duke.

Adam fortified his seven-year-old heart. If Mother didn't love him, he wouldn't allow himself to love her or long for her or need her. The pain in his heart was so enormous he knew he wouldn't be able to bear it if he couldn't relieve it somehow.

He simply wouldn't care. About her. About anyone. Not ever again.

I am a duke now. Dukes don't cry. And dukes don't need people.

CHAPTER TWO

Newcastle, 1816

WITH INARGUABLY MORE THAN HALF her life already lived, Harriet Boyce, the dowager Duchess of Kielder, looked back to find her regrets far outweighed her comforts.

She sat in the sitting room of a dear friend, one of many she'd spent a great deal of time with over the last thirty years, as the gathered group chatted about their plans for the Christmas season. They were all being welcomed to the homes of their children, anticipating a Holy Season spent in the warm embrace of their families. In years past, at least some of her friends had spent Christmas with each other.

Harriet alone had no anticipation of a warm familial welcome.

Her marriage had been contracted at a time when no one of birth considered anything beyond monetary and social benefit when arranging a match. Joseph, the late Duke of Kielder, had been a good man; she had never said or believed otherwise. But they had been horribly ill-suited to one another. And she had been so very young, completely unprepared for the confusion and frustration of their seemingly hopeless situation. She'd made a mull of the entire thing, as had he.

Joseph had been gone for more than thirty years now. In those three decades, she had seldom returned to the home they had once shared. Falstone Castle housed too many difficult memories and heavy emotions. More difficult even than that, it housed Adam, their son.

Her estrangement from him was, without question, the greatest regret of her entire life.

"What of you, Harriet?" Belinda asked. "Where do you plan to spend Christmas?"

"To be perfectly honest, I haven't the first idea."

Two of her friends looked at each other before Juliet spoke. "We cannot like the idea of you being alone. I am certain you could join either of us. Our children would make room."

That was lowering. Harriet was to be an uninvited and, likely, unwanted guest in someone's home. She could be that with her own family.

She and Adam were on better terms now than they had been before his marriage eleven years earlier. She saw him every Season in London. His wife had softened him and eased his frustration with his too-often-absent mother. They'd rebuilt some of their connection. They got on well enough, but only in London.

She'd been invited to the weddings of Adam's sisters-in-law as well as the christening of his little boy, Oliver, a short three years ago. Attending those events, however, had required she travel to her one-time home. All the tension, the resentments, the regrets that stood between them returned with overwhelming force when they were at Falstone Castle.

In the walls of that imposing structure she could no longer deceive herself. She had been a poor excuse for a mother, and she didn't know if that could ever be made right.

"I may be taking a trip to Northumberland near Christmastime," she said. "I am to be a grandmother again, you know."

"So soon?" Belinda asked.

Harriet nodded. "One difficulty for long-torsoed ladies is that estimating when to expect a baby to arrive is made more difficult. Persephone is nearer her time than we realized."

That launched the group into a discussion of confinements that had begun before or after they were anticipated and the difficulties of being very small-scaled versus larger-scaled when carrying a child. Harriet had introduced the topic of Adam and Persephone's expected arrival as a means of turning the conversation away from pity-inspired offerings of lodging, but she found her efforts had only added weight to her own mind.

She hadn't been at Falstone when little Oliver was born. It was more than her pathetic helplessness when faced with physical ailments or pain and suffering. It was Falstone Castle itself. Everything was more difficult there. Happiness. Peace. Any degree of closeness with her son.

But she wanted to be at the castle to welcome this newest arrival. She'd been a failure as a mother, but she would like to be a decent grandmother and mother-in-law. And part of her still hoped there was a way to salvage something of a relationship with Adam, one that could survive the weight of the castle and all the regrets it held.

"So you intend to be there for the birth of your grandchild?" Juliet asked.

The idea grew stronger in Harriet's mind and heart. Adam loved his sweet little family. They meant all the world to him. Showing them her love and devotion would go a long way toward convincing him that she cherished him as well.

And oh, how she longed to have a place in her family. It was her own fault she didn't, and she wanted to make that right.

Adam, she knew, would allow her to visit whenever she wished, but he would not necessarily truly welcome her. Not there. Not to that home where she had abandoned him so long ago.

But nothing was ever mended without effort. She was more than willing to work to claim a deeper connection with him. She loved him; she truly did. But she knew he didn't believe that.

"I think I will travel north," she said in answer to her friend's question. "It has been a very long time since I spent Christmas at Falstone Castle."

* * *

Falstone Forest, Northumberland

Roswell Duncan had been the vicar of Falstone parish for six years now. It was a quiet living, a small parish, isolated and relatively uncomplicated. Anyone hearing him describe a living that required he endure the unpredictable temper of the infamous Duke of Kielder as "uncomplicated" would likely assume he was either jesting or a bit mentally unstable. Yet Roswell found the situation very much to his liking.

The position had come available not long after his late wife had passed away. He'd been looking for a new start, a place where he could begin again and relieve some of the weight on his heart and spirit. He was too old now for a bustling village where his presence and efforts would be in constant demand. This parish had proven perfect.

And lonely.

He drove his humble pony cart along the road that cut through Falstone Forest. Though Christmas remained a number of weeks away, a whisper of it hung in the air. The forest sat quiet, the birds having made their annual migration to warmer climes. Cold nipped at Roswell's face, filling his heart with cherished memories of winters gone by. He particularly enjoyed his sermons as the Holy Day approached, focused as they were on brotherly kindness, love, forgiveness, hope. Christmas was a time of miracles, and he felt in his heart of hearts that one awaited him this year.

Roswell passed through the outer wall of Falstone Castle. He had come to call on the resident family. Though the duke was gruff and often impersonable, the duchess was a favorite. She was kind and thoughtful, welcoming and friendly. He was made to feel like part of her family when he called, a mixture of uncle to her and her sister, who lived at the castle as well, and grandfather to her son, the little Lord Falstone. She was soon to be delivered of another child, and he was anxious to offer what support he could.

"Good afternoon, Your Grace," he greeted as he crossed the sitting room to where the duchess stood, smiling at his arrival. "How are you faring today?"

"Quite well, thank you." She motioned for him to sit.

"How was your trip to Shropshire?" he asked.

"Quick," she said. The family had only just returned from the duchess's family home for the second time in as many months. "But attending my brother's wedding was worth the whirlwind journey. He is so very happy, and I absolutely adore his new wife. It was such a joy to see them begin their life together."

"Are you here to stay for a time?" he asked.

She nodded. "Until well after this little one makes an appearance." She tenderly patted her belly, now rounded enough to reveal the impending arrival expected near Christmas.

Miss Lancaster, the duchess's youngest sister, stormed into the room. She never did make an entrance without some degree of drama. Roswell was rather fond of her, truth be told. If he'd had a daughter of his own, he would very much have enjoyed a theatrically entertaining girl.

"Is Mr. Jonquil coming for Christmas?" she demanded of her sister without preamble.

"No, dearest," the duchess replied. "He will be with his own family."

"Good." She jutted her chin. "One houseguest will be plenty enough, considering we have done nothing but travel from one house to another without so much as a fortnight in our own home, with some degree of peace and quiet."

Peace and quiet? That didn't sound like Miss Lancaster at all.

"I hope Linus doesn't intend to invite him *here* in the future. I might have to run away from home." On that threat, she spun about and left again. Miss Lancaster was something of a cyclone.

The duchess sighed. "I think she is going to be the death of Adam and me."

"But what a merry death it will be." Roswell laughed.

She poured him a cup of tea, offering it with all the grace of a seasoned hostess.

"Your sister indicated you were to have a houseguest," he said between sips.

"Yes," she said. "Adam's mother is coming."

Roswell nearly choked on his tea. The dowager was visiting? Merciful heavens, he hadn't been prepared for that revelation.

She'd intrigued him from the very first. The brief interactions they'd had over the years had only added to that. She was a bit uncomfortable around her son, but she clearly loved him. The lady, who was within a few years of his age, was a beauty, graceful and refined. She was cheerful and friendly, showed concern for the parishioners, no matter that she ranked so far above them all. He liked her very much indeed. And she was coming to Falstone for the Holy Season.

"I look forward to seeing Her Grace again." He was proud of the steadiness of his voice. No one, he was determined, would ever be given sufficient clues to piece together his pointless partiality. "How does His Grace feel about his mother's visit?"

"That is the source of my worries," she said. "Theirs is a difficult relationship."

Roswell nodded. He was aware of their strained connection, though he did not know the reason for it. "What can I do to ease your concerns?"

"I am hopeful you would be willing to visit us often and at length," she said. "Though he hides it well, my husband finds your company to his liking."

Roswell suspected as much but knew better than to say as much to the man all of Society referred to as the Dangerous Duke.

"And you are a calming influence here, on him, on my sister, on my too-often-worried mind. Having you here might prevent disaster."

"I will of course come by as often as you would like," he said.

"I am tempted to suggest you simply stay here for the weeks she will be in residence," Her Grace said. "It would simplify things."

"And it would be far less lonely." He made the admission before he'd realized the words were coming.

True to character, Her Grace responded with immediate concern and kindness. "Then, you simply must stay. No one should be lonely at Christmas, certainly not someone as beloved as you are by us."

"It would not be too much?" he pressed. "You have a houseguest and an expected tiny arrival. I do not wish to be a burden."

She smiled. "Your presence will give my mother-in-law someone to talk with, my husband a reason to keep his annoyance in check, and me the reassurance that I will still be able to enjoy a chat with you over tea. That is the very opposite of a burden."

He accepted the invitation, mind spinning and heart warming with glad relief. It was the first Christmas in six years that he wouldn't be spending by himself. The prospect of being granted the company of the very intriguing dowager duchess only added to the appeal.

This might very well be the best Christmas he'd had in a long, long time.

CHAPTER THREE

Entering the drawing room at Falstone Castle to find Adam standing with his hand on little Oliver's shoulder was like stepping back in time. Whenever Harriet had returned to Falstone while Joseph was alive, this was the scene that greeted her, but with Joseph in the role of father and Adam, the tiny boy, watching her with such obvious uncertainty.

There had been no one there on those long-ago days to bridge the gap between them. Thank the heavens for Persephone. The dear lady crossed the room with arms extended and welcomed Harriet warmly.

In a low voice Harriet asked, "Is Adam terribly upset about my visit?"

"No," Persephone answered with every indication of sincerity. "He is nervous, and you know all too well his tendency to hide that behind grumpiness."

Her own son was nervous about having her visit. That was not reassuring.

She offered a smile to Oliver. He watched her with curiosity but not a great deal of warmth.

Adam nudged him forward. "Offer a greeting."

Oliver took a long step toward her. "Welcome to Falstone Castle." He crossed one arm around his front and the other around his back, then bent at the waist, bowing deeply.

Adorable.

As he straightened, his eyes darted to his mother. "Did I do good?" he asked in a loud whisper.

"Just perfect," she answered.

With a grin wide as the sky itself, he spun and rushed back to Adam, throwing his arms around his father's leg. "I did good, Father."

Adam ruffled his hair. "Well done." His gaze shifted to Harriet. "Welcome, Mother."

Once upon a time, he had rushed to her when she arrived at the castle, telling her in great detail about his interests and plans, begging her to tell him of her most recent adventures. How she'd missed that when she'd been away. How she missed it now.

"Thank you for having me," she said. "It has been a long time since I spent Christmas with family."

"Yes, it has." He scooped Oliver up into his arms.

The little boy poked at and played with the vast web of scars on his father's face. Adam had always been sensitive about them. Not so very long ago, anyone, even his own child, drawing attention to the disfigurement would have deeply disconcerted him. It did Harriet's heart good to see he was doing better in that respect. It eased a little of the guilt she felt every time she was confronted with the reality of what the surgeons had done to him.

Still pushing at the widest of his father's scars, Oliver asked, "When is Mama's baby going to be here? I've been waiting for a long time."

"Not until after Christmas." Adam spoke with gentle patience, something most of Society would likely think impossible. He was feared by nearly everyone; he preferred it that way.

Oliver turned a full-featured pout on his mother. "Can't you get it sooner?"

"No, darling," she said with a smile. "Babies come when they are ready."

Harriet had spent time with this sweet little family in London without feeling like such an outsider. But here, in her one-time home, she never seemed to belong. This had always been Joseph's domain. She had no place at Falstone Castle.

"Aunt Artemis." Oliver wriggled from his father's arms and rushed past Harriet. The duchess's youngest sister had only just stepped inside the room. "Can you get Mama's baby here?"

Artemis's eyes pulled wide with barely withheld laughter. "No, I can't."

Oliver's brow and lips pulled down. He thrust his arms downward with a huff of frustration. That fearsome look mimicked his father so perfectly. It was rather amazing his mother and aunt—and grandmother, for that matter—managed to not laugh out loud.

Persephone crossed to Adam, who set his arm around her without hesitation or embarrassment. How very much he had changed in the years those two had been married. Little Oliver slipped his hand in Artemis's, as comfortable with her as he was with his parents.

Harriet, alone, remained without a companion in the family vignette.

"It is good to see you again, Mother Harriet," Artemis said. "I have a new book of fashion plates I would love to peruse with you. Your taste is impeccable."

"Thank you." The compliment meant more than the young lady likely knew. Harriet felt so utterly unneeded in that moment. To have a role, even as fashion arbitrator, was a godsend.

"I am also in desperate need of your opinion on the coiffure I have adopted in honor of the approaching Holy Season." Artemis turned her head enough to reveal a lovely twist of braids with sprigs of holly tucked tastefully throughout. "Adam says it is a ridiculous affectation I have chosen specifically to annoy him. I say it is gorgeous." Artemis looked at her once more. "What is your verdict?"

"I say it is both."

Absolute, undeniable mischief entered the young lady's eyes as her gaze darted to Adam.

"Let's go to the nursery, Aunt Artemis," Oliver said, tugging her toward the door. "Nurse Mary can get Mama's baby here."

Artemis grinned. "I would love to ask her if she'll try." She allowed her nephew to pull her into the corridor and, no doubt, all the way to the nursery wing.

"We won't keep you, Mother Harriet," Persephone said, still standing in Adam's one-armed embrace. "I am certain you wish to settle in after your journey."

What she had wished for was the warm welcome her friends were anticipating amongst their families, though she knew better than to have set her heart on it. She had time though. This visit was to be longer than usual.

Before she could answer her daughter-in-law, yet another person came inside. For a home famous for its isolation, Falstone Castle was rather bustling.

She turned and came face-to-face with Mr. Duncan. Warmth filled her at the sight of the kind and amiable vicar. She had always liked him. Indeed, visiting with him was an undeniable highlight of her visits to Northumberland.

"Your Grace," he said, a bit of surprise in his voice, but not an unpleasant degree. He offered a bow. "It is always a pleasure to see you here."

"If only everyone in this house felt that way," she whispered.

Mr. Duncan's expression turned concerned.

She smiled, attempting to undermine the confession she hadn't intended to make. "It is good to see you as well," she said.

"I hope you still feel that way by Christmas," he said. "I will be here, in the castle, until then. Beyond, even."

"Two house guests at one time?" She looked back at her son. "Are you certain you can endure that?" She knew all too well his preference for solitude.

"Apparently I didn't suffer enough having to attend a weeks-long house party," he grumbled.

Persephone laughed almost silently. "Pay him no heed. He is not so unhappy about this as he insists on appearing."

"Are you certain?" Harriet pressed. "I fear I am putting you out. I don't usually disrupt your Christmas."

"Having you here is a joy, not a disruption," Persephone said. "Our Christmas will be all the lovelier for having you in it."

Harriet watched Adam, hoping against hope that he shared his wife's assessment. He was as inscrutable as ever.

"Adam," Persephone said with quiet firmness. "Can you not offer your mother a warm welcome? It is nearly Christmas, after all."

"When have you known me to make overwrought emotional speeches?" He tossed Persephone a dry look before turning his attention to Harriet. "Despite apparent current impressions, I am pleased you are here." His eyes darted to Mr. Duncan. "And you as well." With that, he looked back to his wife. "Am I out of your black books now?"

"We'll work on the 'gracious' part of 'gracious host' over the next little while." She tenderly patted his cheek. "But that will do for now."

He pushed out an audible breath. "I had best go make certain our son isn't haranguing the entire staff about assisting in the delivery of his future brother or sister. We will have a mass resignation on our hands."

As he stepped toward the door, Persephone said, "They won't quit. They adore him too much."

Adam looked back at her. "Of course they do. He takes after me." He spoke with utter seriousness.

Persephone laughed and shooed him away. Their relationship was vastly different from the one Harriet had had with Joseph. It did her heart a world of good. After years of sadness and mourning and resentment, her boy was happy.

But was there any place in his happiness for her?

CHAPTER FOUR

As a vicar, Roswell didn't often declare himself "in heaven," as doing so felt a touch too close to blasphemy. But he could think of no other way to describe the two days he'd spent at Falstone Castle. Yes, the duke was often unapproachable, but Roswell had come to know him well enough over the past six years to see the defensiveness beneath it. His Grace, Roswell suspected, was actually a little shy, something he hid behind his fearsomeness. That realization made being at the castle a much more comfortable experience.

Her Grace was kind and congenial as always. Miss Lancaster was a delight, entertaining them all with her excessively dramatic poetry recitations each evening after dinner. The duke made quite a show of being annoyed, but Roswell suspected he secretly enjoyed his whimsical sister-in-law. Through it all, the dowager watched her family with an aching sort of longing.

On his third day of the potentially month-long sojourn in the fortified castle, Roswell sat near the low-burning fire in the sitting room with little Oliver on his lap. The boy had been born after Roswell's arrival in the parish, and he was like a grandson to Roswell, a bright spot in his life these past three years.

"Uncle Linus folds it different," Oliver said, pointing at the boat Roswell was folding from a page of the *Times*.

"Your uncle is a sailor. I believe he has the advantage in all things seafaring." He unfolded the boat, more than happy to begin again. Oliver enjoyed watching the undertaking. "I believe your uncle Linus is married now."

"He married my aunt." Oliver took hold of the corner of the paper right next to where Roswell held it and folded the paper with him. The boy liked to help. "She didn't used to be my aunt. I have lots now. And uncles. And cousins. Papa says the family is a horde. I don't know what that means."

Roswell kept his laugh tucked away. He was certain His Grace had said precisely that, and likely in a grumble. "It means there are a very large number of people in your family."

Oliver looked away from their latest attempt at a paper boat and up at Roswell. "Mama is going to get a baby for the castle, and it'll be our baby. Papa says we can keep it."

"I have heard that," Roswell said. "And I am excited for you to be a brother."

Ladies' voices floated into the room in the moment before Miss Lancaster and the dowager duchess entered. They spotted him and Oliver on the instant.

"Forgive me for not rising," Roswell said. "Doing so would overturn our very precarious shipyard."

"Are you folding boats again, Oliver?" Miss Lancaster asked. "Your uncle would be very proud."

"Grandfather Duncan doesn't fold it right." Oliver made the pronouncement very matter-of-factly.

Miss Lancaster smiled and held her hand out to her nephew. "Let's give your Grandfather Duncan a moment's respite. The next time Linus visits, he can offer some instruction."

Oliver climbed down off his lap and moved happily to his aunt, taking the hand she offered. Miss Lancaster led her nephew from the room. Roswell set the newspapers on the floor once more. To his nervous delight, the dowager sat in the chair nearest his.

"Does Oliver often call you Grandfather Duncan?" She didn't sound upset at the possibility, merely curious.

"He does. My late wife and I did not have children of our own and, therefore, I don't have grandchildren. That Oliver thinks of me that way is a gift, really. I am grateful for it."

She pressed her palms together and brushed the sides of her forefingers along her lower lip, brow pulled in thought. "How do I convince him to think of *me* as his grandparent?"

An unexpected question, to be sure. "You are his grandparent."

She lowered her voice. "He doesn't even acknowledge me. I cannot imagine him sitting on my lap as he was doing with you."

"Do you know how to fold a paper boat? That will win his loyalty in an instant."

Her smile was charming and captivating. This was hardly the first time he'd seen it, but its impact seemed to grow every time. "Perhaps I should ask Linus to give me instructions on the proper technique."

"We can receive his tutoring together," Roswell suggested.

Far from put-off that a gentleman so far beneath her in social standing would speak so informally, she smiled ever more brightly. It did his heart good.

"You know the secret to securing Oliver's devotion," she said. "What do you know of Persephone? How does one go about earning *her* loyalty?"

"Hers is easy to obtain. She wholeheartedly embraces those who live in kindness and generosity of spirit." He appreciated that about the duchess. From the moment he had arrived in Northumberland, she had made him feel welcome. "I have found, though, her approval and loyalty can be easily lost as well. She will not abide unkindness toward her family, or people using their positions of influence or power to harm the vulnerable."

The dowager pressed her hand to her heart. "She is rather remarkable, our Persephone."

"She is."

Her gaze wandered to the low-burning embers. "I wish I had a more motherly connection to her. But I never managed a truly motherly connection to my own son. I haven't the first idea how to go about—" She cut herself off, shoulders drooping a little. "Forgive me. I hadn't intended to spill all of my troubles in your ears."

"If hearing peoples' cares bothered me, then I chose the wrong profession."

The light comment seemed to ease a bit of her burdens. "In London this family and I have plenty enough to talk about as well as a great many distractions. The distance between us isn't as obvious. Here, however, it cannot be missed. I feel it acutely."

The pain in her words caused an echoing ache in him. "You do have weeks here in which to make progress."

"I will confess"—she looked at him—"that was my motivation in coming. I haven't been part of my own family for so long. I want to change that, but I don't know how."

"I could help." His offer surprised even him. He hadn't thought it before he said it, but he didn't regret making the suggestion. "I know the family well, and I would love to see them whole. Without you, I don't believe they will be."

She pressed her fingertips to her lips once more, a bit of emotion apparent in her eyes. "That is such a kind offer. I happily accept. Thank you."

"I will ponder, and you do the same. We'll formulate a plan." He hoped he sounded more confident than he felt. He knew her family wished her to be more a part of their lives; that bit he was entirely sure of. It was his own ability to be a guiding force and a partner of any sort to a lady as independent and genteel as she that he couldn't be entirely certain about. His family barely clung to the outer edges of the gentry. Her family occupied the highest rung of the aristocracy.

"If we can manage in a matter of weeks what I have been unable to do in decades," she said, "I will never again doubt that Christmas is a time of miracles."

CHAPTER FIVE

Harriet ran Mr. Duncan to ground two mornings later in the small sitting room. "I have the perfect idea." She sat near him, eager to share her thoughts. "I wish to do something for Persephone, and nothing matters more to her than her family." She was so excited she could hardly sit still. "Once the baby arrives, she isn't likely to travel for some time. What if her brother and sisters came here for Christmas?"

Mr. Duncan's enthusiasm grew as well. "She would be ecstatic."

"There isn't a great deal of time for making arrangements, and she has enough to be getting on with at the moment," Harriet said, "but I have planned any number of house parties in my time, some with even less warning than this. I feel certain that, especially with your help, I could manage it, as a Christmas gift to her."

"A stroke of genius." He had a way of looking at her, his eyes twinkling and expression filled with approval, that made her feel almost giddy. She couldn't remember the last time someone had had that effect on her. "You do have one very significant difficulty, however."

"What is that?"

"Your son."

That *was* a complication. Adam didn't like guests and visitors. He was very much like his father had been in that respect. "Would he be more amenable if we pointed out that the guests are his family?"

"I suspect his cooperation will be more easily secured if we point out that the guests are *Her Grace's* family."

"He does love his wife. They would do anything for each other."

Mr. Duncan's silver brow tugged in thought. "There's another difficulty. Your daughter-in-law is keenly aware of her husband's preference for peace and solitude. She will likely dismiss the idea of more visitors simply to save him from any perceived misery." He shook his head in mock regret. "We may be forced to lie to them. For their own good, of course."

His was a very subtle sense of humor. She rather liked it. "What if we made the family's visit a surprise?"

That brought more than a hint of uncertainty to his face. "A surprise for whom?"

She laughed lightly. "Not for Adam, I assure you."

He made a show of being very relieved. "I thought for a moment I would be officiating at my own funeral."

"You do think this is a good idea though?" she asked. "Not the funeral, of course—the surprise holiday house party."

"You wished to endear yourself to the duchess," he said. "This will accomplish that in spades."

"And it is something I am good at. I haven't a way with children as I suspect you do. And my relationship with Adam does not lend itself to being helpful on a regular basis. But I am good at planning gatherings." And she enjoyed it. "It will be nice to put that to use here rather than for the benefit of other people's families."

Mr. Duncan rose, the movement slowed a little by age. "Shall we find His Grace and make certain your Christmas gift will not result in a siege or a beheading?"

She laughed again. How good that felt. "He is not as fearsome as he seems."

"Let us hope you are proven correct."

He offered his arm, and she took it. No one could fault Mr. Duncan's manners. Harriet doubted anyone could find fault with his companionship either.

"I suspect Adam is in the library," Harriet said. "If not, he will be in his bookroom, but he does not care to be bothered when he is there. It is his sanctuary."

"Do you have a sanctuary?" Mr. Duncan asked.

She'd never really given it much thought. "I can't say that I do. My little house in London is lovely and cozy, but I wouldn't really consider it a refuge."

He set his hand on hers where it rested on his arm. "Is there nowhere that feels that way to you?"

A weight settled on her heart. "I suppose there isn't. I have longed for a true haven from life's storms but have yet to find one." It was a confession she'd not ever made to herself, let alone anyone else.

"I am sorry to hear that." He kept his hand on hers. It was a comforting and reassuring gesture. "Perhaps in addition to connecting to your son and his family during your visit, you could also see if you can come to feel at home here."

She shook her head. "This was always Joseph's realm. Though I tried, as did he in his own way, I never could gain a foothold here. I'm even more of an interloper now than I was then."

"I firmly believe there is more room for you here than you realize," he said.

"Not once we invite all the Lancasters," she said. "Half of them will likely have to sleep in the gardens."

He smiled at her. "Which half?"

"If Adam has his say, the louder half. Especially Harry."

They laughed as they stepped into the library. Adam was inside and looked up as they entered.

"Good morning," Mr. Duncan greeted.

"That depends on what the two of you are concocting." Adam already sounded vexed, and they hadn't even spoken to him yet.

"What makes you think we are conspiring?" Mr. Duncan asked.

Adam steepled his fingers. "I have an entire flock of sisters-in-law who are perpetually plotting something. I am well-acquainted with a conspiratorial posture."

Harriet slipped her arm from Mr. Duncan's and pulled a chair over to Adam's desk, placing it not across from her son but very nearly beside him. Her choice appeared to surprise him, but he didn't vocally object. "We have been planning something, and we wish for your help."

His eyes darted from her to Mr. Duncan and back. "What are you planning?" The question held more than a hint of misgiving.

"I want to do something for Persephone," Harriet said. "Something to bring her a little joy and happiness."

Adam's expression froze. "Does she seem unhappy?"

"No, not at all."

He looked to Mr. Duncan, clearly still concerned at the possibility of his wife being downcast. "Her Grace is the very picture of happiness."

Palpable relief filled Adam's eyes. He had been such a sweet and gentlehearted little boy in the years before the wedge between Harriet and Joseph had fractured their family. He'd grown cold and distant in the years since his father's death. It did her heart good to see his tenderness once more.

"I know how much Persephone loves to be surrounded by her family," Harriet said. "We"—she motioned to herself and Mr. Duncan—"thought she would be particularly pleased to have her family here for Christmas, especially since, once the baby has arrived, she will likely not be traveling to see any of them for some time."

"You invited a gaggle of my relatives to the castle?" Adam's jaw tightened with each word, adding a bit of a panicked edge to his voice.

"No," Mr. Duncan quickly answered. "We wanted to make certain the idea met with your approval before moving forward. We further thought Her Grace might take even greater delight in the gathering if it were a surprise to her, but we could not manage that without your assistance."

Adam folded his arms across his chest. His mouth set in a sharp line of pondering. Even with his extensive scars, he looked so very much like his father.

Harriet and Joseph hadn't loved each other in the soul-deep way Adam and Persephone did. Indeed, they had spent far too much of their brief time together arguing. But they had been happy at times, as well, and had come to love each other in their own way. Joseph had died before they'd been able to sort out all that had been wrong between them. She missed those tender moments with him and the glimpses of hope she'd once felt for their future.

"Persephone would enjoy having her family here." Adam growled low in his throat and pushed out a tense breath. "Why could I not have married an only child?"

Mr. Duncan smiled. Harriet found she could as well.

For years Adam's grumpiness had weighed on her, serving as proof that he was mired in misery, something she felt certain was her fault. That Adam's best friend, Harry—now his brother-in-law—Persephone, and Mr. Duncan all seemed unconcerned by his gruff and grumbly responses, even going so far as to smile or laugh, set her mind at ease. Perhaps he wasn't as angry as he seemed. Perhaps she wasn't as guilty as she feared she was.

"Will you be including Harry in your invitations?" Adam asked, eying her sidelong.

"Of course."

"That's my Christmas ruined, then." The most fleeting of smiles tugged at the unscarred corner of his mouth.

"You like Harry; admit it," she said.

"I tolerate him because Persephone likes her sister and Oliver enjoys the company of his cousins." Adam rubbed at his temples with his thumb and finger. "The children will be coming as well, won't they?"

"How many do the Windovers have now?" Mr. Duncan wondered aloud. "Twenty-five? Twenty-six?"

"At least," Adam drawled. "But Persephone would be overjoyed to have them all here. I suppose it must be endured."

"We have your approval, then?" Harriet pressed. "Not merely to extend invitations. I have something of a knack for planning gatherings and wish to make this impromptu one as easy on the participants as can be. Mr. Duncan and I would see to everything. We simply need you to help us make it a surprise."

"My advice would be that you not tell Oliver. That boy cannot keep a secret."

"He is so busy trying to force the early arrival of his brother or sister that I doubt he will even notice his grandmother and I are plotting anything."

"For the sake of your plan," Adam said, "I hope he is oblivious."

"Thank you." Harriet reached over and squeezed Adam's hand. It stiffened in her grasp. She pulled back once more.

How was she ever to get through to him if they were still so uncomfortable with one another that a simple touch rendered him so defensive?

CHAPTER SIX

THE THREE MORNINGS FOLLOWING THEIR discussion with Adam, Roswell met the dowager duchess in the breakfast room to discuss their plans before the rest of the family rose for the day. Breakfast had quickly become his favorite meal of the day.

She was witty and earnest, eager to contribute to the happiness of her family but overwhelmed by what she seemed to view as her shortcomings. Though their paths would likely never have crossed in London Society, she didn't act as though she considered him beneath her. And in her company, he felt less alone than he had in more than half a decade.

That third morning, she entered the breakfast room with less enthusiasm than usual.

"Is something the matter?" he asked. "You could not have received responses to your letters yet."

She shook her head. "Not enough time has passed for me to worry about that yet."

"Then, what are you worrying about?" She clearly was.

"Oliver," she said.

"Is he ill?" Roswell hadn't heard as much.

"No."

Roswell briefly touched her arm, drawing her gaze to him. "What is it?"

"Oliver never really looks at me or speaks to me. He hardly notes my presence. I'm not certain what to make of it." Though she had no explanation for her grandson's indifference, it obviously pained her. "I came here to forge a bond with my son and his family, and my grandson is entirely disinterested in me. I don't know how to reach him, but without

Oliver's acceptance, I cannot hope to secure Adam's. Sometimes this all feels so impossible."

"You convinced the Dangerous Duke to agree to an impromptu house party. That, I assure you, is far more impossible than securing the regard of that sweet little boy." Roswell finished his last sip of tea. "You eat your breakfast, and I will go let the nursemaid know that Oliver will be spending his day with his Grandfather Duncan and his Grandmother—" He didn't know how to finish that.

She, to his regret, looked evermore discouraged. "The boy doesn't even have a name for me."

"Never fear. We will make that one of our goals for the day."

His reassurance didn't clear the doubt from her expression. "What if he decides he would rather have no grandmother than have me?"

"He won't."

She took a slow breath, precisely the sort one employed when grasping at a fleeting feeling of hope. "Do you still believe this is a season for miracles?"

"I most certainly do."

She nodded, some certainty returning to her posture. "Then, I will eat quickly, and we will see just how grand a miracle we can manage today."

When Roswell arrived in the nursery, Oliver was decidedly happy to see him, as always. Sometimes the little boy was the perfect mimic of his father: a bit shy, a bit standoffish, sporting an adorable version of his father's fearsome mien. But more often, he reflected his mother's welcoming and congenial nature.

"How would you like to go on an adventure today?" Roswell asked.

Oliver nodded eagerly. "In the forest? With the wolves?"

Winter was not the safest time to be out among the pack of feral dogs that roamed the nearby woods. They gave the castle a wide berth; still, Roswell would not risk it. "I thought, perhaps, an adventure within the castle walls."

Oliver's pout didn't last long. He skipped to his nursemaid and tugged on her apron. "I want to go for an a'venture."

She nodded. "You enjoy adventures, don't you?"

"I want to go for an a'venture with Grandfather Duncan."

Roswell dipped his head when she looked at him. "With your blessing, of course." Nursemaids were the undisputed monarchs of this domain, after all. One did well to treat them kindly and with respect.

"That'd be a fine thing for the both of you," she said.

"The three of us," Roswell said. "The dowager duchess intends to take part as well. In fact, I am hopeful word could be sent to her in the breakfast room to join Lord Falstone and me here when she has finished her morning meal."

"Of course, Mr. Duncan."

Oliver brought him a book, one he'd read to him many times before. Roswell sat in a spindle-back rocking chair, Oliver on his lap, and read while they waited for the dowager to join them.

When she did arrive, the poor lady looked nervous. Still, she smiled at Oliver. "I have not been in here very often since your father was a little boy."

"Papa was a little boy?" That both captured Oliver's attention and, it seemed, surprised him.

"Yes. And this nursery was his nursery."

"Oh." He looked around, as if expecting to see a three-year-old Duke of Kielder wandering around. In a whisper he asked, "How does she know Papa was a little boy?"

"She is your papa's mother," Roswell said.

"Oh."

Roswell kept Oliver in his arms as he stood. "Shall we ask her what sort of little boy your papa was?"

He nodded and looked back at the dowager. This, Roswell knew, was the surest way to build a bridge between Oliver and his grandmother. The boy idolized his father. The duke, therefore, was the link.

"Your papa was a very good boy," the dowager said. "He was strong and brave."

"I'm brave," Oliver said.

Roswell squeezed him and said, "Yes, you are," earning him a proud grin.

The dowager continued. "He loved his papa very much."

"Papa had a papa?" Just how little did Oliver know of his father's family?

"He did," the dowager said. "A mama"—she pressed her open palm to her heart—"and a papa. And a nursery." She motioned around them. "And a castle."

"And a boy." Oliver pointed at himself.

"Yes. He has a wonderful boy."

Oliver looked at Roswell once more. "Can Papa's mama go for an a'venture with us?"

"I would like that very much." He looked from one of them to the other. "This is the adventure I had in mind: Oliver can take the two of us to his favorite places around the castle and the grounds and tell us why they are his favorite."

That would not only help grandmother and grandson develop a more personal bond but would also grant the dowager more of a connection to this home. Her declaration that she had no place that felt homelike still sat heavily on Roswell's heart and mind.

"Ooh. I have favorite places," Oliver said, bouncing in Roswell's arms. He set the boy down, unsure he could hold him if his enthusiasm grew too pointed. "Does—does Papa's mama have favorite places?"

"Your papa's mama is your grandmother," Roswell explained.

Oliver's mouth turned in a pout as he pondered that. "She is Grandmother Duncan?"

The dowager laughed a little, eyes twinkling. "No, dearest."

"Grandmother *what*?" He clearly expected to have a name to attach to the title.

"Harriet," the dowager supplied. "I can be Grandmother Harriet."

Oliver nodded; the gesture looked almost grown-up for a child only three years old. It was the reflection of his father in him.

"Shall we be off on our adventure, Lord Falstone? Your Grace?"

Oliver shook his head firmly. "She is Grandmother Harriet. You have to call her that."

"Ah," Roswell said with a shake of his head, "but she is not *my* grandmother."

The boy pressed his lips together, his brow scrunched. "Then you say *Harriet*," he decided with a firm nod.

Call a dowager duchess by her Christian name? That was very presumptuous. He looked to her, unsure what her reaction would be. The laughter in her eyes set his mind at ease.

"My friends do call me Harriet," she said in a low voice.

"Does that make us friends?" It was a bold question to ask of a duchess, but his hope for a positive answer outweighed his caution.

"We are more than friends," she answered. "We are coconspirators. And"—she wiggled her eyebrows at Oliver—"we are about to be fellow adventurers."

Oliver bounced a bit, taking both their hands in his. "I know my first favorite place."

"Onward," Roswell told the boy.

As they were led out of the nursery, Harriet inched a bit closer to Roswell and, voice lowered, asked, "What am I to call you? If I am Harriet, you cannot be Mr. Duncan."

"My given name is Roswell."

"Roswell," she repeated. "That is lovely."

"Thank you." He was as surprised by her compliment as he was by her invitation to be on more personal terms. "Oliver, however, knows me as Grandfather Duncan. Roswell might confuse him."

"Then, when we are with him, I had best call you Duncan. Otherwise, if you have no objections, I think Roswell will do."

He had a great many questions, but no objections whatsoever.

Their "adventure" took them first to the courtyard that contained the gibbet and stocks. Oliver declared it his most favorite place at the castle because he and his papa spent a lot of time there. If Roswell had been any less acquainted with the duke and his adoration of his son, he might have been alarmed by the explanation.

They were then directed to a side garden, one with winding paths and benches tucked amongst the shrubs and plants. This was, according to their guide, also his most favorite place at the castle, this time because it was his mother's garden and he spent time with her there.

"Aunt Artemis found her leaves for her hair here," Oliver said. "She says every lady should have a Christmas coffer."

The little one clearly meant *coiffeur*. Not an easy word to reproduce.

"Why does Grandmother Harriet not have a Christmas coffer?" Oliver looked legitimately concerned about the oversight. "Christmas is soon."

Roswell helped the little boy choose a few leaves from the garden, none of which were actually Christmas-specific plants, and held him high while he tucked the greenery into his grandmother's hair. The result was every bit as unsophisticated as one would predict, yet the effect was heartwarming.

"When you were my papa's mama," Oliver asked, "where did you go with him?"

She didn't answer immediately. Her experiences as a mother were quite different from what Oliver had described of his parents.

"When your papa was little, he needed to be seen by a great many doctors, so a lot of my time with him was spent while he was in his bed in the nursery either waiting for a doctor to arrive or recovering afterward."

These doctors were, no doubt, connected to the extensive scarring on the duke's face.

"We should go back to the nursery," Oliver said. "It's Grandmother Harriet's most favorite."

"Yes, we should," she said eagerly.

The boy took their hands once more and pulled them toward the garden gate. As they moved along the path, Roswell glanced up, catching sight of the duke watching them from a window above. He was too far away for Roswell to see his expression. Roswell hoped he was pleased that his son and mother were spending time together, and he hoped His Grace wasn't upset to see Roswell playing a role in facilitating the longed-for attachment.

He was growing increasingly fond of this family and evermore enamored of Harriet.

CHAPTER SEVEN

"I am absolutely determined to have a gown made in this style"—Artemis pointed to a particularly fashionable design in her collection of new fashion plates—"but I cannot decide on a color."

"An emerald or a sapphire would be gorgeous on you." Harriet could easily picture it. "Adam will be forced to stand with sword perpetually drawn should you attend a ball dressed in that gown in either of those colors. You would be absolutely stunning."

"He would find that torturous." Artemis smiled mischievously. "I will request the dress be made immediately. It can be Adam's Christmas gift to me."

She had such an odd relationship with her guardian and brother-in-law. One could never be sure if they liked one another or nursed a mutual frustration or both.

"Styles are growing more complicated." The young lady turned her attention to the fashion plates once more. "With so many ruffles and overdresses and layers, it will be remarkable if any lady is able to dance at all next Season."

"We managed to dance in far more complicated gowns when I was your age, even with our wide panniers. I suspect your generation can manage it in these comparatively accommodating fashions."

"Your dances were so lumbering. One could dance a minuet wearing a barrel if need be." Artemis made the observation loudly enough for Roswell to overhear.

"A barrel?" He laughed. "At a ball? Are you hearing this, Your Grace?"

Adam flipped a page of the book he was reading. "I am hearing it, but I am not listening."

Artemis bit back a smile. Harriet suspected she went to great lengths to prevent Adam from knowing she enjoyed him. But why?

"You must admit," Artemis said, "the dances of your day were rather plodding."

"I will admit no such thing." Harriet wasn't actually offended. The young lady's tone was too teasing for her declaration to be taken seriously. "There are few things as graceful as a well-executed allemande." She turned to Roswell, sitting in a chair near the sofa she was sharing with Artemis. "You remember the allemande, I am certain. It has fallen a bit out of favor in recent years, but it was once the most elegant of dances."

"I remember it well," he said. "And I was not terrible at it, though I say so myself."

"How long has it been since you danced it?" Harriet asked him.

"Ages," he answered.

"For me as well," she said on a sigh.

She had so loved to dance. Her late husband had not at all. For the first few years of their marriage, she had simply danced with others who asked her at balls—such a thing was not the least unheard of, neither was it inappropriate—but after Joseph's death, she'd found she struggled to enjoy dancing. Perhaps it had been too stark a reminder of the many things that had never been sorted out between them.

"Persephone could play an allemande," Artemis said.

"I am no musician," Persephone said.

Artemis huffed in dramatic frustration. "You needn't tender a performance worthy of a concert hall. All that is needed is a slow bit of drudgery in honor of very, very old—"

"Best not finish that sentence," Roswell said.

Adam coughed, the sound suspiciously similar to that of someone covering up a laugh. He didn't often allow shows of amusement. Harriet was pleased to be witness to something so rare and personal.

Persephone rose from her chair, her movements a bit more belabored than they had been when Harriet had first arrived in Northumberland. Oliver might be getting his wish for the baby to arrive sooner rather than later. She selected a sheet of music from the small cabinet beside the pianoforte.

Harriet looked to Roswell.

He offered a very regal bow. "I would be honored if you would join me in this allemande."

She curtsied and accepted the invitation. The space near the piano was barely sufficient for the dance they meant to undertake, but it would do. They were the only ones dancing, after all.

"Are you ready?" Persephone asked from the pianoforte.

"Can't be," Adam grumbled. "The vicar's not wearing a barrel."

Artemis laughed out loud. Adam didn't even acknowledge his own quip.

Harriet took her place beside Roswell, the necessary position to begin. "I have not danced in a long time," she warned her partner. "I cannot guarantee I will remember all the steps."

"I find myself in similar circumstances," he said. "We may very well make fools of ourselves. But"—his gaze turned a bit impish—"I doubt Miss Lancaster knows all the steps of the allemande. If we pretend we are performing them correctly, she will never know."

"Our confidence is to be our plaster?" she asked, amused.

"Precisely."

Persephone struck the opening chord. Harriet set her hands in Roswell's, and the dance began. The first few measures were a bit ill-executed as they both attempted to recall the complicated spins and hops and arm positions involved in the intricate dance. But then something remarkable happened. She no longer had to think about what to do; her body simply remembered.

They locked hands around each other's middle, turning in one direction and then the other. They moved forward and backward, up and down. The dance was so specifically choreographed that it even dictated when they looked at each other. Roswell smiled every time they did. At first she simply smiled back. But as the dance progressed and they eased into the long-ago familiarity of the steps, her relief at his silent reassurance allowed her to truly enjoy dancing with him.

She so seldom danced, and when she did, it was always out of obligation to a hostess or in kindness to a gentleman who seemed nervous or overwhelmed. This was the first time in memory she had danced with someone out of sheer pleasure. And it was decidedly a pleasure.

Every time he took her hand anew, a tingle fluttered from her fingers up her arm and she felt her color deepen. If she did not rein in her reaction, it would be humiliatingly obvious.

Persephone trilled the final chord. Harriet dipped the ending curtsy, Roswell the expected bow. The warmth she felt in his gaze caused an answering flutter in her chest.

No one in the room said a word. She wasn't certain anyone was even breathing.

She hazarded a glance at Adam. He watched them with brows drawn, his book apparently forgotten beside him. Artemis was no less intent on the picture they apparently made. She, however, smiled broadly, eyes twinkling.

Persephone, true to character, salvaged the situation. "That was lovely— what I saw of it over my music, at least. I hope Artemis will stop speaking ill of out-of-fashion dances."

"Oh, I think that was my favorite dance I have ever watched," Artemis said. "Don't you think so, Adam?"

His expression still hadn't softened. Indeed, it resembled a scowl even more than it had a moment before. "I have never cared for dancing."

Roswell took a step back, caution entering his posture. He made a quick half-bow to the room and excused himself.

Flustered, confused, and inexplicably disappointed, Harriet returned to her seat, attempting to focus enough to listen as Artemis rattled off her thoughts on other fashions she came across. She had enjoyed the dance far more than she'd expected. Yet, she found herself wishing she hadn't.

Everything was in confusion, and the ache she felt inside, she suspected, originated in her heart.

CHAPTER EIGHT

ADAM DIDN'T OFTEN HAVE TROUBLE sleeping, but he sat on the edge of his bed that night long after the castle had gone silent, his mind spinning. Having Mother at Falstone was always a little uncomfortable, but this time it felt . . . different.

He adjusted his position. If he was going to be awake, he might as well be comfortable. Why was he so bothered by Mother's visit? Bothered wasn't the right word. Confused wasn't it either.

He didn't like uncertainty. He shifted again.

"I love you, Adam," Persephone said from beneath the blankets, "but if I don't get some sleep tonight, I will have to add you to my list of enemies."

He turned enough to look directly at her, grinning despite his heavy mind. "You have an enemies list?"

The blankets shook from her quiet laughter. "Most husbands would be horrified at that possibility. You, however, find it romantic."

"Of course I do." He moved from the edge of the bed to sit beside her. "Who is on your list? Harry?"

She turned so she was lying on her back, looking up at him. "You like Harry, admit it."

Harry was his best friend. But one could not maintain a reputation as the most feared man in the kingdom and admit to something as convivial as having a friend.

Persephone pulled one arm out from under the blanket and rested her hand on her rounded middle. Her condition had grown evermore obvious the last few weeks.

"How are you feeling?" he asked.

"I am well. I'm far more worried about you." She reached out and took his hand. He bent and kissed her fingers, threaded through his. "What is keeping you awake, Adam? So few things ever do."

"Why do you think my mother is here?" he asked.

"She wished to visit her family. Many people do at Christmastime."

That didn't ring true. "She hasn't come to Falstone for Christmas since I was a boy. She has seldom come to Falstone outside of Christmas. Her friends always had more claim on her time and attention than I ever did."

"And you are upset at the possibility of that changing?" Persephone had a way of posing questions that told him he was being ridiculous without the necessity of actually saying as much.

"I wanted her here when I was little, but it's always uncomfortable when she is." He kept hold of her hand. Even after eleven years of marriage, her touch was comforting and reassuring. "I never know what she wants."

"Perhaps she doesn't 'want' anything."

He shook his head. "Why else would she come?"

"Because she loves you, Adam. It is easier to see that when the two of you are in London—as you've said, she's more comfortable there. She has come here to spend Christmas with her son and his family. That certainly shouldn't keep you awake at night."

But it did. It did more this time than usual. He leaned against the headboard. "I never saw her dance with my father. Not even once. They must have; he held balls for her here."

"Are you upset that she danced with the vicar?"

"No." But that didn't ring true. "A little, perhaps. But I shouldn't be. There was nothing untoward about it. And she clearly enjoyed herself. Clearly." She had, in fact, blushed like a young lady at her very first ball.

"I suspect she is growing fond of Mr. Duncan," Persephone spoke hesitantly.

He pushed down the frustration that bubbled at that. It didn't make sense to be upset. Mr. Duncan was an exemplary gentleman. He and Mother were near in age. They had enough in common for a fast friendship to grow between them. He ought to have been happy for her, and yet . . .

A weight settled in his stomach. "My father waited here for her, but she seldom returned and she never stayed. She broke his heart."

"And welcoming her back and celebrating her happiness feels like betraying him?" Persephone always had been shockingly perceptive.

"This still feels like *his* home."

She sat up. The adjustment required effort. He assisted her, adjusting her pillows. Settled at last, she took his hand again and smiled tenderly.

"Do you think, perhaps, it still feels like his home to her as well? That may be why she stays away and why her being here is always so uncomfortable for both of you."

"Father was remarkable. I don't understand how she couldn't see it."

Persephone leaned against him. He wrapped his arms around her. "Do you realize, my dear, that your mother was younger than Artemis when you were born? You have told me theirs was an arranged marriage and that they were horribly ill-suited. Their personalities and interests and preferences could not possibly have been more different."

That was, indeed, true. "But *he* didn't abandon *her*."

"He also didn't go after her." She snuggled in closer. "They both made mistakes. I didn't know your father, so I cannot offer any assessment of his position. But your mother has a good heart. She was so young. I suspect she did the best she could for one who had almost no life experience. She was wrong, yes, but she has tried these past years to make things right."

"She should have tried when I needed her. I was here all alone."

"Adam." Persephone set her hand on the side of his face, gently turning his gaze down to her. "You were a child, and you were hurt. But that little boy you were, the one who ached for his parents, who mourned his father and silently pleaded for his mother to return, that little boy doesn't need you to keep protecting him."

Adam closed his eyes. How easy it was to feel seven years old again, alone in this enormous castle, fearing he would never be happy again. It had been so much easier to decide he didn't care, that people weren't necessary, that being alone was what he preferred.

"Dukes don't need people," he whispered.

"Nonsense. I know for a fact you need me."

He held ever tighter to her. "You have no idea how much."

"And you have a future duke in this home who needs you. And another little one who will soon join us who will need you. And both of them have the opportunity to claim what you longed for all those years ago."

He rested his head against the top of hers. "They have both of their parents and are loved by them. That was what I wanted more than anything."

Persephone twisted as much as she could manage and pressed a kiss to his jaw. "We have a beautiful family, Adam."

"Yes we do."

She settled once more into the crook of his arm. "And your children have the opportunity for their grandmother to be part of their family. You longed for her to be here with you; allow her to be here with them. Give yourself permission to forgive the flawed and absent woman she was, for the pain she caused the boy you once were. He is ready to rest, my dear. He is ready to stop hurting, but he can't if you don't lay down your weapons."

Adam wasn't a crier; he refused to be. But he could feel a lump expanding in his throat. "It is difficult to simply let her back in."

"I know." She tucked herself more closely into his embrace.

"And no matter how hard I try to tell myself I don't care, I will be disappointed when she leaves again."

"I know."

There, in the sanctuary of their room, he could admit to heartaches he would not have dared acknowledge in front of anyone but his beloved Persephone. "I suppose that pain is acute here because of the memory of my father's disappointment."

"He would want you to be happy, Adam. And, I suspect, he would want her to be happy as well."

"Are you saying I shouldn't call out Mr. Duncan for flirting with her the entire time they were dancing?"

"Call him out?" Persephone scoffed. "I plan to send him a note of gratitude, along with a few very detailed pieces of advice."

He could very nearly laugh at that. "You mean to encourage him?"

"I do. And if there is happiness to be found for them, then I applaud it."

"And if he breaks her heart?" Adam pressed.

"Then, I will add him to my enemies list."

He laughed a deep, rumbling, soul-lightening laugh. "I do love you, Persephone."

"And I love you, my darling, ferocious duke. And I will love you even more if you let me go to sleep."

He helped her lie down once more, seeing her settled comfortably, the blanket tucked around her once more. He kissed her lightly as she closed her eyes, weariness apparent in her face.

"Do I need to have a talk with our child, Persephone? It seems to me this new little one is being inexcusably demanding of you."

She smiled but didn't open her eyes. "If this child is half as perfect as Oliver, the sleepless nights and discomfort and pain will be well worth it."

"You are in pain?" He didn't like that in the least.

"A little. I was with Oliver as well, toward the end."

"The end?" His alarm grew on the instant. "Do I need to send for the midwife?"

She looked up at him. "Not that sort of pain, dear. We have plenty of time yet."

He hooked his finger around a strand of hair stuck to her cheek and moved it back in place. "I worry about you, you know."

A bit of laughter touched her expression. "I said that to you not long after we were married. Do you remember what your response was?"

"I would wager it was something grumbled and irritable."

She reached up and ran her thumb along the thickest of his scars. "I like you grumbly and irritable."

Only she and Oliver were ever permitted to touch those scars. It had taken a long time for him to grow comfortable with her doing so.

"What was my answer when you told me you worried about me?" he asked.

"You said, 'Don't.' And I told you I couldn't help myself."

"You cared about me even then. That still amazes me."

She pulled in a sharp breath. Before he could ask what was the matter, she took his hand and placed it on her curved middle. Beneath the light pressure of his hand, the baby moved.

Persephone took a slow breath, her eyes drifting closed. Adam lay down beside her, keeping his hand on her middle, feeling the tiny miracle flutter. He closed his eyes as well.

Dukes don't need people.

He loved his father, admired him, strove to live up to his legacy, but in this he knew his father had been wrong. Adam had a growing number of people he needed in his life, and he wouldn't change that. Not for all the world.

CHAPTER NINE

BREAKFAST HAD BECOME HARRIET'S FAVORITE meal of the day. Morning after morning, while the castle slept, she sat beside Roswell, finalizing their plans to help her carve out a place for herself among her family, reminiscing about their younger years and discovering people they both knew and events they both remembered, talking about things they enjoyed or hoped to do in the years to come. She found in him a friend and companion, but of a different variety than the group of friends she had spent so much of the last decades with. Her heart was growing partial to him.

"Her Grace mentioned during whist last night that she wished her family could spend Christmas at Falstone Castle." Roswell smiled over his teacup. "Won't she be surprised when they all arrive this evening?"

Harriet sighed, utterly pleased with the outcome of their efforts. "I am still amazed we managed to arrange for families from three different counties to arrive here on the same day. What a wonderful Christmas gift it will be."

"Our duchess will be ecstatic," Roswell said.

"She has brought Adam such joy. Before she came into his life, he was unhappy and angry at the world." The pain she'd felt at watching him so lost in his own enmity still echoed in her heart when she thought on those days before Persephone. "If she wants to have her family with her at Christmas, she should get precisely that."

"May I ask you something? I will understand if you decide I am being unforgivably intrusive."

"I have come to know you well enough to not be worried about what you might ask."

He brushed the toast crumbs from his fingertips, then pushed his teacup aside. "How did your son's face become so scarred?"

That was a question she had been asked on a number of occasions, though she had seldom answered it. But she knew without a doubt Roswell would not say anything to cause Adam pain or to indicate they had discussed so personal a topic. She could broach it with him.

"Adam was born without his outer ear. Instead of the cuplike shape that is usually there, his was only a small stub of flesh."

Roswell watched her intently as she spoke. She liked knowing he was genuinely interested in what she had to say.

"His father and I worried his hearing would be diminished by it. And, of course, there was concern he might be mistreated for the oddity of his appearance. We consulted a number of surgeons, all of whom insisted the missing ear was likely just under the skin, that it had, for reasons unknown, become caught there, not emerging as it was meant to."

Roswell nodded, brow pulled in concern.

"One surgeon after another attempted to 'liberate' his ear. By the time we realized there was nothing to be found, his tiny, beloved little face was badly scarred. As he grew, the scars stretched and widened. We should never have let the surgeons operate." Her heart dropped at the memory of all that suffering. "He endured so much pain, and I missed so much of his childhood."

Roswell set his hand on hers, kindly and gently. "Why did his surgeries lead to you missing his childhood?"

"I am not good in the sickroom. Indeed, I am something of a hindrance. I grow so very anxious and fretful. The surgeons asked me to leave so I wouldn't make the situation worse." She had learned to accept this particular flaw of hers, but she still regretted it. "Adam required so many operations, that, during his first three years I was gone more often than I was here. It is little wonder, really, that he was far more devoted to his father than to me."

He squeezed her hand. "Have you spoken with him about all of this?"

She nodded. "Not long after he married, in fact. Our relationship has been better since then, but still far from ideal."

"Which explains why you came here so determined to forge a deeper connection."

She smiled at him. "I want to be his mother in a way I never have been before. But that will only happen if he lets me. I know a large part of that difficulty lies in his uncertainty over my devotion to him."

"Anyone who has watched you here the past fortnight can see you care deeply for him."

What a wonderful thing to say. He warmed her heart so often, so easily. "Perhaps you might offer a few extra pleas to heaven. Adam and I have enough years of difficulty between us that we might need divine intervention to fully overcome it."

"I will petition with every ounce of faith I have." He raised her hand to his lips and lightly kissed her fingers. "But I am not worried."

She felt heat stain her cheeks. How was she within only a couple of short years of sixty and blushing as though she were sixteen?

Roswell spent the rest of the morning with her. They walked in the gardens, despite the cold temperatures. They sat in the library, talking amiably about the past and the future, sometimes sitting in comfortable silence. No matter that this was not home to either of them, with him she felt more at ease at the castle than she ever had before.

Lord and Lady Techney, Persephone's sister and her husband, arrived that afternoon. Daphne—the countess—was a favorite of Adam's. Harriet understood why. They were both quiet; both tended to keep to themselves. And Daphne adored him, something few people could imagine, let alone experience. Harriet was grateful to the sweet girl for loving her dear boy and softening him. The Lancaster family had worked miracles for Adam.

No sooner had the earl and countess and their two tiny children been shown to the nursery than Adam arrived. He shook Lord Techney's hand, not an unfriendly gesture. But Daphne received an embrace so warm and so affectionate no one in the *ton* would have recognized the Dangerous Duke as the one offering it.

"We missed seeing you at Linus's wedding," Adam said.

"I was bringing a life into the world, Adam. That is a difficult thing to do whilst traversing several counties."

Adam stepped back and let out a breath. "Where is this life that kept you away? I fully intend to undertake an argument with that boy."

Most anyone else would have been intimidated by Adam's fierce grumbling. Daphne only patted his face—the side without the scars—then turned to the nursemaid and took the baby from her arms. She placed the tiny little boy, not yet two months old, in his uncle's arms.

He eyed the baby, tenderness well hidden beneath his grouchy exterior. "I understand you didn't name him Adam."

Daphne smiled. "We did not."

"You didn't name the first one Adam either."

"The first one was a girl." She brushed her finger along the baby's cheek. "Ogden Evander is a fine name for this little bean sprout."

He bounced the baby a bit and walked a few steps away. "I believe I will just call him Lord Tilburn."

Roswell moved to Harriet's side. "The fearsome, infamous Duke of Kielder makes a tender picture of domesticity, doesn't he?"

"The late duke was a good father as well. Adam gets that from him."

He slipped her arm through his. "Do you not think you are a good mother?"

That was a question she tried very hard not to ask herself. "I did not show myself to be, though I am attempting to do so now."

"Look at how happy he is," Roswell said, indicating Adam with a nod of his head. "And you facilitated this."

"You are telling me I should give myself a little credit?"

His eyes crinkled. "You should give yourself a great deal of credit, Harriet."

The Lancaster brother arrived in the small set of rooms where the family was. He held the hand of his bride of only a couple of months. How very happy they were. Once upon a time, Harriet had imagined herself being that enamored of the man she was to have spent her life with.

"Linus." Daphne rushed to her brother and hugged him. "I was so sorry to have missed your wedding, but I am so happy for you."

He kept an arm around her and turned her to face his wife. "Arabella, this is my sister Daphne."

Harriet leaned closer to Roswell. "I didn't realize they hadn't yet met. We are offering Christmas cheer to more people than I anticipated."

Artemis rushed in, exuding her usual dose of drama. "Harry has arrived early! They are on their way up here now. *All* of them."

Adam, still holding tiny Lord Tilburn, shook his head in annoyance. "Harry is forever ruining everything."

"That is a fine thing to say about your one and only friend." Harry stood in the doorway, ushering in a little girl, nine years old, and then a boy, a little younger than his sister. They both kept their hands over their mouths, eyes dancing with excitement. Behind them came a girl, about four years old, striking the same pose. Lastly was Harry's wife, Athena, the second Lancaster sister, holding the hand of a gorgeous little six-year-old girl, her spitting image.

"That child is named for me," Harriet told Roswell. "And she is a darling."

He looked over the growing crowd. "This is a fine thing to have arranged, Harriet. For all of them. For Her Grace. For your son." He looked at her once more. "For yourself."

Adam set his bundle in Daphne's arms, then turned to the rest of the room. "We'd meant to surprise Persephone after dinner tonight, but true to form, Harry has created chaos."

Far from offended, Harry chuckled. "Iris and Richard have managed to stay quiet." He motioned to his oldest children, still holding their hands over their mouths. "But they won't last much longer."

"She's in the drawing room," Harriet said. "We could surprise her now."

A quick discussion saw the matter settled. Harriet and Roswell wandered to the drawing room first, settling in casually. Adam followed a few minutes later.

Persephone looked up at him. "You look troubled."

"We are to have guests for dinner," he grumbled. "Unless you'd like me to send them away." He managed to make the sentence sound hopeful. How much of his characteristic gruffness was an act?

"You can be a good host for a single evening, dear." She smiled and rose to her feet.

"Very well." He set an arm around her as he turned back to face the door. "Come in."

Her brother stepped in first.

Persephone took a sharp breath. "Linus! Arabella!" She rushed to them as quickly as her heavily pregnant body would allow and threw her arms around them. "I cannot believe you're here."

"Then you are never going to believe this," Linus said, slipping from her embrace and waving someone else into the room.

Daphne, her husband, and their two little children came into the room. Persephone's hand flew to her heart. "Oh, Daphne. James." Her gaze dropped to the two-year-old clinging to her father's leg. "Cassandra. Oh, you've grown. And—" She took a shaky breath. "Oh, this must be Ogden. I have been anxious to meet him."

"He is Lord Tilburn," Adam said. "They wouldn't name him for me, so I will only ever call him by his title."

"Oh, hush." Persephone playfully swatted at him before embracing her younger sister's family. "I cannot believe you are all here. If only Harry and Athena—" She turned wide eyes to Adam. "Have Harry and Athena come as well?"

He nodded silently.

Persephone turned back to the door. The sister nearest her age entered with her brood to a welcome as enthusiastic as the others received. The youngest of Athena's children was in Artemis's arms, clearly enamored of her youngest aunt.

Iris, the Windovers' oldest, rushed not to Persephone but to Adam, tugging at his jacket as she jumped up and down. "Can we be loud now? I have so"—she stretched the word out long—"many words I need to say and I simply can't say them quietly."

Adam's mouth pulled in a straight slash, and his annoyed gaze settled on the girl's father. Harry only laughed. Even Persephone smiled. Adam was in for a difficult and trying Christmas, but Harriet suspected they all felt as she did: he would endure any level of exasperation if doing so brought his wife joy.

All the Lancasters stood near each other, hugs and greetings exchanged, love emanating from them all. It was a beautiful scene. Persephone had not stopped smiling, even wiping away a happy tear or two.

Adam watched his wife. A tiny, almost imperceptible smile touched his lips, despite Iris making good on her declaration of needing to be loud. He looked at Harriet and mouthed the words, "Thank you."

It was, quite possibly, the very best moment she had experienced at Falstone Castle, the first, she hoped, of many.

CHAPTER TEN

THE CASTLE WAS BRIMMING WITH activity. With seven children under the age of nine running wild down the corridors, the place was decidedly lively. Roswell enjoyed every giggle, every scream of delight, every pounding of tiny feet on the floor, every evening spent watching the children slowly drift off from a day of exhausting play. He was delighted. And watching Harriet interact with the little ones, he suspected she was as well. Yes, she was not as at-ease with her grandchild and honorary grandchildren as some might be, but she clearly loved them, and they quite obviously adored her.

She worried so much about being a good mother to her son, about making right the things she regretted. She gave herself very little credit for the goodhearted and kind person she was. How he wished she could see that for herself.

"Grandfather Duncan." Oliver frantically motioned him over to where he stood, his cold-weather layers a bit askew. "My mittens are stuck."

The little boy's mittens were buttoned to his sweater—an ingenious means of preventing him from losing them—but they'd become entangled in the coat he was attempting to pull on.

"Your nursemaid would have helped you don your outdoor clothes." Roswell tugged the coat sleeves free once more.

"I can do it." Oliver spoke firmly and defiantly.

Roswell chose not to point out that their current predicament indicated otherwise. He adjusted the sweater sleeves enough to slip the boy's hands into his mittens. "Are you excited to gather the Christmas greenery?"

Oliver nodded. "Papa told Mama he will stay here because—because it'll be quiet."

That sounded like their hermitic duke.

"Mama said, 'Adam. Be agreeable.' Then she kissed him."

"And was he agreeable after that?" Roswell asked, trying to keep his laughter firmly tucked away.

"He said he'll go now."

And that sounded like their very astute duchess.

"Will you be joining your parents' team tonight?" Roswell asked.

Oliver shrugged, his aloof expression an exact duplicate of his father's. "Cousin Iris says I should be with her."

"Do you want to be?" He pulled the boy's coat on once more.

"Would—is Grandmother Harriet getting branches?" Oliver asked with a bit of hesitancy.

"I believe she is." He buttoned Oliver's coat. "And I am hoping to convince her to gather greenery *with me.*"

The little boy's eyes pulled wide. "I want to too."

"To gather greenery with me?"

Oliver shook his head. "With her."

"We should ask her." He stood and offered Oliver his hand. "I think the three of us would make an excellent team."

Oliver skipped at his side as they made their way to where the others stood, bundling up for the traditional Christmas Eve outing. Harriet looked as lovely as ever. His heart always flipped a bit the first time he saw her after being apart for a while, even a very short while.

"Grandmother! Grandmother!" Oliver tugged at Harriet's coat sleeve. "We're a team."

She smiled down at him. "We're a team?"

"Grandfather Duncan said so."

That brought Harriet's beautiful blue eyes to him, wrinkling at the corners with a smile. "We're a team?"

"Oliver wishes to join us—you and I—for the greenery gathering."

"Oh." Harriet clasped her hands together. "How utterly perfect. Let us ask your parents though. They might wish you to be on their team."

"Papa will be on Mama's team. That's his favorite part."

In the end, they decided to form a five-person team. They rode out into the forest in one of the four sleighs being employed for the task, each equipped with an armed outrider. Though the wolves hadn't come near the castle in years, the Falstone gamekeeper being quite good at providing ample incentive for the pack to keep to the far side of the forest, His Grace was unwilling to take any chances with the safety of his family.

"I mean to help the girls make a kissing bough," Harriet said, "so we need to make certain we find plenty of holly and a bit of mistletoe."

"No kissing boughs," His Grace said with firm finality.

"The girls wish for one," Harriet said. "We mustn't disappoint them."

"I suspect you'd disappoint a few of the gentlemen as well," Roswell said, a bit cheekily.

Harriet held back a smile. Her Grace didn't bother hiding her amusement.

"Any gentleman who needs a parasitic plant to convince a lady to kiss him doesn't deserve to be kissed," the duke said. "And I will have no unearned affection in my castle."

"Deny your nieces and sisters-in-law this bit of revelry, Adam," Persephone said, "and you will be the one receiving no affection."

He raised an ebony eyebrow, the tiniest twitch to his lips. "Are you threatening me?"

"Rather effectively, in fact," she said.

His Grace didn't smile often, but he did just then. His wife was so remarkably good for him.

Though it was presumptuous of Roswell to do so, he felt the same about Harriet and himself. He was happier and more hopeful with her. She made him smile, made him laugh. Plotting with her had brought him such enjoyment. If only she were staying longer or he could go with her. He could not imagine leaving behind his clerical duties entirely, but he would enjoy traveling a bit, seeing London again, perhaps Newcastle. Going *with her* . . . but he didn't dare dream of such things when he didn't truly know the state of Harriet's affections.

"Stop the sleigh, Adam," Harriet said.

He complied.

"Up in that tree." She pointed. "Mistletoe."

"Fabulous," he said dryly.

Persephone swatted at him. "You have been so agreeable these past few days. Where is *that* Adam?"

"The Well of Amiability has run dry."

She set her arms around him. "Would your well refill faster if we sat here in the sleigh, blanket tucked around us, while our three partners in crime fetch the greenery?"

"It might fill instantaneously."

Her Grace looked to Roswell and Harriet and shooed them out of the sleigh. She had a smile for Oliver. "Will you help them, dear?"

"I'll help, Mama. I'm a big help."

"You always are."

Roswell stepped from the sleigh, then handed Harriet down. Oliver wrapped his arms around Roswell's neck. He held him in one arm and offered Harriet his other hand. She took it. He was absolutely certain in that moment that he would never grow tired of holding her hand. He felt twenty years old again, though, he hoped, not half so inept as he was in his youth. He'd learned to appreciate people more, to value friendships, to view life as a gift not to be wasted.

"This has been a very good Christmas," he said, squeezing her hand. "Oliver is correct: we make a good team, you and I."

He stopped directly beneath the tree, looking up at the obliging branch. "This may be my favorite of our accomplishments so far."

Oliver looked up as well. "What is it?"

"That plant right there"—Harriet pulled her hand free to point at the clump. "Is mistletoe."

He pulled in a tiny, sharp breath. "I know about mistletoe. It's for kissing."

Harriet tapped his little chin. "Yes, it is."

Oliver leaned toward her, holding fast to Roswell's collar, and placed a kiss on his grandmother's cheek.

"Oh, you sweet boy."

Oliver nodded his acceptance of the compliment. He didn't want for confidence. He turned back and placed a kiss on Roswell's cheek as well.

"Why, thank you, Lord Falstone," Roswell said.

Oliver laughed. "People call me that. It's silly." Eventually he would understand titles and courtesy titles, and it would make more sense. "How do we get the mistletoe down?"

"We need a handsaw." Roswell set Oliver down. "Go ask your father if there is one in the sleigh."

As Oliver skipped away, Harriet called after him. "But we will retrieve the saw. Don't you bring it." She looked back at Roswell, shaking her head and smiling. "Can't you just picture him skipping back here with a saw in his hand? He would hurt himself, and then his father would kill the both of us."

"And what a waste of mistletoe that would be." Roswell closed the distance between them, holding her gaze with his. "It is tradition, you know."

She slipped her hand into his once more, not looking away. "I think it may be my favorite tradition so far."

He gave it not another thought but kissed her there under the mistletoe. It was a moment he'd imagined often, though he'd never let himself believe it would happen. The reality exceeded his hopes. She was warm and soft in his arms, and she returned the kiss with a level of enthusiasm that did him good.

And then it ended. Abruptly.

A heavy hand dropped onto his shoulder with more force than was at all necessary. Large fingers dug into his shoulder. "We're here for greenery, vicar. I suggest you focus on the task at hand."

"Adam, really." Harriet crossed her arms, eying her son.

"Go sit with Persephone and Oliver in the sleigh," His Grace said. "I'll see to it the vicar gets the greenery."

She stepped up beside the duke, glaring him down despite being noticeably smaller. "You may think you inherited your fire entirely from your father, but I would suggest you not attempt to browbeat me."

If Roswell weren't already in His Grace's black books, he might have applauded.

"Vicars don't kiss ladies that way," the duke said to her.

Roswell cocked his head to the side. "Actually we do."

He was shot a look that had likely felled many a less-stalwart man.

"Adam." Her Grace's voice reached them from the nearby sleigh.

"I am settling something, Persephone."

"Later, please, dear."

The duke looked to the sleigh but pointed a finger at Roswell. "He was kissing my mother."

"And your child is going to be born in this sleigh if you don't drive me home."

His Grace paled. "Truly?"

She didn't answer. After a moment, Oliver whimpered. "Papa."

They were all quickly in the sleigh, His Grace at the reins, setting the horses at a run back to the castle.

CHAPTER ELEVEN

Persephone's two married sisters were assisting with the delivery, her labor having progressed too quickly for the midwife. Though most husbands spent the hours in which their children were born pacing the corridors or waiting in a nearby room, Adam had refused to leave his wife's side. As Harriet understood it, he had been present for Oliver's birth as well. She had no doubt he was a rock in such situations. She, however, was anything but.

"He must be so disappointed in me," she whispered. "Again."

Roswell, sitting beside her, set his arm around her shoulders and held her close. "I don't think he is, Harriet. His devotion to his little family is boundless." He gently patted Oliver's back as the boy slept against Harriet's shoulder. "You are watching over his precious boy. His Grace will be grateful for that, I promise you."

"Oliver does like me." She leaned a bit against Roswell, turning his arm of support into more of an embrace. She needed that.

"Oliver *loves* you," Roswell said. "He beams whenever he is with his grandmother Harriet."

She turned her head enough to look up at him. "And his grandfather Duncan."

"Well, we *are* a good team, you and I."

This man could make her blush like no one else. She enjoyed it. "I am sorry Adam was so difficult about things out in the forest. It made me almost miss the days when he was entirely indifferent to me."

"The look on his face when he shouted I had kissed his mother was not one of a son who had *ever* been apathetic toward his mother." He held her close to him, quite as if it were an old, established habit between them, a position so familiar there was no need to search for a comfortable arrangement. "But, the Dangerous Duke being the Dangerous Duke, I suspect he has difficulty expressing it. Vulnerability does not come easily to the terrifying."

"Do *you* find him terrifying?" she asked.

His laugh rumbled beside her. "I am too old to be terrified."

"You and I are very nearly the same age," she reminded him.

She was almost certain he kissed the top of her head. "Then, I guess I am not old after all."

"Excellent answer."

He bent his head a little and spoke quietly near her ear. "You sounded like His Grace just then. Formidable, certain, and with just enough fire to warn a person not to disagree with you."

She smiled. "I don't know whether to feel flattered or concerned."

"I hope what you feel is cherished."

She did. She truly did. "I am so glad you have been here at the castle the past few weeks. I've come to know you better than I have in the last six years."

"A dowager duchess can hardly be blamed for taking little notice of the vicar."

She sat up, careful not to dislodge Oliver, and looked him directly in the eye. "What makes you so certain I took little notice of you?"

"My station in life pales compared to yours." He spoke without self-pity, without mortification. He thought it simply a statement of fact.

"Roswell." She did enjoy saying his name. "My grandfather was a vicar. Three of my uncles were vicars. Another uncle was a drunkard who amounted to absolutely nothing, and that was on my father's side, the branch of the family with claims to status and standing. My father saw to it I was married to a duke, but he did so without any regard for my happiness or the well-being of his grandchildren. That is what claim on an elevated station does to too many people. I may be a dowager duchess, but I value far more important things than that."

"Such as?" The tiniest hint of uncertainty touched the question. How worried had he been about this? And for how long?

"I value kindness, compassion, a caring heart." Some little bit of devilment seized her. "And a skilled kisser."

The doubt in his expression disappeared. "If you need further proof of my abilities, I will happily provide it."

"Adam would murder you."

Something like a smirk pulled at his lips. "But I would die a happy man."

Harriet tucked herself into his embrace once more, enjoying the warmth of him and the peaceful, safe . . . cherished feeling he inspired in her. She rested her head against him and closed her eyes, reveling in the moment.

"Where do you travel to when you aren't here?" he asked, his hand gently rubbing her arm.

"London during the Season," she said. "I also spend a good deal of time in Newcastle."

"I haven't been to Newcastle in years," he said. "I enjoyed the time I spent there."

"And London? Did you enjoy London?"

"Oh yes. My late wife's health was poor for the last few years of her life. We weren't able to travel."

"I'm sorry to hear that." She meant it. Heartache and grief were not something she would wish on anyone, but especially not on someone as dear to her as Roswell.

"I always enjoyed London," he said. "I would very much like to go back. And Newcastle as well."

Then, he was not opposed to traveling and seeing some of the kingdom. Her late husband had been utterly opposed to that. It had been an endless source of difficulty between them.

"And are you one who is not inclined to break up travel with extended return trips home?" Roswell asked.

"Not at all. I simply haven't had a warm welcome or a true home to return to."

She felt him go very still, perhaps even holding his breath. Quite suddenly, she couldn't breathe either. Had she said too much? Revealed too much?

"And if that home wasn't a grand castle?" he asked.

"As long as it's a home, the grandness doesn't matter."

He took a deep breath. "Even if it was an extremely humble house?"

The vicarage was humble. Was that what he was worried about? Was that what he hoping for?

She held Oliver more firmly in one arm and, with her other, brushed her fingers along Roswell's jaw. "In this extremely humble house, would I be wanted and welcomed?"

He wrapped his fingers around hers and pressed them to his lips, offering a soft and lingering kiss. "You would be loved."

A rush of heat infused her cheeks even as a sting of emotion filled her eyes and throat. "I would like that very much."

Athena, the sister closest in age to Persephone, stepped into the room, eyes filled with delight. "The baby has come."

"And all is well? Is mother or baby in need of anything?" Roswell asked, a vicar through and through in that moment.

"They are as well as can be," Athena said. "And you—all three of you— are being asked for."

Harriet roused Oliver. His sleep-heavy eyes fluttered a few times before opening enough to look at her. "We're going to go visit your mama."

"Mama?" he asked, his words slurred by the lingering effects of slumber.

"Yes, dear. Her baby has come, and you are to meet your new brother or sister."

He sat up straighter, quickly awakening. "Mama's baby?"

"Yes, dear."

Roswell stood and offered her his hand. She accepted and was soon on her feet, Oliver walking at her side, with his hand in hers. His pace sped up as they made their way down the corridor.

"I think little Lord Falstone is excited," Roswell said.

"He is not the only one."

When they entered Persephone's bedchamber, Adam stood beside his wife's bed with an infant in his arms. Harriet released Oliver's hand, letting him cross to his father.

He looked up at Adam. "Is that Mama's baby?"

"Yes." Adam knelt down in front of his son, affording him a closer look at the newest addition to the family. "Oliver, meet your new little sister."

A girl. And Adam looked at his daughter with absolute adoration.

Oliver bent over his sister, studying her more closely. "Where is her ear, Papa?"

"That *is* her ear. It is simply shaped differently than most."

This little one had inherited Adam's misshapen ear. Harriet's heart sank, thinking of this precious girl going through even a drop of the pain Adam had.

"And"—Adam's eyes met Harriet's—"I will abide no talk of surgeons."

She opened her mouth to insist she hadn't any intention of suggesting such a thing.

"Adam," Persephone protested.

He stood once more, holding his little girl to him like a bear protecting its cub. "No butcher will be allowed anywhere near this child. If anyone lays so much as a finger on my daughter, or even suggests it, I will take her into the forest, and we will live with the wolves."

Persephone shook her head. "Darling—"

"She is perfect, Persephone. Exactly as she is. No one will ever be permitted to say otherwise." A crack of emotion in his voice was quickly swallowed. "And no one will be allowed to hurt her. Not anyone."

"Come sit with Mama, Oliver." Persephone made room for her little boy. "Adam, introduce your mother to her granddaughter."

Adam stood, silently watching Persephone, defiantly and pleadingly.

"Trust me, darling," she said.

His fight did not entirely dissipate. He gave a quick nod and, tucking his daughter closer to him, crossed to where Harriet and Roswell stood. He allowed her only the tiniest glimpse of one rosy baby cheek.

"My dear, sweet boy," Harriet said.

"At least you didn't say 'my poor boy,'" he muttered.

"Your very wise wife told me years ago how you feel about that. I haven't said it since."

His brow pulled in thought. "You haven't."

She slipped from Roswell's side to Adam's and set her arm around him, looking down at his precious little girl. "She is perfect, just as you said. And I would never suggest otherwise. We should not have allowed the surgeons to do to you what they did. We were wrong." She had waited far too long to tell him that. "If I had known then what I know now, *I* would have taken you to the forest, and we would have lived with the wolves."

"Father would likely have stopped you," Adam said.

She raised her chin. "I would have liked to have seen him try."

Adam didn't quite keep his approval hidden. From him it was tantamount to a long and eloquent speech of praise.

"Does this little bundle have a name?" Roswell asked, peering at the little girl.

Adam nodded. "The Lancasters have a tradition of naming their children for figures from Greek mythology."

"A tradition you find 'ridiculous,' if I am remembering correctly your early commentary on the matter," Harriet said.

"Persephone's mother was fond of the custom," Adam said, "and, therefore, so is she."

"What name have you decided on?" Roswell asked.

"Hestia Ardelle."

Harriet pressed a hand to her heart.

"Hestia, of Greek myth, in honor of Persephone's mother. Ardelle, in honor of yours."

"Oh, Adam," she said.

"Perfect," Roswell whispered, looking at her now rather than at the baby.

"Would you like to hold her?" Adam offered.

"I would love to."

Hestia was placed in Harriet's arms with utmost care, the perfect little bundle of light. She had Adam's dark hair and Persephone's milky complexion. One glance at her besotted father told a tale of years of protectiveness to come. Hestia would be treasured and safeguarded.

"What a beautiful family you have, Adam. And what a wonderful father you are. I could not be prouder."

"Oliver has enjoyed spending time with you," he said. "Thank you for being here."

The brush of a feather might have knocked her over in that moment. She'd fully expected his subtle glance of approval to be the extent of praise she would receive from her reticent son. But it wasn't. He'd offered actual words of appreciation.

"Then, it would not be such a terrible thing," she said, "if I were here more often?"

"Not terrible," Adam said.

Roswell met her eyes once more. "Not terrible at all."

Harriet hugged her granddaughter closer, breathing in the fresh baby smell. This had truly been a miraculous Christmas season. Which reminded her. "Happy Christmas, everyone."

Adam looked to Persephone. "Our daughter was born on Christmas Day."

She held Oliver close, rocking him back and forth. "Truly a day of miracles."

Roswell moved to stand beside Harriet and set his arm around her, tucking her and the baby close. "Does this feel like home?"

She leaned into his embrace. "It does now."

CHAPTER TWELVE

"Ask him from at least ten feet away," Harry Windover said to Roswell.

"His Grace has firearms, you realize," Lord Techney jumped in. "Ten feet might not be sufficient."

Roswell smiled. He'd come to the duke's brothers-in-law looking for reassurance and a little advice before undertaking the questionably necessary but decidedly important task of telling His Grace of his intentions where Harriet was concerned. Knowing both of these gentlemen had, at some point, told the Dangerous Duke they wished to marry a member of his family, they'd seemed the obvious source for insight. He hadn't counted on the jesting.

"Suppose *I* arrived armed," Roswell suggested. "Even things up between us."

"Your first lesson as a—we hope—future member of the family," Harry said, "in a fight with Adam, the odds are never even, and never in your favor."

"Your second lesson," Lord Techney said, "is that you can be intimidated by the duke, but if you're actually afraid of him—"

"I'm not," Roswell said with a laugh.

"That will help tremendously." The earl spoke with the surety that can only come from experience.

"More important still," Harry said, "don't ever make his mother unhappy. Adam grumbles and pushes people away and insists he doesn't care for anyone, but he loves his family, and he protects them fiercely."

"I would never do anything to cause her the least pain," Roswell said. "I never could."

"We know," Lord Techney said. "Just make sure *he* knows."

"And if he shoots me anyway?"

Harry slapped a commiserating hand on Roswell's shoulder. "Then, we will make certain you are flatteringly eulogized and that the ladies weep a great deal."

The two gentlemen laughed but not unkindly. Roswell was nudged toward the library, where His Grace had been all morning. This was the moment of reckoning. Roswell didn't mean to abandon his hopes for Harriet if her son proved unamenable, but he wanted her connection to His Grace to continue improving and strengthening. He had no desire to become a wedge between them.

He stepped through the ajar door but glanced back at the other gentlemen. They motioned him on with gestures and expressions of enthusiasm. He would thoroughly enjoy being part of this loving, entertaining, supportive family.

His Grace stood at the far window, looking out over his domain. How easily one could picture his several-greats grandfather doing the same in the days when lords of the manor were more feudal and their "kingdoms" more literal.

"The layer of snow makes the view even more beautiful," Roswell said.

The duke looked the tiniest bit in his direction. "Falstone shines in any season." He didn't sound upset or as if he were correcting Roswell's observation—simply adding to it. That seemed a good sign.

"I consider myself fortunate to live in so beautiful an area of the kingdom." Roswell moved to stand beside him. "I am, however, hoping to add to that good fortune."

His Grace turned enough to lean one shoulder against the stone window frame, arms crossed over his chest. "Why do I suspect this is going to cost *me* a fortune?"

Roswell shook his head. "No money involved, Your Grace. I speak of personal good fortune."

The duke's gaze narrowed on him. He had, over the six years Roswell had known him, shown himself to be as astute as he was menacing. There would be no backing out now.

"Before she leaves at the end of Christmastide, I intend to ask the dowager duchess if she would do me the honor of marrying me."

A dark ducal eyebrow shot upward. His mouth pulled in a fierce line, and his posture stiffened. "You *what?*"

Roswell had expected anger and rejection, so seeing it didn't truly quell him. He simply stood and waited to see how harshly that gale would blow.

His Grace crossed to the bell pull and gave it a firm tug. The two of them stood without speaking as the minutes passed. The duke's instructions to the footman who looked into the library, "Fetch the dowager duchess," was all that broke the heavy silence of the room.

The duke was much younger than he was, far stronger, and decidedly more inclined toward violence, but so help him, Roswell would not abide any harassment His Grace might inflict on Harriet.

She arrived long moments later. Her gaze jumped from one of them to the other, curiosity filling her eyes.

Roswell kept still, voice and vicarly soft fists at the ready.

"This man"—Adam pointed at Roswell, though he watched his mother—"says he wants to marry you."

Oh, mercy.

Harriet's wide eyes turned on him immediately.

Roswell pushed out a deep breath. "This is not the romantic way I had planned for you to discover my hopes on this matter."

A smile tugged at her lips, though she didn't say anything. She didn't look unpleasantly surprised. Thank the heavens for that.

"Harriet, I—"

His Grace held up a hand, a surprisingly threatening means of shushing him. Of his mother he asked, "Does Mr. Duncan treat you well?"

She nodded. "He does."

Still not satisfied, the duke pressed, "Does he make you happy?" His question was posed tensely, just as the previous one had been.

"He does."

Roswell felt a smile form. He made her happy. It was a relief to hear. Then the duke turned to face him.

"Do you resent that she likes to travel and spend time with her friends?"

"Not at all," Roswell said. "I have enjoyed traveling myself. And a group of friends my own age would not be an unwelcome thing."

"You won't make her feel guilt-ridden or unwelcome because she isn't one for remaining constantly at home?" The answer was clearly important to him.

"I know the person she is, Your Grace. And that is the woman I love, not a fictitious version of her."

The duke looked to his mother again. "Do you love him?"

She clasped her hands together, pressing the edges of her finger to her lips. "I most certainly do."

Roswell stepped closer to her. "I have wanted to hear you say that for so long."

"I feel the same about hearing it from you."

"Hold a moment on the miserably cloying aspects of all this," the duke grumbled. "I have another question for our vicar."

Roswell set an arm around Harriet's back and faced the man he hoped would soon be his son-in-law. "What is your question?"

"Are you reconciled to being murdered slowly and painfully if you cause her even an iota of pain or sadness?"

He tucked her in even closer. "I would deserve it."

His Grace nodded firmly. "Then, make your proposal, but do it with an eye to efficiency. I will not endure the drawn-out nausea I experienced with Harry and Athena."

The duke made to step from the room, but Harriet stopped him with a hand on his arm. "You truly don't object to this? I don't wish to cause you any distress."

The tender expression that touched the duke's scarred and usually fearsome visage was shocking. Further still, he took Harriet's hands in his. "Life has required you to walk one difficult path after another. It is time you had someone to walk with you."

"And your father . . . ?"

"Would want us both to be happy." He shrugged. "Persephone said so."

Harriet slipped her arms around her son and embraced him. "I love you, Adam. I wish I'd told you that more often."

Discomfort, emotion, uncertainty all flitted across the duke's face before his expression finally settled on determination. "I love you, Mother. And apparently so does Mr. Duncan." He stepped back, motioning to Roswell with a nod of his head. "Put the man out of his misery, as well as the dozens of Lancasters I suspect are waiting in the corridor for word of all this."

She turned to Roswell, the sweetest, gentlest smile on her face.

He took her hand and raised it to his lips, pressing a kiss to her fingers. "Will you marry me, Harriet?"

"In a heartbeat."

Roswell pulled her into his arms and kissed her properly. In the next instant, a rush of voices and footsteps broke into the library, congratulations being called out and declarations of how very perfect it all was. He kept Harriet in his arms and kissed her again, but quickly so she could receive the well-wishes of her family. Soon to be his family.

Their family.

CHAPTER THIRTEEN

WITH A CHRISTENING AND WEDDING on the same day, Adam had long since reached his limit of interacting with people. But Persephone had told him again and again to be agreeable and had quite specifically forbidden him to toss anyone into the gibbet. He'd made no promises about the stocks.

Persephone sat a bit to the side, holding Hestia in her arms. Oliver leaned against her, watching his sister with the same confused curiosity he had in the weeks since she was born. Mother was right; he had a beautiful family.

He was seized in that moment by a memory, decades old, of standing alone in this castle, his father only recently dead and Mother gone again, absolutely certain he would be alone his entire life. He never could have imagined then how his life would play out. He had Persephone who, by some miracle, loved him. They had two perfect children, who didn't despise him as he'd always feared his hypothetical children would.

He had a family, and it was whole and perfect.

The new Mr. and Mrs. Duncan—Adam doubted he would grow accustomed to that being Mother's name—approached, looking entirely pleased with the day's efforts.

"Oh, Adam," Mother said. "What a perfect day this has been. Thank you for enduring so many people for my sake."

"It was Persephone's idea," he grumbled.

"I will make certain to thank her as well." She threaded her arm through Mr. Duncan's. "We are going to be neighbors now, you know."

Adam nodded. "The wolves should prevent too-frequent visits."

She rolled her eyes at him. "Do not be grumpy with me, Adam Richard Boyce. I know you too well."

More and more people were of that opinion. He had a reputation to uphold. Still, this was his mother. "I am glad you will be close by more often."

"Oh, Adam." She hugged him. "You sweet, lovely boy." She held tight, not stepping back, not letting him go.

He shot a look of frustration to the first person he spotted. Harry, however, was not the most dependable in such situations.

Rather than rescue Adam from the uncharacteristically personal interaction, he cried out, "Mother Harriet," and threw his arms around them both.

An instant later Harry's entire brood of raucous children, his wife, her brother and sisters, and brother- and sister-in-law had joined the enthusiastic embrace, trapping Adam in the middle of it.

He looked over the top of them, directly at Persephone. She didn't do a thing to hide her amusement.

Through his tense jaw he said, "This is what happens when I'm agreeable."

She rocked their children and smiled at him. "I love you, Adam."

He eyed the hug horde. Ridiculous. Utterly ridiculous. Yet, he felt himself beginning to smile. He shook his head, but the shimmer of amusement didn't dissipate. Persephone had brought all this chaos into his life.

The lonely little boy was not alone anymore.

He locked eyes with his beloved again. "I love you too."

"Of course you do," she tossed back.

Of course he did. How could he not? She had breathed life back into more than just these thick stone walls. She'd brought *him* to life as well, had given him back his mother. And now Mother had found her own happiness.

Years of pain had begun to heal at last during that brief, miraculous Christmas at Falstone Castle.

ABOUT THE AUTHOR

© Annalisa Photography, used with permission

SARAH M. EDEN IS A *USA Today* best-selling author of witty and charming award-winning historical romances. Combining her obsession with history and her affinity for tender love stories, Sarah loves crafting deep characters and heartfelt romances set against rich historical backdrops. She holds a bachelor's degree in research and happily spends hours perusing the reference shelves of her local library. She lives with her husband, kids, and mischievous dog in the shadow of a snow-capped mountain she has never attempted to ski.

THE HEART OF CHRISTMAS

ANITA STANSFIELD

CHAPTER ONE
THE SEAMSTRESS

London, September 1820

ADELAIDE MOORE HURRIED FRANTICALLY TO plait her dark-blonde hair before pinning it into a bun that was too sloppy to make her look entirely respectable, but since she'd overslept, she knew opening the shop on time was far more important than the state of her hair. She quickly fastened the starched white apron over her blue dress, both of which were requirements to be worn when officially working. Miss Phyllis wouldn't tolerate her employees to wear anything less than perfection when they might be seen by customers; she considered their manner of dress to be a form of good advertising for a reputable dressmaker's shop. Adelaide had the responsibility of opening the shop and working in the front three days a week, alternating duties with Miss Sullivan—an older woman who had worked there for decades. Her face was pinched and sour, but her gray hair was always perfectly smooth, and never did a stray wisp dare defy her command to remain pinned in place 'til the last hour of the day. Miss Sullivan—whose given name Adelaide still didn't know—wore the required dress and apron with as much perfection as her hair, and not once had she expressed a kind word toward Adelaide in the many months she'd been working here.

Adelaide reminded herself now—as she had many times a day—that she was grateful to have a place to sleep and food to eat, as opposed to the possible alternatives. However, that didn't keep her from praying day and night that a better opportunity for employment might open up for her. Yet with the long hours she was required to work in Miss Phyllis Glade's shop just to earn her room and board, there was hardly time to go out seeking employment elsewhere. With the guidance and training of her mother,

Addie knew she was qualified to manage a household or even to be a lady's maid or companion. But she'd arrived in London more than a year earlier, looking as disheveled and desperate as she had felt. After days of searching for any work at all, only Miss Phyllis had been willing to take her in, and Addie had been grateful. But never would she have imagined still being in this situation a year later.

An eerie mist of fog slithered down the narrow street outside as Adelaide opened the curtains covering the large windows at the front of the shop and unlocked the door. She settled herself into a chair surrounded by displays of fabrics and laces and buttons, as well as lovely drawings of the latest fashions, which Miss Phyllis and her hired seamstresses could create with great expertise. Adelaide's skill with sewing was very minimal, since her only training had been what her mother had given her, which had all been purely for practical purposes—mostly mending and repairing old clothing in order to make it last as long as possible. Her mother's efforts had been focused on the hope that Addie would find work in a higher station. But when she'd come to this town looking for work, Miss Phyllis had been willing to give her meals and a place to sleep in exchange for doing basic stitching tasks. Adelaide had been hungry and out of money, and the offer had been the miracle she'd needed. Although, she'd truly expected to have found a better situation by now—one that actually gave her some income beyond simply having her basic needs met; she needed to be able to buy herself something decent to wear besides the shop uniform Miss Phyllis provided.

Adelaide's stomach growled from hunger as she set to work carefully hemming an elegant taffeta gown. The hem had been carefully measured and pinned by someone with more experience, and Adelaide simply had to make certain her stitches were very precise and even. Sitting in the front of the shop made her feel as if she were part of the display customers were meant to see—a busy seamstress in the midst of all the fabrics and drawings and frills. Someone was always meant to be here in case a customer entered. If Adelaide needed a break, she was to ask one of the seamstresses working in the back room to come and take her place, and if a customer needed any help beyond the simplest questions asked, Adelaide had been instructed to call for Miss Phyllis or one of her highest assistants. The Glade Dress Shop had been so successful for so many years that it employed more women than any other dress shop in the county—or at least that's what Adelaide had been told.

Adelaide glanced at the clock between stitches, dismayed to realize it would be more than an hour before she could even take a very quick break and sneak to the kitchen to grab a scone or bun in order to ease the ongoing grumbling of her stomach. That was the price for having overslept; that and her very sloppy hair, which she hoped no one noticed.

When the fog outside grew thicker, Adelaide had to get up to light a lamp and position it next to where she was working so that she could see her stitching clearly in spite of the stark lack of sunlight. She got comfortable again and hummed a tune her mother had taught her while she worked, which helped her feel slightly more cheerful in spite of doing tedious work on such a dismal day.

The door opened, making the little bell above it ring, startling Adelaide. She looked up to see a man step inside, bringing a bit of fog with him before he closed the door, which made the bell ring again. Adelaide was surprised to see a man here, since this was a woman's clothing shop, but she set her stitching aside and stood to greet him with a friendly smile. "Good morning, sir. May I help you with something?"

"I do hope so," he said, offering a smile in return that made his somewhat plain face appear far more comely. He removed his hat to reveal a head of blond hair that appeared to have been put neatly into place prior to it having come into contact with the hat. "I left my home in a hurry to walk to work—as I always do—and was buttoning my coat as I walked, and . . ." He opened his gloved hand to show her an escaped button. "It fell off in my hand, which is better than having lost it, but . . . I just happened to notice you through the window . . . and it appears you are quite proficient with needle and thread, and I wonder if I could trouble you to sew it back on for me . . . for a fair price, of course."

"I'd be happy to," she said, enjoying the idea of being able to solve a problem so easily for someone who was so kind.

"Oh, that's marvelous!" the gentleman said and removed his coat to reveal the sleeves of his white shirt, topped by a fine waistcoat. "I'll feel far less self-conscious with my customers if I'm properly dressed."

Adelaide took the fine coat from him, along with the button, motioning him toward a chair that was meant to be used by waiting customers. "Make yourself comfortable, and I'll be as quick as I can so you can get along to work."

"Thank you so much," he said and took a seat, pulling off his gloves. While Adelaide was searching for the right color of thread, he added, "It's very chilly for such an early autumn day. Seems like it was summer just a few days ago."

"I believe it was," Adelaide commented with a little laugh and sat down to thread her needle and get to work when she realized she had no idea how much to charge a customer for sewing on a button. It had never happened before; at least not to her.

"You're very good at that," the man said as Adelaide began reattaching the button.

"Oh, this is very simple work," she said. "That's all I do: the simple work. I don't have the skills of the other seamstresses, but I can certainly sew on a button and make certain it never falls off again."

"And that is exactly what I need," he said with enthusiasm. "My name is Theodore Hardwicke, by the way. I work at the bank just a little farther up the street. This is about halfway between my home and work. I've passed by here thousands of times, to be sure, and have never noticed the place before."

Adelaide laughed softly. "A gentleman would hardly need to know the location of a lady's dress shop." Adelaide checked herself, thinking that a married gentleman might very well know of such things; she hoped the comment hadn't sounded presumptuous. Mr. Hardwicke—she was glad to know his name—was likely a decade older than she was and appeared entirely respectable, which made it highly likely that he *was* married.

"Not since my wife passed, I'm afraid," he said, which took her off guard, perhaps because his comment seemed to be some kind of response to words she hadn't spoken aloud.

"Oh, I'm so sorry," Adelaide said with sincerity, glancing up at him just long enough to see that his eyes were focused on her work.

"Thank you, but . . . it's been nearly ten years now. It was difficult, but I've had time to become accustomed to her absence."

"So it's true what they say?" Adelaide asked, keeping her attention completely on her sewing, even while she thoroughly enjoyed some real conversation, especially since she couldn't recall the last time she'd talked about much of anything but sewing with anyone. "That time eases grief over such a loss?"

"Have you lost someone?" he asked instead of answering her question.

"My mother," she admitted, glad for the need to keep her eyes down when the threat of tears stung them at the very mention of her loss. "I cared for my mother through her lengthy illness and also took over all of her responsibilities about the house since my siblings had all left home; they're all older than I am." Adelaide sighed. "She passed just over a year ago."

"It's very fresh, then," Mr. Hardwicke said with a hint of sincere compassion. "Yes," he went on, now answering her question, "I do believe time helps. It doesn't diminish the love, but life goes on and we adjust, and eventually we realize we've adapted. But of course things are never the same."

"Of course," Adelaide said.

"May I know your name, Miss . . . ?"

"Moore," she said, glancing up for only a quick second, but long enough to note that he was looking at *her* now and not her needle. "Adelaide Moore, but my mother called me Addie."

"A lovely name," he said. "And tell me, Miss Moore, how did you come to be working here?"

"Truthfully?" she began, continuing with careful, tight stitches in order to hold the button firmly against the fine fabric. "After my mother passed, I left home, not wanting to remain there, for a number of reasons. I used all the money I had to get as far away as possible. I ended up here, desperately in need of work. Miss Phyllis . . . rather . . . Miss Phyllis Glade," she corrected, certain she shouldn't refer to her employer so casually to a customer, "was kind enough to take me in. She couldn't afford to give me a salary, but she gives me a place to sleep and three meals a day in exchange for doing the tedious work that doesn't take much skill, and which the other seamstresses loathe doing." She laughed softly, more to ease the tension of realizing how much she was talking; she found no humor in the situation whatsoever.

"And do you like your work here?" he asked.

She let out another tense, mirthless laugh. "You ask a great many questions, sir," she said. "Not that I'm complaining. Conversation is nice, especially when I usually work all alone."

"I confess I have an ulterior motive," he said along with his own nervous laugh.

"I beg your pardon?" she said, looking up at him.

"Answer my question first. Do you like your work here?"

"Not at all, sir," she said. "But it keeps me safe and meets my needs."

"Well, then," he said, "perhaps my losing a button was some form of . . . destiny."

"Destiny?" she echoed skeptically.

"I assure you my intentions are entirely honorable, Miss Moore. But I confess that I find you well-mannered, polite, and kind—traits that are not necessarily easily found in such a city as this. And I am very much in need of hiring someone to work in my home with a variety of duties. Perhaps you might consider a change of occupation and therefore be the answer to my prayers."

Adelaide felt frozen and sat there staring at Theodore Hardwicke, her needle poised midair and her mouth hanging open. She swallowed and cleared her throat, reminding herself to respond while at the same time hoping that no one was anywhere nearby in the back room on the other side of a dividing curtain, able to overhear this conversation. She cleared her throat again and came up with a reasonable question. "And what exactly would these duties entail?" She already knew that if he lived alone and wanted a young woman to cook and clean for him without anyone else in the house, she would politely decline. As kind as he was, she knew absolutely nothing about him. And even if he was as respectable as he seemed, she knew it wouldn't be proper for any young woman to work in such a situation; he'd do well to find himself a butler if he lived alone.

"I'll be quick since I need to be getting to work and I know you're nearly finished with that button. My wife passed during childbirth, leaving me to care for our daughter, who is now nine. Thankfully my wife's aunt came to assist when the baby came and has never left since she has no family of her own. She's been wonderful about taking care of everything, which has made it possible for me to work. However, she has recently taken ill—a problem with her heart, which has suddenly become worse—and she's down in bed most of the time. Hence, without her help, we are drowning in chaos. I need someone who can . . . well . . . do whatever needs to be done to keep a household functioning. I assume, from what you said, that you're able to do all of that? You must have some cooking skills. And the ability to watch out for my daughter when I'm not at home. She attends a fine school for girls; therefore, she's not at home for some hours during the day on the same days I work. And Aunt needs some looking after; you've admitted you cared for your mother during a lengthy illness, so I know you're capable of that."

Addie's heartbeat quickened as she listened to Mr. Hardwicke describe a job that felt so perfect for her she wanted to jump out of her chair and shout for joy. Instead she focused on finishing her task so he could be on his way, even while she listened to what he was saying and fought to remain composed.

"We have a lovely guest room that would be yours. You would share meals with the family. And I would also give you a fair salary for your work." He stood, and she handed him his coat, which he put on, then reached inside to pull a small card out of a hidden pocket. "This is where I live," he added, handing it to her. "Why don't you come by this evening at seven if you're interested. We can discuss the details, and you can decide if it's something you can feel good about."

"Thank you," she said, looking at the card in her hand with a printed address on it, along with the name *Theodore M. Hardwicke*. "I'll be there," she added, wanting to say yes to the job offer right there and then but grateful that he was giving her the opportunity to learn more before she decided.

"Excellent," he said with a smile that prompted her to return it with one of her own. "How much do I owe you for the—"

"Oh, don't worry about that," she said with a quick glance over her shoulder to make certain she was alone. She hoped no one had overheard her giving away work for free, but this man had been so kind she didn't want to charge him for such a simple task. "I'm glad to help," she added and meant it.

"I'm certain you are," he said, "but I know very well you are an employee here, and I don't want you getting into any trouble." He set some coins on a table next to an array of fabric swatches. A quick glance told her it was a ridiculous amount of money for sewing on a button. "You have a good day, Miss Moore, and I will see you this evening."

"You as well," she said, and he left quickly, making the bell above the door ring before he disappeared into the fog.

CHAPTER TWO
CHAOS AND DISORDER

ADDIE FINISHED HER DAY'S WORK, overcome with anticipation over her scheduled appointment with Mr. Hardwicke. The hours had dragged by since he'd miraculously appeared with an offer that might very well be the answer to many prayers. She shared a mostly silent and awkward supper with Miss Phyllis and one of the other seamstresses who also lived there. But the other seamstress had a great deal of skill and experience in the creation of fine gowns and therefore was treated with a great deal more respect. Addie had never been treated unkindly—at least not in any outward way—but she had mostly been ignored or barely acknowledged by the women with whom she worked and lived. And Miss Phyllis's other tenant actually had her own room with a comfortable bed, whereas Addie slept on the floor of the parlor since there had been no other beds available and the sofa was far too small and lacking in comfort for sleeping.

Through the course of the meal, Addie could think only of having a room and a bed of her own, not to mention an actual salary as opposed to simply a place to sleep and food to eat. She wondered if Miss Phyllis or the other women would even notice her absence should she decide to take Mr. Hardwicke up on his offer. She doubted Miss Phyllis would notice one less person at the table during their mostly silent meals. And she certainly wouldn't notice that Addie was no longer sleeping on her parlor floor, especially since Addie never prepared her makeshift bed there until after the others had gone to their rooms for the night and always had her bedding folded and put away before they woke up.

While trying not to eat too quickly, increasingly anxious to get out of this place and get to her appointment, Addie reminded herself not to get ahead of the present. Perhaps her interview with Mr. Hardwicke would go badly. Perhaps he would decide she wasn't right for the position after all. Or perhaps she would find some reason to decide that very thing for herself. She trusted her instincts, and she would never knowingly put herself into a situation that might only cause her problems. Until she and Mr. Hardwicke actually came to an arrangement over her agreeing to meet his expectations of someone to help care for his home and family, she needed to keep her own expectations realistic. But oh! How she wanted to be away from here! Mr. Hardwicke's providential need to have a button attached and his subsequent job offer had sparked in Addie her realization of how very much she hated the current state of her life and how desperately she needed a change—even if that change brought on a different set of challenges. She thought of how these ladies might miss the way she had done so much of the tedious stitching they all hated to do, but she doubted that even one of them would notice her absence any more than that.

As soon as Addie had helped clean the supper dishes and put them away, she informed Miss Phyllis she would be going out and felt surprisingly disappointed that this woman she'd lived and worked with for months now didn't express the slightest bit of curiosity over something Addie had never done before. Wrapped in a lightweight cloak, Addie set out into the fog, which had let up somewhat—for which she was grateful, considering that it was now getting dark and she needed to find her way to the address Mr. Hardwicke had given her. She was glad to know the dress shop was—as he had put it—about halfway between his home and the bank where he worked. If he walked the distance back and forth each day, it shouldn't take her terribly long to get there. She hoped not as she considered the time on the clock before she'd left the shop and her desire to be punctual for such a meeting.

Addie was glad she'd often taken walks when she'd had free time and she'd needed to get away from the stifling atmosphere in which she lived and worked. Her familiarity with the surrounding area served her well in being able to find her destination with little difficulty, even in the fog. Addie paused at the iron gate that was a part of the fence dividing the house from the street, with very little space in between. She looked up at the house, which was shrouded by just enough fog to give it an almost magical effect. It was a lovely structure, and large without being enormous; still, it was certainly larger than any home she had ever stepped into. Lamps glowed from windows on both the ground floor and the story above, and a pair of lanterns illuminated the front door between them. Addie took a deep breath, drew in all her courage and hopes, and opened the gate. She stepped through it and closed it behind her as quietly as she could manage, but it squeaked on its hinges and she felt certain anyone in the house could have easily heard evidence that a visitor had arrived. She went up the three steps leading to the door and knocked with the use of a finely crafted brass knocker. The door came open so quickly she felt certain someone *had* heard the gate squeaking.

"Hello," a young girl said with mild skepticism in her eyes *and* a voice that seemed far too advanced for a child. "Who might you be?" she asked, the skepticism more evident. Already Addie felt less confident. She had no experience with children beyond having helped care for a neighbor's children occasionally during her youth.

Bringing herself back to the moment, Addie attempted to come up with a suitable answer to this child's terse inquiry and was inexplicably grateful when she heard Mr. Hardwicke say, "Please be polite, Becky. We've talked about this."

The girl eyed Addie with that same skepticism one more time and hurried away. Addie looked up to see Mr. Hardwicke approaching, a smile on his face that put her at ease.

"I'm so glad you came," he said. "I feared you might not, and I confess I've been hoping very much that I can tempt you to give us the help we need."

Addie hoped for that too, in spite of her concerns for being able to care properly for the skeptical Becky. Trying to remain hopeful but also cautious, Addie returned his smile and said, "I thought we should at least talk about the situation and see if it might work out."

"Excellent," he said and motioned for her to come in.

Addie stepped into the house, and he closed the door. She took a quick glance around, noting a beautiful staircase in front of her, a lovely parlor to her left, and what appeared to be some kind of study or office to her right, with a huge desk buried in piles of books and papers at the center of the room. She assumed this was the room Mr. Hardwicke used for doing some of his business at home, as he had explained to her earlier. The house had a pleasant warmth to its atmosphere, but the clutter and lack of tidiness was immediately evident.

"You must forgive the state of things," Mr. Hardwicke said, his chuckle sounding slightly embarrassed. "At one time, Aunt kept everything perfectly pristine, but her health has slowly declined, and little by little the dust and disorder have accumulated. Now she is too weak to get far from her bed."

"Hence my reason for being here," Addie reminded him. "You certainly must not apologize."

"You're very kind," he said, chuckling again, this time sounding a bit nervous. Addie found it intriguing that the confidence he had exuded earlier today in the dress shop had turned to a mild shyness; she attributed this to the likelihood that he'd not had anyone inside his home, except for when it was necessary for business purposes, in a long time and he was terribly uncomfortable with the disorder.

Following some strained silence through which Addie determined that this was his home, he had invited her, and therefore he must be the one to guide this interaction, he finally said, "Why don't I show you around while we talk about exactly what the job would entail, and you can decide if it's right for you."

"Excellent," she said and removed her cloak, laying it over the back of a chair in the entry hall, being careful to avoid a stack of newspapers there that would prevent anyone from actually sitting in it.

Addie followed Mr. Hardwicke as he guided her through the rooms on the ground floor. He barely motioned toward his study and the parlor, which she'd already taken notice of. They walked through a lovely dining room with an elegant table and chairs enough for eight people. One end of the table was clean, which was obviously where he and his daughter sat to eat—and his wife's aunt, prior to her worsening health. But the other end of the table was covered with a number of odd items that looked like they belonged in many different places and had simply never been put away after being used here.

On the other side of the dining room was the kitchen, which was large and fine. Addie had never seen such an excellent stove, and there were two ovens. She noted that there were no dirty dishes; in fact, some that appeared freshly washed were drying near the sink. However, the remainder of the kitchen was only a little short of a complete disaster. Addie didn't sense that it was dirty as much as simply so out of order that it surely must have been difficult to accomplish any task in here without great stress.

Mr. Hardwicke picked up a lamp, and they walked quickly through the kitchen to a room where the laundry was done, and it too had the same ambience of the kitchen—in essence, it was also in much need of attention. After a peek in there, they walked back through the kitchen and dining room and returned to the entry hall, where they'd begun. While Mr. Hardwicke talked a little about the routine of the household and the needs of Becky and his wife's aunt, Addie followed him down a hall toward the back of the house, where they peeked into a library with more books than she'd ever imagined existed and two comfortable-looking sofas, but it looked as if this room hadn't been used at all in a very long time. She suspected that perhaps members of the family might have come in here to find a book but had never stayed to read due to the amount of dust. She wondered if this room had been cleaned since Mrs. Hardwicke's death; it certainly looked like it had more than nine years' worth of dust.

As if he'd read Addie's mind, Mr. Hardwicke explained. "My wife called the library her sanctuary. She loved to relax here. It's not been used in such a way since before her death . . . as you can see."

"But if it were clean," Addie suggested, "perhaps your daughter might enjoy spending time in this room her mother enjoyed so much."

Mr. Hardwicke made a contemplative noise and said, "I'd never thought of that, but you might be right."

"You wouldn't have a problem with that?" she asked, wanting clarification. "Since it is where your wife—"

"It's been a very long time, Miss Moore," he said. "I have many pleasant memories of Becky's mother. I've not avoided this room because it was her favorite; well . . . perhaps at first I did. And perhaps that's why Aunt avoided cleaning it; I'm not certain because we never talked about it. But I do like your suggestion. However," he chuckled, a little less nervously than before, "you might find that all of the necessary tasks in the household keep you too occupied to take on a project like this." He chuckled again. "Should you decide to take the job, of course."

"Of course," Addie said. She certainly hadn't made her mind up yet, but she couldn't deny that she was strongly leaning toward accepting the position. She felt surprisingly comfortable here. She liked Mr. Hardwicke, and she felt drawn to the challenge of putting this house in order. Her biggest concern at this point was contending with the peevish little Miss Hardwicke. But surely Addie could manage one cantankerous child. Already Addie could presume the obvious likely cause for Becky's temperament. Her father was very busy, and the great aunt who had always cared for her was in very poor condition, which meant her routine had been greatly altered, and likely her sense of security with it. The girl had never known her mother, and her home, with all of its disarray, was likely an uncomfortable place to exist, no matter how lovely and fine a home it was.

Mr. Hardwicke led Addie up the stairs, and from the landing she could see five doors, three of them partially open and the other two closed. He pointed at one of the closed doors and said, "That is the water closet, and all of the bathing items are kept there. In spite of our limitations, Becky and I have tried to keep that room the cleanest, for obvious reasons."

"Very good to know," Addie said, not at all liking the idea of *that* room being as neglected as other rooms in the house.

He pointed to one of the open doors and said, "This is my bedroom. I make some attempt to keep it in order, and of course any cleaning needed in there would be done while I'm at work." He pointed to another open door and said, "That's Becky's room." He lowered his voice slightly, and Addie realized Becky was probably in there and he didn't want his daughter to overhear. "I've attempted to get her to keep it in order, but I confess I'm not very good at motivating a child." Addie simply nodded, thinking that Becky likely had little motivation to keep her own room clean and orderly when the rest of the house was not. "And this is Aunt's room," Mr. Hardwicke said, stepping toward the open door. "You should meet her. I told her you were coming." Addie followed him as he knocked on the open door and peered around it to say, "I have Miss Moore with me. Would you like to meet her?"

Addie heard a woman say, "Doesn't matter whether or not I approve of anyone you might hire."

He didn't argue but rather said, "I do believe you'll like her; she's very kind."

Addie appreciated his compliment and the enthusiasm in his voice as he opened the door wider and guided Addie into the room.

"Miss Moore, this is my wife's aunt Marla. Aunt, this is Miss Adelaide Moore."

"A pleasure to meet you," Addie said, not knowing what to call this woman. She hadn't been told a surname, but using her given name didn't feel appropriate; she wasn't *Addie's* aunt. "You may call me Addie," she added, preferring a lack of formality and hoping it might prompt the same from Mr. Hardwicke and Aunt Marla.

Aunt Marla responded only by speaking with a cynicism that allowed Addie some additional insight into a possible contribution to Becky's less-than-polite nature. "I suppose you're going to come in and take over the house."

"If I take the job, I will simply do my best to put the house in order according to the example you've set all these years." Addie saw the aunt's countenance soften slightly at this hint of respect for her efforts, which was what Addie had been hoping for. She continued by saying, "I'm certain having the house in order and some good meals might ease your concerns and help you relax more and get the rest you need."

Aunt Marla said nothing more, but there was the tiniest hint of something in her eyes that helped Addie believe she might be able to find her way past this woman's crankiness.

"I'll check in on you before bed," Mr. Hardwicke said to Aunt Marla before he and Addie left the room.

He led the way to the other closed door and opened it, stepping inside. Addie followed and could see from the glow of the lamp he lifted higher that it was a typical bedroom, but larger and finer than any she'd ever seen—except for that of Aunt Marla. Her prospective employer said, "On the chance that you take pity on us and accept the job, this would be your room. I would be sure to dust it myself before you come to stay, and even though the bedcover is surely very dusty, the bedding beneath it is all completely clean." He turned to look at her more directly and recited a few more details of what exactly he would need of her, but he promised she would have time to herself at a certain interval of the day and each evening after supper was over and he was at home. Then he told her the amount of money he was willing to give her on top of her room and board, and Addie had to fight to keep from either gasping or choking. Even if this job didn't work out long-term for some unforeseen reason, Addie could make enough money in just a few months to leave London or at least be well-dressed enough to be able to acquire a much better occupation than the tedious stitching she was currently doing.

"If you decide to accept my offer," he said, "just let me know when you would be able to leave the dress shop, and we will greatly anticipate having your help." He chuckled, this time sounding more nervous than ever. "I can't deny that I'm very much hoping you'll agree to at least give us a chance, and as you can see . . . the sooner the better, and—"

"How about now?" Addie said with complete confidence. Everything inside of her knew this was the right choice for her life at this time. And now that the offer had been made and she was fully aware of what she was stepping into, she felt as if she couldn't get away from Miss Phyllis's home and dress shop fast enough.

"Now?" Mr. Hardwicke echoed with a delighted little laugh.

"I confess I very much detest my current situation. I would need to go back only long enough to gather my things from the house, which is behind the dress shop, and leave a note for Miss Phyllis; she'll have gone to her room for the evening by now and doesn't wish to be disturbed, so I—"

"Well, I'd be delighted to have you start immediately," he said, "but you mustn't walk there and back in the dark. I'll get a cabriolet and accompany you."

"Oh, that's not necessary," Addie said. "I can—"

"I insist," Mr. Hardwicke said, and she followed him down the stairs after he'd informed his daughter and Aunt Marla that he would be out for a short while. He took Addie into his study and invited her to sit at his desk, where there were writing materials so she could pen the appropriate communication to Miss Phyllis about her leaving. While Addie wrote, Mr. Hardwicke went out to hail a cab. Addie had no trouble thanking Miss Phyllis for taking her in when she'd needed food and shelter, but she also had no trouble letting her know that she'd found more favorable employment and needed to begin her new job immediately.

Only a few minutes after Addie had finished her note and folded it, she was seated with Mr. Hardwicke in a cabriolet while the hooves of the horse pulling the cab clattered on the cobbled street. Even though there was hardly a word spoken between them, Addie felt a strange awareness of his presence in the confined space of the cab's interior. Pondering how remarkably safe she felt—a sensation quite foreign to her—and the deepening comfort over her decision to work for Mr. Hardwicke, she actually felt some excitement for the future, perhaps for the first time in her life. The goodness of this man seemed to glow all around him, even in the darkness, and she had an instinctive desire to always remain within his proximity.

Once the cab arrived at the dress shop, Addie forced herself back to more practical thinking. Mr. Hardwicke waited with the cab while Addie crept down the alleyway and into the door that had been left unlocked for her. She quickly gathered her very few belongings into the bag she'd brought with her when she'd left home. She set the note for Miss Phyllis on the kitchen table and left the place once and for all, locking the door behind her, feeling more excited and hopeful than she'd perhaps *ever* felt. She prayed that this opportunity was as good as it seemed and that she might be able to truly be of service to this family, just as she was being given a chance at a better life in exchange.

CHAPTER THREE
BENEATH THE DUST

Upon returning to her new home, Mr. Hardwicke again apologized to Addie for the accumulation of dust in the room she was to use, but she assured him that she was certainly capable of taking on the dust and conquering it. "Is that not why you hired me?" she asked him with a smile that didn't begin to express how much lighter she already felt in having left the stifling life she'd shared with Miss Phyllis.

"I suppose it is," he said at the foot of the stairs before he told her where to find clean water and linens. She thanked him and assured him she would manage to see to her own needs and he shouldn't worry about her a bit.

Once alone in her new room, Addie hurried to clean the dust off the bedside table and the bureau; the rest could wait until she wasn't so tired. She carefully removed the bedcover by folding the dusty top inside so particles wouldn't be released into the air only to have them settle elsewhere. She set the folded bedcover aside for laundering at another time. Inside a wardrobe Addie found two spare blankets neatly folded, which had been spared the dust because the cupboard closed up tightly. She spread one of them onto the bed over the clean linens there, which would help compensate for the lack of fire in the grate. Wood, kindling, and matches were available, albeit dusty, but Addie didn't feel cold enough to be motivated to light a fire.

She let out the biggest, loudest, deepest sigh of her life when she crawled into an actual bed for the first time since she'd left home, and this bed was far more luxurious and comfortable than the one she'd used growing up. She'd never imagined living in such a fine place with so many lovely amenities. She fell asleep quickly and slept well, waking just as the light of dawn was beginning to fill the room. Through all the years of caring for her mother and doing everything her mother *couldn't* do, Addie's body had been trained to wake up early so she could make certain everything was in order.

Enthusiastic about taking on her new responsibilities, Addie hurried to get dressed and pin up her hair before she crept quietly downstairs to the kitchen, glad the bedrooms were all upstairs so she could work here and not wake anyone. After taking a few minutes to assess what was available for cooking, and a few more minutes to clean just enough to make working there more feasible and healthy, she lit a fire in the stove.

By the time she heard noises from upstairs, she had washed and sliced some potatoes thinly enough to be cooked quickly in a hot frypan, and she'd also scrambled some eggs, brewed a pot of tea, and found both cream and milk in the cool pantry where she'd found the eggs.

Realizing there was very little food available for meals she would be expected to cook, she knew acquiring groceries was the most important topic she needed to approach with Mr. Hardwicke before he left for the day. At her home in the country, they'd had their own cow and chickens, and she'd been accustomed to acquiring the eggs and milk each day on her own. She knew Miss Phyllis or one of her assistants had gone to the grocer's almost every day to acquire food, but as the woman had sent Addie only a few times, she wasn't at all confident about doing what seemed such a simple task, at least not here in the city, where everything was so different from her country upbringing.

"Good morning," she heard Mr. Hardwicke say, startling Addie. His coming into the kitchen had occurred while she'd been stirring the potatoes, and she'd not heard his approach.

"Good morning," she replied, noting the smile on his face and the surprise in his eyes. Such kind eyes, she noticed.

"You're already up and busy," he declared as if he might have expected to need to wake her. "I don't think we've had a real cooked breakfast in a long time. We usually get by with bread and jam."

Addie just smiled at him again and said, "Have a seat and I'll bring everything to the table." He hesitated for a moment, as if he might be uncomfortable with having her wait on him in such a manner, but he let out a little nervous chuckle and went to the dining room.

By the time Addie had everything on the table, Becky had arrived, also looking pleased with the cooked breakfast but not commenting. As Addie was leaving to let them enjoy their breakfast, Mr. Hardwicke said, "You must join us! It's silly for you to eat alone, and we could use the company."

Becky scowled slightly, which made it easier for Addie to accept her employer's invitation. Instinctively she believed the sooner she could get Becky to *really* express whatever might be upsetting her so much, the sooner they could get past it; at least, that's what she'd learned from her relationships with her siblings. "I'll just . . . get some dishes," Addie said. "Thank you, sir. You're very kind."

She returned to the table to lay a place for herself, surprised to hear Mr. Hardwicke say, "I'll not have you calling me *sir*. Even *Mr. Hardwicke* makes me feel like I'm at work, and when I'm home I don't *want* to feel so formal. Please call me Theo." Addie met his eyes briefly, seeing something warm and inviting there that made her eager to accept his invitation. She, too, preferred a lack of formality, but even in that moment—when she had been here so short a time—she felt a sincere desire to get to know him better, to learn more about him than what might be warranted in her simply working for him.

"Very well," she said and sat down to eat, certain in spite of her desires that it would take time to become accustomed to calling this man by his given name. Perhaps, for the time being, she could just avoid having to call him anything at all.

Breakfast was made less awkward when Becky began to eat so voraciously that Addie might have believed she'd been starved for weeks. But her father seemed much the same, and Addie felt some gratification to think that already she'd been able to make their lives better by giving them something to eat besides bread and jam. While they were eating, Addie asked Theo about acquiring groceries, and he thanked her for reminding him.

"Most mornings," he said, "I leave a list at the grocer's on my way to work. They have delivery boys who will pick things up from the butcher and baker, and they will deliver everything before noon. I have accounts I settle monthly, so all you need to do is be here to receive the order. Any errands you need to do can be done past noon."

"How very convenient," Addie said, liking this plan very much. "I will hurry and make a list before you leave."

"Put down anything you'd like; I'm not certain what you're accustomed to cooking, but we will be glad to eat anything if it's half this good." He motioned with his fork toward his plate.

"It's only some potatoes and eggs," Addie said with a little laugh.

"And very delicious," he said. Becky's eyes agreed, even though she still hadn't uttered a sound. "Mrs. Baird—who has a daughter near Becky's age who attends the same school—will come by for Becky at about half past eight so they can all walk to school together. The dear woman has been good enough to watch out for Becky on the way to and from school ever since she began attending a couple of years ago; in fact, it was her idea for Becky to attend this particular school. She had been friends with my wife, you see."

"That is also very convenient," Addie said, liking the idea of not having to see Becky to school herself, especially with all of the work needed in the house. She added, in an effort to reassure him, "I will take some breakfast and fresh water up to Aunt Marla the moment I'm done making that list. I'm keeping a plate warm for her on the stove."

"Excellent!" Theo declared as if she were literally lifting weight off his shoulders. In fact, he straightened up a little in his chair as he said it, and Addie felt almost giddy at the evidence of easing the burdens of this good man.

Addie looked at Becky and said, "Do you need any help getting ready for school?"

"No," was all Becky said.

Her father added, "She's very good at taking care of herself." He smiled at his daughter, obviously meaning it as a compliment, but Becky's expression showed she didn't necessarily agree.

Not long after they'd all finished eating breakfast, Theo was on his way to work with Addie's list for groceries in hand. Becky went to her room and closed the door, which Addie took to mean she was getting ready for school, while Addie took breakfast and fresh water to Marla's room. The older woman seemed pleased and said politely, "Thank you. You're very kind." But she didn't respond to Addie's attempts at any conversation. It was evident that Marla could get in and out of bed and move around her room enough to see to her own most basic needs, but she was clearly weak and easily out of breath, which was surely the reason she'd stopped venturing beyond the walls of her own room quite some time ago.

Mrs. Baird arrived with her daughter right on time, and Becky was at the door and ready to go. "Thank you for getting yourself ready on time," Addie said to the child. "You are a very responsible young lady; that's clear enough." Becky thoughtfully took in the comment but said nothing. "You have a good day, and I will see you later," Addie said as Becky quickly went out the door and was on her way.

Addie liked the feeling of being alone in the house, except for Aunt Marla, who would not be able to look over her shoulder while she worked since she couldn't leave her own room. She set to work first in the kitchen, knowing that the need for humans to eat—and the fact that good food also lifted spirits—made the kitchen the heart of any home. She wanted *this* room to be the first that was completely clean and perfectly in order. Just as with the little bit of cleaning she'd done in her own new room, she found that beneath the dust everything in this house was fine and lovely. It was all simply long overdue for some personal attention. She made good progress with scrubbing everything from ceiling to floor and in between, so much so that she was nearly finished when the groceries were delivered at about half past eleven.

While putting the abundance of food items away where they belonged, Addie made sandwiches from fresh, soft bread that had come from the bakery, freshly made butter from a jar, and slices of cold roasted beef that had come from the butcher. Addie hadn't even realized butchers sold cooked meats, but apparently they did. She had put beef on the list, and a raw piece of flank had come, as well as an ample supply of the cooked slices. Addie lit the stove, since the breakfast fire had gone out, and she hurried to put the flank into a pot in the oven. She washed and sliced some apples, which she added to the plates beside the sandwiches and put the plates on a tray along with two glasses of milk before she headed up the stairs, hoping Aunt Marla wouldn't mind if they shared lunch, as opposed to Addie simply delivering her meal.

"What's this?" Marla asked, her eyes going wide as she turned from staring toward the window, where the persistent fog made it impossible to see anything but some tree branches. While Addie was setting the tray on the large bureau, Marla added, "Theo generally brings some food up before he leaves that will keep through the day. It keeps me from going hungry, but it's never been very appetizing."

"I can imagine," Addie said and took a deep breath before she turned more toward Marla and asked, "Would it be all right if I eat lunch in here with you? I always ate in my mother's room with her when she was bedridden, and I confess I'm quite lonely for company; I was hoping you wouldn't mind."

Marla looked freshly astonished. "I'd be glad for your company, dear," she said. "Theo's far too busy with his work, and little Becky has mostly kept her distance since my illness grew worse." Marla was far more talkative than she had been this morning, and Addie hoped that was a good sign.

"I'm so sorry for that," Addie said and realized the older woman was getting out of bed.

As Marla moved toward a small table with two chairs on either side, Addie set the food there. Once they were both seated and Marla had volunteered to offer a blessing on the food, they both began to eat. Marla commented more than once on how good the food tasted and how nice it was to have company. She asked Addie many questions about her life and what had brought her to be in the employment of this household.

Addie felt surprisingly comfortable telling this woman about how her father had been a heavy drinker, and a cruel one at that. Somehow he'd managed to keep a job, which had prevented them from being destitute, but all of Addie's siblings had left home the moment they were old enough to find their own employment and lodgings. Since she'd come from a rather small village in the country, most of them had moved rather far away. Addie told Marla how she had stayed to care for her mother, who had been unable to get out of bed at all. She too had wanted to leave, but she had known her father would never take care of her mother. So Addie had done her best to keep the house in order, care for her mother, and avoid her father when he was drunk.

"As soon as my mother passed and the burial was complete," Addie concluded, "I packed up what little I owned and used the small amount of money I'd managed to put away to get myself to London. I was blessed enough to get work for a dressmaker, but she only gave me room and board. That's where Mr. Hardwicke found me just yesterday when he needed a button sewn onto his coat. This job is an answer to my prayers; I only hope I can do it well."

"I'd say you're doing very well so far," Marla said, eating her lunch so slowly that Addie became aware of how her weakness and difficulty breathing made it hard for the poor woman to do anything normally. But Addie matched her pace as they visited over a lengthy lunch. Addie thought of the cleaning she could be doing, but she'd accomplished a great deal this morning, and there was a beef flank in the oven for tonight's supper.

"And what about you?" Addie asked, hoping that her own candid confessions might prompt Marla to be more open about her circumstances. Having a woman in the house in whom Addie could confide and with whom she could chat had great appeal. "How did you come to live here with Mr. Hardwicke and Becky?"

"I suspect Theo likely mentioned a little to you, but I know him well enough to know that he likely didn't expound much." Marla smiled slightly. It was evident she liked Theo; it was as if she were teasing him even though he wasn't there. More seriously, she went on. "My niece—the late Mrs. Hardwicke—was my only living relative. Her parents had both passed, and I had promised her mother that I would watch out for Rebecca— that was her name, and Theo named the baby after her, always calling her Becky to establish the difference. Rebecca's baby was due about the middle of January, according to the doctor's calculations, so we decided through letters that I would come for Christmas and just stay until she'd had the baby and had recovered enough to manage on her own. Theo was very generous in providing the money for my traveling expenses." Addie saw Marla's expression darken, and it was easy to guess the path of her thoughts even before she said, "And then when the baby came, it was so difficult for her, and . . . Rebecca lived less than an hour after our little Becky was born—only long enough to hold her for a few moments." Marla sighed.

It was evident time had eased her grief, but memories of that horrible Christmas still clearly brought sorrow, which was certainly understandable. She sighed again and declared, "Theo asked me to stay—begged, more like. He told me he couldn't possibly work and care for an infant, and he was right. He could hire someone, but he preferred that Becky have family to care for her, and I couldn't dispute that. Besides, I had no one else. So as soon as the baby was old enough to travel and the weather had warmed, we went together back to my home in the country to get the rest of my things, which didn't amount to much. I've been here ever since. It was a few years ago that I started having some little bouts of weakness and getting out of breath. But it's gradually worsened. The doctor has been useless. He's just told me if exerting myself causes the problem, I shouldn't exert myself."

Addie didn't know enough to be able to agree or disagree with the doctor, but she did say, "Well, I will do my best to take very good care of you from now on. And I hope we can become friends as well."

Marla smiled and reached across the table to squeeze Addie's hand. "You're a kind girl," she said.

"I've very much enjoyed visiting with you," Addie declared. "If it's all right with you, we'll make a habit of it."

"I'd like that very much," Marla said before Addie declared the need to get some more work done before Becky came home from school.

Addie spent the remainder of the afternoon in the kitchen and felt good about all she'd accomplished by the time she heard Becky coming in the front door. Addie put on a cheerful face to greet the child, but Becky seemed little more than annoyed to have Addie there. Every question about how her day had gone was met with simply, "All right." After Becky said "all right" more than a dozen times, Addie said, "Would you like to join me and Aunt Marla in her room for tea?"

"Tea?" Becky asked, her eyes showing a glimmer of enthusiasm. "We've not had tea since Auntie became too ill to work in the kitchen."

"Then it's high time we did," Addie said. "I've made a cinnamon cake and some cucumber sandwiches. Why don't you wash up and take one of the plates upstairs, and I'll be up shortly with the rest; the tea kettle is already hot."

Becky went to the kitchen and did as she was told. Marla was even more pleased than Becky to be sharing tea in her room. She too tried to get the child to talk about her day at school, her friends, anything, but Becky was quiet and subtly solemn. But the child obviously enjoyed the cake and sandwiches. Marla suggested lightly that perhaps she couldn't talk to them because her mouth was always full. Becky seemed to like that idea and kept eating. Once she'd had her fill, she excused herself politely but couldn't get out of the room fast enough.

"I keep hoping she'll come around," Marla said with a sigh once alone with Addie. "She was always a content and cheerful child, but in the last year or so she's become more as you see her. And when I became too weak to care for her and her father as I'd been doing, she became especially solemn. Sometimes she gets downright snappish, although it never lasts long since she knows her father won't have it. Still, I worry over her."

Addie didn't know how to console Marla's concerns, other than to say, "I'll do my best to keep an eye on her—as much as she'll let me. Hopefully it's a stage she'll pass through soon enough."

"Oh, I do hope!" Marla said before she profusely thanked Addie for the tea and the company.

"I assure you I enjoyed myself likely far more than you did," Addie said as she gathered everything onto a tray and left the room, exchanging a smile with Marla before backing out the door.

She set to work on cooking supper and managed to finish cleaning the kitchen while potatoes and vegetables were cooking that would be served with the beef flank that was still roasting its way to being perfectly tender. When the food was nearly ready and Addie knew Theo was due to arrive home soon, she went upstairs to tell Becky she needed her to lay the table for supper and also a tray to be taken up to Aunt Marla. Becky argued with Addie rather vehemently until Addie said nonchalantly, "Very well. I'll do it myself. And this evening I'll discuss with your father what he feels your responsibilities should be. In my family every person had chores to do that contributed to the household because every person lived there and benefitted from the house being in order and the meals cooked. But I shall leave that up to your father."

Becky said nothing but huffed past Addie and hurried down the stairs to do as Addie had asked, and she did a good enough job of it that Addie knew she'd done it many times before. Becky was just finishing up when her father came home, full of excited compliments about the smell of supper, the way Becky had laid the table, and the cleanliness of the kitchen. While he washed up, Addie took a supper tray up to Marla and then returned to put the food on the table with Becky's reluctant assistance.

Since it had been mandated that Addie eat with Theo and Becky, Addie did her best to ease the silence by asking Theo about his day at work, but he wasn't much more forthcoming than his daughter. But Addie continued to gently press him to converse, and he finally smiled at her with a subtle sparkle in his eyes that prompted an inexplicable warmth inside of her. Theo told Addie about a humorous incident that had happened at the bank that afternoon, frequently looking at her as if she were some kind of angel descended from heaven. He complimented her on the excellent meal at least three times and expressed his gratitude for the positive difference she had already made in their home. Addie felt a little embarrassed over so much attention being given to her efforts, but she responded graciously and continued to encourage him to talk about his day; she found she truly enjoyed listening to him talk. Becky just ate her meal—once again as if she'd been starving—completely oblivious to the conversation and long glances being exchanged by the adults at the table.

Later that evening, after Marla too had offered Addie deep gratitude for such a fine meal, Addie felt a mixture of fulfillment in her new employment and concern for the people with whom she now lived. She focused on her fulfillment while Theo put his daughter to bed and Addie put the kitchen in pristine order, ready for the start of another day.

Before Addie went to bed, Theo thanked her again for a fine supper, and added, "It's so nice to have you here. Already everything feels better. Marla told me she very much enjoys your company, and Becky was delighted to have tea. So . . . thank you." He smiled at her in a way that provoked a fluttering in her stomach, which she credited to how good it felt to simply receive acknowledgment and appreciation for her efforts.

"Of course," Addie said. "I'm just doing my best to accomplish what you hired me to do."

Addie told him goodnight and checked with Marla to see if she needed anything. She was able to help Marla with a few personal things that were much appreciated, before she went to her new bedroom and slept well after such a busy day.

CHAPTER FOUR
ADELAIDE'S QUEST

ADDIE QUICKLY SETTLED INTO A fairly comfortable routine in the Hardwicke household. Each day she made progress with putting the house in order and finding the beauty in each room as the dust and clutter was done away. She and Marla became friends, sharing the ability to talk and enjoy each other's company in a way Addie had only experienced with her own mother. And Addie became comfortable enough to actually call her employer by his given name. In fact, she began to enjoy his company so much that she sometimes feared the possibility of not being able to remain here forever. In spite of Theo's somewhat shy nature, he was clearly growing more comfortable conversing with her, and Addie enjoyed their interactions very much.

It didn't take long for Addie to observe the typical habits and personalities of this family she worked to care for. Marla was weaker on some days than others, but she found satisfaction in doing as much for herself as possible. Addie did her best to help Marla achieve a balance between self-reliance and not doing too much. Rebecca Hardwicke's aunt was a kind and insightful woman who was often full of laughter as they chatted over lunch and tea. But there was also a sorrow about her that Addie didn't fully understand since Marla seemed hesitant to talk about anything sad.

Becky became more cooperative as the weeks went by, although Addie suspected that was mostly due to the girl's realization that Addie wasn't going away and her father wouldn't be pleased if Addie reported to him that his daughter had been disrespectful. While Addie didn't like the idea of tattling on Becky to her father—and as of yet it hadn't become necessary—she realized the very threat of it was the only thing that seemed to give Becky the incentive to do what had become her daily chores.

Addie expected Becky to lay the table for breakfast and supper and help prepare her great aunt's food trays. She also required the girl to keep her own room in order. Over the course of nearly a month, working in small increments each day, Addie had helped Becky sort through and organize all of her belongings and put her room in orderly condition. Becky never complained aloud, but Addie knew the child hated the project—until the results started to become evident. Then Becky's enthusiasm increased, and when everything was in order, the child offered the first real smile Addie had ever seen.

"Now," Addie told her, "if you make up your bed every day and put things away after you use them, the room will always stay tidy, and you'll enjoy your time in here much more. And once a week you'll need to dust everything the way I showed you."

"Thank you, Miss Addie," Becky said, and Addie felt as if she could have fallen like a rock to hear such words coming from this child who had barely addressed her at all in the time she'd been living and working in the same home.

Addie swallowed carefully, her fulfillment deepening at the hint of tears making her eyes tingle. "You're very welcome, Miss Becky," she said.

They exchanged a smile, and both admired the lovely room. It was decorated in pastel spring colors, with floral patterns in the curtains and bedcovers, almost making it look like a garden in bloom now that it was all in order. There were shelves of pretty dolls and storybooks and other toys, some of which Becky was too old to ever play with again, but she had declared their sentimental value and had chosen to keep them.

After that Becky was a little less petulant about doing her daily chores, and a little less silent, although she still never said anything that was actually conversational. Still, Addie was thrilled with the progress they'd made, and it gave her hope she could yet come to understand this little girl better and perhaps help her to be happier, as a child living in such a fine home with a loving aunt and father should be.

One afternoon after Becky came home from school, Addie asked the child to join her to go down the hall to the library. Becky looked confused as she asked, "Is there something you want me to read?"

"Reading is wonderful, as I know you are aware," Addie said, "but that's not why I brought you here. Did you know this was your mother's favorite room? She loved to relax here."

Becky said nothing, but intrigue shone in her eyes. Addie went on to repeat what Becky's father had told her, and then she asked if Becky would be interested in helping her remove all the dust and put the room in order a little at a time, just as they'd done with Becky's bedroom. "And then," Addie said, "perhaps you might like to come here and read or do other things you like, or maybe we could have tea here occasionally."

"Just like my mother," Becky said with enthusiasm and agreed whole-heartedly to helping Addie with the project.

Less than a week later the library was clean and in order, and it became common for Becky to do her schoolwork or read or draw in the room that had been her mother's sanctuary. And sometimes she even began humming as she did so, which Addie couldn't help but smile at.

As autumn left in a sudden rush, making it very cold outside, Addie reached the point where she felt that she'd achieved the goal of putting the entire house in order. She'd scrubbed and dusted and organized every room, including the cellars and pantries below the kitchen. With all of that finally completed, she established a new routine that focused more on maintaining the order of the house, and she was able to spend more time cooking and baking things her mother had taught her to make prior to her illness. The family was appreciative of her culinary skills, and Addie began to enjoy mealtimes every day. Breakfast and supper with Theo and Becky were mostly devoid of conversation, but she had become comfortable with them and was glad to not be alone. Comparing their company to that of Miss Phyllis and the other seamstresses made Addie deeply grateful for the quiet comfort of being here with these people.

Addie often found Theo looking at her with some kind of intrigue in his eyes. At first she had a tendency to look away, but over time she felt her own intrigue growing and she found it easier to return his gaze, as if they were silently attempting to assess each other's character or perhaps reach each other's minds. Addie wondered if he might be more prone to share adult conversation with her if Becky weren't always present at meals, but knowing Theo had a definite shyness about him, she wondered if he actually preferred having his daughter there, making it easier to avoid talking. Addie hoped they would eventually find opportunities to talk more, since she had grown to admire him very much and felt a sincere desire to get to know him better. And she sensed he felt the same about her.

Each day, Addie very much enjoyed lunch and tea with Aunt Marla; most of the time Becky joined them for tea and seemed to like behaving very maturely while she listened to the adults do most of the talking. Sometimes Becky wanted to have her afternoon cake and sandwiches alone in the library, apparently enjoying the idea of doing what her mother had done. Whether Becky was present or not, Addie enjoyed spending time with Marla. Through every conversation they became closer and more comfortable with each other. As Marla explained the details of her physical symptoms and what the doctor had told her, Addie felt a little confused but didn't comment. Who was she to question what the doctor had said? And yet she'd had a great many conversations with the local doctor from her hometown throughout the course of her mother's long illness, and there were some things about Marla's ailments that Addie didn't understand. The reasons for her weakness seemed inconsistent, and Addie couldn't help wondering if Marla was mostly just exhausted both emotionally and physically due to the burden she had been carrying in the household. Addie sincerely believed her mother's health problems had been mostly due to the hardships of her life; according to Addie's own observations, emotional and physical challenges sometimes went hand in hand, and she wondered if that was the case with Marla. But she kept her thoughts to herself—at least for now.

Theodore Hardwicke was the most confusing conundrum in the household. While Addie had a deep desire to become more comfortable with both Marla and Becky and perhaps be able to help with whatever might be troubling them, which they were not willing to discuss, Addie was most fascinated by Theo. She'd never heard an unkind word come out of his mouth, even when he'd been very frustrated with his daughter. He was always appreciative of Addie's efforts and highly complimentary over every piece of evidence of her hard work as the house had gradually transformed. He paid her a generous wage, some of which Addie had used to get herself some much-needed new clothes. She'd taken to going into town one afternoon a week between lunch and tea while Becky was at school. And she felt deeply blessed with the abundance Theo Hardwicke had brought into her life. Yet, she felt strangely preoccupied with him and deeply concerned for reasons she couldn't quite decipher. Sometimes she actually felt a fluttering deep inside when she heard the door and knew he'd come home from work or when he entered a room, always greeting her with a warm smile and kind words. But it was the subtle sparkle in his eyes that affected her most, making her wonder if he too felt the same quickened heartbeat whenever they encountered each other.

Theo always shared meals with his daughter when he wasn't working, and he always read a story to Becky at bedtime and tucked her in for the night. But beyond that, he spent nearly every waking minute in his study—a room which Addie had been able to clean and tidy only to a point, since he had books and papers scattered about in what seemed to be a kind of strange order she hadn't dared disturb. Occasionally someone came to the house in the evening to meet with him about business, but whether or not he had anything official to attend to, Theo hovered in that room, surrounded by his piles of books and papers but not doing much of anything with them. He always left the door open about halfway, which Addie came to believe was a habit he'd developed from needing to care for his daughter and be able to hear her if she needed anything. Now, it gave Addie a perfect view of Theo sitting at his desk as she discreetly passed by the study going in and out of the parlor and dining room to do her work.

With the house in order, Addie had found more time to relax in the evenings after supper. Once the parlor had been restored to its inviting condition, Addie had quickly realized that in spite of her efforts to keep an inviting fire burning there throughout the evening, the room was always empty. Therefore, she had taken to relaxing there with a cup of tea and a good book—right across the entry hall from Theo's study. She hadn't intended to seek out a place to sit where she could discreetly spy on him, but it just so happened that the most comfortable spot at the end of a sofa gave her a perfect view of him through the open doorway. Every evening he sat at his desk, where more often than not he was just staring toward a window, where the drapes were usually closed, and doing absolutely nothing.

Addie was careful to remain discreet in her observations, always keeping a book poised at the right angle to quickly dart her eyes toward it should Theo move even slightly. She didn't want him to know that she was watching him, and she felt certain he wouldn't necessarily like the fact that her concern for him was growing. For all of his kindness and generosity, and for all of his trying to do right by Becky and Marla, Addie had been here long enough to see that he was deeply unhappy, even if he had excellent skills in being able to hide it. She thought of the man she'd met in the dress shop and how cordial and cheerful he'd been, and she realized now that he'd been putting his best self forward. She felt certain he always did so when interacting with anyone in the outside world, just as he did here at home. He'd always been cheerful and kind to her, and she couldn't deny the intrigue they had for each other, even if it had remained unspoken. But when he was alone and he believed no one was watching, his true feelings came to the surface.

A part of Addie felt mildly guilty for spying on her employer this way, but something deeper in her spirit instinctively believed that someone needed to know just how unhappy Theodore Hardwicke truly was. Becky was only a child; her father was meant to care for *her*. Marla was too ill to do anything at all beyond making it from day to day, and in all the years she'd been here, she'd clearly not been able to understand or ease Theo's burdens.

Addie felt deeply grateful for the new life Theo had given her. She'd quickly grown to love living in this home and keeping it in order, but more so, she'd grown to love caring for this family. And most of all, she'd come to love being anywhere near Theo himself. Instinctively she felt safer and more comfortable and confident in his presence than she'd ever felt in her entire life. Now that she'd taken on the chaos and disorder of this neglected house and conquered it, she felt compelled to take on the vague cloud of sorrow beneath this roof and see if she couldn't help ease it into the open and see it replaced—even if only a little—by some happiness and joy. As it stood now, she was caring for three people in this house who all seemed to be suffering from the same affliction, and yet they were all completely disconnected from each other beyond the minimal necessary interactions.

Addie believed Becky was starved for a more meaningful relationship with her father—something beyond the way he went through the motions of his simple morning and evening routines with her and sharing mostly silent meals. Becky had never known her mother, but Addie now wondered if she had ever truly known her father. Theo clearly loved Becky and wanted the best for her, but he was lost somewhere inside his own mind most of the time, and blatantly unreachable. With as much as Addie had come to know Marla and feel comfortable talking to her, she knew this woman had done everything she could to help keep this little family together following the tragic death of her niece. But something vital was missing in this house, and Addie desperately wanted to help this family find it. For all that the house was lovely and in perfect order, it did not feel like a home, and Addie was determined to find a way to help change that. Perhaps it wasn't in her power to do so, but she had to try. Her conscience demanded it.

* * *

Addie began to diligently pray for divine assistance in her quest, but days turned to weeks with no ideas and no progress. She continued to enjoy her interactions with Marla, but there were certain things Marla simply avoided talking about, and Addie felt certain there were some clues in those tender and difficult memories, which remained hidden.

Becky continued to be her quiet and reserved self. Occasionally she had a friend over to play, or she went to Mrs. Baird's home to play with her daughter. Beyond that the child's life was as dull as her father's. Becky enjoyed being in her room now that it was tidy, and she enjoyed even more spending time in the library, but she was clearly accustomed to spending most of her time alone. And while the girl had completely stopped being unkind toward Addie, she always politely declined Addie's offers to spend more time with her. It seemed obvious that it wasn't Addie's company the child craved and needed. Addie had attempted to get Theo to open up more about his feelings by inquiring more sincerely over his well-being, but it had quickly become evident that she couldn't get him to talk about the emotions he held close to his heart without crossing a boundary that simply wasn't appropriate for hired help.

Addie tried not to feel discouraged, and she continued to pray, certain God was mindful of the situation; losing hope simply because answers had not come according to her own desires and limited perspective would demonstrate a great lack of faith. She had come to feel increasingly comfortable with every member of the family, and she couldn't deny her growing affection for—perhaps even attraction to—Theo. But for all of their outward attempts to be cheerful, Addie was constantly aware of an underlying current of sadness and perhaps even loneliness no one would talk about.

Addie awoke on a dark and especially cold morning early in December that motivated her to stoke up the fire in her room and add some wood before she crawled back into bed to wait until it was warmer before she got ready for the day. She could hear wind mercilessly pelting heavy rain against the windows and hated the way it seemed to express her mood. While Addie enjoyed the work she did here, and the comfort she'd found in being a part of this household, she'd become increasingly discouraged with the dismal mood of the house, just as she'd come to feel increasingly responsible for doing something to help change it.

Addie finally forced herself out of bed, hurried to get dressed, and put up her hair before going downstairs to light fires in the kitchen and parlor so the rooms would be warm before Theo and Becky came down for breakfast. Theo always made certain there was plenty of firewood and kindling in each of the bedrooms before going to bed so that he could warm up his own room, and Becky was old enough to do the same for herself. Addie had taken on the task of sneaking quietly into Marla's room to stoke the fire and add wood so the room would warm up before Marla awoke.

While Addie was putting breakfast on, she was surprised to realize she hadn't yet seen Becky, who normally would have laid the table with all of the necessary dishes by now. Addie hurried to lay the table herself, wondering if she should go and check on the girl. A moment later Theo entered the room and said, "Becky isn't feeling well. I think it's best if she stays home from school today. Will you be all right with helping her—?"

"I can do whatever needs to be done," Addie assured him, and he gave her a wan smile and a nod of silent appreciation. "Does she have a fever?"

"She doesn't feel warm to me," he said. "She just said she doesn't feel well. If she's worse by the time I get home, we'll send for the doctor, but I suspect it's just one of those things that will pass."

"Don't worry," Addie said and sat across from him, thinking how strange it felt not to have Becky there. She'd never shared a meal alone with Theo. "I've had a lot of experience with illness. I'll take good care of her."

"I'm certain you will," Theo said, giving her another appreciative nod and one of those intriguing gazes that made Addie's stomach flutter. But he looked quickly away as if his concern for his daughter had overpowered his every other thought.

Addie tried to think of something—anything—to say that might initiate some pleasant conversation, but her mind remained blank and the meal passed in silence. Being alone with him at the table, she was overcome more than usual with the strange sensations that had become more and more familiar, which she could only describe as a deep fascination with this man— and an even deeper desire to see him show some sign of happiness.

Addie finally cleared her throat as if that might help her gather some courage before she said in her most gentle voice, "Theo . . . is there anything I can do to . . . ?"

"To what?" he asked when she hesitated, his tone nothing but curious.

"To help?" she went on.

"You've helped so much already," he said with conviction. "The house, the meals, the—"

"I've done what you hired me to do," Addie said, "but that's not what I mean. Forgive me if this is none of my business, but . . . you seem so . . . sad. It's evident that the death of Becky's mother has left a deep impact on all of you, but perhaps . . . if you talked about it . . . perhaps if you . . . well . . ." Addie felt suddenly nervous and subsequently stuck. Theo didn't appear offended or upset by what she'd said, but she simply didn't know how to clarify her motives other than to say, "If you ever feel the need to talk . . . I'm here."

"Thank you," he said and smiled. But that was all he said other than, "You're always so kind." Following minutes of silence while he finished eating, Theo complimented her cooking as always and thanked her again for her efforts before he left the table, and not many minutes later he was off to work. Addie was once again left feeling concerned and disappointed, wondering why she had come to feel so personally responsible for Theo Hardwicke's happiness.

Addie took Marla's breakfast up to her and made certain she had everything she needed. Then she peeked into Becky's room to check on her. She was surprised to see the child sitting in the middle of her bed, wrapped in a blanket and staring toward the rain now drizzling down the windows since the wind had calmed down. Becky looked sad but not necessarily ill. Addie took a deep breath and stepped into the room, wondering if this change in routine might be an opportunity to help Becky know she truly cared and wanted to help her.

"Your father told me you're not feeling well," Addie said and sat on the edge of the bed, glad when Becky didn't protest. "Can you tell me what hurts, sweetheart?" Addie had never called her that; it had just jumped out of her mouth, but Becky didn't react negatively, so she pressed on. "Are you achy all over? Does your head ache? Does your belly hurt? Or your throat?"

Addie was surprised to see Becky's hand unconsciously go to her heart; she absently rubbed the center of her chest, while it was evident she didn't even realize she was doing it. She looked at Addie and said, "You've been very kind to me. When you came, I was afraid you wouldn't be. One of my teachers at school isn't very nice, but the other two are. Some of the girls are nice, but most of them are not. But you've been very kind to me. I'm sorry if I wasn't kind to you. I think some of the girls at school made me think I could be happier if I behaved the way they did, but my father told me how important it is to be kind no matter how other people behave. My father is the kindest person I know. I don't want him to think I'm not like him, because I want to be like him. And I want to be like you."

Addie was utterly stunned by Becky's little speech. It was not only surprisingly mature and insightful, but it had clearly been well-thought-out, and there was no denying that it came from the heart; her sincerity showed clearly in her countenance.

Addie tried very hard to think of the best thing to say. Instinctively she knew that putting too much attention on her apology or her growing self-awareness would only create an awkwardness that might dispel the openness that had suddenly appeared. "How very grown up you are!" Addie said and impulsively reached out a hand to press it over Becky's silky hair that was so near the color of her father's. "That's very mature to realize such a thing, Becky. And I believe you are *very* kind. Sometimes when people have feelings they don't understand or know what to do with, it can make them impatient or frustrated, and that might come out sounding unkind, but I think maybe you just have some feelings you don't understand." Becky looked deeply intrigued, and Addie hoped she was on the right path as she added, "Do you want to know what I think? And if you disagree, you can tell me." Becky nodded and Addie said, "I think you're unhappy, Becky. I think you love your father and Aunt Marla very much, but I believe they're unhappy too, and that might make you feel lonely." Addie leaned a little closer to Becky and whispered, "Can I tell you a secret?" Becky nodded. "I think all of you are unhappy and even lonely, but none of you know what to do about it."

Tears welled up in Becky's eyes, then rolled down her cheeks as she nodded very slightly before admitting, "I'm not really ill. I just didn't want to go to school."

"I understand," Addie said, still whispering. "I'll keep your secret if you keep mine, and . . . well, I was thinking that together you and I might share a secret project."

"Like what?" Becky asked, wiping at her tears.

"What if we see if we can figure out how to bring more happiness into this house? I'm just a maid here, you know. I'm not a part of the family. But I think you could figure out what the problem is, and then we could figure out together how to fix it. Or we could at least try to make it a little better. What do you think?"

Becky looked both intrigued and skeptical. "Do you really think we could do that? Do you think we can make our house happier?"

"I really do," Addie said, "and I think the first step is getting everyone to talk about why they are so unhappy. So before you are able to help your father and your aunt, perhaps we could work on what makes *you* so sad. Do you want to talk about it, Becky? You don't have to, but—"

Addie stopped when Becky assaulted her with a tight hug, going on her knees so she could reach all the way around Addie. Addie returned the child's embrace, tightening her hold when she realized Becky was crying.

"It's all right, sweetheart," Addie said and just let the child cry for several minutes before she drew back and wiped at her tears. Addie pulled a clean handkerchief from her apron pocket and handed it to Becky. "It's good to cry when we feel sad, you know," Addie said. "It helps get all of that sadness out of us."

Becky nodded in agreement, then confessed to crying frequently at night when she was alone. She knew her father loved her, but she also knew he was very sad even though he tried to hide it. What shocked Addie most was Becky's belief that it was her all her fault; since her mother had died giving birth to her, she felt certain she was to blame for the sorrow felt by her father and aunt. Addie was glad for Becky's confession because it gave her the opportunity to explain that this was certainly not the case. The dear girl seemed somewhat hopeful from Addie's reassurance, but not entirely convinced.

When Becky was apparently finished with her confessions, Addie took her by the shoulders and said with a cheerful voice, "Why don't we talk about ways we might work together to make Aunt Marla and your father happier, and I have a feeling helping them might help *you*. What do you think?"

Given the fact that the conversation Becky had just shared with Addie had cheered her up already, Becky was easily convinced that talking about feelings as opposed to holding them inside was a good place to start. She eagerly agreed to attempt to talk with her father and simply tell him how she felt, and Addie would talk to Marla. They made a pact to follow through on their mutually agreed-upon assignments before the day was done.

Now more cheerful and bright than Addie had ever seen her, Becky jumped out of bed to get dressed while Addie went down to the kitchen to heat up the girl's breakfast. Addie met Mrs. Baird at the door to tell her that Becky would be staying home today but would likely be able to attend school the following day. While Becky was eating, it occurred to Addie that having this time with Becky—especially in light of the conversation they'd just shared—might be exactly what they needed to get past the awkwardness and strain that had been between them since they'd met.

Becky was thrilled when Addie asked if she would like to help bake a cake for dessert that evening. Becky clearly enjoyed being taught how to measure and mix the batter ingredients and how to make certain the oven was the correct temperature for the cake to bake properly. It was evident that for all of Marla's cooking for the family, she had never included Becky in her efforts, but it was something the child liked enough that Addie felt certain it would be to the benefit of both her and Becky to have her help with the meals whenever possible.

Since Addie knew as well as Becky did that neither the girl's father nor her aunt would approve of her staying home from school if she wasn't actually ill, Becky agreed to spend the afternoon in her room playing quietly with the guise of resting. Becky promised Addie she would attend school diligently from tomorrow forward unless she was legitimately ill, and Addie promised that her reasons for staying home today would remain a secret between them. While Addie made it clear to Becky that she didn't believe being dishonest in any way was acceptable, she suggested that sometimes the heart or the spirit might not feel well and therefore they could be honest about the need for Becky to stay at home and rest. Becky liked this idea very much, and it seemed that their being coconspirators had warmed Becky toward Addie a great deal.

When it was time for tea, Addie took a tray to Becky's room with some little sandwiches and two types of biscuits that had come from the local bakery. Becky was pleased by the snack and thanked Addie.

"Now," Addie whispered, "I am going to do my best to talk with Aunt Marla over tea and see if I can't find a way to help her be happier. You stay quiet in here, little miss, and we'll hope for the best."

Becky nodded with enthusiasm and surprised Addie with another hug before Addie left the room to share tea with Marla as always. She silently thanked God for the enormous progress that had occurred today in her relationship with Becky, and she prayed to have a conversation with Marla that might go half as well. She believed her consistent efforts at simply being helpful and kind in this household over the course of the last few months had softened this family toward her, and perhaps that was the very reason Becky had finally been willing to open up. Addie only hoped the same might be true for Marla; she was an adult who had been here when Becky's mother had died and every day since. Surely she had some insight as to the cloud of sorrow that consumed this house.

CHAPTER FIVE
CRACKED HEARTS

Tea with Marla was enjoyable as usual, although Addie desperately wanted to get past all of the casual chitchat and have a more serious conversation. She finally set her teacup aside and leaned forward a little toward where Marla was propped up with pillows in her bed.

"Marla," she said in an earnest voice that got the older woman's attention, "may I ask you something I believe is very important? You don't have to tell me if you don't want to, but . . . I've been in the house for a while now, and . . . well, may I just speak candidly?"

"Of course, dear," Marla said. Her brow furrowed slightly in concern, but her eyes showed curiosity.

"It's just that . . . I know you and Becky and Theo all love each other very much, and you live in such a lovely house, but . . . it doesn't feel like a home, Marla. The three of you are so very . . . well . . . perhaps disconnected. And you all seem so sad. Both you and Theo do well at being cheerful when you interact with others, but . . . I can see the evidence; I can feel it. And little Becky feels it too. I'm just . . . well . . . I'm wondering *why*, Marla. I know your niece's death was very difficult for you and Theo. Surely your memories of her are precious, and you will always miss her. But . . . is it her absence that is causing all this sadness so many years later? Or is there something else I don't understand? I want to help, Marla. But . . . I'm not sure I would know what to do without understanding the reasons."

Addie had been so focused on getting the difficult words out into the open that she didn't notice until she'd stopped talking that tears were streaming down Marla's face. "Oh, my dear," Marla said, reaching for Addie's hand, "you have brought such a light into this house. I'm not certain any of us realized how sad and tired we've become . . . or perhaps we just haven't known what to do about it. I'm not certain I have anything helpful to tell you, but I'll try."

"That would be wonderful," Addie said, squeezing the older woman's fingers.

"Would you get something for me?" Marla asked. "It's in the bottom left bureau drawer—a box."

"Of course," Addie said and went to the appointed place, opening the drawer to see nothing inside *except* for a box that looked as if it had endured many years and much hardship. It barely seemed to hold itself together as Addie carefully lifted it into her hands and delivered it with great caution to Marla's lap. The dear woman pressed her aging hands over the top of the box as if it were priceless, and her tears increased.

"I brought this with me when I came for Christmas nearly ten years ago," Marla began with nostalgia in her voice. She sighed and went on. "Here in the city Christmas isn't celebrated much, except for perhaps having a finer meal, but in the country where I grew up—where Rebecca grew up—we made more of a celebration of it. We had a tradition in our family of spreading pine boughs about the house, especially on the mantel. We went to a great deal of trouble of decorating the mantel with ribbons and candles. It was always the four of us: my sister—Rebecca's mother—me, and our parents. We had such lovely Christmases. We always hung these on the mantel." She pressed her hands lovingly over the box. "We each had one. Our father had given them to our mother as a gift when we were very young, with the intention of making them a part of our Christmas traditions. When my sister married, she took hers with her, and she told me once that she'd given it to Rebecca, but Rebecca told me when I came to visit that she'd dropped hers and broken it and had had no choice but to throw it away." Marla lifted one hand off the box long enough to wipe at her tears. "After she died, I had the silly thought that it had somehow been a foreshadowing that her life had been coming to an end. Silly, I know."

"I don't think it sounds silly," Addie assured her. "It sounds like the kind of thing I might have thought; whether or not something like that is true doesn't really matter, does it? But how such things make us feel certainly matters."

"Yes, I suppose so," Marla said and sighed more deeply, as if she were releasing years of pent-up sorrow. "Rebecca went into labor before we even had a chance to start decorating for Christmas, and . . . well . . . things went wrong very quickly. It's a miracle little Becky survived. Of course it was . . . shocking . . . horrible . . ." Marla sniffled and pulled a handkerchief from inside the sleeve of her nightgown, which she pressed beneath her nose.

"I can't even imagine how terrible it must have been," Addie said.

Marla drew in a courageous breath and pressed forward with her story, just as she had surely pressed forward with her life at the time. "It was an easy decision for me to stay and help care for Becky. Theo and I together did our best to do what needed to be done, but we never talked about our grief, even though we were both certainly brokenhearted over losing our precious Rebecca." She focused her attention more on the box. "We did nothing to celebrate Christmas that year and, in fact, haven't done so since. All of my intentions to bring with me the traditions I'd grown up with and that Rebecca had learned from her mother all melted away with her passing. I think it was four or five years before I found the motivation to even open this box. My intention when I'd first come for Christmas had been that we would hang these on the mantel, just as it had been done in my childhood, and that the two that had been passed to me from my parents would be for Theo and Rebecca since hers had been broken. But Christmas never happened, and the box remained in the drawer for years. Then . . . , when I did open it . . ." Marla began to weep so intensely that she couldn't speak.

Addie moved instinctively to the edge of the bed and put her arms around Marla. "It's going to be all right," Addie said to her, a warmth surrounding them both that seemed evidence of the miracle taking place. Marla recounted in detail her experience of losing her niece to an untimely death and how deeply it had impacted her. The way she wept made it evident she should have talked about it long before now. It was increasingly obvious that Theo and Marla had bottled up their grief and had never allowed the cork to pop off in order to bring their feelings into the open. If Addie had to leave this house tomorrow, she prayed she could leave this family more at peace and capable of finding new happiness. But she never wanted to leave. This place had come to feel more like home to her than even her own home had ever felt, and these people had come to feel more like family than the one she'd left behind, with the exception of her mother.

Marla's crying finally settled, but she still seemed unable to speak as she carefully handed the box back to Addie, nodding as an indication that Addie open the lid and look inside. Addie took a deep breath and did so, wondering what beautiful items she might find hidden away that had represented Christmas to Marla and her family. She saw nothing at first but a great deal of crinkled tissue paper that looked as old as the box. As she was slowly pulling it back, Marla said with new tears, "I thought it was packed carefully enough to be protected during my journey here, but . . . clearly it was not."

Addie gasped as she looked down to see—lying on more crinkled tissue paper—three white porcelain hearts, each with a little hole near the top through which a faded piece of red ribbon had been threaded and tied so that they could be hung on a nail or hook. But each one of the hearts had been badly cracked, so much so that Addie didn't dare even touch them or try to lift them out of the box, certain they would break right in half.

"Oh my," she managed to say before tears of her own bubbled up and spilled down her face. Staring at the cracked hearts, Addie felt as if she were looking at a clear and undeniable representation of the three people who lived in this home, the people she'd been hired to care for, the people she'd grown to love. Their hearts were broken, and Addie wanted nothing more than to find a way to help mend the cracks so they could find new happiness in their lives and share life like a family instead of simply living completely separate lives beneath the same roof.

* * *

Becky was anxious to hear if Addie's conversation with Marla had done anything to help in their mutual quest to bring more happiness into their home, but Addie felt the need to ponder the things Marla had shared with her. She also didn't feel it would be appropriate for her to share with Becky all that Marla had confided without first asking permission. Addie simply told the child that she believed it had gone well but that it was only a beginning and they needed to be patient. Becky seemed to understand, even though she also seemed a little frustrated and disappointed, but Addie distracted her by asking if she would like to help prepare dinner. Becky was so excited by the opportunity that Addie marveled over how far the child had come now that she'd finally come to trust Addie and they'd been able to connect with each other at a heartfelt level.

When Theo came home from his usual day of working at the bank, he was very pleased Becky was feeling better, and equally pleased with Becky's announcement that she had helped Addie prepare their evening meal. Theo hugged his daughter with more enthusiasm than Addie had ever witnessed, which made her think that perhaps there was some divine orchestration taking place in the way events were lining up on this day that had already brought about some positive steps toward healing. Knowing Becky intended to have a serious conversation with her father later that evening, Addie was pleased that the mood between them seemed as good as it had ever been.

Addie took a tray up to Marla while Becky finished putting food out on the table in a very mature fashion. She knew she couldn't stay and visit with Marla right then, since Theo and Becky wouldn't start eating without her, but she *did* say, "I enjoyed our visit earlier, and I want to thank you for being so candid with me."

"I believe it was very good for me to talk about those things," Marla said with a sad smile. "And a good cry was likely long overdue."

Addie returned her smile and added, "I wonder if we might be able to talk some more . . . perhaps after I've got the kitchen cleaned up after dinner."

"I'll look forward to it," Marla said and thanked Addie for the delicious-looking meal.

Addie was surprised at how talkative Becky was throughout dinner, and she could see that Theo was surprised as well—pleasantly so. And while they were eating dessert, Becky said to her father, "Would it be all right if we talk about something when we're finished eating? In your study?" Addie took the last to mean that Becky considered this to be an important meeting, not unlike those she had observed when people came to the house to conduct business with her father.

"That would be all right," Theo said with a mixture of confusion and pleasure.

"Good," Becky said and stood up to help clear the table without being asked; it was a chore she'd never helped with in all the time Addie had been there.

While Becky was in the kitchen, Theo leaned across the table toward Addie and whispered, "What kind of magic has taken place here today? She's like a completely different child."

"We just . . . talked," Addie said with a shrug and a smile. She hurried to use the few seconds of privacy left to them and added, "Now that she's opening up more, I think we simply need to hear the things she has to say and do our best to respond appropriately."

"Of course," Theo said, as if Addie had spouted words so wise he could hardly take them in.

Was he, in truth, simply a man without any knowledge of how to have a relationship with a child? Of course, such things had to be learned and practiced just like any other kind of knowledge, and Addie didn't know enough about him to have any idea of his upbringing or how it might have affected his inability to handle the delicate situation that had resulted from years of not talking or sharing feelings in this household. She hoped the conversation between Becky and her father went well.

After the two of them went off to the study, Addie resisted the urge to eavesdrop and forced herself to hurry through the necessary tasks of putting the kitchen in order and cleaning the dishes so she could visit with Marla before the usual time the older woman went to sleep. Father and daughter were still in the study with the door closed when Addie finished and went upstairs to find Marla anticipating her visit.

Addie sat in a chair near the side of the bed and once again thanked Marla for all she had shared earlier. She then asked permission to share those things with Becky, along with her belief that knowing more about her mother and the events surrounding her death might help the child. "Even though there is much sorrow in this story," Addie said, "it is the story of the beginning of Becky's life, and I believe she has assumed some things that are not true. If those things could be spoken of openly, she might be able to express her own emotions more easily and be happier as a result."

"How wise you are!" Marla said and reached for Addie's hand, squeezing it gently.

"My mother was very wise," Addie declared. "She told me herself that she hadn't chosen wisely in marriage, but as soon as she realized that, she consciously sought to gain more understanding of life and its struggles, if only to be able to endure her marriage to my father in the best way possible."

"And you learned well from her," Marla said, then sighed deeply while her eyes became distant with contemplation. "I *do* think Becky should know the things I told you, but I would very much like to be the one to tell her."

"All the better!" Addie agreed with some excitement; she had believed Marla wouldn't want to talk about the situation to Becky when it had been so emotional for her. But Addie felt certain this was ideal.

"And I would love for you to join us," Marla said, which also pleased Addie since it meant she wouldn't have to once again resist the temptation to eavesdrop. "I know you are interacting with Becky a great deal, and if we all talk about this together, then perhaps you can help her adjust to things that should have been talked about a long time ago." This brought forth more tears in Marla, but she readily admitted once again that she believed she'd been holding too much back for too long and crying it all out was long overdue.

Just as Addie and Marla were wrapping up their conversation so Marla could get ready for bed, they heard Becky come up the stairs and go into her room. "She was talking to her father," Addie whispered to Marla. "I hope it went well."

Marla nodded in firm agreement before Addie stood and embraced this woman who had come to feel like her own aunt, a relationship she'd never before had the privilege of enjoying. "I'll check on you before I go to bed," Addie said and kissed Marla on the brow before leaving the room.

Addie knocked on the half-open door of Becky's room and heard her call, "Come in."

Addie stepped inside and purposely closed the door, wanting privacy. She quickly scanned the child's countenance and was pleased to note that Becky seemed in as good of spirits as she had earlier.

"Did everything go all right?" Addie asked, intensely curious but knowing she needed to respect the child's boundaries, especially when she was just barely coming out of a fragile shell in which she'd likely lived for the majority of her life.

"Yes," Becky said and smiled, but more to herself than to Addie. While Addie was wondering how she might ask for even a little specific information, the child declared she needed to do some reading to be caught up on a school assignment before she got ready for bed. Addie left her to do so, pleased at the progress taking place in spite of her disappointment over not knowing what exactly had transpired between Theo and Becky.

Addie went back to the kitchen to make herself a cup of tea that would help her relax, as she often did before getting ready for bed. While she was waiting for the kettle to boil, she was startled to hear Theo say, "There you are."

"Did you need something?" she asked, realizing how lost in thought she'd been.

It took him several seconds to answer, during which time she realized he was staring at her with a warm gaze she couldn't construe as anything but affection. While she tried to convince herself that his regard for her was only due to her efforts in his home, a swarm of imaginary butterflies all at once began to flutter inside her, making it difficult to fully draw in her breath. The amount of time they spent gazing at each other in silence should have been awkward, but it wasn't; it was as if they both understood the need to simply take each other in, along with the feelings growing between them. Without a word spoken, Addie was able to acknowledge to herself now more than ever that she had truly grown to love this man, and she suspected he felt the same for her. Perhaps, with time, these feelings could be acknowledged outwardly; for now, she felt certain his focus was more on his daughter, as was hers.

"Only to tell you," he finally said, still with that affectionate gaze, "how grateful I am for all you've done for us. From the conversation I just had with my daughter, it's evident your influence here has far surpassed your household skills and cooking—and that's really saying something." Addie wanted desperately to ask what had been said between him and Becky, but she didn't want to appear as nosy as she felt. "I grew up in a home where difficulties were never talked about," he went on, "and emotions were never even acknowledged. Rebecca helped me understand the need to be able to talk about such things, but when she died, I'm afraid I reverted to my old ways. It was so refreshing to simply share an open conversation with my daughter. We talked about her mother's death," he continued, much to her relief, "and I was rather shocked to realize she blamed herself. Of course, I assured her it was not her fault. She also expressed concern over her belief that I'm not happy."

"*Are* you happy?" Addie ventured to ask, her heartbeat quickening in orchestration with the ongoing fluttering.

"Happier than I have been in a long time, I believe," he said and smiled slightly. He cleared his throat and looked down briefly, as if to clear his head and force himself to break the gaze between them. "Becky and I have agreed to talk with each other about how we feel from now on. I'm certain her suggestion must have come from you. Anyway . . . thank you . . . for everything."

Addie felt suddenly overcome with the urge to cry, so thoroughly happy that no words could possibly come out of her mouth without releasing an onslaught of tears. She simply nodded and tried to smile. He nodded in return and left the kitchen. A moment later she was able to let out her breath and allow a few tears to fall, releasing some of the pressure in her head. They had come far in one day, and with some help from above, perhaps they could all work together to make this household a happy one.

CHAPTER SIX
MENDED HEARTS

THE FOLLOWING DAY, WHEN BECKY came home from school, she helped Addie prepare sandwiches and biscuits for tea and carry everything needed upstairs to Marla's room. The usual tea was anything but usual as Marla tenderly told Becky things about her mother the child had never known, including about her mother's death, and assured her once again that it had not been her fault. All three of them shed some tears as Marla spoke of it, Becky asked some questions that Marla answered kindly, and Addie simply observed a healing miracle taking place. When Marla had Addie get out the cracked porcelain hearts so she could show Becky, the child only looked sadly at them for a moment before she looked up with glee in her expression and declared, "We need to find something else to hang on the mantel for Christmas! And we need to have Christmas the way you had it in the country, Auntie Marla!"

"I think that's an excellent idea," Marla said, laughing with delight. "And what about your birthday, little miss? It's not many days before Christmas, and we need to celebrate that!"

"I've never liked celebrating my birthday," Becky admitted, and Marla looked stunned. "I tried to be happy, but I knew it was the day my mother died. Can't I just share my birthday with Jesus?"

Marla and Addie exchanged a tender smile before Marla looked at her great niece and said, "If that's what you want, my dear, then that's what we shall do."

They started talking about plans for Christmas that incorporated the traditions Marla had grown up with—the same traditions Becky's mother had celebrated—as well as some things Addie's family had done. Becky talked about traditions she knew some of her school friends did for

Christmas with their families. Even though they were simple, Becky was clearly nothing but thoroughly excited to make Christmas everything she had come to believe it should be.

The next day after school Addie took Becky shopping. They perused shop after shop while Becky insisted they had to find just the right thing to hang on their mantel along with the pine boughs they'd purchased from a street vendor. They also purchased some bright-red ribbon to weave among the branches and some new candles to be lit as part of their new Christmas traditions. Becky wanted to get gifts for her father and Marla, and Theo had provided plenty of money for their shopping excursion. The little girl was frustrated over not finding anything that resonated with her to hang on the mantel, but she was quickly able to find gifts that pleased her and made her excitedly anticipate the arrival of the holiday, when she would be able to give them.

As the streets of London began getting dark, Addie was glad she'd planned a simple, cold supper that could be put on quickly once they arrived home. She tried to insist that they needed to return home, but Becky begged to go into just one more shop. She dragged Addie by the hand toward it as if some external force were leading her there, although Becky declared she'd never been inside before; she'd only seen through the windows a few times while walking with her father to church. They casually wandered through the slightly odd shop, where a kind, elderly man made interesting jewelry and simple pieces of home decorations, mostly from melting down silver and other metals and fashioning them into unique designs. While Becky was perusing the shop within Addie's view, Addie was taken with some pieces of pottery and glass vases that had been broken and then mended by fusing the pieces together with glistening metal that surely made the items more beautiful than before they had been broken. An idea was just beginning to formulate in Addie's mind when she heard Becky declare with loud enthusiasm that she'd finally found the right thing. Addie noticed the shopkeeper smiling at the child's excitement as she went to see what Becky had found.

"See!" Becky declared, pointing to the figure of an angel, crafted uniquely from a combination of glistening gold and silver metal, with a white ribbon strung through a tiny loop at the top so it could be hung decoratively. "It's like my mother!" Becky added, her eyes glowing with a light Addie had never seen before. It was as if something or someone beyond their world—perhaps Becky's mother indeed—had guided the child to the lovely memento that had the potential to serve as a reminder of her lost mother.

"We'll take it," Addie said with enthusiasm to the shopkeeper, who smiled more brightly even though he didn't say anything.

They paid for the angel and returned home with their other purchases, which were all set aside in order to have dinner since Theo was already home from work. Becky insisted on waiting to show her father all they'd bought to decorate the parlor with for Christmas; she wanted to surprise him.

That evening after Theo had tucked his daughter into bed, he found Addie in the kitchen and asked if they could talk. Addie attempted to suppress her quickened heartbeat and fluttering stomach as he motioned her toward the parlor and they sat across from each other.

"I need to thank you," he said.

"You've thanked me far too many times," Addie said, truly unable to recount how many times he had expressed his gratitude.

"And yet you've gone so far beyond what I hired you to do; you've been caring and helpful in ways that have nothing to do with your job. I'm grateful," Theo said earnestly, "and I need you to know that."

"Thank you," she said, trying to be gracious in accepting his compliment. "And I'm grateful for the good life you've given me here."

"The pleasure is entirely mine," he said with a smile. Then he looked away and cleared his throat tensely before adding, "I understand you've had some serious conversations with Marla and Becky, and it's occurred to me that it might be well for you and I to have the same. I hope you don't mind."

"Not at all," Addie said hopefully; to have Theo open up to her would be a miracle she had been praying for.

Addie settled more comfortably into her chair as Theo talked of his childhood here in London as the son of a banker. He'd always had financial security, but he'd been keenly aware from a young age that something was lacking in his home—something he'd wanted when he started his own family—and Rebecca had had the qualities he'd been looking for to fill that gap.

Addie kicked off her shoes and tucked her feet up beneath her as they continued to talk and share stories from their lives. She felt so comfortable she never wanted their conversation to end. But they talked for so long they both began yawning until neither of them could talk at all and they resigned themselves to getting some sleep. But Addie found it difficult to relax with the giddiness she felt over her growing affection toward Theo and her memories of the way he often looked at her and how it made her feel. Miracles were indeed taking place. She only hoped she could truly stay here with this family forever.

* * *

With just a few days until Christmas, Addie sneaked the box of cracked porcelain hearts out of Marla's bureau drawer while Marla was napping soundly. While Becky was at school, Addie took the hearts to the shop where they'd purchased the angel and showed them to the shopkeeper; she needed a fine craftsman.

"Do you think you could mend them?" Addie asked him. "The way you've mended other things that have been broken?" She motioned toward the display of vases and pottery. "The hearts are very precious to someone I care about, and I would love to give them as a Christmas gift, but if you don't have time to do this before Christmas, I understand and—"

"Of course I can mend them," the old man said with a proud grin, as if she had just given *him* a precious gift. "And it would be a joy to have them finished before Christmas. You can come pick them up Christmas Eve morning. I can't promise exactly how they'll turn out; I just follow my instincts when I do such things . . . as if an invisible hand is guiding me. But I promise you they'll be beautiful and whole once again."

Addie thanked him profusely, and as she walked home, she considered the implications and symbolism of what the old man had said in relation to what Christmas truly meant. Her mother had raised her on the teachings from the New Testament, and they were seared joyfully in her heart. If Christ, for whom Christmas was named, could mend any broken heart, then what this man could do symbolically with the porcelain could be a lovely reminder to this family of the reasons Christmas was celebrated.

The day before Christmas Eve, Becky didn't have school—and she wouldn't until the new year—so Addie had her help make some gingerbread cookies the way Addie's mother had taught her. They cut them into many shapes before baking, but Becky especially loved making hearts. Most were made for eating, but there were some they cut holes in near the tops so that a ribbon could be threaded through after overbaking them in order to hang the hardened cookies from the mantel for decoration. At Becky's insistence these were all hearts—four of them, one for each member of the family; Addie was deeply touched by the way Becky declared her to be a part of the family, and she couldn't help hoping it would always be that way.

Thinking of Theo usually quickened her heartbeat, and she hoped more than ever that it might be possible for her to one day officially become a part of the family. The way he often looked at her strengthened that hope, although nothing specifically to that effect had ever been said between them. She could only pray she had not misinterpreted his feelings—or her own.

They were in the midst of their baking project when Marla appeared in the doorway of the kitchen, holding to the wall as she worked on catching her breath.

"Good heavens!" Addie declared and hurried to Marla, brushing her hands on her apron. "You must sit down." Marla did so, but with a big smile on her face. "Is this a Christmas miracle?" Addie asked.

"Perhaps it is," Marla said. "I've actually been feeling better, and I realized this morning that if I was careful, I could likely make it down here and join the fun." She took hold of Addie's hand and looked at her with tears rising in her eyes. "It's occurred to me, my dear, that perhaps I'd just grown so weary and sad that my heart stopped working for me as it should. But you have brought so much healing and happiness into our home, Addie, and while my health may not be optimal, I do believe my heart is not nearly as broken as I had believed it to be."

Addie had to contend with her own tears as she bent over to embrace Marla tightly. "Oh, it *is* a miracle!" She drew back, and they exchanged a smile before Becky intruded and also hugged Marla tightly, making the older woman laugh.

"We're making hearts to hang on the mantel," Becky told her aunt, "since the other hearts were broken."

"Oh, how lovely," Marla said and visited with them while they finished their baking project and then ate warm gingerbread cookies together.

After the kitchen was all cleaned up, the three of them shared lunch before Marla made herself comfortable in the parlor to observe and offer some opinions while Becky and Addie put pine boughs through which they'd woven ribbons on the mantel. Candles were set amidst the boughs, and the new gingerbread hearts were hung on tiny nails that had already been nailed into the wood; Addie wondered if it had been done for this exact purpose in years past. Thinking of the porcelain hearts that were being beautifully mended, she was glad to note there were many empty nails discreetly placed in the ornately designed wood so that they were barely visible.

When everything else was completed, Becky showed Marla the angel she had found, and the older woman wept as Becky told her it was like her mother and would always be hung on the mantel for Christmas from now on. Becky wiped her aunt's tears and kissed her cheek, and they hugged tightly before the darling girl hung the angel in the center of their gingerbread hearts. The three of them admired the finished results in silence, while Addie inhaled the aroma of fresh pine from the boughs and felt her heart overflow with joy at the thought of how far this family had come in having their own broken hearts mended.

When Theo got home from work, Becky was waiting for him, giddy with excitement to show her father what they had done to prepare for Christmas. He was clearly overjoyed with the results and the fact that Marla was sitting in the parlor. He *also* enjoyed a gingerbread cookie before eating dinner. And Becky was thrilled when he told her he would not be working the next two days and they could spend time doing whatever she wanted.

The next morning after the kitchen was cleaned up following breakfast, Addie was glad to have Theo at home so she could leave Becky in his care and walk to the shop where she had left the hearts to be repaired. When the shopkeeper showed her the results, Addie gasped and then couldn't keep from letting a couple of tears slide down her cheeks. "Oh, they're magnificent!" she declared, marveling that they were dramatically more beautiful than they had been before they had cracked.

The cracks had been mended with glimmering metal in a way that made each heart even stronger, and the shopkeeper had put the same silvery substance around the edges and in some designs on each of the hearts so that the mended cracks looked as if they had always been part of an intended pattern. Each of them was slightly different, and yet they all clearly went together.

"I'm so glad you are pleased," the old man said.

"Very pleased!" Addie told him and was even more pleased when he offered to put the hearts into individual little boxes which were tied closed with different-colored ribbons. Addie paid his fee from her own money since she intended to give these to Theo, Becky, and Marla as Christmas gifts.

Addie felt happier than she perhaps ever had as she returned to the house that had become her home to find these people she'd come to care for all gathered in the parlor while Becky and Theo played a rousing game of checkers and Marla cheered them on. Addie joined Marla in observing; she'd never imagined checkers to be so exciting, but Becky kept giggling for no apparent reason as her father discreetly allowed her to win, and the child's laughter was infectious.

That evening after dinner, they all gathered in the parlor and lit the candles on the mantel before Theo read the Christmas story from the book of Luke in the Bible. After he was finished, Addie said, "I know Christmas gifts should be opened Christmas day, but I have something for each of you that I believe should be opened tonight."

"Oh my!" Theo and Marla said almost exactly together. Becky just beamed at the prospect of a Christmas gift.

Addie handed each of them one of the boxes and tried to watch all three people at the same time as they untied the ribbons and lifted the lids. Marla gasped and began to cry. Becky squealed with more excitement than Addie had ever seen from her or any other child. Theo's lip quivered before he pressed a hand over his mouth. Once he'd gained his composure, he looked up at Addie and said in a husky whisper, "It can't be."

Addie just shrugged and smiled, trying to maintain her own composure before she briefly explained how she had managed to get the hearts repaired.

"They're more beautiful than ever!" Marla declared. "It's another miracle!"

"Amen," Theo said, still fighting back emotion.

Becky carefully but with enthusiasm hung each of the newly mended hearts on the mantel. The silvery lines glistened in the candlelight, which prompted everyone to silently admire the beauty.

"But Addie doesn't have a heart!" Becky declared with sudden enlightenment and disappointment.

"You mustn't worry about that," Addie said, then impulsively decided to express her feelings honestly. "I've never been happier, and I'm so grateful to all of you for giving me a new home. I hope never to leave. That's all the gift I could ever need."

Becky hugged Addie tightly and said, "You mustn't *ever* leave!"

"Amen," Theo said again, and Marla echoed the word.

While Theo read a bedtime story to Becky in her room and Marla went back upstairs to get herself ready for bed, Addie worked in the kitchen on some preparations for tomorrow's Christmas feast. She felt giddy with excitement and realized that even though Christmas had been acknowledged throughout her childhood, it had never felt like this. Her mother had tried, but her father's negative influence had always drowned out so many of her mother's good efforts. Here, in the Hardwicke home, Addie realized she was overcome with an indescribable peace and joy she'd never experienced before.

"I'm glad you've not gone to bed yet," she heard Theo say and looked up to see him standing in the doorway of the kitchen. "I have something for you, and I didn't want to wait until morning to give it to you."

"Me?" she asked, not having expected a Christmas gift from Theo Hardwicke.

"Of course," he said as if nothing could be more natural.

Addie wiped her hands on her apron and stood to face Theo as he handed her a little box tied with a ribbon. Her heart quickened at the familiarity; it looked exactly like the boxes she had given to the others. Had he actually purchased something for her from the same shop? She gingerly untied the ribbon and lifted the lid, then found it difficult to breathe as she looked at what was inside. Once she'd accepted it wasn't her imagination, she looked up at Theo, silently questioning how this could be possible.

"I know you're aware that Rebecca had possession of the fourth heart in her family's collection and that it broke. She was so upset when she dropped it, and she attributed her clumsiness to being so pregnant. She refused to let me help her pick up the pieces, but I felt unsettled when I watched her throw them into the trash bin. She went upstairs to take a nap, and I dug out the pieces and hid them. I knew a kind shopkeeper with the skill to repair things most people would think were not repairable. I had passed his shop many times. So I took the pieces to him, and this is what came back to me. It was intended to be a Christmas gift for Rebecca, but . . . well . . . you know she wasn't here by the time Christmas came. I put it in the back of a drawer and hadn't looked at it until yesterday, when it occurred to me that I needed to give it to you."

"But . . . why?" Addie asked, unable to wipe away her tears since her fingers were clutching the little box so tightly.

"Because . . . Adelaide Moore . . . you have mended all of our hearts—especially mine. And I need you to know how I've grown to care for you . . . to love you." Addie gasped while Theo took a deep breath as if to gather courage and added on his exhale, "I'm not certain how you'll feel about what I really want to say, but I have to say it. I agree completely with Becky:

you mustn't ever leave. And I'm desperately hoping you'll take pity on me and allow me to court you." Addie gasped again but let him finish. "I know it's strange since we live under the same roof, but we have Marla and Becky as chaperones, and . . . I hope you'll eventually agree to be my wife . . . and never leave." He took another deep breath and said, "Please say yes—not because I'm hoping you will but because it's what you want. Of course I expect you to be completely honest."

"Yes," Addie said quickly and sincerely. "Yes, yes, yes."

Impulsively she hugged him, carefully holding the little box in one hand. He returned her embrace with a fervor that made her feel as if she could soak up all the love he was feeling for her, and she hoped that he could feel the same in return.

As they drew away from their embrace, Theo looked at her and smiled, with no evidence of any shyness or reticence. Before Addie had a chance to anticipate such a glorious moment, he lowered his lips to hers and kissed her. Perfect joy permeated through every part of her heart and spirit. This was indeed a Christmas of miracles.

ABOUT THE AUTHOR

ANITA STANSFIELD HAS MORE THAN seventy published books and is the recipient of many awards, including two Lifetime Achievement Awards. Her books go far beyond being enjoyable, memorable stories. Anita resonates particularly well with a broad range of devoted readers because of her sensitive and insightful examination of contemporary issues that are faced by many of those readers, even when her venue is a historical romance. Readers come away from her compelling stories equipped with new ideas about how to enrich their own lives, regardless of their circumstances.

Anita was born and raised in Provo, Utah. She is the mother of five and has a growing number of grandchildren. She also writes for the general trade market under the name Elizabeth D. Michaels.

For more information and a complete list of her publications, go to anitastansfield.blogspot.com or anitastansfield.com, where you can sign up to receive email updates. You can also follow her on Facebook and Twitter.

OTHER BOOKS AND AUDIOBOOKS

BY ESTHER HATCH:

The Roses of Feldstone

A Proper Scandal

'TIS THE SEASON ⟨TO⟩ BE DARING

ESTHER HATCH

To my children—
Your father and I dreamed of you long before you arrived, and you are
everything we dreamed of and more.

ACKNOWLEDGMENTS

THIS IS A SHORT STORY, and yet somehow my list of those I need to thank is still very long.

To the members of my family writing groups: Alice Patron, Laura Rupper, Paula Anderson, Lindy Hatch, Audrey Mangum, Monique Bird, Tammi Bird, and my mother, Elsie Bird Mosher—thanks, as always, for getting me started and keeping me going. You may be tired of getting your names on this list, but I can't really write an acknowledgments section without you.

To my fellow authors: Joanna Barker, Bridget Baker, Heidi Kimball, Clarissa Wilstead, and Megan Walker—thank you for helping me out with this one and for being a support in good times and bad. Authors are amazing people, and I have somehow managed to sneak in through the back door and hang out with the coolest of the cool.

Susan Warnock and Kim Dubois keep my manuscripts legible. I'm so grateful to have them on my side.

My last-minute readers, Amy Kate Parker and Colleen Lynch, were an immense help, and I didn't give them much warning or time. Thanks for rising up when I needed you.

Lisa Kendrick, April Young, Becky Mielke, Debbie Jorgensen, Melissa Paynter, Abby Merkley, Karin Smith, and Heidi Maxfield—all of you have helped me craft books and cheered me on through the trenches of motherhood. Words cannot express what that kind of friendship means to me.

A special thanks to the three other authors in the anthology. We all know I am getting the best end of the deal by having my name on the cover with yours. It is an honor to work with you and something I never would have dreamed possible just two years ago. Thank you, Covenant Communications, for inviting me to be a part of this project. Kami Hancock, thank you for editing my story; you know your stuff.

And finally, thanks to my family. Writing is a job that never leaves, and our lives have changed since I chose this path. I'm so grateful to have you to ground me in real life. My stories are all love stories, but more importantly, they are stories about the formation of family. I hope my love for families comes through in every book I write. Thank you so much for being supportive and proud. I couldn't do it without you.

"With mirth and laughter let old wrinkles come."
—Shakespeare, *The Merchant of Venice*

CHAPTER ONE

London, 1814

I SHOULD HAVE BEGGED MY parents to let me stay at home with Rose. Not that it would have done any good.

Mama dragged me by the arm to the opposite side of the stuffy, overly flowered ballroom. "Elizabeth, tonight you have a very special chance with Lord Fagerlund. Rumor has it he is finally looking for a wife."

"*He* is? Or is his mother looking for him?"

Mama waved her free hand in response, the fan that dangled beneath it swooping about in circles that only emphasized her point. "It is the same thing."

Since my mother's excitement at marrying me off was quite different from my own, I highly doubted that. "Lord Fagerlund is over forty years old."

"But he is a baron." It was her final point, and one I could never argue with. The only thing Mama wanted more than to marry off her daughters was to marry them off to someone of rank. Papa was a baronet with a small holding, and while it had never bothered him that he didn't sit in the House of Lords, Mama was bound and determined to get a son-in-law who did. "Besides, it isn't as though you are a spring chicken. This is already your second Season. Eighteen is the perfect age for someone like Lord Fagerlund."

I might be the perfect age for him, but there was no part of me that felt he would be perfect for me. But one could never win an argument with Mama, so I never tried. Lord Fagerlund was broad and thick, like a workhorse, and despite his age he still had all of his dark hair. He stood in a group of comparatively slender gentlemen who were watching the dancers on the floor. Based on their raised eyebrows and smug laughter, they weren't complimenting anyone's dance skills. We had been introduced to Lord Fagerlund earlier in the Season, but Mama had ruled him out, not due to his age or disdain for others but due to his obvious lack of motivation to marry.

I trailed behind Mama until she pushed her way into his group. The two men on either side of Lord Fagerlund stepped aside to make room for us. I didn't have to look up from my slippers to sense the looks of scorn and surprise on their faces. Mama was anything but subtle in her search for her next son-in-law. With five daughters, Mama's main goal in life was to do her duty and marry off each of us. Then she would finally find peace. After me there was only Rose left, and since she was thirteen, Mama would have to wait at least a few more years to start parading her around. But still, Mama was nearly to her goal, and at the moment, pawning me off to Lord Fagerlund was her only objective.

"Lord Fagerlund!" Mama batted her eyes and hit him playfully with her fan. "What is a young man such as you doing standing here instead of dancing?" She pulled me closer to her and then pushed me in Lord Fagerlund's direction. A familiar sickness rose up in my stomach. I didn't dare look up at Lord Fagerlund's face. More than half the men Mama approached this way did end up dancing with me. But a few didn't. I wasn't even sure which was the outcome I preferred. They were equally dreadful.

Lord Fagerlund cleared his throat in a way that meant he was going to fall into that minority of men who would find some semi-polite excuse not to be on the dance floor. "I am afraid I am not up to dancing this evening, madam. I came with the purpose of spending the evening with close friends."

Heat rose to my face. I changed my mind; not dancing was worse. I turned and started to walk away. I wasn't going to spend another minute in the company of a man who was rude by nature.

Mama still had my elbow and hauled me back. "Conversing is so much more interesting than dancing. I quite agree with you, Lord Fagerlund. Don't you feel the same, Elizabeth?"

Mama hadn't mistaken his intention to get rid of us. His thick lips were set in a snarl, but Mama's false smile was plastered on her face, and her feet were rooted firmly in place. If I didn't do something, we would be accosting Lord Fagerlund all night.

"Oh!" I said, and for the first time, the lofty baron turned his muddy-brown eyes on me. "The Elliots are waving me over. I had better go speak with them. Enjoy your conversation with Lord Fagerlund, Mama."

I extracted my arm from Mama's and scampered away before I could see either of their reactions. I walked as quickly as my gown would allow, managing to bump into only a few women on my way across the ballroom.

Why did Mama have to try so hard? I wasn't bad-looking or a social outcast, but I was starting to feel like one. I needed an escape from all of this auctioning to the highest bidder—or any bidder—feeling. I wasn't some cast-off piece of furniture.

"Elizabeth!" Fanny Elliot beamed when she saw me approach. Her hair was golden and shone in a way that always made me regret my own dark hair. Her mother stood next to her, an older and plumper version of her daughter. "I am glad you are here tonight."

"Mama wouldn't dream of missing it. Apparently Lord Fagerlund is looking for a wife."

Fanny's eyes flashed. "Lord Fagerlund is a clodpoll."

"Lord Fagerlund is both a man and unmarried, making him quite acceptable as far as Mama is concerned."

Fanny shook with laughter. Mrs. Elliot shushed her. "Your mother wants to provide for her daughters. Marrying off five young ladies is a daunting task."

"Daunting, yes," I said. "But I need a break from it, at least for the rest of this Season. I have no prospects yet, and it is already the first week of December. I don't see how a few more months of awkward introductions will produce any kind of improvement in my situation." I had never spoken the sentiment out loud before, but as soon as I heard my words, a burning need to flee blossomed in my chest. I hated it here. I hated the small talk and the flirtations that were impossible for me to understand. And the smell of so many bodies confined together in one room would only intensify as the evening wore on.

If something didn't change, I would be spending the next few months in similar ballrooms, trying to avoid Mama and the men she wanted me to pursue. My chest tightened. Months of evenings just like this, when I would so much rather spend my time at home with Rose. "Isn't there some way a woman can be excused for the Season?"

"Well, you could get engaged." Mrs. Elliot said with a shrug. "That would solve some of your problems."

"With no men interested, I believe we can skip over that idea. Do you have any others?" I needed some evenings at home, some quiet time away from the crowds and the pressure of the marriage mart.

Fanny reached for both of my hands, her face glowing. "You could damage your reputation."

"Fanny!" Her mother hit her softly with her fan. "Miss Davenport would never do such a thing." Mrs. Elliot was right. I never would. I wouldn't even know how to. And even though the last thing on earth I wanted was for Mama to find me a husband, I still did like the idea of marrying *someday*.

"No. Listen, Mama, not irreparable damage." Fanny dropped my hand and reached for her mother's elbow. "Just enough that her mother would give up on this Season and try again next year."

Mrs. Elliot frowned. "Even still, Miss Davenport would never dream of such a thing."

I ignored Mrs. Elliot's objections. If the damage was slight enough . . . "What kind of damage would be repairable next Season?" I asked. Mrs. Elliot's mouth dropped open, but she quickly shut it again, glancing around us to make certain no one was eavesdropping on our conversation.

Fanny chewed on her lip. "Well, you couldn't do anything too outrageous."

"Nothing outrageous at all!" Mrs. Elliot shook her head. "Fanny, I wish you would stop this subject at once."

"But it is such an entertaining one." Fanny's eyebrows jumped up and down.

I nodded my head in agreement. Already the room seemed less stifling. If there was a way to excuse myself from attending even half the social functions of the Season, I was willing to entertain the idea.

"Mrs. Elliot, I believe this is worth considering," I said, and her shoulders slumped. But I knew she would never tell Mama. She was as much my friend as was her daughter. "What kind of scenarios are you thinking? I could attend a ball having forgotten my gloves." That was the type of mistake that wouldn't truly ruin me, but the embarrassment could make Mama hesitate to attend the next ball or two.

Fanny shook her head. "I don't think forgetting your gloves would get you out of much."

"Perhaps if I made some wrong acquaintances, Mama would try to keep me away from them. No one actually dangerous—just inappropriate and unapprovable."

Fanny pursed her lips together in thought. "Well, there is Lord Hawthorne."

Mrs. Elliot shook her head. "No. Not Lord Hawthorne."

"I've heard quite a lot about him. Mama doesn't like him. But we haven't been introduced. Isn't he a rake?" Mama had strictly avoided Lord Hawthorne after an unpleasant episode her friend Mrs. Jepson had had with him. Apparently, after being introduced to her daughter, he'd let them know in no uncertain terms that he had no intention of ever pursuing a relationship with any women of good breeding.

"No," Fanny said. "He is a lot of things, but not a rake. Society could have forgiven him that." Her face softened. "With his appearance, I could have forgiven him that." She received a second, harder whack from her mother's fan.

"Lord Hawthorne is completely out of the question." Mrs. Elliot ran her fingers over her closed fan. "He has no idea how Society works. He doesn't concern himself with rules and rank. Just last week he refused an invitation to dine with Lord and Lady Hampton because he had a prior engagement with a woodcutter." Mrs. Elliot waited for our reaction, but we must have disappointed her. She widened her eyes and fanned her face as if it were the middle of summer. "A woodcutter! For what purpose does one even meet with a woodcutter?" She shuddered as if the thought of meeting a woodcutter were unimaginable. "I know I've never met with one. Miss Davenport, he is just careless enough to put you in a situation that *would* ruin you and then walk away with a smile on his face, completely unaware that he had done anything wrong."

"What do you mean *ruin* me? Fanny said he isn't a rake. Was she wrong?"

"No. He wouldn't do anything to undermine your character in that way. At least, I don't think he would. He did have a rather serious episode with a young lady two years ago, but when everyone was quite sure they were to be engaged, he stopped all communication with her. There isn't a mother in Town who would be happy to see him showing interest in her daughter, even though he is an earl. They all know he isn't to be taken seriously. And it is one thing for a man nearly to get engaged and not follow through, but for the woman? Her reputation would be in tatters. No self-respecting mother would risk it."

Everything Mrs. Elliot said made it clearer that Lord Hawthorne was exactly the man I needed to free me from the rest of the Season. Mama disliked him, and the rest of Society didn't take him seriously. An earl

Mama hadn't chased around a ballroom? He *must* be improper enough to get me the reprieve I was hoping for. "I must procure an introduction."

"An introduction?" Fanny laughed. "You don't need an introduction to Lord Hawthorne. He doesn't care a fig for such things."

"Not to be introduced? How would I even start a conversation?" I shook my head directly after asking. If I was going to extricate myself from the rest of the Season, I would need to shock Mama completely. I needed to throw caution to the wind and be inappropriate for once.

"Is he here tonight?"

"Your mother most likely steered you away from him," Fanny said. "But yes, I believe I saw him earlier, conversing with one of the servants." She surveyed the ballroom once again. "There he is." Her eyes widened, and her eyebrows rose. She pointed discreetly with her fan. "That's him, leaning against the wall, looking like he would rather be inspecting the woodcutter's pile than be here."

I followed Fanny's eyes and knew Lord Hawthorne immediately. His sandy-brown hair was disheveled, rather than meticulously styled like that of so many other men. Staring intently at his fingernails, he had one leg kicked back behind him with his foot resting on the wall. Those gold-trimmed wallpapers must have cost the Greenwoods a fortune, but Lord Hawthorne treated them as if they were lining the wall of a stable. More than anything, though, just as Fanny had said, Lord Hawthorne looked as if he would rather be anywhere else but here.

I understood the sentiment perfectly.

"I am going to speak with him."

"Miss Davenport, I am sure your mother wouldn't approve," Mrs. Elliot said.

"That is precisely what I am counting on."

Mrs. Elliot squawked and moved to stop me, but Fanny held her back. I smiled to myself. It was good to have such a friend.

Lord Hawthorne never looked up as I approached him. From across the room Mama shot me a questioning glance, but she had moved on from Lord Fagerlund and was deep in conversation with Mrs. Jepson, and conversations between those two never ran short. She was probably boasting about how quickly my sister Dorothea was able to catch a husband.

The closer I got to the infamous earl, the more handsome he was. Even leaning against the wall he was taller than most of the men in the room. His shoulders were broad, but his hips narrow, and his eyes, which I had yet to see, were shadowed by thick, dark lashes. He paid no attention to anyone, but the few ladies nearest him couldn't take their eyes off his striking features. I didn't blame them. How had this man escaped my notice all Season?

I stopped just a few feet away from him. Not daring to look back at Mama to see whether she had noticed my location, I jumped right into a conversation before I ran out of courage. Or worse, someone—most likely my mother—interrupted us.

"Lord Hawthorne?"

His hand dropped to his side, and his foot fell off the wall. He straightened, with a smile that deepened as he took in who was addressing him. His eyes were blue, and although they had seemed dull and bored when he first looked up, they sparked with interest as he looked to either side of us for someone who should have introduced us. When he realized there was no one, the corners of his mouth rose to reveal a deep crevice that dimpled one side of his cheek. The blue of his eyes had become effervescent, as if by calling out his name I had provided the most entertainment he had had in months. I felt the corners of my mouth rise. This man's smile was contagious.

"At your service," he said with the slightest of bows.

"Truly?"

He raised an eyebrow. Then, sizing me up and down in the most inappropriate manner, his smile spread even farther across his face. "Most definitely."

Every other man I had talked to this Season had struggled to find a way to escape me. But Lord Hawthorne stood at attention, waiting for whatever I would say next. He didn't even know my name, nor did he ask it. We just stood there smiling at each other. I shook my head slightly to clear it. There was a reason I had approached Lord Hawthorne, and it wasn't to look at him.

"I am glad you said that. Because I would like to propose a plan for the two of us."

He put a hand to his waist and leaned forward. "I cannot wait to hear it."

"It is quite untoward."

"I specialize in untoward." He stepped closer to me, and the air seemed to brighten around us. "Ask anyone in this room."

"I did," I said, and he stopped his forward motion. "It just so happens I am in need of a gentleman—"

He threw up his hands. "I am going to have to stop you there. I am not comfortable being used as a gentleman. I am not sure I deserve the term."

"But you are an earl." I had never heard of anyone of rank being hesitant to use the title of gentleman. He shrugged his shoulders as if to say his lineage was no fault of his own. I sighed. "I am in need of a man, then."

"Aha, there I can help you. For what purpose do you need a man? If it is for marriage, I am afraid I cannot agree to that, at least not until we have ridden in Hyde Park together, and it's much too late in the evening for that. Dangerous place at night, I am afraid."

A laugh escaped my mouth. It was absolute madness that I had never made this man's acquaintance before. He straightened his spine, obviously pleased to have elicited such a reaction from me.

"No, not that, I assure you. Quite the opposite, in fact."

"The opposite of marriage? If you are looking for a divorce, I am afraid I can't help you after all. One must first marry for a divorce to take place, and as I said before, we haven't even had a ride in Hyde Park yet." His jest was taking it too far. I tilted my head to one side and grimaced. His shoulders sank at my reaction. "Too much?"

"Quite. And no, I am not looking for a divorce." My voice lowered when I said the word. Even trying as hard as I could to be inappropriate, it was hard for me to say *divorce* out loud. I was going to have to get better at this. I was far too accustomed to following rules. "I am trying to secure a reprieve from attending these blasted balls with my mother."

He covered his mouth with his hand at my outburst. I had never used such language, but something about Lord Hawthorne made me feel it was best to let all of my inhibitions slip. I was more likely to get him on my side. He looked left and right, seemingly delighted by my indiscretion but still concerned about my reputation. My nerves settled slightly.

Lord Hawthorne was the right man for this task; I was sure of it.

His face went stony for a second, his smile dropping and his eyebrows furrowing. "Is your mother perhaps wearing a light-pink gown with a dozen more ruffles than it needs?"

My head whipped around. She was marching toward us. Apparently preventing my acquaintance with Lord Hawthorne took precedence over one-upping Mrs. Jepson. Without thinking, I reached out and grabbed

Lord Hawthorne's hand. "If you are willing, I want you to associate with me as much as possible in the next few days. Enough so that Mama will stop bringing me to these infernal balls." He was quiet. "Please?" I added. I wanted this more than I dared to admit.

He placed his free hand on top of mine. It was warm, and even through my glove a spark of energy seemed to flow from him and into me. "I have never heard of a more worthwhile goal." He was suddenly soldier-straight and as solemn as a saint. "I would be honored to help you in this most noble of causes."

I bit my lip to stop another laugh, and once again his eyes flashed with pleasure. He liked to make people laugh. Well, I could do worse than spending a few days with a man determined to entertain me.

"There is only one thing I must know before we begin this great endeavor."

"What is that?" I lowered my voice, knowing Mama must be nearing us.

"Your name."

A soft laugh escaped my lips. *I suppose there are reasons for social customs after all.* How would he even know where to find me if I didn't tell him that? "My lord, I am quite certain you are about to hear it."

"Elizabeth Davenport," Mama hissed from a few feet away. I raised an eyebrow at Lord Hawthorne, and his face split into a smile. I suddenly understood his desire to make others laugh. "Come with me now. I have someone you must meet." She reached for my arm and, with only the slightest of nods in Lord Hawthorne's direction, wheeled me away from the most interesting man in the room.

CHAPTER TWO

"But Mama, I thought you would be pleased I took a liking to him. He's an earl!" I was sitting next to Mama at the breakfast table and tried but failed to snatch Lord Hawthorne's card from her hand. Father looked up briefly, then went back to reading his morning newspaper.

Rose's green eyes were as wide as saucers. "An earl is asking you to ride in Hyde Park?" Rose managed to reach around the breakfast table and grab the card from Mama while her attention was on me. "Lord Hawthorne," Rose practically squealed. "Even his name sounds handsome. When did you meet him?" Oh dear. Rose was going to like Lord Hawthorne. He was exactly the type of person she would approve of. She would need to be told.

"I met him two days ago at the Greenwoods' ball. He is handsome and interesting. You would like him, Rose."

"There isn't a serious bone in that man's body." Mama rose from her seat and stalked toward the fireplace. "He has offended every person of good character I know. And even if those things could be forgiven, all of London knows he isn't looking for a wife. He had the most perfect opportunity to snatch up the darling of the Season two years ago, and he let the chance slip through his fingers. Not to mention what he said to Mrs. Jepson. He made it very clear that he wasn't looking for a wife and had no interest in well-bred young ladies like her daughter. He may come from a good family, but the only thing you will gain from him is a damaged reputation. I will not have you wasting time on a man who won't commit."

"But an earl, Mama!" Rose's eyes shone with mischief. "If she could catch him, Elizabeth would do much better than Dorothea. She managed only a knight."

"Marriage isn't a competition, Rose," Mama said.

Rose and I shared a look. In almost every regard Mama made it very clear that marriage was, in fact, a competition.

"Besides, I don't care if he is the king of Sheba. Elizabeth, you are not riding with him in Hyde Park. You must send your regrets."

Rose bit her fingers to keep from laughing at, or correcting, Mama. Despite her lack of fortitude, I managed a straight face. At least, I hoped I did.

I put my hand out, and Rose reached across the table to hand me Lord Hawthorne's card. "He and his sister are arriving in thirty minutes," I said. "There isn't time to send him a reply." A brilliant move on his part.

"Again," Mama said, "who doesn't allow time for an answer to an invitation? And Hyde Park at this hour? It is unfashionable, at the very least."

"At any rate," I said, standing up, "I won't receive an earl in my morning dress. I am going upstairs to change."

Mama looked down at her own dress and apron. And then stood up frantically. "You are right. Even a dastardly earl is an earl." Mama rushed out the door before I had the chance to tell her a man who would happily spend an evening with a woodcutter probably wouldn't object to her wearing an apron.

Twenty-five minutes later I descended the stairs. I had taken better care of my appearance than I had in months. At my request Mary had arranged my hair in an elaborate design, with braids wrapped around my head and pulled back into a loose knot. With most of the time spent on my hair, I had quickly donned my favorite blue day dress, placed my grandmother's pearl necklace around my throat, and pinched my cheeks. Lord Hawthorne had agreed to spend time with me; the least I could do was try my best to be pleasant to look at. Heaven knew he was going to provide me with the same satisfaction.

I would be meeting his sister and her husband—Lord and Lady Rothschild. Mama hadn't said anything negative about them. They must not be quite as unfashionable as Lord Hawthorne.

Mama was ready and waiting in the drawing room. Gone was her apron, and in place of her morning dress was her very nicest day dress. I eyed the costly fabric. She wore that only when the highest quality of guests were arriving. This just wouldn't do. Mama could not get her hopes up about Lord Hawthorne. Or even tolerate him.

At the exact moment he was set to arrive, there was a knock at the front door. Mama and I both jumped. Papa was nowhere to be seen; most likely he had retreated to his study after breakfast. I didn't know where Rose had escaped to. Mama and I would have to receive our guests alone.

There was a clamor of feet, and the drawing room door flew open. Rose swung into the room, her dark hair bouncing and her feet sliding on the hardwood floor. "I am not too late, am I? Did Mama toss the earl out on his ear?"

The butler, Mr. Sparrow, cleared his throat behind her, and just at that moment Lord Hawthorne appeared. He gave Rose a smile and a wink. "I truly hope your mother has no plans of throwing me out on my ear. Typically when I am thrown out of houses, I try to make it a point to land on much more cushioned parts of the body."

I snorted, Mama gasped, and Rose let out a peal of laughter.

"I like this one," Rose said. "You should keep him."

Lord Hawthorne straightened to his full height and raised a solitary eyebrow in my direction. "Keeping me was never part of the arrangement."

"Arrangement?" Mama frowned. "What sort of arrangement do you have with my daughter?"

"Oh, Mama. He simply means our carriage ride." I placed a hand on Mama's arm and sent a stern look to Lord Hawthorne. "What else could he mean?"

"What else indeed?" The earl sent a wink in my direction while Mama's face was turned. A wink! I had never been winked at in my life.

I rather liked it. It was as if my whole world had been turned upside down just by this one man's entrance into it.

"Well," Mama harrumphed. "If there are to be any arrangements made, I fully expect to know about them. Rose, you may return to the nursery." Rose was thirteen and yet was still expected to spend most of her time in the nursery. Mama didn't tolerate children well. And until her daughters were ready to marry off, they were children to her. "There is no need for you to be here at the moment. Lord Hawthorne must want to sit down to tea and speak with me before taking Elizabeth."

"Actually, Lady Davenport, I am here only to take Miss Davenport for a ride. I am afraid a visit, as delightful as that sounds, will have to wait until next time. My sister and her husband, Lord Rothschild, are waiting outside, and my horses are ready to run. They haven't been exercised in over a week."

Mama's face went white, then red. Rose stopped halfway up the stairs; she never could handle not being privy to an exciting conversation. Mama sputtered, sounding like a tea kettle about to boil over. "Run? You plan to run your horses?"

Lord Hawthorne gave her the type of smile that would send most ladies into a swoon. My breath caught slightly even though I knew better. He was putting on an act because I had asked him to. It may have been smarter to pick a man who was both unacceptable and unattractive. As it was, his smile might just win over Mama. "My carriage is solid," he said. And my horses' instincts are unsurpassed. They would ride into battle if I asked them to. They can handle Hyde Park."

"Elizabeth, may I speak to you? Just outside the drawing room. Actually, in your father's study. I need his advice on something."

Lord Hawthorne glanced at the clock on the mantel, then bowed slightly to show a short delay would be acceptable. I followed Mama to Papa's study, and she quickly shut the door behind us.

Papa reluctantly looked up from his paper.

"The earl wants to run his horses in Hyde Park!"

"Well . . ." Papa turned a page of his newspaper. His dark hair was slicked back and away from his plump face. "If he is an earl, I suppose Society will let him do as he pleases."

"John!" Her voice rose at least two octaves. "Our daughter will be in that carriage. What if it turns over or they fall into the Serpentine? What if Mrs. Jepson sees them? She will remind me of it for years. You can't just run horses in Hyde Park."

Papa slammed down the newspaper he had been trying to read, even with the two of us in the room. "Blast it all, woman. Where the devil is a man supposed to take his horses to run in London, if not in Hyde Park? I find it a capital idea. I am inclined to make my mount run in the park every so often. It would keep him in shape for the hunt I have planned in the spring."

Mama tried everything short of crying, but Papa wouldn't take the time to come into the drawing room and forbid the ride. If something wasn't related to hunting, he wasn't interested, and my affairs had nothing to do with hunting. For once I was glad to have a father who didn't want to interfere.

When we returned to the drawing room, Lord Hawthorne held a small frame in his hand. He placed it back on the mantel where he had found it.

"That is fine workmanship," he said of the framed embroidery.

"That is Elizabeth's. She is always working on something or other, whether embroidery or knitting. Why, at some point she had better have twelve children, for she has knitted more than double that in booties."

"She has, has she?" Lord Hawthorne cocked his thick eyebrow once again. I was beginning to think that would be something I would see often from him. "Is that more than double twelve *pairs* of booties or just double twelve? For you do need two of them per every small person, you know."

"Pairs," Mama said. "I am not sure what she plans to do with them."

"My children will wear them, Mama, and they will need more than one, so I am not concerned about having too many."

Please just let us leave for Hyde Park.

I didn't want to stand here while Mama talked about my normally demure self. Lord Hawthorne would have no interest in the type of woman who sat at home knitting booties. Not that I was trying to interest him. I was merely using him, and he didn't seem to mind it. But he might start to mind if he realized how uninteresting I was.

"Shall we begin our ride to Hyde Park, then?" I asked, gesturing toward the door. "Your sister is waiting . . ."

"You won't show me these booties your mother mentioned? It would take only a moment to have a look at them." He raised both of his eyebrows this time. "I find myself quite intrigued by them."

My face felt warm, despite being far from the fire. "They look like any other booties you would see."

"Oh no, they don't." Mama jumped at the opportunity to make me more uncomfortable in front of Lord Hawthorne. "She took extra care with each one. Roses and violets embroidered on the tops of some and boats and balls on others."

I'd had enough. Stalking over to Lord Hawthorne, I grabbed one of his arms and pulled him toward the door. He laughed in surprise but didn't pull away.

"Elizabeth!" Mama was shocked at my behavior, and so was I, but I couldn't stand here another minute and let her tell Lord Hawthorne what a dull life I led. I didn't love embroidery or knitting, but if I was going to be forced to spend hours on it, I would spend it on things I cared about. That was all.

Lord Hawthorne twisted in order to bow to Mama as I propelled him through the door. The movement made the lean muscles under his jacket harden and pull. I dropped my arm. How could I be so inappropriate? But even after I released him, I recalled the feel of the thickness and strength of his forearm.

In front of our house sat two phaetons. Two. A bundled-up couple sat in one, and the other stood empty. Our supposed chaperones would be in a completely different carriage. Phaetons were small, with room only for two people. Not only that, they were open so the couple sitting in one would be exposed to anyone walking or riding nearby.

"We are going to ride alone?"

"No, Lord Rothschild and my sister will be right behind us."

"Mama was under the impression we would all be riding together." I had been under the impression that we would be riding all together. I hadn't counted on us being alone. I didn't know Lord Hawthorne, not at all. I assumed he was taking me to Hyde Park out of the goodness of his heart or, more likely, because he liked the idea of upsetting a matchmaking matron like Mama. But what if he had something more nefarious in mind?

"Yes, she was supposed to be under that impression. But that would hardly be considered scandalous, now would it?"

Lord Hawthorne's carriage wasn't ostentatious, but it looked clean and well cared for. The horses that pulled it were a deep chestnut. He had no driver, so we would be completely alone. Not completely unheard of, but definitely inappropriate.

As far as my plan went, it was perfect. But my poor heart felt differently. I had felt his arms under his jacket and knew it would be no work at all for him to overpower me. I closed my eyes and forced myself to think of Lord Fagerlund. Strangulation was a chance I was willing to take.

We walked over to his sister's carriage, and he made the introductions. They were so bundled under the blankets I didn't get the best look at them, but Lady Rothschild had the same sandy hair as her brother. Lord Rothschild was plump but jovial. They didn't stop smiling as Lord Hawthorne introduced us. What exactly had he told them about me?

Lord Hawthorne helped me into his carriage. Most of the men Mama had paraded me around to had been thin and stringy gentlemen who'd smelled of smoke and bear fat from their slicked-back hair. As I brushed past Lord Hawthorne on my way into the sleek phaeton, he smelled of only one thing.

Soap.

Men didn't smell of soap. If they didn't reek with smoke and bear fat, they reeked of liquor. Only children smelled like soap. For some reason the thought put me at ease. Surely a man who smelled of soap wouldn't accost a woman.

The carriage shifted as Lord Hawthorne climbed in after me. He placed a warm brick at my feet and settled a blanket over both of us. "To Hyde Park?" he asked.

I nodded, suddenly unable to form words.

He took the reins and, with a click of his tongue and a flick of his wrist, the chestnuts jolted forward.

"Now that I have you alone . . ." Lord Hawthorne glanced sideways at me. He must have felt my nervousness, for unlike his usual carefree and boisterous manner, he spoke softly, as if he was afraid I would dart away. I straightened in my seat. I was no shrinking violet. I was the one who had gotten us into this situation. "Would you mind telling me more of your plan? How exactly do you want to use me?"

"*Use* is a rather negative word, don't you think?" Words had finally come, and to my relief, they had even made sense.

"Perhaps, but accurate." He smiled, and though I could see only his profile as he watched the horses, his cheekbones seemed to rise with the motion. "Please don't misunderstand; I have no objection to being used— at least, not by fair women such as yourself. I only want to establish exactly how I will be used, in order to play the part correctly."

I nodded in response as I thought through exactly how I wanted Lord Hawthorne to help me. "I want an escape from the Season. I am quite through with being paraded around by Mama. It is ridiculous. I feel as though I am suffocating."

"You don't want to be paraded around?"

"I do not."

"And you believe I can help you with this how?"

I sneaked another glance at him. "You are just the right amount of inappropriate. I need to damage my reputation a bit, but not too much. I will marry someday, I suppose, but I want to be finished with this Season. I have been introduced to all the gentlemen on Mama's list, mostly in a very mortifying manner. The only ones who can look past that embarrassment are the ones dull enough not to mind Mama's machinations. Therefore, the few men willing to spend time with me bore me to tears."

"All of them?" He turned to look at me for a moment with feigned hurt.

"Well, you don't count."

"Because I am not a gentleman?"

"Because we haven't been introduced. At least, not properly."

Lord Hawthorne barked out a laugh and pulled the carriage to a stop. He turned and lifted one of my hands in his. "Miss Elizabeth Davenport"—that smile again—"I would like to introduce myself. I am Lord Hawthorne. Or Charles—I will allow you to call me whatever you feel is necessary to further this most noble goal of getting you out of every social commitment we can until the end of the Season." He nodded solemnly and then placed my hand back under the blanket.

"There, now we have been introduced," he said.

I snorted.

"What?"

"That hardly counts as an introduction."

"Well, that is all right with me, as long as it is all right with you. I am not sure I want to be lumped in with those boring men anyway. We will remain unintroduced, and it will make every interaction that much more scandalous."

I smiled. "Perfect."

"And now, I must ask . . ." He still hadn't moved the horses forward, so he looked directly at me. "Exactly how scandalous will you allow me to be?" His half-smile this time was a rakish grin that somehow was not intimidating at all. Even when his eyes found my lips I knew he must be jesting. It was impossible for this man to be serious.

"As I said, just scandalous enough to get me out of this Season. I can't have my reputation marred completely. I would like to marry."

"After all, someone needs to father those twelve children. Or was it twenty-four?"

"A child needs more than one pair of booties," I answered back, even as my fingers fidgeted under the blanket. Why did Mama have to bring those up?

"How many does a child need? Two? Three? I am merely trying to judge what your future holds."

"Oh, I was barely thinking of numbers while knitting and embroidering those. When confronted with hours of time for needlework or knitting, most ladies embroider hankies or tat lace to go on their dresses. I just wanted to work on something more personal to me. If I was going to spend the time on it, I wanted it to be something interesting."

"And you find children interesting?"

"Doesn't everyone?"

He finally looked forward and slapped the reins down on the horses. "No, not everyone."

He was right. Mama had never really seemed the type to enjoy children, despite having five of them. Rose was practically an adult but was often still relegated to the nursery so she would be out of the way. She was still liable to say something too open and honest in public, and Mama, most of the time, felt it was easier to tuck her away than deal with the comical situations she created.

"At any rate, I wouldn't like to do anything that would truly upset my future husband. I suppose I don't care too much what Society thinks of me, but I imagine I will want his good opinion."

He nodded, and we rode for a while in silence. Lord Hawthorne didn't want to marry. Did he think I was old-fashioned or unoriginal because I did? Not that it mattered what he thought. Lord Hawthorne was only a tool I was using to further my own purposes. But when I glanced at him, the corners of his lips were pointed down.

When the gate to Hyde Park came into view, Lord Hawthorne turned to me. "So we have one rule: we won't do anything to compromise your future wedded bliss. If this unknown husband of yours wouldn't approve, we won't do it." I nodded, and he gave a brief nod in return. "However, you do realize that if you would like word of our actions to reach your mother, we will need to do something a bit drastic."

"You did mention going fast."

"That goes without saying."

"What else did you have in mind?"

His eyes sparked in a way that made me nervous. "Miss Davenport, do you drive?"

CHAPTER THREE

THE REINS WERE LOOSE IN his hands, as if he was ready to turn them over to me at the drop of a hat. I did drive, but I hadn't done it often. Papa occasionally let me try the reins when Mama wasn't around.

"It isn't exactly scandalous for a woman to drive a carriage."

"No, but if we went fast enough, it would cause a stir."

I chewed on the side of my cheek. "It would, wouldn't it?"

"Are you up for it?"

"Truthfully, I am not sure I am. I have driven before, but never very fast, and not in Hyde Park, where there are so many other carriages."

He smiled and brought one arm over my head. His clean scent engulfed me as quickly as his arms did. Lord Hawthorne placed the reins in each of my hands, but didn't let go of them. Men had held me at certain points in dances, but there was always movement and the expectation of nearness. Lord Hawthorne's arms didn't move. They were steady around me, and very unexpected. My back was pressed against his solid chest as it rose and fell with a deep breath. I stilled, reminding myself not to squirm or look uncomfortable. His words were mere inches from my ear. "I will help you."

"Now?"

"This is a driving lesson." He shrugged, and I felt, rather than saw, the motion of it. "Nothing overly scandalous about that."

"With your arms around me?"

"Do I distract you?"

With his voice in my ear and his warm breath on my cheek, how could he not? "Honestly?" I asked.

"I wouldn't expect anything else."

"Yes, your arms distract me a great deal."

His reaction was to pull me tighter to him. He leaned his head forward and to the side until his cheek lightly grazed my own. "If you are distracted while driving, I am afraid I have no choice but to help you." With that, he slapped the reins down on the horses' flanks, and we were off with a jostle that pushed me even deeper into Lord Hawthorne's arms. Wind whipped at my hair. The phaeton bounded forward at a pace that made the trees rush past.

I let out a small scream and shrank down into Lord Hawthorne. He, however, seemed to grow with the excitement of it all. He leaned forward, chest puffed up and hands steady around mine. His arms were much warmer than the blanket or the brick at my feet, and even with the brisk winter air hitting my face, I barely felt the cold. We passed one carriage, then another.

His sister was left far behind. So much for a chaperone. Men and women dressed in the height of fashion scowled at us as we flew by them. The chestnuts were responsive to each of Lord Hawthorne's moves, and his phaeton was truly well-cared-for. I never heard a squeak of complaint from it.

After making a turn that brought us up next to the Serpentine, I relaxed enough to take in the view of the park. There were no leaves on the trees and, with the weather being clear the past few days, no snow on the ground. Lord Hawthorne must have sensed my confidence building, for his voice was once again warm in my ear.

"Are you ready to try it on your own?"

Was I? I sneaked a glance at him. His eyes were sharp and flashing with the thrill of our ride. No man had ever been that happy while spending time with me. My lungs filled with air, and I matched his smile. I was a grown, capable woman; I could do this. "Yes."

"What was that?"

"I said yes. Yes, I am ready to drive on my own."

"Good. Although, quite unfortunate for me." He squeezed each of my hands quickly, and then he was gone. The cold December air enveloped my arms and back. Only my left side, where he still sat close to me, remained warm. Perhaps I should have said no.

I maneuvered the carriage around a turn, and a carriage going a very leisurely pace appeared in front of us. Lord Hawthorne was forgotten for the moment. I quickly pulled the reins to one side, but not too quickly—carefully and precisely—just as Lord Hawthorne had done moments ago. We flew past the carriage in a matter of seconds, and I couldn't help the laugh that escaped my throat. Lord Hawthorne did the same. We passed many more carriages after that one. Each time the thrill of the ride brought laughter to our lips. Halfway through the park I slowed his steeds until they were walking unhurriedly. I handed the reins back to Lord Hawthorne, and his hand rested on mine, just longer than needed, before he took them.

"Thank you," I said. "I haven't had that much excitement in months." Not months, truly. I had never had such an exhilarating afternoon. The ride through the park wasn't even the most thrilling part. Spending time with Lord Hawthorne was like nothing I had ever experienced. He lived life fully, and he *enjoyed* it. Duty and pleasing others, two things which occupied my mind more often than not, were forgotten.

"Well then, it sounds like I need to find many more entertaining things for you to do."

His face shone, reflecting the light of the sun. In his words was a promise of many more afternoons and evenings together. I had never looked forward to anything more. Rose was the only other person in the world with whom I cherished spending my time. But Rose didn't make my face flush or my heart wish for her warmth. I missed Lord Hawthorne's arms around me. But I shouldn't. He wasn't a permanent fixture in my life. Not like Rose was. He never would be.

I had chosen him because he had no interest in forming an attachment with anyone. I needed to keep my goal in mind. There was a reason I was spending so much time with Lord Hawthorne, and it wasn't because it was enjoyable. That was merely an extra benefit I hadn't counted on.

"We need an end date," I said.

"Pardon me?" His eyebrows came together as if he was confused by my sudden change in subject. But if I was already missing his arms around me now, after one outing, how much harder would it be if this were to continue for an extended amount of time? "An end date for what?"

"For our agreement. I can't expect you to be slightly scandalous with me indefinitely." I kept my voice light, as if it didn't bother me to think of going back to being Mama's perfect daughter. It was going to be hard enough to live without the brightness Lord Hawthorne had brought into my life already. I couldn't get too used to having him around.

He quirked his head to one side, as if thinking about the idea.

"If we haven't made my mother give up on the Season by Christmas, then we stop. I will be just one more woman you showed interest in and then ultimately stopped caring about."

His brow furrowed. "Is that what you think of me?"

"What? No, it's just what I've heard. My friend told me you were nearly engaged to a woman—"

"Miss Green."

"Yes, well, she couldn't remember her name, but it must have been Miss Green, I suppose." I didn't like the sound of her name. Miss Green? I was surprised Lord Hawthorne would be interested in a woman with the name of Green. It wasn't exactly inspiring. "What happened to her?" I tried to keep the curiosity out of my voice, but I wasn't sure I succeeded.

"She married. She found another earl who suited her taste better. Thank goodness."

His last words opened up my lungs, and I felt the smile return to my face. "So she didn't break your heart?"

"No, I suppose she didn't." He flicked the reins once more. I gasped and grabbed hold of his arm as the carriage jumped forward faster than we had ever gone. Just as it had so often that afternoon, a gurgle of laughter escaped my lips. He glanced my way. "She never laughed with me like this. Nor did she knit copious amounts of booties. It is hard to mourn the loss of a woman like that."

My hand was still on his arm. How quickly I had become comfortable with this man I barely knew. Our arrangement would last only the three weeks until Christmas. Actually, it was only until Christmas *at the latest*. If Mama truly felt worried enough to stop my Season, then it could be over even sooner. He would be gone. I pulled my hand away and tucked it back under the blanket. If I continued to be so casual with Lord Hawthorne, I would run the risk of missing him when he was gone.

We arrived at my house even sooner than expected, thanks to Lord Hawthorne's superb driving. He jumped down, then assisted me down as well. With my hands still on his shoulders and his still holding my elbows, we stood there for a moment.

"Thank you, Lord Hawthorne. I am quite certain Mama will hear of our ride this afternoon."

His wicked half-smirk returned to his face. "As will mine."

"Oh, I didn't even think of your family." How had I not thought of his consequences when coming up with this plan? "Will this cause much trouble for you?"

"My family is used to it, but I would wager they will be interested in meeting you. My sister barely had a chance to speak with you. You may get a formal introduction after all. At least, to my mother."

"Oh." Lady Hawthorne. What did I know of her? Nothing. But no mother would be happy with a woman using her son as I was using hers. He released my elbows, and I dropped my hands and turned to the house. I managed only a step before stopping. "Would you like to come in with me? We can speak of the Germains' ball while we wait for your sister to return. If you push for extra dances, perhaps Mama will excuse me from attending and I can spend a pleasant evening at home instead of being in company."

A muscle clenched in his jaw, but it was gone before I was even sure I'd seen it. "Of course," he said and bounded forward to catch up with me. Side by side we ascended the steps to confront Mama. It felt good to have someone on my side.

CHAPTER FOUR

FOUR DAYS AFTER OUR EVENTFUL carriage ride, Mr. Sparrow shut the door behind Mama and Papa on their way to the Germains' ball. I ran up the stairs to join Rose in the nursery. This was to be the first ball I had been invited to attend that Mama had let me miss. After our ride together, Lord Hawthorne had more than delivered on his promise to pretend to want to dance with me. He had been perfect, adding just enough humor to each of his sentences for Mama to feel strongly that there wasn't a serious bone in his body. Her frown had deepened at every jesting comment. A connection with him could never be permanent, and Mama knew it. That night at dinner she had informed me that Rose had been left at home alone too often and I was to stay with her during the ball. *Apparently* I had a headache, and she would let everyone know.

Lord Hawthorne was remarkable. The plan had worked even faster than I'd thought. A twinge of regret at not being able to inform him tonight how well he'd done touched my heart. But I supposed he would hear of my headache and know.

Rose and I read and relaxed the whole evening. As the night wore on, we left the nursery, went to our room, and unpinned our hair. Rose lay on the bed with her head in my lap while I combed through her long dark tresses. She was already nearly as tall as I was, and she still had years to grow.

"You don't feel disappointed about missing the ball?" she asked.

"Not one bit. It is such a relief." Or it would have been just a few days before. But, oddly, I did feel a bit of emptiness at not being able to attend.

"But whom do you think Lord Hawthorne is dancing with?"

I laughed. "I am certain he is dancing only with the women he wants to dance with. He makes a point of doing only what he wants."

"Then, he must have wanted to go on that carriage ride with you."

My hands stilled, the comb halfway through Rose's hair. I looked down at it and decided I was done. Setting the comb down, I began instead to massage Rose's scalp. Lord Hawthorne had seemed to enjoy our time together. "I suppose," I finally said.

"What if you were the only girl he wanted to dance with? What do you think he would do then?"

"Rose, don't get into your head that anything will happen between Lord Hawthorne and me. If he had wanted to get married, he would be married by now. He has had ample opportunity and has shown no interest in it. That is why he is the perfect person to help me. Mama knows he is pursuing me only on a whim. And you know even better. As I told you earlier, he is just helping me enjoy more free time at home with you."

"Yes, but you did just say he does only what he wants. He must want to help you."

I finished massaging her head and leaned forward to place a small kiss at her temple, as was my habit. "Oh, Rose, I don't think it is quite that simple."

"Why not?"

"Well . . ." I couldn't think of a reason Lord Hawthorne was willing to help me when he didn't seem to care about anyone else in Society. "I think he truly despises social customs, and I have dropped an opportunity right into his lap to ignore them. I think he couldn't resist."

There was a soft knock at our bedroom door, and Mary poked her head in. "Miss Davenport," she said hesitantly. "There is a gentleman downstairs in the drawing room. He is hoping to have a word with you."

"A gentleman?" I jumped up out of the bed. Rose and I still wore our dresses and aprons, but our hair was down. "Who would call at this time of night?"

"I wasn't going to let him in, not with Sir John and Lady Davenport out of the house, but he went on and on about how he is an earl and earls can do whatever they want."

Rose gasped, and my hands flew to my hair. "Where is he?"

"I told you, I put him in the drawing room. He wouldn't listen to reason, and Mr. Sparrow has his night off. I don't know what possessed me to open the door. But there was no one else to do it. Mrs. Beecher had already turned in for the night. I didn't think a gentleman would be at the door so late, or I would have woken her." She paused and placed her hand over her heart. "He is right you know, about earls getting to do whatever they want. I couldn't really keep him out. Or at least, I wasn't sure how. Mr. Sparrow may have been able to, but he was so . . . well, persistent, and—"

"Handsome." I finished for her.

Mary's face went scarlet. "Yes."

"Rose and I will go down and see what he needs, but can you help us pin our hair back quickly?"

Three minutes later, with our hair pinned back in hasty knots, Rose and I descended the stairs. What was Lord Hawthorne thinking? I knew he didn't care at all about convention, but to come practically in the middle of the night while my parents were not at home? And he knew they weren't. He must have seen them at the ball.

We opened the drawing room door, and Lord Hawthorne spun around to greet us. He was in his blacks. His suit was tailored to perfection, even if his cravat was loose. He had been handsome before, but his boyish looks and clear skin had brightened somehow in the time I had gotten to know him. He burst into his crooked smile at the sight of us, and I reached for Rose's hand to steady myself. It was almost painful to look at him. He was life and energy. How had I managed to live eighteen years without those two things?

"Miss Davenport, my goodness, it is good to see you." His eyes, while bright, were slightly haggard.

"Shouldn't you be at the Germains'?" We had left the door open, but still, Lord Hawthorne shouldn't be here.

"Yes, well . . . a funny thing happened." He pulled on his already-askew cravat. "I realized I hate balls."

"You have always known you hate balls."

"Yes, but this one was even more tedious than usual." He ran his fingers through his loose, clean hair, which I knew smelled of soap. "Because you weren't in attendance."

Rose snickered, and I squeezed her hand to silence her. This situation had to be handled delicately.

"That was our plan though—to help me escape those tedious balls."

"Yes, I do realize that. However"—he scrunched his face together—"I have just decided I detest that plan."

"You can't just decide you detest my plan after you have already agreed to it."

"Of course I can." His face relaxed, and his jaunty grin returned. "As I told your sweet maid who let me in, I am an earl. I can do whatever I want."

"I thought you hate Society and all of its pompous nature," Rose said from just behind me.

My face warmed. With an answer like that, Lord Hawthorne was sure to know we had been speaking of him.

"Yes, well, when it suits my purpose, I do like to take advantage of it." Lord Hawthorne winked at Rose. "And it suits my purpose not to attend any more balls where your sister isn't present. It was so dull. Not a single person asked me to do anything even the slightest bit inappropriate."

"What do you propose, then?" I hadn't counted on him showing up again. Nor did I know what to do with him now that he was here.

"We either both attend balls, or neither of us does."

That was simple. "Don't go to the balls, then. I am surprised you kept going even before I came along."

"That would break my mother's heart." He shrugged his shoulders. "She is the one person in London who still thinks there is hope for me."

"So you wish to evade them, but in a way that won't disappoint your mother?"

"Yes. Or you could start attending them again. That would at least make them bearable. I am afraid our outing at Hyde Park has spoiled me. I refuse to make dull conversation with any more of London's prattling women. All I see in them now is how unlike you they are."

"Lord Hawthorne." I frowned, closing my eyes and heart against the implication of his words. Had he said similar things to Miss Green before informing her that he wasn't interested in marriage? When I opened my eyes, he was closer than he had been before. I must remember to keep my eyes open at all times.

"Yes?" He leaned forward, waiting for my reply. How could I tell him to be wary of how he spoke to me? Especially in front of young and impressionable Rose. I knew he didn't care about being careful with his conversation, but she was going to hound me about it for days.

"I see no way to convince your mother to keep you from Society. My reputation would have to be quite derelict for her to discourage our association. And as I have said all along, I am not willing to actually put my reputation in complete ruins."

"Then, it's settled. You will start attending balls again."

I put my hands on my hips. That is not what at all what I had meant. "So we went to all of that trouble to get me out of only one ball?"

"First, it has been no trouble. And second, if I remember correctly, you promised to remain in this agreement until Christmas."

"I said if it didn't work by Christmas, we could stop the pretense."

"'Tis the same."

I gritted my teeth. Lord Hawthorne was impossible to argue with. He smiled in response. It seemed a grin from him could be a response to anything. "On Christmas Eve all the pretense will be over, but please come to all the events until then and make them bearable for me. I promise to keep them from being unbearable for you." He reached for my hand. I hadn't bothered to put on gloves; I had been too concerned with my hair. He wasn't wearing his either. As the warmth of his skin touched mine, all of my resolve melted away. His promise to me would be easy to keep. The next two-and-a-half weeks would be much more than bearable. But after Christmas, when I needed to adjust to life without the light he carried with him? Could I be satisfied with my quiet existence ever again?

It was difficult to think coherently with his hand still holding mine. He was so close and so intriguing. "But what of Mama? Our plan has already begun to work. She may confine me to my room for the rest of the Season as it is."

He leaned forward and rubbed his thumb over the top of my knuckles. "Let me worry about your mother. I know just the thing to persuade her."

* * *

The next morning a card arrived inviting Mama and me to tea with Lady Hawthorne. Although the invitation came from his mother, I knew who the orchestrator behind it was. Trust Lord Hawthorne to recognize the one thing Mama couldn't resist: a chance to socialize with someone of rank.

Two days later Mama and I were in a carriage, headed not to a party or a ball but to an intimate tea at Lady Hawthorne's home on Grosvenor square. Mama's smile couldn't have been any larger.

"You must not talk of anything silly, Elizabeth. And especially don't mention your ride in Hyde Park with Lady Hawthorne's son."

"I am certain she knows we were in the park together that day."

"Yes, but we must hope she didn't hear how brazen you were. Why, Mrs. Jepson heard from Mrs. Candle that you were practically in his arms, racing along at an unpardonable speed."

"I wasn't in his arms, Mama. He was just showing me how to drive the phaeton."

"Why would you want to know how to drive a carriage? We have people for that."

I nodded my head, not mentioning the fact that Papa had taught me earlier. It would have exasperated her more. "I know."

"Please, just don't ruin this for me. It isn't often we get the chance to associate so intimately with a family from the peerage. Who knows what doors this could open for us?"

"Of course," I agreed, knowing full well that the person who would need to be controlled was Lord Hawthorne, and the chances of him controlling himself were roughly none. He probably wouldn't be joining us though; the invitation had been from Lady Hawthorne alone.

Lord Hawthorne's home was a dark-red brick, just like all the other homes on this side of the square. Although we had ridden around the square often, I had never been inside any of the homes here. We were immediately ushered into the drawing room, where Lady Hawthorne and Lord Hawthorne's sister sat. Lady Rothschild was arranging the teacups. Now that she wasn't bundled up for a carriage ride, I could see that she was young and vibrant, a lot like her brother.

Lady Hawthorne spoke first, her voice refined and very unlike her son's. "Ah, Lady Davenport. It is such a pleasure to meet you. And I have heard much about your daughter." Mama's face drained. But Lady Hawthorne's demeanor showed nothing of disdain or contempt. Her smile was broad, and she looked genuinely pleased to see us. "This is my daughter, Lady Rothschild, whom Miss Davenport has already met. She will be staying with us until the new year. We love Christmastide in this household, and with no more young ones of my own to spoil, I insisted she bring my grandchildren. Please sit down."

Mama and I sat slowly, both watching the two women for signs of what this tea would bring. Lord Hawthorne wanted Mama to bring me to social events again. But had he communicated that to his mother? How would he? I couldn't believe he would have told his mother I was using him to stain but not ruin my reputation.

"You have five daughters, I hear," Lady Rothschild said while pouring tea. "Your home must be very full of life."

"The eldest three are already married," Mama said. "So it is just Elizabeth and Rose at the moment. But when they were all at home, oh, the headaches I would get from all the noise. Rose is much younger than Elizabeth, and if it weren't for her, we would be enjoying a quiet home at last."

"Oh," Lady Hawthorne said with a smile. "But you will miss the noise."

Lady Hawthorne didn't know Mama. The last thing she would miss about having children was the noise we had created. I wasn't sure what exactly her grudge with Rose was. True, she would have been nearly done raising children if Rose hadn't been born, but I had mothered Rose much more than she ever had, and I didn't mind it a bit. I found mothering to be a much more enjoyable pastime than daughtering.

Mama cleared her throat and acted as though she were thinking about it. "Perhaps you are right."

The conversation became more comfortable as we spoke of our estate and what times of year we spent there. When husbands were mentioned, Lady Hawthorne stated how much her late husband had loved to hunt, which of course opened up an opportunity for Mama and Lady Hawthorne to commiserate about the amount of time their husbands spent hunting. The longer the conversation went on the more comfortable Mama became. Apparently, Lady Hawthorne had not invited us over to berate me for parading about Town with her son.

Whenever hunting was brought up, my mind naturally wandered. The room we were in was warm, the fireplace almost twice the size as ours at home, and the furniture of the best quality. The wooden chairs we sat on seemed to be ancient, passed from one family member to the next, but treated with utmost care to the point that they shone.

The drawing-room door cracked open so slowly I was sure I was the only one who noticed. A stuffed lion suddenly flew through the air and landed at Lady Rothschild's feet. Mama screamed, her hands flying to her face.

Lady Rothschild leaned over and picked up the toy. "Phoebe?"

A small blonde head peeked in the door.

"You may come in," Lady Hawthorne said. A small child who couldn't have been older than three walked in with shoulders hunched, looking side to side. "You aren't in trouble. Come have some tea."

Phoebe's face lit up as she skipped to her grandmother's side, reaching automatically for a biscuit. Just as she settled down on Lady Hawthorne's lap, the door swung wide and Lord Hawthorne burst through it. He wasn't wearing a jacket, and his shirtsleeves were rolled up, showing the skin of his forearms. What must have been a cravat at one time was now wound about his head like a turban.

"Phoebe!" He gave his niece a stern look. "What are you doing in here?"

He strode toward his mother. He hadn't looked at me yet, but he must have known we were there. Surely he was the one who had arranged the meeting.

"Come along; back to the nursery. Let the ladies have their tea."

Phoebe looked up at her uncle with one eye closed and her nose scrunched. "But you were the one who threw Mr. Lion."

Lord Hawthorne stepped back, and one hand went to his heart. "I did?" Lady Rothschild's eyebrows rose, and Lord Hawthorne finally turned to look at me and Mama. He was quiet as he took in my appearance, then rubbed the back of his neck. His finger grazed over the bottom of his makeshift turban, and his eyes went wide. Pulling the material off his head in a lightning-quick movement, he gave me a nod of greeting. If I didn't know any better, I would have thought he was nervous. "Why would I do that?"

"I can only imagine," Lady Hawthorne said with a smile. "Charles, I believe you have already been introduced to our guests. This is—"

"No, stop." Lord Hawthorne turned to his mother. "We haven't been introduced, and I forbid it."

Lady Hawthorne glanced at Mama. "Charles, of all the silly things . . ."

Mama gave me a look that was somewhere between *watch out for this man* and *I was right*.

"Did Uncle Charles throw in your lion?" Lady Rothschild asked her daughter. Lady Rothschild's eyes were bright with mischief, and she snuck another glance at me. Between this and our carriage ride, I had become much more interesting.

"Don't pester the child," Lord Hawthorne said, handing a second biscuit to his niece. "What reason would I have to throw a toy into the drawing room? Phoebe, enjoy your biscuit. Don't worry about answering any questions."

"She almost never opens doors on her own, Charles." Lady Hawthorne spoke as if Lord Hawthorne were the child, not Phoebe.

"Well, isn't that interesting?" Lord Hawthorne slid the cravat back and forth in his hand. "I wonder how it opened, then." He snuck a glance at me, and I couldn't hold his gaze. His cravat, his home, and his actions were more than I could bear. If I held his gaze for more than a moment, I would probably have to rush out of the room in order to breathe correctly. He was different here, amongst his family.

Mama was shifting uncomfortably in her chair. She didn't know how to handle a situation such as this. She slid her hands down along her dress. "Perhaps it was the wind?"

Lady Rothschild laughed. Phoebe squirmed in her grandmother's lap. "It wasn't the wind. Uncle Charles was chasing me and—" Lord Hawthorne put another biscuit in her mouth.

"Perhaps Phoebe and I could join you for a moment?" Lord Hawthorne asked. "If Lady Davenport doesn't mind. I find I do feel the need for a cup of tea."

"Of course I don't mind." Mama straightened in her seat, looking more comfortable now that her opinion had been asked on something. "I am not above taking tea with children. I profess I never did it with my own, but they weren't interested in adult conversation."

"Well then, it is settled." Lord Hawthorne pulled a chair over from near the fireplace and set it next to my own. "I don't know why you didn't invite me in the first place."

"You were invited," Lady Hawthorne said. "You were the one who said you wanted to give us a chance to talk."

"I said that?" he asked as he sat down. His legs were at least half a foot away from my own, but it brought to mind the time we had sat much closer in his phaeton, his arms around me. I reached for my tea. Anything to distract me.

"Yes, Charles."

"I suppose Phoebe couldn't handle not seeing Miss Davenport," Lord Hawthorne said. "It isn't every day a young lady who drives a carriage as fast as she does visits the house."

Mama's face went white, and she grabbed the edge of her seat. "Elizabeth is usually very well-mannered."

"Is she?" Lord Hawthorne asked, eying Mama. "That is unfortunate."

I coughed lightly and set my teacup down. If he wanted me to get permission to join him at any future balls, he had better stop making comments such as those. But that was his dilemma, not mine. If he couldn't get Mama to allow me back in the Season, well, my plan had worked, and that was the end of it. I would get my peaceful evenings with Rose. Peaceful, empty evenings with Rose.

"Perhaps Miss Davenport would like to help us prepare for our Christmas dinner," Lady Rothschild said. She gave a sideways glance to her brother. "Charles could use someone well-mannered to help him choose games."

"Indeed I could." Lord Hawthorne nodded. "And Miss Davenport has been a model of decorum at each of our meetings." He gave me a gravely serious look, as if just sitting near me had turned him into a saint.

I pulled my lips tightly together, not wanting to laugh out loud. I had never been more scandalous than the times I was with Lord Hawthorne.

Lady Hawthorne stirred her tea. "Oh, that is an excellent idea. Charles wants the games to be a surprise for me, but his surprises have a way of getting a bit out of control. Miss Davenport could be just what we need to keep things reasonable." An image of the two of us racing around Hyde Park flashed in my mind. I wasn't sure Lady Hawthorne was correct about my influence over her son. If anything, he was the one who influenced me. His enthusiasm for life was contagious, and when I was with him everything seemed larger. It was as if a vast existence that had never touched my being before had been opened up to me. "Will you come next week? We will have dinner, and then I will leave you young people to plan our family's Christmas games. Charlotte, Lord Rothschild will be here Monday night, won't he?"

"Yes." Lady Rothschild clapped her hands. "Between the four of us, we will be sure to plan a Hawthorne Christmas that won't be forgotten."

Lord Hawthorne looked hopefully at me, and I turned to Mama. She set down her teacup and smiled at Lady Hawthorne. "We would love to come," she said. "I am quite the evening planner myself. Why, I have the drollest twist on whist, which I love to teach others."

Lady Hawthorne and her daughter exchanged a look. Either Mama hadn't caught that she wasn't invited, or she'd willfully chosen to ignore it. I assumed the latter; I hoped Lady Hawthorne believed the former.

Lady Hawthorne paused for only a moment. "Oh, but you would need to keep me company. You could show me the whist game in the morning room. It sounds fascinating."

"It really is." Mama nodded. "And if the young people can't come up with something suitable, then at least you will have it as a fallback."

Poor Lady Hawthorne. I had played that particular version of whist, and it was even worse than the original. While she would have to keep Mama busy, I would be spending Monday evening with Lord Hawthorne and his lovely sister and her husband. I was quite certain it would not be the type of social activity I was used to.

CHAPTER FIVE

THE NEXT DAY I STOOD outside the dressmakers, having spent the last two hours being poked and prodded for the purpose of ordering two new gowns. Mama was still inside, but I needed a chance to breathe after such an ordeal, and she said I could wait outside. My scheme to remove myself from any social engagement had failed miserably. Instead it had gotten us another invitation. Two, if I counted tea the day before. If only I had a scheme to be excused from shopping with Mama.

We weren't in the most fashionable part of town, but Mrs. Balton made fine dresses for three-quarters of the price that dressmakers on Bond Street did. There were shops of all kinds nearby: a watchmaker, shoemaker, and milliner's shop were across the street, and right next door to the dressmaker was a woodworking shop.

The woodshop door opened, and a gentleman laden with slats and sheets of wood walked out. His burden was so heavy and awkward that it covered his face.

"Are you sure you can handle that?" the shop owner called out to him.

"I could handle it on one foot." To prove his point he stood and hopped on one foot in my direction. The jovial quality of his voice was unmistakable, even if I couldn't see his face.

The shopkeeper laughed. "Looks as though you have it. I shouldn't have underestimated you." He let the door swing shut.

Lord Hawthorne may have been completely capable of carrying his load on one foot, but he couldn't actually see, and he was headed straight toward me.

"Excuse me, sir," I said.

The man paused and set down his raised foot. "Who is that?" He stepped forward, and I jostled to the side, almost getting away without incident; however, the sleeve of my dress caught on one of the longer boards, throwing both me and the precarious stack out of balance. He dropped his load and the wood crashed to the ground. It *was* Lord Hawthorne, and he looked as surprised to see me as I had been to hear him.

"Miss Davenport?" He blinked, reaching for my elbow to ensure I was steady. "What are you doing here?"

I steadied myself, and he dropped his hand. "I am waiting for Mama." My mind was reeling over the fact that we had met here in the street. "She is finishing up our order with the dressmaker."

"Well, that is fortunate. I was just thinking about how long it had been since I last saw you." Lord Hawthorne bent over to pick up some of the wood pieces.

"We saw each other just yesterday."

"Is that all? I could have sworn it had been much longer." He riffled through the wood, picking out the larger pieces. Some were wide and flat and others more slender. What was he planning on making? Or, more likely, what was he planning on having someone make for him?

"These just don't seem to be stacking quite as well, now that I am doing it myself." He had three of the larger pieces in one hand, while, with the other, he was leaning over to grab a few of the smaller ones.

"Here." I walked over to him. "Let me help you."

He looked up from his bent-over position. "That would be much appreciated." Just as I was about to bend down to help stack the wood more properly in his arms, he plopped two small rods into my hands. "My carriage isn't far." He bent over to grab a few more off the ground and deposited them in my arms. "We will wait for your mother. Then I'll lead the way."

He continued bending over and stacking more and more wood into my arms. Most of them were small thin slats, so it wasn't heavy, but what would Mama think when she saw me?

The creaky shop door opened behind me. I locked my eyes on Lord Hawthorne's and raised my eyebrow. Even he must see the ridiculous position into which he had thrust me. He glanced behind me, and a smile lit up his face. "Lady Davenport! How fortunate." He reached down and snatched the last two spindly rods of wood. "I didn't really want to load Miss Davenport up with any more wood than I had to. Do you mind taking these?"

Lord Hawthorne held the wood out in front of him. Mama looked at him and then at me. I could see what she was thinking. *Is this man out of his mind?* She furrowed her brow and gingerly took one of the spindles between her forefinger and thumb. It dangled beneath her outstretched hand as she kept the offending object as far away from her body as possible.

Lord Hawthorne waited for her to take the other one, but when she didn't, he loaded it on top of the two larger pieces he carried. "I can manage this last one, I suppose. Follow me. The carriage is just up the street."

"Up the street?" Mama's eyes widened in horror.

"It can't be far, Mama. Surely we can help the earl."

Lord Hawthorne had already started on his way, expecting the two of us to follow. Instead of walking after him, Mama shuffled over to me. "What if someone sees us? Carrying wood? In broad daylight? Doesn't he have someone who can do it for him?"

"He does." Whether or not Lord Hawthorne was hoping to perpetuate our ruse, he was doing an excellent job. This was exactly the type of behavior that was sure to disgust Mama. "*We* can do it for him." I marched forward, determined to follow Lord Hawthorne.

"But-but—" Mama sputtered. "What if someone sees us? Your father is a baronet. His family shouldn't be traipsing around London with a burden. What would people think?"

"I would hardly call that a burden." Her one measly stick was still held out in front of her as if it would burn her dress.

"I don't like this Lord Hawthorne. His mother is worth knowing, for certain, but I want you to stay away from him, Elizabeth."

"But Lady Hawthorne seemed so interested in your whist game."

"That is true, and I would love to see it being played among her set. After I have taught it to her, and after she has seen the merit in keeping me as a friend, you must quit any contact with Lord Hawthorne. I told you what he said to Miss Jepson, didn't I? He isn't interested in ladies of quality. And if he considers Miss Jepson a lady of quality, then he must be even less interested in you. After all, your father is a baronet, and hers is a nobody. He has money, to be sure, but no title like your father. Lord Hawthorne is the worst kind of man. One who doesn't know his place or duty."

I twisted around and hushed Mama. It was improbable Lord Hawthorne could hear us as far ahead as he was, but at times, Mama's voice was known to carry. I leaned toward her, careful not to disturb my small load. "I know he isn't serious about pursuing me, Mama. I assure you, you don't need to remind me of it." Lord Hawthorne was the first man I had met who fascinated me. I never knew what to expect when we were together, and yet I had always known his interest would be only in passing. "As soon as your friendship is secure with his mother, I will stay far away from him."

Just as I said that, Lord Hawthorne turned around and smiled at us with that lopsided grin that seemed to say, *Isn't this fun?* I smiled back, but my heart wasn't in it. It wasn't just for Mama's sake that I would need to avoid Lord Hawthorne. He was steadily stealing my heart; I would need to cut all ties with him if I wanted it to stay my own. He was like a vibrant strand of thread in a piece of embroidery. My eyes were constantly drawn to him, whilst everything else around him seemed dull. But vibrant color is to be used sparingly, or the piece will look garish. I would enjoy this moment of color, then go back to the tans, browns, and whites to which I was accustomed. Eventually, I would adjust again to life without color.

I picked up my pace in order to distance myself from Mama's complaints. Lord Hawthorne was waiting for us at a corner, and I quickly caught up to him.

"Your mother doesn't carry wood often, I take it."

She had pulled her bonnet down low, and her stick was still out in front of her. With her eyes on the ground, we watched her bump into two different people. She would have been a lot less conspicuous if she had only walked confidently. "No. She doesn't really carry anything, actually."

"For what purpose does she use her arms, then?"

Like so many other things about him, his question caught me by surprise. What did Mama use her arms for?

"She drags me around ballrooms with them so I can meet eligible bachelors, I suppose."

Lord Hawthorne grunted. "She should carry more wood."

"I will suggest that to her." I laughed. "But I don't think she will agree with you."

Mama reached us, and together we crossed the road.

"Why do you need all of this wood?" Mama asked, still hiding her face as best as she could.

"A puppet theater for my niece and nephew. It is to be a surprise for them on Christmas."

"A puppet theater?" Mama asked. "But are you having your men build it? Surely it is simpler to buy one."

"My men aren't making it. I am."

I tilted my head to one side. What kind of gentleman made his own Christmas presents? Lord Hawthorne did, I supposed. It was probably long past the time to assume anything about the man. The different sizes of wood made more sense to me now. The larger flat ones would be walls. The spindle-shaped ones could hold a curtain. Lord Hawthorne would go home and turn these rough shapes into something enjoyable and exciting. Did the man never stop being incredible? He would make two children very happy on Christmas.

Mama sputtered more at his answer. "Why would you make a puppet theater?"

Lord Hawthorne gave her a quizzical look. "For a Christmas surprise," he said slowly, each word longer than the next. Then he looked at me as if to say, *Didn't I just say that?* "My carriage is just around this corner. It was a busy day today, so I couldn't leave it in front of the woodshop."

True to his word, we came upon his carriage moments later. It wasn't his phaeton we had ridden in earlier, but a more sturdy and less nimble landau. His coachman jumped down and immediately came to Mama and me. At first he reached for my larger load, but Mama jumped in front of me and handed him her stick. He took it with a slight bow and looked askance at his master. Lord Hawthorne didn't seem to notice it as he waited for his man to take my more substantial load. The coachman dumped what now looked like a small amount of wood onto a sheet of undyed muslin lying in the carriage bed. Lord Hawthorne followed suit, then brushed off his clothes.

"Thank you for your help. May I offer you a ride back to the shop or to your carriage?"

"No," Mama said much too quickly. "We are quite capable of making it on our own. And your carriage seems to carry enough of a burden." She motioned to the stack of wood we had just transported. "I am not sure where we would fit."

"I could move the wood around a bit. It really is no trouble."

"I don't think you are going to convince her," I said. "But thank you for the offer. We shall return to our errands. Your niece and nephew are going to be very pleased with your present. Even more so because you made it yourself."

"I hope you are right." His eyes flashed in the familiar way they did when he made me laugh. I loved how he got enjoyment from pleasing others. "I didn't mean to keep you. But we will be seeing you on Monday. I am eager to see what you think of some of the games I have planned. And Mama has been wondering exactly what kind of rule changes you have for that whist game, Lady Davenport."

"I will be there, but Elizabeth may stay at home if she develops another one of her headaches."

"Miss Davenport, you suffer from headaches?" His brow furrowed in concern.

"Only recently." I smiled at him and then raised an eyebrow. "About the time we met, actually. I believe I had one on the night of the Germains' ball, didn't I, Mama?"

She jabbed me softly with her elbow, and I stopped talking.

Lord Hawthorne's face relaxed with my explanation, but it took on a rare serious expression when he turned to Mama. "Well, Mother will be very disappointed if Miss Davenport can't make it. I know she wants to ask her opinion on some of the decorations for our family Christmas party."

"I would be happy to offer my expertise, in the event my daughter isn't well." Mama stepped forward and in front of me.

"Yes, but Mother was quite particular about wanting to hear a young person's ideas."

Mama scrunched her eyebrows together in confusion. "But my ideas are much better than Elizabeth's. She hardly notices things like decorations."

Lord Hawthorne smiled at me. "Neither do I. Hopefully my sister will help her. At any rate, if Miss Davenport doesn't come, Mother will be quite upset. Whether Miss Davenport is interested in helping with planning or not, Mother has taken a liking to her."

"I will do my best to be healthy, Lord Hawthorne," I said. The thought of Mama spending the evening alone with the Hawthornes was unimaginable. Even if I had to threaten to stop taking care of Rose, I would be there.

"I trust you will." He looked pointedly at Mama.

As Mama and I walked away, his manservant leaned his head in toward Lord Hawthorne's ear. "You made them carry wood, milord? Those two ladies?"

"Oh, John. She offered to help."

"Even the mother?"

I lost the conversation then, as we had travelled too far. I would have loved to hear Lord Hawthorne's reasons for believing Mama had no objections to carrying his wares about London.

* * *

Mama never mentioned my headache, so Monday evening we arrived at Grosvenor Square once again. It was hard to keep my eyes off Lord Hawthorne. After running into him on the street six days ago, I half expected him to crop up anywhere we went. But he hadn't, and I'd had to wait nearly a week to see him again.

After dinner with Lord Hawthorne and his family, Lady Hawthorne regaled Mama with questions about her whist game while they left the dining room for the drawing room. Lord Hawthorne jumped up from his seat as soon as the door closed behind them.

"What have you in store for us this year, Charles?" Lord Rothschild asked, his slightly pudgy cheeks rounded with his smile. Lord Rothschild was a few years older and a few inches shorter than Lord Hawthorne, but he had been fairly lively during dinner. He was a good companion for Lady Rothschild, and they seemed genuinely happy. "Nothing too dangerous, I hope."

"Just dangerous enough, actually. Stay here while I fetch John; he has something for us."

Lord Hawthorne left me with his sister and her husband. "Does he usually come up with dangerous ideas?"

"Yes," they both answered at the same time, then laughed.

"Although, as Charles said"—Lady Rothschild exchanged an amused look with her husband—"usually just dangerous enough. Not enough to warrant a doctor."

"And Lady Hawthorne allows it?"

"Mama allows Charles everything." Lady Rothschild shrugged her shoulders. "He is her darling."

"Which is fine with you." Lord Rothschild smiled. "Since I am your darling."

"Are you trying to say that I am not also Mama's darling?" Lady Rothschild narrowed her eyes at her husband. "I was under the impression we both were."

"Well, yes, you are right. That is exactly what I meant. Only that you don't mind sharing the title with him since you also have me."

Lord Rothschild's wife raised one eyebrow in his direction. I hadn't known many married couples to interact playfully. Was this common for them? Or was tonight a special occasion, with Christmas preparations to be made? The only time Papa and Mama interacted at all was when Mama forced him to. I rubbed my hands down my dress. I had never been part of an evening with such a small number. Everyone else was so familiar with each other. Hopefully they couldn't see how nervous I was.

Lord Hawthorne returned with a candle, even though the entire house was well lit. Behind him, the servant who had helped him purchase wood followed with a low, flat bowl. He carried it carefully, each step measured out evenly so as not to upset whatever was in the basin.

"Oh, Hawthorne, what have you planned now?" Lord Rothschild asked.

"You are about to find out." He set his candle down on the sideboard, and the servant set the bowl next to it. Lord Hawthorne then proceeded to blow out the rest of the candles in the dining room.

"Rothschild, would you mind snuffing out the candles on the table?" Lord Hawthorne asked. Lord Rothschild stood from his seat and reached for the candelabras. With each of their puffs, the room grew dimmer, until only the fire from the fireplace and the small single candle on the sideboard lit the room. Lord Hawthorne silently sauntered over to the three of us still at the dining table. He stood directly behind my chair and leaned forward so his mouth was only inches away from my ear. "Now," he whispered—I didn't know if it was from the low lighting or his breath sliding along my cheek, but gooseflesh rose on my arms—"if you would all follow me to the sideboard, we can get started."

Lord Hawthorne stepped to the side and offered me his arm. I stood and took it, hoping he didn't notice the small bumps still raised along my skin. In the darkness I doubted he could.

The four of us took places around the sideboard, and I could finally see what was in the bowl. It was a dark liquid and, based on the smoky-sweet smell, brandy.

"We aren't going to be slogging down a whole bowl of spirits, are we?" Lord Rothschild said.

"No, although after the ladies leave, if you are interested, that may be an option." Lord Hawthorne reached into his pocket and retrieved a small package wrapped in a cloth. Opening the cloth, he revealed a pile of raisins. What could he have planned for a bowl of brandy and some raisins? I tried to read his face, but it was too dark and I didn't want him to catch me staring at him. "We will be playing snapdragon."

Lady Rothschild sucked in a breath, and Lord Rothschild cursed. Apparently, they knew what snapdragon was, which put them already ahead of me.

"Snapdragon?" I asked, my voice barely carrying across the sideboard. It was unfortunate the braver Elizabeth hadn't shown up tonight. I could have used some of her audacity.

"Snapdragon." Lord Hawthorne raised the packet of raisins and showed them to us. "They are all dark raisins except one. Whoever gets the golden raisin and manages to eat it wins a boon."

"How will we even know if we got the golden raisin?" Lady Rothschild asked. "You don't expect us to spit them out, do you?"

Lord Hawthorne pursed his lips together. "Fair point." He glanced around the room until his eyes rested on the front of my bodice. "Miss Davenport, would your mother notice if your dress was missing a button?"

My dress had three buttons running down the center of the fabric over my bosom. They were the same color of the fabric, and there was no chance Mama would not eventually notice. My hands flew to my chest, and heat rose to my face. "She would notice."

"Well then." Lord Hawthorne felt his own clothing, stopping his hands near his neck and tearing out a button underneath his cravat. He pressed the button into one of the larger raisins, which didn't completely cover the button, but it seemed Lord Hawthorne felt it would suffice. "There. Now anyone who eats the raisin with the button wins a boon of their choosing."

Lord and Lady Rothschild both nodded and proceeded to take off their gloves. I followed suit, not knowing why. I was simply relieved my dress was no longer the object of everyone's attention. "You still haven't explained to me what snapdragon is."

"Oh." Lord Hawthorne slid his lips across his thumb to remove what must have been some raisin residue. "It is easy. There are practically no rules. Just eat as many raisins as you can." He then dumped all of the raisins into the brandy.

"Do you count to three?"

"No." He smiled and in the dim light looked almost devilish. But devilishly good, if that was possible—as if he knew we were about to have a lot of fun, and he was the one responsible for it. He rolled up his sleeves to expose his lean, corded forearms. Lord Rothschild did the same. "You wait for the game to start." He picked up the candle, and his wicked grin spread wide across his face. "And . . ." He dipped the candle low over the bowl, and it became apparent what he was about to do. I stepped back just as the bowl burst into flames. "Start!"

Lord Hawthorne blew out the candle, set it down, and without taking a moment to think about it, his fingers rushed into the bowl. They came out lightning quick and flashed to his mouth. He snapped his mouth closed as soon as his fingers reached it. Neither Lord nor Lady Rothschild had ventured into the bowl yet, and they watched as Lord Hawthorne chewed.

"Well, did you get the prize?" Lady Rothschild leaned forward over the table.

Lord Hawthorne paused his careful chewing and a hand flew to his cheek as if he had bitten into something. But then he relaxed. "Sorry, but no. You are going to have to try for it yourself."

Lady Rothschild shook her head and poised her hand above the bowl. The low blue flames flickered as she hesitated. "I don't know how you talk me into these things." Before she could put her fingers in, Lord Hawthorne's hand shot into the bowl once again.

"There is no taking turns," Lord Hawthorne said after popping a second raisin into his mouth. "You don't have to wait, and I want that boon for myself."

All three of their hands rushed to the bowl, and after watching them all come out unscathed, I threw myself into the fray. I placed my hand above the dish and felt the heat from the fire. I dashed my hand down but pulled it back before even reaching the brandy. It was hot. Not unbearably so, but it was hard to train myself to ignore my instincts. I tried a second time, this time coming at the bowl from the side so fewer of the flames would reach my arm. I darted my hand in and out as quickly as possible and was surprised not to feel the heat until lifting it out of the bowl. Raisin still aflame, I quickly popped it into my mouth, as I had seen Lord Hawthorne do. The raisin sizzled in my mouth with a sharp spot of pain, and then it was extinguished. I bit down on it.

No prize.

I went for the bowl again. Soon we were all laughing. Many of the raisins were being dropped before making it to our mouths. We put out the raisins' flames with wetted fingers and threw them into our mouths again and again. At one point Lord Hawthorne bumped me with his hip so he could reach his hand in before mine. I would have thought it inappropriate had I not been so upset about missing my chance to get one more before him. He had better not have snatched the prize.

The next time he leaned forward to grab another, I returned the favor and bumped his hip. Out of the corner of my eye I saw him turn in surprise, then chuckle as he once again dove in with his hand. There were only a few raisins left now, and the next time I dipped my fingers in I couldn't get one. They were getting harder and harder to catch. I gave up and decided to watch the three of them battle it out for the last of them. Lady Rothschild saw the wisdom in this and leaned back as well.

The two men still leaned forward, trying to spot the raisins through the low-burning blue flames. Their faces lit up eerily, yet their smiles were contagious. Was this what a family could be like? No sitting around with knitting and embroidery? No gossiping about who was marrying whom? Just pure enjoyment? Lord Hawthorne placed a raisin in his mouth and glanced up at me for a moment. Our eyes met, and in the firelight his shone an almost iridescent blue. And in an instant I knew. Whoever was lucky enough to marry Lord Hawthorne would live this way. She would have laughter, love, entertainment, and belonging. There would be trust and conversation. Oh, the conversations—always on the verge of laughing, but never at the expense of others. I stepped back away from him as a fire in my chest grew to be more painful and hot than the bowl of brandy in front of us.

I wanted to be that woman. I wanted to spend the rest of my life with Lord Hawthorne, not just the next few days. I had allowed myself to be too long in his company, and now it was too late. No matter how we left things, I would never be the same. I would marry a stuffy, proud gentleman who was looking for a wife. He would most likely be old and not as interested in me as he was in marrying because that was the way things were done.

Lord Hawthorne's forehead furrowed as he leaned forward in my direction. Concern flickered in the shadows of his face.

"There is one left in there." Lord Rothschild's voice jolted my eyes away from Lord Hawthorne's. "I am going to get it. It must be the one with the prize." He threw his hand into the bowl and fished around longer than he should have. He grimaced as he shifted his hand in the bowl, feeling for the last raisin. He was spending too long in there.

Lord Hawthorne grabbed his forearm and pulled it out. "Don't be a fool; I got the prize long ago."

"What?" Lord Rothschild shook his hand and jumped up and down, blowing on his exposed skin. "Why didn't you say so?"

"Because he wanted to keep playing the game as long as he possibly could." Lady Rothschild shook her head at him. "You should know that by now." She reached for her husband's hand and inspected it. "Are you hurt?"

"No, just a few singed hairs. But Hawthorne, you devil, you should have told us. Another half-second in that bowl and I would have been burned."

"Sorry, but I got it on the third raisin. Everyone had their hands in the bowl, and no one noticed." He was still looking at me from the corner of his eye as he spoke. "There was no way I was going to stop the game then. Not when we were having so much fun."

"Yes, well, it is *fun*, isn't it?" I said. My breathing still hadn't returned to normal. All that mattered to Lord Hawthorne was that he was having fun. It didn't matter if he was hurting others in the process. It didn't matter to him that being near him was the same as having a hand hovering over a bowl of burning brandy. I could dip my hand in, but it couldn't stay. Not if I didn't want to get burned. The only intelligent thing to do would be to leave the fire alone.

Lord Hawthorne was still looking at me strangely, but Lord and Lady Rothschild hadn't noticed.

"Well, what will be your prize, then, Lord Hawthorne?" Lord Rothschild's deep baritone interrupted our gaze.

Lord Hawthorne tore his eyes away from mine and looked down into the slowly dying fire still in the bowl. He rubbed the back of his neck with his hand. "I was going to ask for a kiss."

My heart stopped.

"A kiss from whom?" Lady Rothschild laughed as her eyes flashed in my direction.

"No," I said before he could answer. Lord Hawthorne was fixated on the flames in the bowl. "It would violate our one rule." No future husband of mine would want me kissing Lord Hawthorne. It was an excuse—the only excuse I could think of—but I prayed he wouldn't see it that way. A kiss from Lord Hawthorne would leave me very badly burned indeed.

A muscle worked in Lord Hawthorne's jaw. His shoulders drooped, and he placed both of his hands on the sideboard. "I'll give the boon to Lord Rothschild. After all, I was less than honorable in the way I played. It is the least I could do."

Lord Rothschild shrugged his shoulders. "I was going to ask for the same thing. Nearly, anyway."

"Oh, Jim." Lady Rothschild toyed with a curl that had escaped her chignon. "You can have a kiss anytime you want. Why would you use a boon on that?"

"Oh, vanity." He leaned forward and kissed his wife heartily on the lips. "I was going to ask Miss Davenport to kiss dear Charles. It seemed like he needed it."

No. No, this could not be happening. Lord Hawthorne wasn't looking at me, thank the heavens. My face must have been white as a sheet. And to have Lord Rothschild kissing his wife so heartily while my heart was contracting so painfully . . . I needed out of this room. I needed out of the darkness and away from the eerie blue light still softly burning in the bowl.

Lady Rothschild softly swatted her husband's shoulder. "You can't make Miss Davenport kiss Charles. That would be completely inappropriate."

"It is a game. The servants hang mistletoe all around the house this time of year and take good advantage of it, as have I." He smiled at his wife, and if it weren't so dark, I would think a blush had risen to her cheek. "A kiss in a game like this is completely acceptable. You can't deny a boon. Society would forgive, but more importantly, Society would never know, for it is just the four of us here."

"She won't do it, Rothschild." Lord Hawthorne was smiling, but it was an empty smile—the kind I had seen on others so often, but never on him. "She is right to refuse. Let's move on from this subject. It is my boon to bestow, and if you don't want it, I will give it to Miss Davenport. She may do what she wants with it."

The servant was relighting candles, but the room didn't seem to be growing any lighter. My vision was as dark as my future, a future that would never hold another game of snapdragon or a wild ride in Hyde Park. I should never have approached Lord Hawthorne. Mama was right. It was best to stay away from men who weren't interested in marriage. This one was breaking my heart.

The laughter of the game was now forgotten, and an awkward silence filled the room instead. I had intruded on this family's lighthearted game. I was Elizabeth Davenport. I knitted and cowered before Mama. I didn't spend my evenings laughing and playing risqué games. I didn't belong here. "If it is all right with you"—I inched a little farther from Lord Hawthorne;

it was time I distanced myself from him—"my desire is to go home. I find I have grown tired."

"Granted," Lord Hawthorne said before the other two could protest. "I'll have John ready your carriage and let Mother know."

Less than a quarter of an hour later I was outside on my way to the carriage. Mama was already stepping up into it with help from the same servant who had been with Lord Hawthorne on his wood-gathering trip. Lord Hawthorne stood awkwardly on the side of the path, his smile still empty. I wanted to explain myself. But how could I let him know how he had touched my heart in just a few short weeks? A kiss, for him, would be amusement, and just one more game for his entertainment this evening. It would have been easy for him and searing for me.

"I am sorry not to have granted your boon."

"Not as sorry as I am to have missed out on it," he assured me. "But you are correct. I am sure a kiss, no matter how innocent, would upset that future husband of yours."

His words made my mouth grow dry. When we had first spoken of a husband, I had had a picture in mind. A kind man—someone Mama would have introduced me to. And unexpectedly, we would have found something we liked in each other. I'd have been happy with him. That surprisingly decent man in my dreams had been enough at one point. Before I had met Lord Hawthorne. How long would it take before I felt that way again?

CHAPTER SIX

WHY DID GUARDING ONE'S HEART have to be so painful? Mama leaned forward in the carriage once again to pinch my cheeks. She had made certain I had dressed in my loveliest of gowns. It was white, as fashion dictated, but had small pink roses around the neckline. I had matching ribbon woven into my dark hair. But apparently my disposition was off, and that was still bothering her.

"Why are your cheeks so pale this evening, Elizabeth? There must be some way to get some color into them. It is the Christmas Eve ball, and everyone who is anyone will be there. You can't go in there looking like a ghost." Mama leaned forward and bumped Papa's knee with her reticule. "Sir John, does it seem to you that Elizabeth is unwell?"

Papa opened his eyes and glanced around the carriage as if orienting himself to his surroundings. "Yes, m'dear," he said slowly, rubbing his cheeks before leaning his head back to return to sleep.

"If it weren't for the fact that Lord Fagerlund will be there tonight, I would have required that you stay home. Rumor has it his mother is getting desperate and he is about to give in and do what she says. I've arranged for you to have the first dance with him. Don't ruin this, Elizabeth. Who knows when another chance like this could come around? I was worried your association with that no-good Lord Hawthorne would damage your chances with him, but Lord Fagerlund's mother actually said it piqued his interest. He is looking forward to your dance together."

He was the only one looking forward to it. The last thing I wanted was a dance with Lord Fagerlund. He was good-looking enough, despite his age. But his disdain for others did nothing for his character. And the fact that my ride in Hyde Park with Lord Hawthorne had piqued his interest made me even more wary of him. Nothing about this evening held any appeal to me. Lady Hawthorne hadn't written; nor had Lady Rothschild. I was no longer even certain Lord Hawthorne would come to this infernal ball. He would most likely be happier celebrating at home. Christmas was tomorrow, and I was in no mood for it. Lord Hawthorne and his family would be playing games tomorrow night. Would he really invite his mother to play snapdragon? I couldn't imagine it. But I wouldn't ask him. After tonight, our interactions would be at an end.

Twenty minutes later I cursed myself for not defying Mama and refusing to dance with Lord Fagerlund. His smile twisted something deep inside my gut. It deepened each time he placed his hand at my waist, and all too often his eyes wandered to the neckline of my dress. It was the first dance of the evening, and I was already wishing to leave. There had been no sign of Lord Hawthorne. He most likely wouldn't be coming. I hadn't wanted to say goodbye to him, but not seeing him at all left a hole in my heart.

"You look particularly lovely this evening, Miss Davenport," Lord Fagerlund said as we came together for a turn. "How have I not noticed that impish gleam in those emerald eyes before?" My hand was in his, and his thumb slid over the top of my hand in a completely unnecessary gesture. Only two weeks ago Lord Hawthorne had done something similar while we were practically alone in my own home, but somehow the two movements produced opposite reactions in me. Lord Hawthorne's touch had convinced me to remain with him, while Lord Fagerlund's induced only a desire to run.

My back was ramrod straight as I avoided his eyes. "I assure you I haven't an impish gleam."

One side of his mouth rose. "That isn't what I've heard. Any young woman willing to ride alone with a gentleman in Hyde Park must have more sides to her than she shows in a ballroom."

"His sister and brother-in-law were there. We weren't alone," I said. He tipped his head to one side and lifted a shoulder, as if to say he had heard differently. Indeed, we had been separated from them for most of the ride. If I had known that would attract the likes of Lord Fagerlund, I would have insisted we stay near Lord Hawthorne's sister.

We broke apart, and my hand was grasped by a young man who looked as if he were barely out of university. I had been introduced to him at the beginning of the Season. Mr. Jenkins or Ekins—I couldn't exactly recall, as we hadn't spoken since. What a difference his soft, light touch was compared to Lord Fagerlund's heavy-handed grabbing. He smiled quickly but didn't speak a word before we finished our steps. I could feel Lord Fagerlund nearing even before he reached for my hand. How could Mama think this was the type of man I would consent to marry?

Lord Fagerlund leaned down to kiss my hand after the set, but I pulled it away with a firm "thank you" before his lips came too close. His chuckle followed me as I stormed away, not caring that I was without an escort as I crossed the ballroom. Never again would I dance with Lord Fagerlund. I would tell Mama as soon as I found her.

"Do you think Lord Fagerlund is going to be that husband you've been working so hard to be loyal to?" Lord Hawthorne's voice was bitter.

I spun to see him just to my right. He must have just come from the crowd, or I would have seen him sooner. We were in one of the few open spaces in the ballroom, and I hoped no one had heard his comment. I was not used to seeing him with a frown on his face. It didn't suit him.

I closed the distance between us, hoping no one would hear my reply, "Of course n—"

"I can promise he will not give you that same courtesy," he continued before I could finish my answer. "That man hasn't a loyal bone in his body, and it makes me ill to see his hands on you."

"No." I reached his side and could see that not only was he frowning, but he had dark circles under his eyes as if he hadn't slept well. "As I've told you before, it isn't as though I have a man picked out. And if it makes you feel any better, having his hands on me makes me ill as well."

"Then, why did you dance with him?"

"Mama arranged it," I said.

His jaw clenched in disapproval. "Since when do you do things to please your mother?"

"Since birth, Lord Hawthorne." I sighed. This was the end of our time together, and he might as well know the truth about who I was. "My whole life. And yes, it is suffocating and unbearable at times. You and I met in the one instance in which I was feeling brave and reckless, but that typically isn't me. I am not usually driving carriages in Hyde Park at breakneck speed. I don't walk up to unknown men and introduce myself. I sit at home and knit, and when I am bored with knitting, I embroider." I took a deep breath and willed my eyes to stay dry. "I have practically reared my younger sister and would rather be in her nursery than anywhere else. That is who I am, Lord Hawthorne. I cannot live up to this wild, abandoned person I portrayed myself to be. Tomorrow is Christmas, and I will go back to doing whatever Mama asks, only I hope there will be fewer balls due to my behavior with you."

"So you really have been using me." His fist clenched, and his jaw tightened.

"I thought I made that clear from the beginning," I said softly. What else could he have thought I was doing?

"You did. I just thought . . . well . . ." He cleared his throat and rubbed his face hard.

"What did you think?" I shouldn't have asked. But I had to know.

He slid his hand down his cheeks, his fingers pulling at the rough, unshaved skin. "I thought perhaps you enjoyed spending time with me as much as I did with you."

How did he know exactly how to break my heart?

"Of course I have enjoyed my time with you. Enjoyment should be your middle name."

"I never did properly introduce myself. For all you know, it is my middle name."

I couldn't help the smile that pulled up the sides of my mouth. For the first time this evening, his did the same. "That is much better. A frown doesn't suit you, Lord Hawthorne."

"So you find me unattractive? Is that the problem?"

With his soft hair, intense eyes, and that crooked grin? Impossible. "I assure you that is *not* the problem," I said, and his smile grew broader, deepening the lines on either side of his mouth in a way that made me want to reach out and touch them. "The truth is, I don't know whom I will marry, but I would like to be a loyal wife to whomever he turns out to be. And I know you aren't looking for a wife, so I need to be careful and abide by our rule when we are together."

He narrowed one eye and placed a hand at his hip. Had I said too much? "So if you had thought I was interested in marrying you, you would have kissed me five nights ago? You wouldn't have used the boon to leave?"

I sucked in a breath and hastily checked our surroundings. No one was within hearing distance. Lord Hawthorne seemed a lot less concerned. Of course.

My heart matched the beat of the dancer's feet hitting the floor. I would have kissed him. I had thought of it a thousand times since his invitation.

"I have no way to answer that." I would have kissed him in front of his sister—and enjoyed it—if I had thought there was even a remote chance of us becoming husband and wife. My eyes flew to his lips, so often curved into a smile. I had almost kissed him, even assuming he had no interest in marrying me, which was why I had begged to leave.

A couple walked toward us. Our small empty space in the ballroom was about to be invaded. Lord Hawthorne took hold of my elbow. "Dance with me, Miss Davenport, before your ever-meddling mother forces you into some other man's arms." He looked earnest, as if his happiness hinged on my answer. "Christmas is tomorrow, and if you never want to see me again after tonight, I will stay away from you. But as for tonight, we still have our agreement, and I hope you will give me the honor of a dance."

At least the next dance was the reel. I wouldn't have been able to handle the touching involved in the cotillion.

I nodded, and Lord Hawthorne held out his arm and escorted me to the center of the ballroom.

The first bouncing bars of the reel played, and a grin split Lord Hawthorne's face. Even with several feet between us, his energy was contagious, as was everything else about him. His head bobbed from side to side in a most ridiculous manner, matching the beat being played, and for the first time, the reel felt hilarious. He leapt to his left in such a grandiose movement when the music started I almost missed my own steps. He pranced—there was no other word for it—nearer and nearer to me. I couldn't help the small chuckle that escaped my lips. Lord Hawthorne. What in the world was I going to do without him?

We passed each other, my dance steps much higher than usual, following the example of my partner. His hand grazed my arm as he passed, even though there was no need for it. Anyone watching, however, wouldn't have noticed. They would have been fascinated by Lord Hawthorne's silly faces and overexaggerated leaps. I noticed though. A jolt of energy passed from him to me, and my legs lifted even higher. This was not how a reel was supposed to be danced. It was high-energy, for certain, but never quite this high. Laughing, I passed another man to my left, who gave me a quizzical look. Yet, when I turned, I noticed his feet were farther from the ground than when I had first seen him.

The ladies that were now closest to Lord Hawthorne were undergoing a similar effect. Soon the whole dance floor would be laughing and leaping like Lord Hawthorne. Even the band seemed to catch on to what was happening, and the music's tempo, already invigorating, sped up by degrees.

Lord Hawthorne passed another lady while I passed a gentleman, but our eyes had already found each other's. His were sparked with mischief. Mine might have looked the same. I may have missed my chance to kiss Lord Hawthorne, but I would enjoy this dance; I would never have another one like it. I would deal with the pain of loss later. This dance was time for abandonment. I kicked my legs up even higher, and this time when we passed each other, it was I who slid my hand along his arm.

His eyes darkened perceptibly, and he missed a step. I craned my neck behind me long enough to see him perform an extra turn to get one more look at me. But then he was off to pass by another dancer. Our game continued throughout the dance. Each time we passed each other one of us would reach out and slide a finger along the other's arm. Once Lord Hawthorne pretended to stumble and bumped his shoulder into mine. He paused in his dancing to hold me by both elbows. The warmth of the room and all the dancing seemed almost suffocating. But a second later we were off and dancing once again.

Exhaustion was starting to set in for everyone. The music had reached almost a feverish pitch, and by the final note, several ladies let out large sighs of relief and slumped sideways in fatigue. Thankfully, no one fainted. A smatter of laughter filled the room. Lord Hawthorne had done this. Single-handedly, he had brought energy to the whole ballroom. Everyone smiled and relaxed in a way the elite of London never did.

Lord Hawthorne held out his arm, and without hesitation I took it. How well our arms looked intertwined. Perhaps it was because I was exhausted from our energetic dance, but I found myself leaning in toward him. It was our last evening together, and he had made it a memorable one.

Across the ballroom Fanny Elliott stood next to her mother. They must have only just arrived. Both of their mouths hung open in surprise. Not far from them sat Mama. She wasn't speaking to anyone. Her mouth was a contrast to everyone else's in the room. The corners turned down in a frown so severe she looked frightening.

I quickly looked away. There wasn't anything I could do about Mama. She would be happy enough after Christmas, when Lord Hawthorne no longer sought my company.

Movement across the ballroom caught my eye. Lord Fagerlund was striding directly toward us. His face was also not smiling, but it wasn't frowning either. He looked grim and purposeful, as if he had made up his mind about me. Fanny was too near Mama; I wouldn't go toward her, but perhaps I could lose myself in the crowd.

"Thank you, Lord Hawthorne. I must admit I have never had a dance like that before."

"I must admit I am happy to hear that." He was smiling as if he had no care in the world, just as he should. My heart reached for him, but I knew there was no future for us. I had made him smile one last time, and that would have to be enough.

His smile faltered as he followed my eyes to where Lord Fagerlund was still crossing the room in our direction. The last thing in the world I wanted was to have Lord Hawthorne privy to any conversation Lord Fagerlund would have with me.

"It has been a lovely evening." I unraveled my arm from Lord Hawthorne's before he had a chance to complain.

"Miss Davenport—" he began, and I held both of his hands in my own as I tried to convey all of my feelings to him.

"Thank you, Lord Hawthorne. Not just for the dance—for everything. You have performed every task I asked of you marvelously, and as you promised, not a moment has been dull. I'm prepared to deal with Mama now on my own."

His eyebrows furrowed, and his grip tightened on my hands. "No. There is no reason we cannot remain . . . friends."

Why did he have to make this so difficult? This was our agreement— only until Christmas. I had my dance, and now I needed to move on and find a life of my own choosing. At least now I felt prepared for that. My nose started to twitch, and I knew if I didn't leave soon Lord Hawthorne's last memories of me would be of me breaking down in tears.

"Goodbye, Lord Hawthorne. It has been a pleasure." I pulled my hands from his grasp and dodged through ladies and gentlemen until I was hopeful neither Lord Fagerlund nor Lord Hawthorne would see me. Neither lord was my future.

I turned and nearly ran into a young man. It was the barely past-university man I had turned with during my dance with Lord Fagerlund.

"Mr. Jenkins, pardon me. I didn't see you there." Other than our short encounter on the dance floor and an introduction earlier in the Season, I had spent almost no time with him. He didn't look confused when I said his name, so I assumed I had gotten it right. Mama must not have felt him quite up to snuff, or she would have made sure our paths had crossed more often. He was young and quiet, but handsome, in a slender and graceful way.

"Miss Davenport, it is good to see you again. I trust you have been well this evening."

I nodded in response but was immediately distracted. Lord Fagerlund had seen us and was pushing his way through the crowd once again.

Mr. Jenkins coughed a small nervous cough. "May I have the honor of your next dance?"

My eyes flew to his. "Yes." It came out breathless and full of relief. His eyes brightened, and his shoulders pulled back.

"Shall I escort you to the refreshment table while we wait for the next set?"

I nodded and took his arm, happy to be moving away from Lord Fagerlund.

"It looked as though you were quite enjoying yourself during the reel," Mr. Jenkins said.

I laughed softly, still nervous for some reason, even though there was nothing threatening about Mr. Jenkins. "Yes, I did."

"I hope you will enjoy our dance as well."

"I am sure I will." I scanned the room. Lord Fagerlund was staring at us, a deep frown marring his face. Lord Hawthorne was nowhere to be seen. Had he left? Was that truly our last goodbye?

Mr. Jenkins placed his free hand on my arm. "There is something different about you tonight. I find it very becoming. It is as if your eyes are lit by some fire within."

He was the second man to say something to that effect tonight. Did I really look so different? "I don't know what you are saying."

"I am not sure either." He ducked his head, and some of his blond hair fell forward onto his forehead. "But I am very much looking forward to our dance together."

I enjoyed dancing with Mr. Jenkins. He was careful to touch me only when the dance called for it. Our conversation stayed on appropriate subjects like the weather, and when I glanced over at Mama, she didn't exactly look happy, but neither did she look worried or annoyed. Why had I not spent more time in his company this Season? It might not have been so dreadful if I had.

"Thank you, Mr. Jenkins," I said as we bowed to each other after the dance.

"The pleasure was all mine." He smiled deeply, and although there was no hint of devilry or a spark of mischief in his eyes, it was still a nice smile in its own way.

I weaved through person after person to make it to the other side of the ballroom, where I had last seen Mama. I hoped to sit out the next dance with her. My line of sight to her was covered by the crowd until I was only a few feet from her, which is why I hadn't noticed that Lord Fagerlund was standing next to her. I stopped. I couldn't dance with him again tonight. They hadn't noticed me, so I turned and prayed they wouldn't.

"Mr. Jenkins is a very nice man." Lord Hawthorne had come up behind me. "He seems the type who would be able to handle twelve children."

"Lord Hawthorne," I turned and hissed at him. There were people everywhere. It wasn't the type of thing that should be said out loud, let alone in a ballroom. But at least he was still here.

"Dance with me for the rest of the evening."

My heart seemed to catch in my throat, and I couldn't answer.

"Lord Fagerlund is headed this way, and if I don't dance with you, he is bound to ask you."

"I was hoping to sit this one out."

Lord Hawthorne took my arm and propelled me toward one of the glass doors that led to the balcony. I could see a few groups of people had gathered outside. It was a mild night for the middle of winter, and the ballroom had grown quite hot. As he opened the door, a blast of cold air shot through me. Not the most mild of nights after all.

"We can cool off out here, and then I hope you will honor me with another dance."

"You do understand I can't dance with you for the entire evening."

"Why? So you can dance with Lord Fagerlund a second time? He has been ogling you all night."

"I have no plans to dance with Lord Fagerlund either. He may not be opposed to marriage like you are, but I am opposed to marriage with him."

"I am opposed to marriage? Where did you get an idea like that? I've never understood why you assume I don't want a wife. Every time you mention a future husband, I want to punch him in the jaw and then perhaps challenge him to a duel." Lord Hawthorne was tense, his arms straight at his sides and his fists balled in tight knots. "He comes up so often I am beginning to think you do have the man picked out."

Two could play at this game. "You've never wanted to marry any of the other young ladies here, and they are much more qualified than I am." If he wasn't against marriage, why did he tell Mrs. Jepson he wasn't interested in the women of the *ton*? If Mama had arranged an introduction to him, he wouldn't have given me the time of day. No, the only reason Lord Hawthorne had agreed to spend time with me was because I had given him a chance to do so with no commitment involved.

"I will ignore your comment about your qualifications for now, but rest assured, I disagree most vehemently with that statement. But the other young ladies? You mean, perhaps, Miss Green?"

"And Miss Jepson."

"Miss Jepson?" Both of his eyebrows rose in surprise. He shook his head and rubbed his forehead with his hand. "I do remember Miss Jepson. She wouldn't look me in the eye. Her mother practically told me her daughter would approve of my having a mistress. In front of the poor girl. Miss Jepson may be sweet, but I refused to stand there and let her be degraded by her own mother for any longer than she already had been."

"But you never showed any interest in any of them. Miss Green for a while, I suppose, until—"

"Until I realized she wanted to have children but not raise them. Until I saw that she cared more for what Society thought of us together than what we actually felt for one another. I was young and naïve, and I suppose I have been less so since then with the women to whom I am introduced. Do you think they want an introduction because they desire what *I* have to offer? No. I am actually quite certain most of them didn't even approve of my personality, let alone like it. They want my title. They want to gain the best match possible for the Season. And now I want to ask you, Elizabeth"—my name sprang easily from his lips, as if he had been thinking of me as Elizabeth for days—"are those the reasons you wanted to spend time with me?"

"No," I said breathlessly. "Spending time with you has never been about raising my social circle. I needed someone like you to help me. I'd never considered you would want to marry me, so your being an earl had nothing to do with our arrangement."

"And that is one of the reasons I asked you to spend the rest of the evening with me. I didn't do it because I wanted to start rumors or to bother your mother—as much as I would enjoy that—or because I am completely incapable of understanding what the consequences are. I asked only because I wanted to be with you, the one person invited to this ball who doesn't care about my title more than you care about me. And I am accustomed to doing what I want." His hands finally relaxed, no longer clenched tightly into balls but hanging loosely at his side. He shrugged, opening the palms of his hands toward me. "I find myself always wanting to be where you are. When you came for tea and met my mother, I told myself I would stay away. My best chance at getting your mother to approve of you spending time with me was to stay away, but I couldn't. You were in my home. *My home.* Sitting and drinking tea, looking as if it didn't affect you at all to be so near me."

"You couldn't see me—not until you came in." I had been affected. I had been quite affected.

"No, but isn't it true?"

I thought back to the way I had examined everything in the room, wondering which items belonged to Lord Hawthorne and where he usually sat when he was there. I had been anything but indifferent, though I may have looked the part. He walked farther into the darkness of the balcony, and I followed.

"I was more intrigued than you have painted me to be."

"Were you?" He turned to glance at me but didn't stop walking. "I find that very interesting."

We reached the balustrade. He leaned over the side, looking down into the garden. Sliding his hands back and forth on the cold marble, he didn't turn to look at me. "Do you know that everything you have touched feels different to me now? I smile every time I drive my phaeton because I picture your hands on the reins."

My breath caught in my throat. Lord Hawthorne had changed how I viewed everything. Dancing would never be the same now. It was as if some part of each of us had invaded the other's life, and I didn't think I would ever be able to expel him. My hands ached to reach for him. If only I could see his face and know how deeply he cared for me. I stepped closer, running one finger along the back of his arm, as I had when we danced.

He must not have felt my touch, for he continued to look out over the balustrade without even flinching. "If you want to start obeying social customs now," he said, "that is all right with me. I don't go around trying to break them. It just seems to happen sometimes. But I want to be your only partner for the rest of the evening. I will not sit by idly watching you dance with other men."

"Even knowing the implications?"

His hands paused. He at last turned to look at me, eyes burning in the darkness of the balcony's night air. Only then did he notice my finger still touching the lowest part of his sleeve. He stepped closer and placed his hand over mine, trapping it between his arm and hand. The air heated around us until I could no longer feel the cold. "Especially knowing the implications. I hate Lord Fagerlund, and I hate that future husband you keep mentioning. I would like nothing more than to have everyone in that room know we belong together."

A small portion of my heart opened to the idea that perhaps Lord Hawthorne wasn't the man Mama had portrayed him to be. If I hadn't known him to be quite unreachable, how would our relationship have been different? "But Christmas is tomorrow. It is the end of our agreement."

"Oh, hang Christmas. You were the one who came up with that idea. I don't know what put it in your head. I only agreed because it meant you would spend at least that amount of time with me."

I swallowed. Every word that came out of his mouth seemed to grant me more life. A life of color. "If we go out there and keep dancing together, people will assume we are to be married." He didn't run away. He didn't shrink to one side.

"Perhaps we should get married, then. You know how set I am on following all of Society's expectations." His smile was a half-smile, like he was jesting. But his eyes were intense and piercing. I didn't know which to believe.

"You never do things for the sake of Society."

"True, but I think I may love you, so . . . perhaps I should. Just this once."

My breathing stopped, and my mind silenced. I wasn't certain I had heard him correctly. I couldn't have heard him correctly. "You *think* you may love me?"

"Yes, most definitely." He pulled my hand up to his chest until it rested over his heart. The sensation of his heart beating under my palm filled me with longing.

I dared not move. Not until I knew for certain what Lord Hawthorne's intentions were. "As in, you may love me at some future point, or you may love me here and now?"

"Here and now." He squeezed my hand. "And at every future point."

"But you aren't certain?"

He shrugged his shoulder, and then his half-grin lit up his face. "I am certain I will never love any of the featherheads in that ballroom behind us. Not like I might love you."

I smiled. He wasn't going to give me a straight answer. But I began to think it might not matter. Nothing with Lord Hawthorne ever went as planned. He wasn't about to start being conventional now. "Again, might . . ." I prodded.

He pulled on his cravat, loosening it. I thought of all the times I had seen this man's cravat loose or undone or even wrapped about his head. He was like no man I had ever known, and the few times we had been in each other's company were some of the happiest in my life. All because I had thrown caution into the wind and pursued something I wanted, for once. Perhaps it was time to do it again.

"Charles." His hand stilled at his cravat, and his eyes flew to mine. They were filled with something—hope or fear—but whatever it was, he was not indifferent to me calling him by his Christian name. "I want a second chance at using my boon. The one you gave me. Using it to leave you was a mistake." My fingers shook as I reached for his cheek and touched the corner of his mouth with my thumb. That same corner that so often rose when he was pleased or amused or had made someone happy.

He drew in a deep breath at my touch. "Anything."

"I simply want what you wanted."

His lips parted. "But your rule—"

I didn't give him time to finish. I was going to take what I wanted and hope that, once again, it led to happiness. I curled my fingers behind his neck and pulled his face toward mine. His hair was as soft as I had imagined. Only inches from his mouth, I paused. His eyes were wide with wonder. He wrapped his arms around my waist, and my name was a whisper on his lips. "Elizabeth." He lowered his head toward mine, and I raised mine up to meet his. His shoulders were stiff and hard, but as our lips met, they relaxed, as if all the weight of the world had been lifted off him.

The cold was forgotten as the heat from Charles surrounded me, lingering everywhere he had touched and spreading into my heart. I had been wrong about being burned by Charles. Nothing about him was sharp or painful. He wasn't a bowl of burning brandy. He was sunshine and warm blankets. Every caress of his lips on mine fueled a fire in my heart, but it didn't burn. It gave life.

He pulled away from me and placed both hands on my shoulders. His hair was even more disheveled than normal, and I was the cause of it. Pleasure rippled through my being at the sight of it.

"I'm tired of being jealous of a nonexistent man." He sighed. "Can't I be your future husband? I want to be the father of those twelve children. Our children, Elizabeth." His grip on my shoulders tightened, and I could see Hawthorne children scrambling about our feet, laughing and smelling of soap. My heart opened even more, to include not just Charles but them. The corner of his mouth rose. "We will have so much fun with them."

A laugh escaped my lips. Oh, dear Charles. "If Mama heard you calling children fun, she would think you even more preposterous. They are hard work."

"But for us, the two of *us*, they would be a pleasure. Tea will always be noisy at our house." Lord Hawthorne's eyes shone, and this time I knew it was with hope. Everything about him was contagious. When I was with him, life was more vibrant. I was more vibrant.

And I could picture it. We would make a family, one where children were a blessing and not a disturbance. We would gather around the fireplace at Christmastime and put a yule log on the fire. We would tell the story of how we fell in love during this Christmas season. If the servants left mistletoe around the house, Charles would be sure to make good use of it. It was a life I had never in my wildest imagination considered. I didn't know people could be so happy. Lord Hawthorne pulled me closer to him.

"It is rather untoward of me, isn't it, to ask you to marry me just because I might be in love with you? Because I want to spend my days and nights with you and raise a family with you?" He ran his gloved fingers up my bare arms as if to reassure himself that I was still there. "There is a very real chance I am doing this all wrong."

"I have never known you to be very concerned about doing things the right way, nor have you ever been anything other than untoward."

"So . . ." He cocked his head to one side. Lines of worry crept into his forehead. "Is that a no?"

I laughed. A few couples standing not far from us turned to see what was so amusing. "No."

"No, as in yes?" He stepped in even closer. I could feel his warmth everywhere now. On my arms, through my dress, and on my face and neck. "Yes."

"You will marry me." He threw my hands around his neck and reached for my waist. After spinning me around once, he paused in his celebrations, set me down, and furrowed his brow. "Why would you do that?"

I laughed softly. "Well, Charles, I may not have made this clear earlier." I stepped forward and placed my hand on his chest, just above his heart, so I could feel it beating again. It was racing, just like my own. He was so solid, so real, and so warm, and now, he was to be mine. "I think I might be in love with you too."

Lord Hawthorne covered my hand with his own. His eyes closed, and I felt the rhythm of his heart pick up speed beneath our hands. He leaned forward until our faces were only a breath away from each other. "I think I am about to do something very untoward."

"I should hope so."

The corners of his mouth rose in the smile I loved so much, but I caught only the beginning of it before his mouth was pressed softly against my own. He pulled my hand away from his chest and placed it back at his neck. Then both his hands were at my waist, pulling me closer to him. Lord Hawthorne—Charles—was here with me. This was real. I curled all of my fingers into his hair, so soft, clean, and natural. Nothing about Charles was counterfeit; even his hair was uninhibited.

He lifted his head, his eyes wide, as if he was as incredulous as I was about the events of the last few minutes. "Let's get married tomorrow. I am actually quite certain I love you. I should have mentioned it before."

A soft chuckle escaped my lips, still only inches from his. "On Christmas?"

"I'd forgotten about that." He kissed the corner of my mouth.

"We can't get married on Christmas," I said. His face crumpled into a pout, which, for some reason, made me smile. "Now that we are engaged, you will have to listen to some reason, at least. Banns take three weeks."

"Three weeks, then, and not a moment longer." His lips grazed the tip of my nose as if everything were finalized and taken care of.

"We can't list them tonight or tomorrow."

He groaned. "Three weeks and two days, then. But that is it. I will not wait any longer."

"I wouldn't expect you to. After all, you are an earl. You do whatever you want."

"That's right." Charles stood straighter, his smile broad. "Should we go tell our families?"

"Not yet." Mama would be surprised, but as long as Charles was willing to marry me, she wouldn't actually be upset. His rank alone qualified him as a husband. "Poor Rose. She isn't going to be happy about this."

"What? Rose didn't like me? She certainly hid that well." Charles looked offended.

"She will have to put up with Mama on her own after we are married. And Papa made a new hunting friend who invited them to his estate during Michaelmas. She will have to face our parents and this new family at Feldstone Manor on her own."

"I don't think you need to worry about Rose. From the little I saw of her, she will be able to handle your mother and whatever else life throws at her. You have raised her well."

He was right. Rose had done a lot of growing up in the past year, and in truth, she was more suited to dealing with Mama than I had ever been. Rose wouldn't be pushed around or embarrassed by her. She wouldn't stand for it. "But we should invite her to come stay at times."

"Anytime you want. You will be the wife of an earl." He touched my nose with his finger. "You can do whatever you want."

I smiled slowly and tipped my head to one side. "Whatever I want?" I knew what I wanted, and it wasn't to leave the balcony to speak with my parents. Not yet. This moment with Charles would forever remain the brightest in my life, and I wanted to bask in it longer. "Well then, I think I would like to be untoward a little longer."

His blue eyes darkened. "I am going to kiss you again, Miss Davenport— Elizabeth." He turned his head slightly so he could place a kiss on the palm of my hand. "And I am going to do it in a way that I am certain your future husband will heartily approve of."

A man cleared his throat behind us, but we ignored it. I was going to have to get used to doing things differently than expected if I was to be Lord Hawthorne's wife. I wrapped my hand around his neck, and he pulled me once again to him. My eyes closed as his fresh, clean scent invaded my senses. His kiss was more confident this time. More urgent. His arms crossed at my back, and each hand enveloped one of my shoulders. He growled slightly under his breath, and my laughter broke our kiss, but not for long. This would be us. Laughter and kissing. And perhaps a growl here and there, thanks to my enthusiastic fiancé. Together we would weave a pattern of color with our children, bright and beautiful. Perhaps it would seem garish to some, but to us it would be perfect because it was ours, the life we had created together.

ABOUT THE AUTHOR

ESTHER HATCH GREW UP ON a cherry orchard in rural Utah. After high school, she alternated living in Russia to teach children English and attending Brigham Young University in order to get a degree in archaeology. She began writing when one of her favorite authors invited her to join a critique group. The only catch was she had to be a writer. Not one to be left out of an opportunity to socialize and try something new, she started on her first novel that week.

OTHER BOOKS AND AUDIOBOOKS

BY JOANNA BARKER:

The Truth about Miss Ashbourne

Miss Adeline's Match

Secrets and Suitors

THE CHRISTMAS DRESS

JOANNA BARKER

To my mom and dad,
for always making Christmas magical

ACKNOWLEDGMENTS

FIRST OF ALL, THANK YOU to my publisher. I've always wanted to write a Christmas story, and I was excited when they asked me to contribute to this collection. I'm grateful for their dedication to publishing good literature and am so glad to be a part of it.

Thank you to my editor, Kami, for your thorough edits and for supporting me as I went through last-minute changes to make this story stronger. This book is much better for having had your eyes on it!

Thank you to my critique partners and beta readers: Heidi Kimball, Jessica Christian, Arlem Hawks, and Esther Hatch. This story needed every bit of the help you gave it, and I am so appreciative of all your time and talents.

CHAPTER ONE

Yorkshire, 1816

Blast her bonnet.

Nell Addington raced across the wide lawn as frozen grass crunched beneath her boots, desperate to keep sight of her bonnet tumbling in the wind. The treacherous breeze had snatched it from her grasp as she'd removed it to pin back a stray lock of hair. Now the cursed thing was bouncing and bounding over the lawn, its ribbons flailing behind as if teasing her to catch them.

Nell's breaths came in great gulps, puffing out again into the cold December air. No matter how she pushed herself, her legs could not keep pace with the swiftness of the wind. It certainly did not help that she still clutched her portmanteau, filled with fabric samples and fashion plates. It banged against her knees as she ran, and bruises were sure to follow.

The wind calmed, and her bonnet came to a stumbling halt on the grass. Nell tossed her heavy bag to the ground and dashed forward again, determined to catch the elusive headwear. But just as she reached for it, the wind stole it once again, hurtling it toward a line of oak trees. She let out a sound of frustration, sharp against her throat. She would never catch it. What would she do? She could hardly present herself at Oakhurst Park without a bonnet.

She shook her head and started off again, her legs already burning from the long walk from town. She had to get her bonnet—she had to. Perhaps the trees would stop it.

Unfortunately, her wish came true. As her bonnet approached the trunk of an enormous oak tree, leaves dancing in the wind, it swept upward, entangling itself in the branches.

Drat, drat, drat! Nell came to a jolting halt beneath the tree, staring at the bonnet dangling over her head. Her hands found her waist as her lungs heaved for air. Though she was nearly four and twenty, she was hardly tall enough to reach the lowest shelf in her mother's kitchen, let alone the branches now above her. Jumping for the bonnet would never result in success—only a great deal of exasperation.

She checked the pocket watch pinned to her pelisse, the wind dancing all about her. It was nearly ten o'clock. She'd imagined arriving at Oakhurst Park early, calm and collected, for her appointment with Mr. Hammond and his sister. Now, not only would she be late, but she would be bonnetless, disheveled, and red-faced.

Mrs. Shaw would not be pleased to hear about this. The modiste demanded perfection from her seamstresses, in both their sewing and their comportment. Unfortunately, while Nell excelled at the first, she struggled with the second.

She really must get the bonnet. She could not allow Mrs. Shaw any reason to be disappointed in her, especially not for something so ridiculous as a lost bonnet.

She turned to the thick tree trunk, unyielding in the wildness of the wind around her. A branch jutted out, about level with her eyes. She could climb it and scoot out to where the leaves held her bonnet captive, then drop down without any further mishap. She'd climbed much taller trees during her childhood; the land surrounding her father's vicarage had included a great many trees just like this one.

The wind whipped her hair over her face as she marched to the base of the tree and took hold of the low branch. She took a quick breath and began to pull herself up.

"Pardon me."

Nell jumped at the voice, her surprised yelp snatched away by the wind. She dropped back to the ground and stumbled a step before catching her balance. A man on horseback stood at the edge of the tree's branches. He peered at her from beneath his hat, watching her with amusement.

Mr. Jacob Hammond. It had been more than five years since Nell had last seen him, but she recognized him in an instant. She'd certainly spent enough time in her youth admiring his clear blue eyes and dark hair, the angular lines of his jaw. But as she stared at him now, heat flooded her face, clashing with the cold wind.

"I am sorry," he said. "I hate to interrupt what surely would have been quite the entertaining venture. But I wonder if I might be of assistance."

He urged his horse forward, stopping beneath her bonnet. With the added height of his horse, he could easily reach it. His fingers moved deftly over the ribbon and straw, untangling it from the branches.

Nell watched with an odd detachment, as if this mortifying thing was happening to someone else and not herself. What was Mr. Hammond doing here? He was supposed to be at the manor house, waiting to meet with her.

Mr. Hammond succeeded in freeing her bonnet from the tree and dismounted. "Might I be so bold as to ask whose hat I have rescued?"

Did he not recognize her? She could hardly blame him; it had been years, and they hadn't spent much time in each other's company to begin with. But her shoulders still dropped slightly.

Then he squinted and took a step forward. "I must apologize again. I know you, do I not?"

She swallowed and managed to nod, but before she could say anything, he snapped his fingers. "Ah yes. You are the vicar's daughter. Miss Addington, isn't it?"

He *did* remember her. And though there was a time when she would have been rather thrilled to have caught his notice, now she wished his attention was focused anywhere but on her. She finally convinced her lips to move. "Yes, sir."

"And do you often have trouble keeping hold of your bonnet, Miss Addington?" His words teased her, but his eyes were kind.

"Only when I am foolish enough to remove it."

He stepped forward and presented the bonnet to her. "Well, there you are. No harm done."

"Save to my pride." She took it, remembering her coiffure at the same time. She raised a hand to her head and grimaced at the tangled mess her fingers encountered. "And my hair."

He raised his eyebrows but thankfully did not comment. She cleared her throat as she tied her bonnet once again over her hair, glad to have it hidden. "Thank you, Mr. Hammond. I am grateful for your assistance."

He tipped his hat. "Happy to oblige. Might I ask where you are off to? Bit windy for a stroll, don't you think?"

She bit her lip, glancing away. She'd anticipated this from the moment Mrs. Shaw had received Mr. Hammond's note three days before, asking for a private consultation at Oakhurst Park for his sister, Alice. Nell was not ashamed of being a seamstress, not really. It was honest work, at least.

But Mr. Hammond had known her when she had been the daughter of a respected vicar. Five years ago she'd had soft hands, pretty dresses, and no worries to keep her awake at night. That was certainly not the case now. She had to be presentable, of course, or her clients would not want her. But she wore a plain blue gown, embellished only with a few tasteful ruffles, and her hands were calloused from the constant pricking of needles. And who knew what gray shadows lingered beneath her eyes these days?

She raised her chin. It hardly mattered what Mr. Hammond thought of her. "I am actually here to meet with you, sir. Mrs. Shaw sent me from the modiste shop."

She watched carefully, knowing too well the awkward silence that would follow. She'd repeated this conversation many times with former friends over the years. Their eyes would fill with pity, their voices dropping in tone as if she were on her deathbed. And then they would make excuses to leave and never call upon her again.

Mr. Hammond did not do any of these things. He tipped his head to one side, squinting. "From the shop?" he repeated. "Are you working there now?"

Nell gave a swift nod. "Yes, as a seamstress."

"Oh." He did not sound pitying, for which she was grateful, although his voice held a curious lilt. But it was hardly polite to question a lady about her drop in social status, and he was ever the gentleman. "Well, shall we go up to the house? The wind is growing wilder by the minute, and your bonnet may not withstand another journey across my estate."

He earned a small smile from her at that. He was just as amiable as she remembered, though somehow he had grown *more* handsome. Or perhaps it was simply because she felt so unkempt in comparison. And here she'd thought she had outgrown her girlhood fancy for him. She gulped against the sudden dryness in her mouth. "I'm afraid I abandoned my bag during the chase," she said, her cheeks once again tinging with heat. "Just over there." She nodded across the lawn.

"I am sorry to have missed that bit of your performance."

"It was rather dramatic, I assure you."

"I have no doubt." He took his horse's reins, gesturing for her to join him. They started across the lawn, the wind still tugging at her hem and bonnet. She kept a hand firmly clamped to her head; she had no desire to repeat that embarrassment. The memory burned within her. Had she truly been prepared to climb a tree while Mr. Hammond, of all people, looked on? It was little wonder Mrs. Shaw constantly lectured her on her behavior.

They reached her portmanteau, and before she could protest, Mr. Hammond took it up, holding it in his left hand as he led his horse with his right.

"Please, let me carry it," she said quickly. "You've your horse."

He gave her a wry smile. "I shall manage well enough, Miss Addington. My mount is not known for sudden bouts of recklessness, unlike your bonnet. Best to keep your hands free."

"You shall tease me about that forever, shan't you?" The words left her mouth before she realized it. Nell pressed her lips closed; it was not her place to speak so informally to a man of his station, no matter their past acquaintance.

He only grinned. "So long as opportunities continue to present themselves."

He started off again, and she followed, the wind rushing about them, blowing her dress behind her.

"So tell me," he said, speaking loudly so as to be heard. "How is your family? Your parents and sisters? I cannot say when I saw you all last."

Nell blinked, shooting him a sideways glance. Did he not know? "My mother and sisters are well," she said hesitantly. "My eldest sister is married now, with a young son." She cleared her throat. "My father passed four years ago."

Mr. Hammond came to a jolting halt, staring at her. And though she had seen no pity in his eyes before, when she'd mentioned her position at the shop, she certainly saw it there now.

* * *

Jacob Hammond was not easily surprised. He considered himself rational and intelligent and a good judge of character. There was rarely much that could take him aback.

But at Miss Addington's news of her father, he admitted an unprecedented shock. The vicar had died? How had he not known?

The answer was perfectly obvious; he hadn't attended services in the six months since his return to Oakhurst Park, and he had spent five years in London before that. Even still, a knot tightened inside him. He ought to have known.

"I am sorry," he said, his words embarrassingly inadequate. "I was unaware."

Miss Addington did not show any signs of offense, but then, she'd always been a bit difficult to read. Even in their few interactions from years ago at church services and various social functions, he could remember her dark-blue eyes, intelligent and inquisitive as she observed those around her. Now those eyes avoided his, looking off to her left as they began walking again, starting up the last stretch of lawn.

"I can hardly expect you to stay abreast of every bit of news from the village," she said, her voice soft. "I'm certain you are very busy."

"Yes, well, this is something I should have noted." His voice was tight in his throat. If Father hadn't been such a cantankerous fool, then perhaps Jacob might've spent more time in Yorkshire. As it was, he'd only returned after his own father's burial, another reason he had been unaware of a new vicar in the place of Mr. Addington.

But these were ridiculous thoughts to have, when the woman beside him had suffered much more than he.

"Truly," he added quietly, hoping she could hear his words over the wind. "I am sorry for your loss. I thought most highly of your father, I hope you know."

She nodded. "Thank you, sir. He would be glad to have your good opinion, I have no doubt."

Their conversation came to a rather awkward pause, though Jacob had no one to blame but himself. Surely he should have realized that with her working for the modiste shop, she could hardly be in a good position. Instead he had drudged up her difficult memories.

Miss Addington rescued him by clearing her throat. "In your note to Mrs. Shaw, you mentioned this appointment is to be a surprise for your sister?"

"Yes, yes," he said, eager for the new topic. "Alice hasn't any idea I've arranged this. She would hate for me to make such a fuss. In truth, she hates being the center of any amount of attention, which is why I insisted on a private meeting at Oakhurst."

"I see," she said. "And what have you in mind for her?"

He waved a hand. "Oh, I haven't the slightest clue. Only that I am entirely through with seeing her in black and gray. We are long finished with mourning, and I intend to see her properly outfitted."

Miss Addington tipped her head to one side. "She is to have a new wardrobe completely, then?"

He did not hesitate. "Yes. Everything must be new." He would spare no expense on Alice's behalf. She had endured far too much in the past years, even more than he had, although their father's relentless manipulation and mistreatment had left unseen scars on them both. It had been six months since his father's death and nearly five years since he had last seen the man, but even now he could hear that harsh, deep voice shouting as Jacob rode away for the last time.

"Very well," Miss Addington said, bringing him back to the present. She spoke briskly, her voice all business. "I've brought fabric samples and several fashion plates. We shall surely be able to decide on some designs and colors. It will require a few weeks, but I am certain we can meet your needs."

Miss Addington seemed keen to present herself as all that was professional and proper. But a hand still clasped her bonnet as she surveyed the nearby landscape. He fought a smile at the image of her standing beneath the oak tree, fully prepared to climb the branches and rescue her bonnet. He could not imagine any of his female acquaintances in London attempting such a feat.

"Excellent," he said. "I am certain you shall do a splendid job of it. Your shop came most highly recommended to me by Miss Fowler. She could not say enough good about it."

A strange expression came over Miss Addington; her jaw tightened, and her eyes squinted. "Oh yes," she said, her voice strained. "Miss Fowler is a frequent patroness. I am pleased she speaks well of our work."

Odd. Why had the mention of Miss Fowler set her so ill at ease? He nearly pressed her but stopped himself. He hardly knew Miss Addington; he had no reason to pry into her thoughts.

"I am actually quite glad it is you who came," he said instead.

"Oh?" She glanced at him, her honey-colored hair dancing about her face in the breeze. "No doubt because of my amusing dash across your lawn."

He grinned. "Yes, there is certainly that." His grin slowly faded as Oakhurst Park appeared ahead from around a bend of trees. The stately manor looked forlorn in this weather, though it was still nothing short of impressive in terms of size and elegance. Just as his father had wished it.

He shook his head and applied himself once more to the conversation. "No, I am glad you came because of Alice. She at least knows you."

Miss Addington pulled back her chin. "Does she? I wouldn't think she would remember me after so long."

"Ah, but you underestimate the impression simple kindness can have on a young girl." Alice had not known much kindness in her life, with their mother having died in childbirth and their father withholding any shred of affection.

"Kindness?" Miss Addington repeated, peering up at him. "What do you mean?"

He raised an eyebrow. "You made faces at her during services for years just to make her laugh. You think she would not remember you?"

Her cheeks pinked. "Oh dear, those faces were certainly not meant to be seen by anyone other than Alice."

"I could not help but notice." More of Jacob's memories came back to him the longer he spoke with Miss Addington. He remembered the silly faces, the small bouquets of wildflowers she had left on Alice's spot on their family pew, and the constant encouraging smiles. Miss Addington did not seem to smile much now, which he thought rather wasteful. She had a lovely smile, if he recalled. "You were very kind to her."

She bit her lip. "It was not much, I know. I only imagined life without a mother would be difficult indeed and did what little I could to help."

He nodded, swallowing. People like Miss Addington were a rare occurrence. Perhaps that came from her upbringing; Mr. Addington had been a wonderful leader to their parish, and certainly his daughter had inherited his compassion.

"In any case," he said, his voice gruff, "I have no doubt she shall be glad to see you. Which is fortunate for me. She dislikes surprises, so I am hopeful she will be less likely to throw something at me after you leave."

Miss Addington laughed, a delightful ringing sound that was taken away far too soon by the wind. "Does she do that frequently?"

"Only when I am particularly overbearing and intrusive."

"She is lucky to have a brother to worry over her," she said a bit wistfully. She had only sisters, he knew.

"She does not often think so," he said with a slight laugh. In truth, Jacob likely worried too much. But Alice was all he had left. She was his responsibility, and he was determined to see her happy.

And he was beginning to think that Miss Addington might be an excellent cure for Alice's reticence. She was easy to speak with and had such a pleasant manner. Surely the two women would spend much time together in the next few weeks, with fittings and such.

Though he would not mind stealing a bit more of Miss Addington's time for himself. He cast a sidelong glance at her as they started up the long drive to the front door of Oakhurst. Miss Addington wore a half-smile, her blue eyes vivid even on this blustery day. It had been far too long since he had so enjoyed a conversation, and he was keen to repeat it.

CHAPTER TWO

"What do you think of this red?" Nell slid yet another square of fabric across the table. Alice took it and felt it between her fingers, her face revealing nothing of her thoughts. She considered the fabric, and the silence of the large parlor at Oakhurst bore down on them like the gray clouds that hovered outside.

Heavens, was it always so very quiet here? Nell could not imagine living in such solitude. She had always considered her small home with Mama and Diana as painfully cramped, but now she was grateful for its warmth in spirit.

Alice handed back the fabric. "It is too bold, I think."

Nell held back a sigh. Alice had said the same of every color, save for the whites and pale blues. But Alice did not have the complexion for such light colors. With her pale skin, she would appear wan and gray. And the black mourning dress she wore now certainly did her no favors, especially against her dark hair. Nell had an eye for such things; it was one of the reasons she was one of the more popular seamstresses at the shop, though Mrs. Shaw would never admit it. But that did not stop her from sending Nell out on such appointments as this. Having a vicar's daughter working at the shop gave Mrs. Shaw a certain credibility, and she would be a fool to waste such a commodity.

But that was beside the point, which was that Alice needed color—life—in her dresses.

"Miss Hammond," she began, sliding the stack of fabric to the side. "I cannot help but think you would look lovely in some of these brighter colors. Is there a reason you are reluctant to try them?"

Alice sat stiffly in her chair across the table, hands clasped in her lap. She was quiet for a long moment. "I've never worn anything like them," she finally admitted, her voice a near whisper. "My governess—my former governess—never allowed it. And Father would have hated it, I am certain."

Ah, that shed some light on her reluctance. Nell was hardly surprised. Though she could not claim more than a bare acquaintance with the late Mr. Hammond, she'd known him quite well through reputation as a hard, cold, and unforgiving man. She could only imagine what mix of emotions Alice had suffered since his death.

But Alice's father was no longer here. He had no authority in her life now.

"Well," Nell said. "I am afraid to say that, as you are seventeen years old, you are unlucky enough to have to make such choices yourself. It is a difficult task, I am aware, but I think you shall be able to manage well enough if you put your mind to it."

Alice looked up, her eyes wide. Nell bit her tongue. Had she taken her teasing too far? She hadn't meant to offend.

But then Alice took a deep breath and reached out again for the square of red silk. Nell pressed ahead.

"Truly," she said. "I believe a blue or red silk would look lovely against your hair and complexion."

Alice ran her fingertips over the smooth surface of the fabric. "I suppose we might take the risk with one gown."

Progress. Nell nodded. "Perhaps this red? We might be able to have it ready by Christmas. You could wear some holly and berries in your hair and look very pretty indeed."

Alice shook her head. "We have never held much in the way of Christmas celebrations. Father——" Her voice broke, and she cleared her throat. "Father thought it a bit rustic for us."

No Christmas? Nell could not imagine such a thing. She had only the fondest memories of her childhood Christmases: gathering greenery with her father and sisters to decorate the house with on Christmas Eve, warming herself beside the burning Yule log, helping her mother roast the goose and boil the plum pudding.

Nell examined Alice, pretending to straighten her stack of fashion plates. The young lady wore her dark hair in a careful twist atop her head and had not relaxed her posture in the entire half-hour they'd been speaking. She'd shown only the slightest surprise when Mr. Hammond had introduced Nell—well, reintroduced—and Nell had certainly doubted Mr.

Hammond's claim that Alice remembered her at all. She spoke only if Nell questioned her, and then in that quiet whisper of a voice.

Nell folded her hands on the table. They'd both suffered the loss of their fathers, and she could not imagine they'd felt their grief in the same way. But perhaps she might lend some understanding.

"When my father died a few years ago," Nell said gently, "one of the hardest things to endure was change. I wanted everything to remain the same as when he had been alive."

Alice stared down at her hands in her lap, not reacting at all. Nell took a quick breath and continued on.

"Christmastide was especially difficult for me," she said. "Father so loved this time of year, for the love and spirit it kindled. But in the past years, I have found much peace in our traditions and memories." She paused, allowing her words a moment to register with Alice. "Perhaps Christmas might lend you the same opportunity to find peace. There is always time to start anew, and what better season than now?"

Alice did not move for a long moment. But then her shoulders relaxed by the slightest margin, and she leaned forward.

"Would you tell me more?" she asked softly. "Of you and your family and your Christmases together? I think it lovely." She gave the smallest of smiles, and Nell's heart warmed at the sight.

"Of course," she said. "Of course I will."

* * *

Jacob sat at the desk in his study, listening to the sounds of laughter and conversation drifting down the hallway. He could not make out the precise words, but it hardly mattered. Alice was *laughing*.

Oh, she sometimes laughed with him, but always shortly, and usually in annoyance at his teasing. But this . . . this was real laughter, joyful and contagious. He could not resist a smile, and he turned to stare out the wide window, warmth growing in his chest the longer he listened to their voices.

If he'd known Miss Addington would have had such an effect on Alice, he'd have dragged her here months ago. As it was, he was ashamed to have allowed her to pass so easily from his thoughts. He hadn't thought of her or her family in years, not since he had left Oakhurst Park after his clash with Father. Living in London for more than half a decade had distanced him both physically and mentally from Yorkshire, and he was still realizing the costs of that separation. Alice, of course, was always his biggest regret. He'd missed so many years of her upbringing, driven away as he'd been by their father's insufferable cruelty.

His smile faded as he watched the wind whipping the empty tree branches outside. Even beyond the grave Father took and took. Would they ever be free of him?

Jacob turned back to his study—his father's study. He had redecorated it entirely the minute he'd returned to Oakhurst Park. He'd torn down the dark curtains that framed the windows, filled the shelves with his own books and belongings, and ordered the gamekeeper to use his father's enormous desk as firewood, replacing it with one much better suited to the space. But he still had far too many memories of this room to find comfort here.

He stood and went into the hallway, following the now-quiet voices, a soft hum that beckoned to him. He stopped outside the closed parlor door, listening. He did not want to eavesdrop, but neither did he wish to interrupt.

"—if you are not kissed, then it is said you shall not marry that entire year. But I do not put much faith in that method of predicting the future."

Jacob raised an eyebrow. That was Miss Addington's voice. What on earth was she talking about?

"And what of the berries? Is there not something to do with the number of berries?"

Alice's words were quiet, but he could nearly hear the smile in her voice.

"Oh yes," Miss Addington went on. "Every time there is a kiss beneath the bough, a berry is plucked. Once they are gone, there can be no more kissing."

Alice gave a short giggle. "How very unfortunate for the couple wishing to be caught next under the bough."

"Indeed," Miss Addington said dryly. "They shall be forced to find another."

They laughed together, and Jacob shook his head in silent amazement. Was that truly his Alice? The sister who had spent most of the last six months refusing to leave the house? Miss Addington had already done more good for Alice than he had since his return to the estate, though certainly not for lack of trying. There must be something singular about female companionship that simply provided what he could not.

The women's voices continued on in the parlor—speaking about wassailing—and Jacob listened. Alice asked so many questions, spoke with such lightness. Was it Miss Addington who had inspired such a response, or was it the subject?

Christmas. He had never given the holiday much thought. But Alice was certainly showing an interest, even beyond the kissing bough. He walked slowly back down the hall to his study, his eyes skipping over the familiar paintings and furnishings. Was this perhaps the chance he had been looking for to heal some of the broken edges between him and Alice? Could they rebuild their little family, with pine boughs and Yule logs?

He hardly knew where to begin. But he was fortunate to know someone who did. He could only hope Nell Addington would continue to prove generous. Because he very much needed her help.

CHAPTER THREE

AFTER TALKING WITHOUT RESTRAINT FOR over an hour about Christmas, Nell and Alice required nearly two more hours of serious consideration before they were able to decide upon the colors, styles, and fabrics for six new dresses.

After Alice decided upon the neckline for the last gown, they retreated to her bedroom for Nell to take her measurements. Nell tried not to stare at the numbers. Alice was a skinny thing. Did she not eat properly? Had Mr. Hammond noticed?

After returning to the parlor, Nell began collecting her things but paused when a knock came at the open door. Both women turned as Mr. Hammond stepped inside the room. Nell's fingers fumbled over her measuring tape as he cast her a warm smile.

"How goes the dressmaking?" he asked, coming farther into the room and clasping his hands behind his back.

Nell cleared her throat. "Very well, Mr. Hammond. We were just finishing for today."

"Wonderful," he said. "And what happens next? I admit I lack a working knowledge of sewing."

Nell smiled as she returned her measuring tape to her bag, already packed full again with her materials. "First I will need to sew a pattern from linen."

"And how long does that take?" Alice asked curiously.

"No more than a few days for a single dress." Nell fastened the buckle on her portmanteau. "Once it's ready, I will need to return for a fitting. Unless you wish to come into the shop."

Alice shook her head. "No, I would prefer here."

Nell smiled gently. "Of course." There was no use in pushing Alice further than she wished to go. And Nell hardly minded coming to Oakhurst. Not when it had such an agreeable owner. She glanced at Mr. Hammond, who watched her intently, the corner of his mouth hinting at a smile.

"After that fitting, I can start with the proper fabrics," she went on. "It is difficult for me to say exactly how long it will require, but I can guarantee the first dress within two weeks."

"Just before Christmas, then," Mr. Hammond said.

"Yes, a day or two before would be my best estimate." She turned to Alice. "Which dress should you like me to begin first?"

Alice bit her lip. "I hardly know. What do you think?"

Nell did not hesitate. "Oh, the red. I am ever so eager to see it on you. I have no doubt you will be stunning."

Alice did not look entirely convinced, but she nodded. "All right, then. The red it is."

"Lovely." Nell took up her bag and offered a curtsy. "Good day, Mr. Hammond, Miss Hammond."

Mr. Hammond bowed, which was kind of him considering she was naught but a seamstress. "Good day, Miss Addington."

She allowed herself one last look at him as a dark lock of hair fell across his forehead, his blue eyes warm and sincere. Then she turned and left the room, scolding herself for her weakness. There was no point in indulging in such a way. Yes, Mr. Hammond was handsome, but she could not see him as anything more than a paying patron of the shop. Surely he saw her as nothing more than the seamstress she was.

She went to the front door and waited while the footman fetched her things. She took her gloves from him first, thinking another walk in the brisk breeze would do her good. She had spent far too much time today with flushed, hot cheeks.

"Miss Addington, a moment please."

Nell nearly dropped her gloves at the sound of Mr. Hammond's voice. She turned as he came down the hall with long strides.

"Did I forget something?" she asked, clutching her gloves.

He stopped beside her. "No, no, I simply wanted to offer to call the coach for you. It is far too blustery out there for you to be walking back to town."

"Oh, you needn't trouble yourself." That irritating heat was already pricking in her cheeks. This man had a special talent indeed, inspiring such prominent blushing from her. "I don't mind the walk."

He waved her off. "It is no trouble, I assure you. Not after—" But he shook his head, cutting off whatever he had been about to say. "It is no trouble," he reasserted.

Nell nibbled her lip. There could be no harm in accepting his offer, could there? "All right, then," she said hesitantly. "If you are sure."

Mr. Hammond wasted no time in dispatching the footman to the stables with orders to prepare the coach. When he turned back to her, Nell had managed to compose herself, though her heart still beat too fast.

"It sounded as though you and Alice got along splendidly," he said, clasping his hands behind his back. "I heard you laughing from my study."

She swallowed. "Oh, I hope we did not disturb you." Did he think her idle, chattering away the afternoon?

"On the contrary." His tone softened. "I was glad to hear it. Alice could do with a bit more laughter in her life. She could do with a great deal more. She seems quite taken with you."

His eyes moved over hers, as if he meant more than what he had actually said. She cleared her throat. "I'm quite fond of her as well," she said. "She is a sweet girl, if a bit quiet."

"Yes, she is." He paused for a moment. "Miss Addington, I must admit I overheard a bit of your conversation with her. I hope you will not think me so very terrible."

She blinked up at him. He had been listening? Her ears burned hot. Had he heard their discussion of kissing boughs? They'd talked of them for a good ten minutes. "That depends entirely on what you overheard."

His lips twitched. "Nothing of importance, I assure you. Just a bit about your Christmas customs is all."

He *had* heard about the mistletoe. It was painfully obvious from the amusement in his voice. Oh, she could just melt into the floor here and now.

"I mention it," he said, "only because of Alice's reaction to your stories. She seemed rather captivated by the idea of Christmas."

Nell struggled to find her thoughts, tangled as they were in an embarrassed mess. "Yes," she managed. "She questioned me near to an hour."

Mr. Hammond nodded thoughtfully. "Perhaps you might be able to offer your opinion on an idea of mine, then. I had a notion that I might—"

But his voice was cut off as the sound of jangling harnesses and hoofbeats met their ears, coming from outside the house. Mr. Hammond furrowed his brow. "That can't be the coach yet. Pardon me, Miss Addington."

The footman was still gone to the stables, so Mr. Hammond strode to the door himself, opening it just as the coach outside came to a stop. Nell's shoulders stiffened. Miss Fowler descended from the equipage, her auburn hair somehow shining even on this sunless day. Nell immediately recognized the dress she wore, a frilly pink day dress with far too many ruffles. It was one Nell had slaved over for a week, working endless hours to finish it for an impossible deadline. Well, nearly impossible. She always met her deadlines.

"Oh," Miss Fowler said upon spotting Mr. Hammond at the top of the stairs. "Acting as your own footman now, are you, Mr. Hammond?"

The woman's voice was teasing, and her familiarity irked Nell. But why should it? Mr. Hammond had said Miss Fowler was a friend. Nell's irritation must be because the woman had interrupted whatever he had been about to tell her, that's all. She was vastly curious about whatever was on his mind.

Mr. Hammond gave a polite smile as Miss Fowler climbed the front steps. "Just this once, I'm afraid."

He gestured for her to step inside out of the cold. She spotted Nell in the next instant. "Why, Miss Addington," she exclaimed. "Whatever are you doing here?"

Nell could not find her voice. What a day she was having. First her bonnet and encounter with Mr. Hammond, then her rekindled friendship with Alice, and now the appearance of her least-favorite customer. She nearly expected it to start snowing, just to continue the unexpectedness of the day so far.

"I just finished a consultation with Miss Hammond," she finally managed.

Miss Fowler's eyes took in every stray hair upon Nell's head. Why hadn't she been quicker to tie on her bonnet?

"She came at my request," Mr. Hammond said, stepping forward. "I was inspired by your recommendation of Mrs. Shaw's shop."

"Oh yes." She cocked her head to one side, a delicate curl framing her face. "They do excellent *work* there. That is, *you* do excellent *work*, Miss Addington. I have been so pleased with your latest creations."

These were nothing less than her usual pointed remarks, but they cut a bit deeper with Mr. Hammond present. It was often the way of women to include a veiled slight within a compliment. Mr. Hammond likely had not noticed the light but calculated emphasis Mrs. Fowler had used, yet Nell felt her words keenly, reminders that she was just a seamstress, far beneath Miss Fowler.

The woman had always treated her with vague disdain, even before Nell's father had died. Mama said it was because Miss Fowler was jealous of Nell, though Nell could not figure out why that would be. Even when Nell and Miss Fowler had circled through the same society years ago, Miss Fowler had always worn prettier, more expensive clothes and had a list of accomplishments that put all others to shame. But the poor girl never seemed to have many friends. Perhaps that is what Mama had meant.

"Thank you," she said quietly. "I am glad you are pleased."

Miss Fowler barely seemed to hear her, already turning back to Mr. Hammond. "I was passing on my way to town and decided to pay Miss Hammond a little visit. It has been far too long since I last saw you both."

Nell watched the exchange from beneath lowered lashes. Mr. Hammond did not appear particularly delighted to see Miss Fowler, she thought. At least not in the way Miss Fowler did to see him; her eyes never left the man's face.

Mr. Hammond frowned. "I'm afraid I have appointments this afternoon, but I am sure Alice will enjoy your company."

He did not seem very certain of that statement, glancing back to where Alice remained in the parlor. He spoke with careful politeness, and Nell was quite certain Miss Fowler's admiration of the man was rather one-sided. Not that it mattered to her at all. But she enjoyed—far too much—the satisfaction of that knowledge.

Miss Fowler kept a perfectly pleasant expression on her face, though her jaw tightened slightly. "How unfortunate. But Miss Hammond and I shall entertain ourselves well enough."

The footman returned then from the stables, and Miss Fowler began handing over her things. Mr. Hammond glanced back at Nell, as though he meant to speak once again.

"What weather this is," Miss Fowler said loudly as she removed her gloves. "I've never seen such terrible wind, have you?"

She was clearly addressing Mr. Hammond, so Nell did not bother with an answer. She turned to peer out the open front door, hoping to catch a glimpse of the coach coming round. If only she hadn't accepted his offer, she might have been gone already.

"No, indeed not," Mr. Hammond said. "Though it does have its benefits, don't you think, Miss Addington?"

Nell's gaze flicked to him. His brow lifted innocently, but he must have meant their meeting earlier. Mustn't he? Her heart quickened. "Yes," she said, touching one hand to her bonnet. He grinned. "I daresay you are right."

Miss Fowler gave a little laugh as she handed her cloak to the footman. "Well, we shall hope you are not swept up in the wind on your way home, Miss Addington." She turned to Mr. Hammond and stretched out her hand. "Won't you show me into the parlor? Perhaps I might steal just a few minutes of your time."

Mr. Hammond finally turned to Miss Fowler. "I'll just see Miss Addington off first."

Miss Fowler's smile twitched, her eyes narrowing by just the slightest measure. But before she could speak, Nell spotted the blessed vehicle coming up the lane from the coach house.

"The coach is here," she blurted. "Do not wait on my account, Mr. Hammond. I will see myself out."

"There," Miss Fowler said, stepping to his side and taking his arm. "Let us go in, Mr. Hammond. I am anxious to see Miss Hammond."

Mr. Hammond hesitated still, but Miss Fowler tugged him down the hall. "Good day, Miss Addington," he called back.

Nell did not even have time to respond before they disappeared into the parlor, the door closing behind them. She sighed. "Good day, Mr. Hammond."

CHAPTER FOUR

Jacob was unused to time passing so slowly. His was a busy life, and he spent his days meeting tenants, overseeing the estate, and returning correspondence. But since Nell Addington had made a rather unexpected reappearance into his life five days before, he had found each day passing with an odd sluggishness. He went too often to his study window, where he could just see the lane leading from the road, and he reprimanded himself constantly. Alice had said Miss Addington would write to set their next appointment. Of course she would not appear without warning.

But he could not help himself. The memory of her chasing down her bonnet, her lovely pink cheeks and sparkling eyes—they had captivated his mind more than he would ever admit. He could not remember the last time a woman had so overtaken his thoughts.

It was likely because Alice spoke of her so often. Since her morning with Miss Addington, his sister had mentioned her nearly every day, wondering how she was getting on with the pattern for the dress or recounting some silly tale the seamstress had told her. Jacob hadn't seen this much life to his sister since she was a child; Father had always insisted a woman was valued for her silence and obedience, not her opinion. As a result the bright, lovely child that had been Alice had transformed into the detached and impassive woman he'd returned home to.

But now . . . now he had begun to see a bit of her old self returning, shining through. He tried not to show his amazement every time she spoke, though he doubted he entirely succeeded.

That was not to say Alice didn't still resort to her previous quietness, because she certainly did. But whereas he'd previously had to pry words from her mouth, she now spoke with little prompting and with less reluctance than before.

They had just settled in for the evening in the drawing room near a snapping fire built to ward off the December chill outside. Alice had taken up a book, and he sat at the desk, penning a letter to his uncle in London. But before he had written two words, Alice's voice broke through his thoughts.

"Did you know that the townspeople go wassailing on Christmas Eve?" she asked.

Jacob looked up, squinting at her across the room. "Wassailing?"

"Yes, they go door-to-door singing songs, visiting one another."

"I know what wassailing is," he said wryly.

She raised an eyebrow in challenge, lowering her book. "It did not sound as though you did."

He ignored the slight. "Why the sudden interest in begging food from your neighbors?" he teased. "Do I not feed you well enough?"

In truth, he worried over his sister's health almost as much as he did her quietness. She was terribly thin, and though he encouraged her to take second helpings at every meal, she only picked at her food.

"I only thought it sounded curious," Alice said, not rising to his bait. "I certainly cannot picture Miss Fowler participating in such an event."

He gave a short laugh. "No, neither can I."

The young lady was a persistent visitor to their house, and though she came under the pretense of seeing Alice, Jacob was not oblivious to her true aim. But he was not interested in marriage or a wife. Or, at least, not in Miss Fowler as a wife. She was a pretty girl, no doubt, and she made an effort with Alice, for which he was grateful. But there was also something a bit odd about the woman that he could not quite lay his finger on.

"Miss Addington goes with her family every year," Alice said, her fingers moving absently over the leather binding of her book. "And then her mother invites anyone who would like to come to their home for food and hot drinks."

Now that was an image Jacob had no difficulty creating, unlike with Miss Fowler. He could easily picture Miss Addington bundled up against the cold as she sang and laughed with her friends and family.

"It sounds like a pleasant way to pass an evening," he said.

Alice nodded and turned back to her book. She did not speak again, and silence reclaimed the room.

Jacob sighed. He was often at a loss for how to continue these conversations. He'd so long been absent from Alice's life that he was still coming to know her again, a difficult task considering her reticence. He set down his pen and turned to face her once more.

"Alice," he said. She looked up from her book. "I had an idea the other day."

"What idea is that?" She did not sound irritated—just distracted, as if she would much rather be reading. He pressed on.

"I was thinking we might invite some friends for a dinner on Christmas Eve."

She tilted her head. "Friends? We haven't any friends."

He grinned. "I have friends. They just happen to live in London."

"And you'll invite them?"

"No, not them." This conversation was getting away from him. "I was thinking the Alfords, perhaps."

He'd proposed the safest option first, so as not to scare her off. The Alfords were old friends of their mother's before her death. They still stopped in every now and again to see them, though they were getting on in age. Alice liked them well enough. Certainly she would not refuse them.

She mulled over the idea, setting her book in her lap. "I suppose that could be pleasant."

"And what of the vicar and his family?" he suggested.

"Mr. Jameson?" She squinted at him. "You've not attended services since your return, and now you want the vicar in our home?"

"I've been busy," he protested. In truth, it was not religion or the vicar he was avoiding. The cemetery was simply far too close to the parish. He had no desire to visit his father's grave, now or ever.

She nodded, albeit a bit reluctantly. "All right, then. The vicar and his family. Anyone else?"

Jacob frowned. "I suppose we ought to invite Miss Fowler and her father. She would be put out with us if we did not."

"I'm not convinced that would be so terrible a thing," Alice muttered. Jacob coughed to cover his laugh. Alice was not fond of Miss Fowler's visits. They generally resulted in an hour or two of stilted conversation, with Miss Fowler doing most of the speaking. Jacob could usually excuse himself with an invented alibi, but Alice did not have that luxury.

"I promise not to seat her near you at dinner," he said with a grin.

But Alice did not seem to hear him as she leaned forward slightly. "Might we invite Miss Addington?"

Jacob sat back in his chair. He had already thought of inviting Miss Addington. "I worry about taking her from her family on Christmas."

"We could invite her family as well," Alice suggested.

Jacob tapped his fingers against the surface of the writing desk. "They have their own traditions, Alice. I wouldn't want them to feel obligated to accept an invitation from us."

She frowned. "I suppose. But I should like her to come."

As would I.

"At least I shall see her tomorrow," she went on.

"Tomorrow?"

"When she comes for my fitting." Alice was already raising her book again.

His stomach performed a rather spectacular flip. "Oh," he said as nonchalantly as he could manage. "Did she send a note?"

She did not look up. "Yes, yesterday."

He cleared his throat. "What time is she coming?"

"Two o'clock."

Blast. He had a meeting with a tenant at that time. He could only hope the meeting would be quick and that he would not miss Miss Addington's visit entirely.

He glanced out the window, where darkness had settled over the landscape. Ice crystals had already begun creeping across the glass, despite the fire in the grate. Nell would have to walk the long way from town in such cold.

Perhaps he might do something about that.

* * *

"Eleanor!" Mama's voice rang up the tiny stairwell and echoed into the bedroom where Nell stood squinting in the mirror, attempting to fix her coiffure the best she could. Mama was the only one who called Nell by her given name. Papa had called her Nell from the start, but Mama had always insisted on Eleanor since it had been her mother's name. Nell, however, far preferred her shortened appellation.

"Yes, Mama?" she called back, slipping another pin into her hair. She had looked such a mess the last time she had gone to Oakhurst, and she was determined not to repeat the experience.

"You had better come down. Quickly, now."

Nell straightened at the peculiar tone in Mama's voice. The last time she had sounded like that, the neighbor's pig had gotten loose and run rampant around the neighborhood.

"I am coming," she shouted, then took one last cursory glance at her light-brown hair. She sighed. It would have to do. She simply did not have Edith's thick locks or Diana's golden color. Her sisters had certainly been more blessed in their appearances than she had been. But at least Mrs. Shaw had allowed her to leave the shop early to dress for her appointment, since the plain gray gown she wore most days would certainly not impress anyone.

She took her bag from the bed she shared with Diana, already packed with the dress pattern she had finished only yesterday. She smiled in anticipation. The design she and Alice had chosen from the fashion plates had been a complicated one, and she'd rather enjoyed the task of recreating such a pattern. She hoped Alice would be pleased.

She hoped Mr. Hammond would be pleased as well.

"Eleanor!"

She turned and hurried down the stairs. "What on earth is all this fuss about?" she asked, setting down her portmanteau as she took her bonnet from the hook on the wall.

Both Diana and Mama stood at the front window, peering outside. Diana turned and waved her forward frantically. "Come and see," she hissed.

Nell furrowed her brow as she strode across the small room, furnished only with a well-worn sofa and two rickety wooden chairs. "What are you two gawking at?"

But then she immediately found herself gawking as well. Just outside their home, on the tiny lane that connected it to the rest of the town, waited a coach. But not any coach. It was Mr. Hammond's. She recognized it from last week, when it had taken her back to the modiste's shop.

"The coachman says he is waiting for *you*," Mama said, turning to peer at her. "Is he mistaken, Nell?"

Nell shook her head, still staring out the window at the team of two horses prancing restlessly. "I think Mr. Hammond must have sent his coach for me again."

"Again?" Diana echoed, exchanging a glance with Mama.

Nell did not respond. Why would Mr. Hammond do such a thing? They were barely friends—hardly even acquaintances, really.

Diana echoed her unspoken question. "Why has Mr. Hammond sent you a coach?"

Nell glanced up at the sky, where clouds hung heavily in the sky, a threatening gray. "Perhaps he thought it would rain and did not wish for me to arrive soaking at his estate."

That was certainly not beyond belief. He was thoughtful; she knew that much. Or perhaps he simply felt sorry for her and this was an act of charity. She frowned at that, turning from the window and tying her bonnet beneath her chin. She still could not come to terms with the fact that hers was a family in *need* of charity. The sitting room was sparsely furnished, with faded and wobbling furniture. There was never a penny—or a moment—to spare in this home. Diana worked as governess for a strict mistress, teaching her spoiled daughters, and Mama took in whatever spare work she could find, be it mending, washing, or cleaning. For a moment, Nell's mind dashed back to another time, when Papa had been alive, when they'd lived in the vicarage in comfort and peace. Now they had neither of those.

"You'd better go out." Mama went to the door. "No use keeping the poor driver waiting in the cold."

Nell took up her bag again and followed Mama, stepping out into the brisk afternoon air. After kissing her mother and Diana, she approached the coach hesitantly.

"Good day, Miss Addington," the coachman said, opening the door for her.

"Good day," she stammered. "Pardon me, sir, but do you know why Mr. Hammond sent you?"

The coachman shook his head. "I couldn't say, miss. I only do as I'm told."

She nodded and allowed him to take her bag and place it inside before handing her up. She sank back against the cushioned seat as the carriage started off, her thoughts spinning.

Mr. Hammond was just being kind. There was nothing more to it.

But the mixture of warmth and anticipation inside her whispered of possibilities she had yet to admit to herself.

CHAPTER FIVE

Nell half-expected Mr. Hammond to greet her at the front door, as he had Miss Fowler the week before. But instead she was met by the footman, and then Alice's maid whisked her upstairs without Nell catching so much as a glimpse of Mr. Hammond. She pushed back her disappointment. She had come for Alice, after all.

"Good afternoon, Alice," she said brightly after the maid showed her into Alice's bedroom.

Alice looked up from where she sat by the window, dressed in a simple black gown. Heavens, Nell would be glad indeed when they could be rid of all the black and gray. They did Alice no favors.

"Hello." Alice stood to greet her, the slightest smile pulling at her lips.

Nell had never been one to waste time on pleasantries, and she doubted Alice particularly enjoyed them either, so she went straight to business.

"I am eager to see what you think of this," she said, setting her portmanteau on the table. "I cannot deny that I spent a bit more time than necessary on this pattern. I wanted it to be exactly right for you."

"You have me curious, to be sure," Alice said, moving closer. "I thought this was just the simple dress made of linen."

"Oh, it is," Nell said. "But this is where the true beauty of a dress comes from, the lines and cut of the pattern. Frills and lace can only do so much. It is the shape of a dress that truly complements a woman."

She was entirely correct. During the whole of the fitting, Alice's eyes continually strayed to her image in the mirror. Nell could hardly blame her; the plain cream of the linen fabric was already a vast improvement over the black, not to mention the style was much more fashionable than the dresses she'd worn before in Nell's presence.

"Miss Wittingham would never have liked this dress," Alice said a bit mischievously.

"Is that your governess?" Nell asked, pulling the bodice flat against Alice's stays, determine to get the best possible fit.

"Not anymore, and quite thankfully. She was rather horrid, reporting every one of my failings to Father."

Nell couldn't contain her curiosity. "What happened to her?"

"Jacob dismissed her." Alice's voice grew quiet. "It was the first thing he did when he arrived after the burial."

A question had been lurking in Nell's mind since her last visit, but she'd hardly thought to find an opportunity to ask it. "Why was it your father and brother did not get along?"

Alice sighed, looking away from the mirror to the window. "It was rather complicated, but it had more to do with their natures than anything else. Father was—" Her voice cut out, and she shook her head. "Father was not a good man."

Nell's heart ached, and she set down her box of pins, stepping forward to take Alice's hand.

"They disagreed on everything," she went on quietly. "Father oversaw his tenants and servants without any shred of kindness, and he insisted Jacob do the same. In the end, Jacob decided he could no longer live in the same house, live under Father's rules. He went to London to stay with our mother's brother."

"He left you?" Nell could not stop her question. She could not imagine kind Mr. Hammond abandoning his sister to a cold and cruel father.

But Alice shook her head. "Do not think badly of him for it. I was but twelve years old at the time. He had his own life to live. And he was always very good about writing to me and sending little gifts." She squeezed Nell's hand. "I am glad he came back. I missed him."

"You are lucky to have such a brother." Nell loved her sisters but had often wondered what it would be like to have a brother. Certainly their lives would be much different, with a man to help support their family after Papa's death.

"I am lucky," Alice said. "Though you mustn't tell him that, or I shall never hear the end of it."

Nell laughed, and the somberness of the conversation fled. They spent the rest of the fitting speaking on lighter topics, and the afternoon passed far more quickly than even their first meeting together. Alice still spoke slowly and quietly, but the more time they spent together, the easier it was to understand her nature and simply allow her to talk as she wished.

"That is that," Nell finally said as she packed away her pins and pattern. "I am terribly pleased at how well it is looking already."

"I admit I am anticipating seeing it completed," Alice said, fixing a stray hair in the mirror. "You've captured my imagination quite thoroughly."

"It will be even better in reality. I promise."

"I shall hold you to it." Alice turned with an eyebrow lifted. "I am hoping to wear it to our Christmas Eve dinner."

Nell crinkled her brow. "I thought you did not celebrate Christmas."

"*Father* did not," Alice corrected. "But apparently Jacob is quite keen to start our own traditions. He wants to organize a dinner with our friends, such as they are."

Mr. Hammond wished to celebrate Christmas? Nell's thoughts went back to their conversation in the entry, when they had been interrupted by Miss Fowler. Was that what he had wanted her opinion on? It must have been.

"I think it sounds perfectly lovely," Nell said firmly. "You ought to spend the day with those you love."

Alice nodded, a flash of disappointment crossing her expression. But before Nell could question her, Alice cleared her throat and turned the subject. "Would you like some tea before you go? Jacob has hours yet before he'll be finished with his work."

Nell was already late in returning to the modiste's shop. Mrs. Shaw was expecting her back. But there was such loneliness in Alice's eyes that Nell could not bring herself to refuse. She glanced down at her pocket watch. Nearly four o'clock. She could spare a few minutes, though she would need to work later tonight to make progress on her projects.

And she could not deny that a small part of her—oh, why lie?—a very *large* part of her hoped Mr. Hammond would join them. Her heart quickened just at the thought of meeting him again, hearing his deep, teasing voice.

"Yes, thank you," she said. "Tea would be lovely."

* * *

Jacob had returned from his appointment an hour ago. But instead of going to his study, where he had a stack of letters to return, he found himself in the library, staring at a book. He had yet to read a word and could not have told anyone the title; in truth, he was only in the library at all because it was the closest room to the stairs. Considering how very quiet his house was, it would be nearly impossible for anyone to descend without his hearing it.

He glanced at the clock on the mantel above the fireplace. He knew from his coachman that Miss Addington had arrived two hours earlier. How long did a fitting generally take? Far too long, by his estimation.

Finally, he heard voices and footsteps on the stairs. He recognized Alice's higher tones and Miss Addington's mild alto. His stomach lurched, and he set his book down, going to the door he'd left propped open. But instead of passing him and continuing to the front door, the two women went down the hallway, away from him. Jacob furrowed his brow. Where were they going? Clearly they had no idea they'd just foiled his brilliant plan of asking Miss Addington to stay for dinner.

He stepped into the hallway. Laughter echoed back down the hallway, and he followed it as he had a week ago, when Miss Addington had first visited. The parlor door was ajar, and this time he did not stop to eavesdrop. He knocked and stepped inside. Alice and Miss Addington sat near the fire, and at his entrance, Miss Addington leapt to her feet and curtsied as he came farther into the room.

"Good day, Alice, Miss Addington," he said, offering a bow in return. "How went the fitting?"

"Very well." That delightful pinkness climbed Miss Addington's face, bringing out the lovely shape of her cheeks. "Alice makes for an excellent subject."

Alice had remained seated at his entrance. "That is certainly not true. The most that can be said for me is that I did not move too terribly much and cause Nell to stab herself with pins."

Jacob took the armchair beside Alice's, wishing there was an empty seat beside the one Miss Addington returned to.

"Hush." Miss Addington—Nell—arranged her skirts about her ankles. "You looked lovely. And you will look even more lovely in the finished gown."

Alice gave a small shake of her head as if protesting the compliment, then turned to Jacob. "I've just rung for tea, if you'd care to join us."

"I would be glad to," he said, trying to focus on his sister and not the woman across from him. Although, that might have been a mistake as well.

Alice was staring at him oddly, likely because he was acting very oddly. He rarely left his study before dinner, consumed as he was in the business of running Oakhurst Park, and here he was, interrupting their tea.

He cleared his throat and glanced back at Nell. "I am glad the fitting went well."

Now it was her turn to give him a bewildered look, and rightfully so. They'd already discussed the fitting. Blast, he was making a mess of this. It was not as though he'd never talked to a woman before.

Just never a woman quite like Nell Addington.

"Yes, it went well," she said, speaking slowly, no doubt because she thought him dimwitted. "I imagine we'll be ready for a final fitting within a week."

Even though the conversation was slow as molasses, the thought that she would be returning again gave a lift to his heart.

"Mr. Hammond," Nell said before he could say anything else senseless, "I wished to thank you for sending the coach this afternoon. That was very thoughtful of you."

Alice raised one eyebrow, he saw from the corner of his vision.

"You needn't thank me," he said. "It is far too cold for anyone to be walking that distance."

Nell shook her head. "I should like to thank you just the same. Though I am certain my mother and sisters will be bursting with questions when I return tonight."

"As will I," Alice murmured from beside him, thankfully too quietly for Nell to hear.

He ignored her. "You mentioned before that your elder sister is married now. And you've a nephew?"

"I do indeed," she said with a smile. "He is two years old and something of a menace, if Edith is to be believed."

Jacob grinned, leaning forward. "My uncle in London has several young sons, so I do not find such a claim difficult to accept."

Alice gave a short laugh. "You needn't look to other boys as the example for that, Jacob. I cannot count the number of times you were in trouble as a child."

"Me?" Jacob shook his head. "You must have me confused with another brother. I was the picture of obedience."

Nell raised an eyebrow. "Oh, indeed? Never a teasing word or mischievous prank from you?"

"Never," he said.

"And what about that occasion you secreted a toad into services?"

She remembered that? He could not have been older than twelve at the time; he barely remembered it himself. His lips twitched, though he kept his expression serious.

"A toad?" he repeated. "I recall no such event."

Nell leaned forward. "Truly? I remember quite clearly. It escaped from your pocket and made quite the fuss leaping about the church. People were climbing up on their pews as if the poor toad was a plague sent from heaven."

He raised his chin, as if just remembering. "Ah yes, that does strike a memory. If I recall, your father had to duck behind the altar to hide his laughing."

"And old Mrs. Wilkins nearly fainted at the fright." Nell was grinning. "Although, I thought it the most exciting Sunday I'd ever had."

He had but a dim memory of her then, the quiet middle daughter of the vicar, but he could well imagine her laughing eyes and delighted smile. "I suppose I was no saint. But I am glad to have provided you with some excitement."

In truth, Jacob had played more than his share of pranks as a youth. Father had been so controlling, so callous, that Jacob had spent much of his childhood searching for ways to rebel against him.

Alice stood up beside him, and he jumped slightly. He'd almost forgotten his sister was there.

"I've just realized I forgot to ask for some of Cook's lemon tarts with our tea," she said. "Will you pardon me for a moment?"

She did not wait for a response, going to the door. As she stepped into the hallway, she cast a knowing look over her shoulder at Jacob, then disappeared around the corner.

Clearly he was not nearly as subtle as he thought, seeking the two women out as he had. Alice had seen through his charade in an instant. He glanced back at Nell. Her brow was furrowed at the empty hallway where Alice had disappeared.

He cleared his throat. "Alice is particularly fond of lemon tarts."

Nell turned to him, uncertainty written over her features. "Is she?"

"Very," he said emphatically.

She sighed. "I thought for a moment I had offended her somehow. We've talked a great deal, but she can be difficult to read, don't you think?"

"Yes, indeed," he agreed. Anything to keep her mind from that pointed look Alice had given him as she'd left. He cast about for a topic, but Nell spoke first.

"Alice mentioned the two of you are hosting a Christmas Eve dinner."

Jacob's leg was bouncing; he stopped, sitting forward in his seat a bit. "Er, yes, we are."

"I think that is wonderful. She seems happy at the prospect." She paused. "Well, happy for Alice, anyway. She does hold her emotions very closely. But I gathered she was looking forward to it."

"Yes, I think she is." Did Nell wonder why they had not invited her? There was no bitterness in her voice, no searching for an invitation as she spoke with quiet calmness.

Even though he had told Alice the night before that they should not invite Nell, that surely she wished to spend the day with her family, neighbors, and friends, he found his resolve quite vanished. Nell had that effect on him.

"Miss Addington," he said, and her name felt cumbersome on his tongue. He wished he could simply say *Nell*, but that would likely frighten her off. "If you have no previous commitments, we would be most glad to have you attend the dinner."

Nell straightened her back, her shoulders tight. "Please, Mr. Hammond, I hope you do not think I was begging an invitation by mentioning the dinner. It was only that Alice—"

He shook his head. "No, no, of course not. We had thought to invite you, but we worried that you might feel obligated to accept. I know Christmas is a special time for your family with your father gone."

"Oh." Her face softened. "It is very kind of you to consider that."

"And you are more than welcome to extend the invitation to your family, if you desire," he said quickly.

Her whole body seemed to brighten. "They would be delighted by an invitation, I am sure."

"It shall just be a small gathering. The Alfords have already accepted, and we have also invited Mr. Jameson and his family, and—"

Nell's face fell. His comment about the Fowlers died in his throat.

"What?" he asked, leaning forward. "What did I say?"

She blinked, as if just realizing he was there. "Oh, nothing. Nothing at all."

He did not believe that for a moment. "You are a terrible liar, Miss Addington. What is troubling you?"

Nell pressed her lips together. He waited, determined to hear what worried her.

"It is just my mother," she said softly. "She finds it difficult enough to attend church with Mr. Jameson in Papa's place. I'm afraid she and Mrs. Jameson do not see eye-to-eye on how the parish ought to be run. It would be terribly awkward for all involved to have them at a dinner together."

"I see." Jacob truly did not see at all, considering he did not know the Jamesons in the slightest. He forced a smile. "Well, I promise I shall not be offended if you decline. I shall only mope about for a day or two."

"Only a day or two? Perhaps I ought to be the one offended."

She still held her shoulders a bit stiffly, but he was glad she was willing to jest with him. "Oh, very well, a week, then. But not a day more."

"Very well." She bit back a smile. "I do wish to come. Perhaps I might be able to slip away from our family celebrations for a time."

His stomach performed quite the acrobatic feat at her words. She wanted to come.

"Alice would certainly be pleased," he found his mouth saying.

Though she kept a smile on her lips, a flash of disappointment crossed Nell's face. At least, he *thought* it was disappointment. Was it possible that she felt what he did between them, a current of attraction that caused his words to trip over themselves?

He leaned forward. "That is, I would be pleased to have you come. Truly."

Her gaze flicked away for a moment before returning to him, soft and sweet. "I shall make my best effort, then." There was a look in her eyes he could not quite name, but it filled him with a thrilling warmth, deep in the center of his chest.

"Good," he said, and then he could not think of what else to say. Did all men lose their heads near a pretty woman, or just him?

Thankfully, a maid appeared at the door at that moment, carrying their tea. As the lemon tarts were still missing, Jacob could only assume Alice continued to carry on the pretense that she had set off in search of them. He found he did not mind; even as slow-witted as he was around Nell, he was loath to give up a single moment of their time together.

They fell into easy conversation as they sipped their tea, discussing his time in London with his uncle and more of her family and her life in town.

They laughed together over stories of her nephew's naughtiness, and they shared news of old acquaintances from their youth.

A half-hour passed before Nell noticed the clock on the mantel and gave a little jolt. "Oh dear," she said, setting down her tea. "I meant to spend only a few minutes. I must be getting back to the shop. Mrs. Shaw will be—"

Her voice broke off, and her face flushed red. Her employment at the modiste shop had not come up in their conversation. Was she embarrassed by her position there? Did she think he cared one whit that she worked for a living? Since he was a child, watching how his father had treated others—how he'd cared only for wealth, status, and power—Jacob had refused to allow such things to have importance in his own life. Nell could have been a pauper or a princess and he would have liked her all the same.

"I am sorry I kept you so long," he said. "Please, let me send for the coach again." She shook her head, but he held up a hand. "I insist. It's growing late, and I'll not have you walking home in the dark on my account."

Her blush deepened. "Thank you," she said. "I would be grateful."

He stood and offered her his hand. She took it, and his pulse quickened at the feel of her hand in his, small and warm. He helped her to her feet and resisted the urge pull her closer. He cleared his throat, releasing her hand and stepping away.

"Thank you for the tea," she said in a soft voice before she turned away, leaving the faintest aroma in the air, a light, lively scent that reminded him of summer and sunshine.

"You are welcome," he managed.

Nell went to her bag, abandoned alongside the sofa. "You'll pass on my goodbye to Alice, won't you? I can't imagine where she's gone off to."

Jacob was not certain how Nell had not seen straight through Alice's weak excuse, but he was not eager to question it. "Of course. You needn't worry over her. Let us get you on your way."

"Oh, are you leaving, Miss Addington?" Alice's soft voice came from behind, and the two of them turned to see her standing in the doorway.

"Yes," Nell said. "I'm needed at the shop, I'm afraid."

Alice furrowed her brow. "And what of the snow?"

"The snow?" Nell echoed.

Alice only gestured behind them. Jacob and Nell turned as one to the large window that overlooked the gardens. Jacob's mouth parted. A blur of snowflakes twirled past the window, the light dimmed by the thick clouds and the coming evening. He stepped closer, examining the ground. More than an inch of snow already and increasing by the second. The wind blew the snow against the window in a fury, and cold leached through the window.

"I cannot believe you hadn't noticed," Alice said, watching him most carefully. "Whatever were you speaking about?"

Jacob did not trust himself to look at Nell, certain her face would be as red as his. He ignored Alice's question. "Why did you not come sooner? We might have hurried a coach for Miss Addington."

Alice cleared her throat. "I was in the kitchens and noticed only a few minutes ago."

He did not believe her for a second, but what could he say? He glanced out the window again. He couldn't in good conscience send Nell out in such weather, not to mention his coachmen and horses. But would Mrs. Shaw be angry with her?

He exhaled and turned to Nell. "I am sorry, but I do not think you should be out in this mess, especially as it will be dark soon."

She bit her lip. "Oh."

Alice stepped forward. "We are more than happy to have you spend the night. I shall tell the housekeeper to prepare a guest room for you."

Nell's eyes widened, traveling back and forth between Alice and Jacob. "Oh no, I could not presume that of you. I can take a spare servant's room."

"You certainly will not." Jacob spoke before he'd even formed the thought. But the idea of Nell in a cramped, cold bedroom was ridiculous. "We've more bedrooms than we know what do with. There's no need to banish yourself to the attic."

"None at all," Alice said firmly.

Nell opened her mouth as though she meant to argue again but then sighed. "I am grateful for your hospitality," she said. "I only hope my mother will not worry overmuch."

"I am certain she will understand you could not return in the midst of a snowstorm." Jacob had to work to keep his voice even, to stop a wide grin from stealing over his face. This was working out much better than he'd planned. He would have an entire evening with Nell, and perhaps even tomorrow, weather willing.

He'd never much cared for snow, but now he found himself wishing it would never stop.

CHAPTER SIX

Nɛʟʟ ᴡᴏᴋᴇ ᴛʜᴇ ɴᴇxᴛ ᴍᴏʀɴɪɴɢ with a start. She jolted up in bed, hands clutching the covers around her, blinking rapidly in the near dark. She could see only the barest shapes in her room—a desk by the window, a vanity near the door.

Oakhurst Park, she reminded herself. She was at Oakhurst Park.

She took a deep breath, calming the rush of anxiety that came from waking in an unfamiliar place. Except the anxiety had not come solely from her sudden awakening. No, she'd been dreaming, she was certain. Mrs. Shaw had been shouting at her for not finishing her work on time, dismissing her in front of the other seamstresses. Nell knew it hadn't actually happened, yet that did not calm her much. Because it *could* happen. If she had just left yesterday when she should have, instead of fooling about with tea and flirtations with Jacob Hammond, she would be home even now, readying herself for work.

Nell threw off her covers, gritting her teeth against the sudden chill, and padded to the window. She pulled aside the curtains and groaned at the sight of snow still falling. The wind had ceased its frenzy, but there would be no chance of returning home anytime soon.

Mrs. Shaw had to understand that. She had to realize that Nell could not control the weather, that she could not walk the four miles to town in a blizzard. Nell took a steadying breath and dropped the curtain, hurrying back to her bed and burrowing into the covers.

If she was being perfectly honest with herself, Nell was torn between dismay and excitement. Because if Nell had left yesterday afternoon, she never would have been able to spend such a wonderful evening with Jacob and Alice. They'd played card games and laughed late into the night, toasting cheese and bread over the fire in the drawing room. Jacob's eyes had been on her continually, and even now her face warmed at the remembrance of the firelight flickering across his handsome features.

Nell covered her face with her hands. She could not be imagining it, could she? Was she so desperate that she was inventing a connection between them that was not there?

But she could not deny what she felt when she was near Jacob, the constant awareness of him, the thrill that ran across her skin when he grinned at her. It was not so very impossible, was it? She was a gentleman's daughter, after all, even if she was in lowered circumstances at the moment. Perhaps she was not such a fool to dream of something more.

Though it was early yet, not quite six o'clock, Nell struggled to find sleep again, her body far too used to the long hours she often worked. She finally gave up her warm bed and dressed in her gown from yesterday. She spent a bit more time on her hair than normal, glad she had asked Alice to borrow some curling papers. At least she would have proper curls.

Once dressed and ready, she faced her room, which was gradually growing lighter as the sun rose behind the thick clouds and flurries. Jacob and Alice would likely not be awake for hours yet.

Nell glanced out the window. The snow still fell, but in a merry sort of way, not like the fierceness of last night. She so loved the first snow of winter. A walk in the snow, bright and cold, would feel wondrously invigorating. She threw on her thick woolen cloak and her winter gloves, grateful she had dressed warmly yesterday in anticipation of her walk. Then she slipped from her room and descended the stairs.

She found the garden door and stepped out into the snow, her feet sinking into nearly a foot of it. Raising her hood to shield her hair, she inhaled deeply, the crisp, clean smell of the snow striking deep into her lungs. Oh, but she adored this time of year. It was her favorite, and not just because of Christmas. She had more memories than she could count of playing in the snow, just her and Papa. Edith had been too "grown up" for such adventures, and Diana had been but a baby. She and Papa had sledded, ice-skated, and built snowmen, and she'd loved it all.

A sharp pang ricocheted from her chest. Heavens, but it never seemed to get easier. Perhaps one day she might look back at her times of happiness with Papa and not feel such emptying pain.

She shook her head, determined to enjoy the sight before her. Though snow in town was still beautiful, it was usually destroyed all too soon by carriages and animals and people. At Oakhurst, there was no one to ruin the perfect lines of soft snow. Well, no one except for Nell. She started through the garden, slipping out the gate to reach the snow-covered lawn. She wanted the openness, the freedom of the wide space. She spun, tipping her head up to the clouds and closing her eyes as the snow fell against her face, melting in her lashes.

If only her life could be as carefree as a snowflake in winter, twirling about without worries or doubts.

Nell gave a sigh even as she fought a chuckle. She was certainly waxing dramatic this morning. She had worries, yes, but her trials made her stronger. She was glad she had changed, even if she was not glad for how the changes had come about.

Nell gathered a ball of snow and pressed it together tightly in her gloved hands. She drew back her arm and fired the snowball into a nearby tree, watching it burst into a white puff as it hit the bark.

"Excellent aim, Miss Addington."

Nell spun, her heart in her throat. Jacob walked toward her, his eyes bright and cheeks red in the cold. He was bundled up in his greatcoat and thick scarf, his boots nearly buried in the snow.

She somehow managed to find her voice. "Thank you. It's been years since I've had much practice. I am glad I've not lost all of my skills."

He came to stand beside her, clasping his gloved hands behind his back. "And who was the unfortunate target of all that practice?"

"Papa, mostly," she said. "Though I may have sometimes saved a few for Edith as she returned from town."

He shook his head. "An ambush on your own sister? I would not have thought you capable of such mischief. My toad in church does not seem nearly so terrible now, does it?"

She could not help her grin. "Ah, but Edith deserved a snowball much more than the poor old ladies of the congregation deserved a toad. She was ever so vain at the time, always fussing about her clothes and hair."

He laughed. "Oh yes, I've heard a snowball to the head is the best way to combat vanity."

"It certainly proved effective."

They stood smiling at each other, the snow falling softly around them. Nell's heart was beating too fast, galloping through her chest. A man had never looked at her like Jacob was now—as if he would never tire of looking at her.

She inhaled a deep breath and turned away, bending to scoop up another ball of snow. "I hadn't realized you were awake already."

"I couldn't sleep."

There was a question begging to be asked, but she could not bring herself to speak it aloud. Did his lack of sleep have anything to do with her?

She straightened, turning toward him again to see him also beginning to form a snowball, the flakes clinging to his woolen gloves. "I saw you from my window." He nodded to the house behind them. Nell glanced back, heat coursing through her at the thought of him watching her from his bedroom. Had she done anything particularly silly while outside? She hoped not.

"I cannot resist a new snowfall." She tossed her snowball at the tree again, missing it entirely.

"That was a poor effort," he teased. "Have I disrupted your focus?"

He had no idea just how much. "Of course not," she said. "I am bound to miss every now and again."

Jacob faced the tree, his snowball ready in his hand. He threw it with much more force than Nell could ever manage, and it exploded into the branches, sending a shower of snow below. He turned to her, grinning.

"I should be happy to instruct you on throwing a proper snowball," he said. "Since it has been so very long, you said."

"You needn't show off." Her scolding words were made harmless by her smile. "Or I might have to temper your vanity like I did Edith's."

He raised an eyebrow. "With your inconsistent aim, I am willing to take my chances."

She gave a laugh of protest and brushed the snow from her gloves. "Truthfully, I would not fare well against an armed and determined opponent. Edith was simply an easy target. I far prefer building snowmen."

Jacob formed another snowball, lobbing it lazily out over the field of snow. "I cannot say I've ever built a snowman."

Nell stared at him. "Truly? I am shocked at you, Mr. Hammond. A man of your taste never built a snowman?"

He gave a sharp laugh. "I was far too busy catching toads."

"Well, we shall simply have to fix such a travesty." Though the hem of her dress was wet, her feet already growing cold in her boots, Nell had no desire whatsoever to go inside. She bent and began forming a ball of snow, far larger than her previous snowballs. "Come help me."

"You are not simply luring me closer so as to take me by surprise with that enormous ball of snow, are you?"

She laughed. "That was not my intention, but you have certainly put the idea into my head now."

Jacob moved to stand beside her. "I think I shall risk it."

Nell could no longer feel the cold—not her wet stockings or the snow on her face or the dampness settling into her cloak. Just Jacob being beside her brought enough warmth inside to forget it all quite easily.

* * *

As Nell showed Jacob how to roll the ball through the powder, its size growing with every pass, he watched *her* more than her actions. Her cheeks and nose were a cheery pink, her smile quick and her eyes alive. The hood of her cloak had fallen around her shoulders, and though he could tell she had made an effort with her hair, her pins had already loosened, sending honey-colored spirals about her ears and neck.

His fingers itched to touch the curls, to see if they felt as soft as they looked. But he kept his hands at his side, pretending to pay close attention as she instructed him on building their snowman. He hardly needed the lesson; he'd built dozens of snowmen as a boy. But he did not intend to reveal that now, not when she was allowing him to stand so close, their arms brushing as they rolled the enormous ball of snow. They laughed as they slipped about, but eventually she declared it a suitable size.

They made two more balls, and though they were smaller than the first, it still required their combined strength to lift the snowman's midsection atop the first ball. Once the head was in place as well, Nell dug through the snow to find a few pebbles and used them to fashion eyes and a crooked smile.

"Finished," she said, stepping back to admire their work.

"Really?" Jacob crossed his arms and scrutinized the snowman. "I think the poor fellow looks rather cold."

"That tends to happen when one is made of snow."

He grinned. "Yes, but we can certainly make what efforts we can." He unwrapped the thick scarf from his neck and wound it about the snowman's neck. "There. Now he is finished."

"You did quite well for your first attempt," Nell said. "I think with a bit more practice, you could be quite the expert."

Jacob brushed the snow from his gloves. "I am hoping there will be many such snowmen in my future."

She brushed a curl back from her face. "Perhaps you can build them with your young cousins in London."

"Or perhaps I should have a few children of my own so I might teach them."

Nell swallowed. The tips of her ears were red, though from the cold or blushing he couldn't tell.

"My father always built them with me," she said, pulling her hood back up, regretfully, hiding those tempting curls of hers. "I should think your children will be lucky to have such memories as I do. They are some of my happiest."

She did not look particularly happy, grasping her elbows and staring absently across the snowy landscape. There was more pain inside her than she let on with her cheerful countenance and determination. Jacob very nearly reached for her, took her in his arms to comfort her. But they stood in full view of the house. It was hardly proper for them to be outside alone, let alone embracing.

"You must miss him very much," he offered instead.

Nell managed a smile. "I do." Her smile faded as she examined him. "And you? Do you miss your father?"

"No," he said immediately. "No, I do not."

She furrowed her brow. "Was he—" She stopped and shook her head. "I am sorry; I should not pry."

"I don't mind." Surprisingly, Jacob spoke the truth. He generally disliked talking of his father, but sharing with Nell was easy. Natural, even. "If you are wondering what he was like, you simply need to think of the worst rumor you heard about him, because it was very likely true."

She let out a slow breath. "I can think of some fairly terribly rumors."

"I do not doubt it." Jacob shook his head. Word of the late Mr. Hammond's ill-treatment of his servants and tenants had spread widely through town. He'd overworked and underpaid his staff, and the tenants struggled desperately to keep up with his constantly rising rent.

And that was only what others knew of his father. Jacob knew far too much more. He knew that even before she'd died in childbirth, his mother had been wan and distant, as if wasting away. Father had treated her the same way he'd treated his children, with unyielding control and belittlement. The way he treated everyone.

Five years ago, on a cool autumn day, Jacob had returned from a ride to find his father shouting at a maid, furious with her for rearranging his desk when she'd cleaned. Jacob had arrived just in time to see the man raise his hand to strike the maid, the poor girl cringing away. Jacob had caught his father's hand and forced him to stop. Father had turned his anger on Jacob, and the resulting barrage of shouts had ended in Jacob packing his things and leaving before the afternoon was out.

But he hardly wanted to tell Nell all that now. She did not deserve to have such images in her head. She had stayed quiet, watching him, waiting for him to continue. He took a steadying breath. "I did not want to leave Alice, but I could not stay a moment longer. Going to live with my uncle was the only path I could see to one day rescuing her from him. I worked for my uncle, saving my money for when she reached her majority and could choose to live with me. But then . . ."

"But then he died," she finished for him.

"Yes," he said. "Is it terrible of me to say I was only relieved upon receiving word of his death? Should a son not feel grief at his father's death, or regret at the very least?"

She stepped forward and touched his arm. "I think you are allowed to feel whatever you'd like. No one else may dictate your emotions. He was your father, yes, but you do not owe him anything you do not wish to give."

There was such gentleness in her clear eyes; he'd never felt as understood as he did at that moment. He hadn't ever discussed his emotions freely with anyone, not even Alice. The tension in his stomach—the guilt over his lack of grief—loosened. He hadn't even realized he'd held such feelings in check until he spoke of them.

"Thank you," he said softly. "I did not know I needed to hear those words."

She squeezed his arm, and he moved before he could stop himself, taking her hand in his.

"Truly, Nell," he said, savoring her name on his lips. "I am grateful. You have made a world of difference, for me and for Alice."

Her hand tightened around his own. "You are welcome," she whispered.

He wanted to kiss her, likely more than he'd ever wanted anything in his life. But he could not. As master of the house, with her being a guest, he was currently charged with her well-being. He could hardly take advantage of their situation in such a way. No, when he kissed Nell for the first time, it would be with no worries of impropriety. He would make sure of that.

He forced himself to drop her hand and step away. "Come," he said. "Let us get you into the house. I imagine you are half frozen."

She nodded, and they started back to the house, their steps muffled in the snow. Even as their conversation moved to other things, his mind was working, piecing together the puzzle of his feelings for Nell—and what they meant for his future.

CHAPTER SEVEN

THE SNOW CONTINUED ALL MORNING, and equal amounts of pleasure and fear fought within Nell. The longer the snow fell, the longer she could stay at Oakhurst—stay with Jacob. But the longer it fell, the longer she neglected her work at the shop. She already knew she would be terribly behind.

Jacob was an excellent distraction from her worries, at least. Their time in the snow had brought a warmth to her stomach that had yet to dissipate, likely because they hadn't spent a moment apart since then. After coming in from building their snowman, they'd dried off in front of the parlor fire, eventually joined by Alice when she awoke. She'd given them a knowing smile, and Nell began to think her search for lemon tarts the day before had not been entirely innocent.

"And how long have the two of you been awake?" Alice asked, seating herself beside Nell.

"Oh, not long." She took up her tea to avoid Alice's eyes. For some reason, she did not particularly want to share the memory of her morning with Jacob, even with Alice.

"Good," Alice said. "I should hate to miss anything."

"That is very unlike you," Jacob said. "You are generally keen to miss most things."

Alice gave a little laugh. "True enough. But not Nell's visit. It has been so lovely to have her here."

"I quite agree," Jacob said. She expected his usual teasing grin, but his eyes were serious, intent upon hers. "It would be a shame to waste a minute of it."

Nell set her tea down, her stomach swooping. Heavens, he should not be allowed to look at her like that. It was indecent, it was. Especially as she could not think of a thing to say in reply.

Thankfully, noise from the window distracted all of them. Jacob stood and strode to the window. "It's the Alfords."

"The Alfords?" Alice repeated, with a lilt of a question. Nell was just as confused. The snow was nearly a foot high now.

"They've a sleigh," Jacob said. "Rather small, but does the job."

A few moments later, a footman led the Alfords into the parlor, and the two parties exchanged greetings. Nell knew the kind older couple fairly well. They'd often invited her family for dinner parties and such when Papa had been alive. Since his death and the onset of Mrs. Alford's illness, they rarely hosted such events.

"Whatever are you doing here, Miss Addington?" Mr. Alford asked. "Not precisely the best weather to go out visiting, is it?"

Nell smiled. "I ought to ask the same of you. I was here yesterday for a fitting with Alice, and the snow came upon us suddenly. We are still waiting for a break in the storm for me to return home."

"Ah, and we had rather the opposite idea," Mrs. Alford said. "We have been so cooped up in the past weeks with the cold that we decided to take advantage of the snow." She smiled fondly at Nell, looking stronger than Nell had seen her in months. Mrs. Alford was often ill, with a weak constitution. To see her out and about was a very good thing.

"Miss Addington," Mr. Alford said, "if you are in need of transportation to town, I should be delighted to offer you a ride. Perhaps Mrs. Alford might stay and visit with Alice while I take you."

"Oh," Nell said, taken aback. Jacob frowned but said nothing. "Yes, thank you. That is most thoughtful of you to offer."

"We can be off as soon as you'd like." He smiled kindly, reminding her of her father for the briefest of moments. "I'm certain your mother is worried over you."

"Of course," she said. "I'll gather my things. Thank you again."

There was nothing for it but to go upstairs to her room to retrieve her portmanteau from her wardrobe and her drying cloak and gloves from before the fire. She was grateful for Mr. Alford's offer, truly she was. But she could not help her disappointment at leaving Oakhurst.

She returned to the parlor, going first to Alice and giving her a small embrace. "I am grateful for you putting up with me for the last two days."

"Do not be ridiculous," Alice said as she pulled away. "I quite enjoyed it." She lowered her voice as she glanced at Jacob. "I daresay we both needed a bit of company. Oakhurst has been lonely as of late."

Alice's voice was not teasing like earlier. She seemed to mean her words quite seriously. Though Nell could understand why Alice would be lonely, with her reserved nature, she had never thought of Jacob as lonely. But perhaps Alice was right. Jacob had left another life in London to return to his childhood home. He'd left friends and family there. A sharp pain pricked her heart. Had he left a woman there?

She shook her head. She should not torment herself with such thoughts. She gave Alice a last smile before turning to Jacob.

"Thank you for your hospitality, Mr. Hammond. I am glad not to have spent the night buried in snow."

"No, we could not have that." He smiled. "We are happy to have been of service."

She wanted to say so much more, but the Alfords and Alice stood watching, so she offered only a curtsy and turned to Mr. Alford.

"Ready, then?" he said brightly.

Alice took Mrs. Alford's arm, leading her to the couch by the fireplace, and Jacob moved after them. As Nell followed Mr. Alford to the parlor door, she allowed her head to turn back to catch a last glimpse of Jacob.

He had stopped beside an armchair, one hand on the wooden frame, and his eyes lingered on Nell. She smiled and gave a little wave, which he returned. And then she turned and stepped out into the snow, already wishing she was back inside the warm parlor with Jacob and Alice.

* * *

Jacob pulled his scarf more tightly around his neck to guard against the chill that worked its way through to his skin. The mid-December air held a bitter cold, which normally would not bother him. But as he'd been pacing up and down the main road of town for the last hour, waiting for a glimpse of Nell, he was rather more susceptible to the weather than normal. He could only hope the townsfolk had not noticed him shivering away as he stole glances at Mrs. Shaw's shop.

But his patience and near-frozen fingers were finally rewarded. Just as the sun dropped to touch the edge of the trees on the horizon, the shop door opened and Nell stepped out, bundled up in her thick cloak and gloves. Though it had been only two days since Jacob had seen her, his wind-chapped cheeks took on a new warmth, as if the sun had suddenly broken through the dense gray clouds overhead.

Two days had been far too long.

Nell fiddled with her reticule as she started up the road, thankfully walking in his direction. He preferred not to chase her down the length of the street, though he certainly would have if she'd chosen to walk the other way.

He straightened his hat as she drew closer, wishing he had ridden his horse instead of walking to town. At least then he would have reins to occupy his hands. But he hadn't wanted to bother with a horse, not when he had such hopeful plans.

When Nell finally looked up and spotted him, she came to a jolting halt.

"Mr. Hammond," she sputtered, her cheeks red, though that certainly could have been an effect of the cold and not his unexpected appearance. But he flattered himself that perhaps his presence played a part.

"Miss Addington, what a surprise to see you again so soon." He gave a low bow, and she curtsied in return.

"And you as well," she replied, a bit breathlessly he thought. Or perhaps his desperate imagination had invented that detail as well.

"Where are you off to?" he asked. "I just finished an errand myself."

"Oh." Her smile faded, and her hands moved with quick, jerky motions as they brushed back a lock of hair and tugged straight her skirts. She was dressed warmly enough, but her gray dress and sturdy bonnet were far plainer than what she had worn when she'd visited Oakhurst Park. "I am just leaving—" She coughed. "That is, I am walking home."

Was she still ashamed about her work at the shop? He thought he'd made it clear before that he could not care less that she worked for a living. But it seemed she still cared, since she was plainly ill at ease about being ambushed at the end of her workday. Jacob could not deny that she seemed tired, her shoulders drawn and shadows lingering beneath her eyes.

"I happen to be heading in that exact direction," he said, "if I may be so bold as to trespass on your evening."

She furrowed her brow. "You happen to be walking to the north edge of town near the church?"

Jacob somehow managed to keep an unconcerned expression on his face. "I am indeed."

Her cheek twitched. "Then, I would be glad for your company." She did not question him further, and she fell into step beside him as they started off. "And what errand has brought you to town today?"

He had prepared for such a question. "I came to see Mr. Littleman. My pocket watch has refused to keep proper time for the last week."

"How very impolite of it," she said. "And was the problem solved to your satisfaction?"

"He says it should be simple enough to fix."

"Mr. Littleman said that, did he?" Nell clasped her hands behind her back. "And how did he manage that when he's gone off to visit his sister in Lyme for the next week?"

Devil take it. And he thought he'd been quite sly. Nell tilted her head to one side with an innocent expression.

He shook his head slowly even as he fought a grin. "All right then, you've found me out. And since surely dishonesty is as serious a sin as vanity, I expect I deserve a snowball to the head."

She shook her head, fixing him with a stern expression. "I'm afraid there is a far worse punishment for inventing falsehoods."

"And that is?"

"Telling me why you did so, of course."

She was right. That was much worse than a snowball. He had some pride, after all. Admitting he had waited about for her in the cold for a good portion of the afternoon was rather embarrassing. He'd thought to keep that fact to himself for a great deal longer. Likely forever, if he'd had his way.

And yet, a large part of him itched to know what she would say if she knew his thoughts. She had asked, after all.

"All right, then," he said. "Here you have it. I came to town with the sole purpose of waiting for you outside the shop."

Her steps faltered before she hurried to catch him again. "Is this about Alice's dress? I've only just started it. You ought to have come in—"

"I didn't come about Alice's dress," he interrupted. "I simply wanted to see you."

"Oh." And then she finally seemed to realize the true meaning of his words. "*Oh.*"

When she said nothing for a long minute—or was it an hour?—Jacob's thoughts dashed in the worst possible direction. He was hardly an expert in romance, after all. Surely he was supposed to be more subtle in his attentions. Instead he'd likely just frightened Nell off. Did she not feel what he did? His doubts clamored about in his head like race day at Newmarket. What if she had just been acting as a friend that day in the snow when he'd nearly kissed her? Perhaps she felt nothing toward him at all besides fondness and camaraderie.

He forced himself to steal a glance at her. A shy smile had captured her face, entirely relieving the burden of exhaustion she'd worn before. "I'm glad you came, then," she said softly.

A freeing breath escaped his lungs. He hadn't been wrong. At least, not entirely. But he was glad to accept this promising path instead of the outright rejection he'd been imagining not moments before.

"Although, I daresay you regret seeing me now." She again fussed with her hair. "I look a mess."

He very nearly took her shoulders and shook her for being so obtuse. But that was likely not the best course to follow when he was attempting to court her. "Not for a minute," he said instead. "You are as lovely as ever."

Her hand dropped from her hair. "Thank you," she finally said.

They walked in comfortable quiet as they passed the last of the shops in the main square of town. Other shoppers and townsfolk bustled around them, not seeming to pay them any mind.

"Miss Addington," he said slowly. "I hope you do not mind me asking or think me prying. But I have been thinking much on the subject and cannot resist my curiosity any longer. Your father was rather well-situated before his death, was he not? The last thing I wish to do is intrude, but—"

"But you are wondering why I've been forced to take up the position I have?" She spoke in an even tone, though it could not be an easy topic for her to discuss.

"Yes, I admit that is my question exactly." He did not press her. If she wished to change the topic, he would allow her, of course. But he hoped she would trust him, allow him into her confidence. He hoped he might help her, just as she had helped him come to terms with his father's death.

She sighed. "There is truthfully not much to the story. Papa was certainly well-compensated as vicar, and we lived a comfortable life. But he never saved as he should have. There was always one thing or another that needed his help, his money—a friend fallen on hard times or a widow left with young children. I loved my papa, but he was generous to a fault. None of us ever knew how little he had saved for us until it was too late." She blinked, her gloved hands tightening around fistfuls of her skirt. "He assumed he had more time to care for us, provide for us. He begged our forgiveness on his deathbed."

Jacob took her hand and slipped it through his arm, pulling her as close to his side as he dared. Would that he could do more for her, ease her aching heart.

"I don't blame him; I truly don't," she went on. "But it has been a difficult adjustment, I shan't lie. There is always some bill to be paid or a roof to repair. And working at the shop has been a trial in and of itself." She shook her head. "But I should not complain so. I hope you do not think me selfish. I know I have many blessings to be grateful for."

"I think you the furthest thing from selfish," he said gently. "And just because you recognize your blessings does not mean your trials hurt any less."

"I know you are right," she said, her voice unsteady, thick. "And yet I feel guilty for thinking I deserve anything more than what I already have."

For a moment he thought it had begun to rain. But no, that was a tear that wound down Nell's face, not a raindrop. The tear stopped at the corner of her mouth, and he pulled her to a stop. His hand moved before he could think, curving around her cheek and brushing away the wetness with his thumb.

"You are so much more than your position in life, Nell. You mustn't ever limit your happiness based on what you think you are worth."

She gave a watery smile, and his stomach took a sudden tumble, much like her bonnet had across his lawn that first day. Blast it all, but why did he keep putting himself in a position to kiss her when he clearly could not? A woman passed just as that thought crossed his mind, eying him shrewdly. He dropped his hand and tugged Nell gently as he moved forward again, their steps falling back into an easy cadence.

"Thank you, Jacob," she said. "I daresay we could all use a reminder of that every now and again."

They made to cross the road then, and a blast of chilly wind caught them as they stepped from the shelter of the buildings. Nell clamped a hand to her bonnet as they hurried across the street, and he could not help himself from leaning close to her ear. "There aren't any trees nearby, but I would hold tight to that bonnet all the same."

She laughed, relieving the solemnity of their conversation thus far. "I am lucky enough to be accompanied by a great rescuer of bonnets, so I am not overly worried."

As they continued on, the rest of their conversation contained a great deal more laughter, thankfully. Jacob would much rather make Nell laugh than cry, though he could never regret the things she had shared with him. He could not deny that the more he came to know her, the more determined he became. Nell was a light, a lantern in a storm. And he would do all he could to help that light burn brighter.

CHAPTER EIGHT

NELL COULD HARDLY SLEEP THAT night, memories of her evening with Jacob dancing through her mind. After he had accompanied her to her family's little house near the church, she'd invited him inside for tea, half hoping he would refuse. After all, she had no better seat to offer him than the worn and faded sofa, and tea served from a chipped cup.

But he'd accepted without hesitation, and she'd had no choice but to lead him inside and introduce him to Mama and Diana. They'd welcomed him warmly even as they'd sent Nell a dozen sly glances. And though Jacob had spent only a short half hour in their little sitting room, he had won over her family as certainly as he had won over her heart.

Because she was a fool if she could not admit she had fallen completely in love with the man. It was his own fault, really, for being so wonderful. He lifted her burdens without even seeming to be aware that he did it, so naturally kind and thoughtful was he.

Her blissful thoughts carried her throughout the next few days, making even her long hours at the shop bearable. Mrs. Shaw had not been particularly pleased with Nell after her absence during the snowstorm. The woman had assigned her the worst, most tedious tasks, which was saying quite a lot considering how tedious her profession was as a whole. Nell cut and measured and stitched from dawn until long after the sun had set, her eyes straining in the candlelight to see her stitches.

Mrs. Shaw ended her punishment only a few days before Christmas, finally allowing Nell to continue her work on Alice's dress. The modiste knew very well that even despite the delay, Nell would have it finished by the promised date, even if it meant long days and even longer nights. Nell worked as quickly as she could without compromising quality. The red silk she and

Alice had selected was difficult to work with, slippery as an eel. But the fabric was smooth and soft, with a beautiful sheen no matter the lighting. It would look exquisite, she had no doubt. She carefully cut the pieces according to the pattern she'd created, making adjustments for the changes she'd made at Alice's fitting. The dress came together beautifully: a simple bodice with ruffled sleeves, with a more ornate skirt of embroidered layers. She grinned as she worked, already knowing how stunning it would look on Alice and anticipating Jacob's approval and pride in seeing her skill. Or at least, that is what she imagined during those long minutes and hours and days of endless sewing.

Two days before Christmas, Nell breathed a sigh of relief. It was finished. All that needed to be done was the final fitting. Her heart beat wildly inside her as she penned a note to Alice, asking her for an appointment the next day, Christmas Eve. She could be to Oakhurst Park in the morning and finish the final alterations that afternoon, just in time for the Hammonds' Christmas Eve dinner.

And she could see Jacob, if she was very lucky.

She sent her note with the messenger boy the shop employed and waited for a response. But none came, and she left the shop late that night wondering if the boy had gotten lost or if Alice had fallen ill. But wouldn't she have still responded to the note if she were ill? Wouldn't Jacob?

Nell had the sneaking suspicion that sleep would not come easily that night.

* * *

Jacob's pulse thrummed within him as the coach neared the modiste's shop. Just knowing how close Nell was sent a burst of energy to his limbs, and he tapped his foot restlessly.

"Nervous, are we?" Alice said from beside him, one corner of her lips curving upward.

He forced his leg to still. "Nervous for what?"

She gave a short laugh. "You must think me rather dim not to have realized that you've set your cap for Nell."

He chuckled. "No, not dim. I'd just hoped you were less observant than usual."

"You've no luck there. You are far too obvious." She examined him closer. "You like her very much, don't you?"

He cleared his throat and straightened his cravat, though he'd already done it a dozen times since entering the coach. "I do; I admit it freely."

She gave a nod. "Good. I would hate for you to marry anyone I could not stand. As it is, I could not be more pleased."

"Married?" Now his face rebelled against him, pricking with heat. "You've already married me off, have you?"

"Haven't *you?*" she asked with a raised eyebrow.

He stared out the window, avoiding her gaze. Because she was right. He had already begun to imagine the life he and Nell might have together—a life of laughter and joy, understanding and contentment. He'd missed her from the moment he'd left the warmth of her home a few days ago.

But he had barely begun to formulate a plan for their future, let alone speak of that plan to Alice. He changed the subject. "Are *you* not nervous?" he asked her. "I cannot remember the last time you came into town."

Alice's smile faded, and she swallowed. "I am nervous," she said quietly. "I hate being gawked at."

"Nell will be there," he said. "She will help you. This is a good thing for you, Alice."

She sighed. "I know. I cannot stay at Oakhurst forever, no matter how I might wish to."

The coach slowed to a stop, and Jacob helped Alice down the step. He barely noticed the passing townsfolk, focused as he was on the fact that he would be seeing Nell in just a few seconds. Alice took his arm, and he led her into the shop.

He spotted Nell across the room, helping another customer. She did not immediately see them, involved as she was in her conversation, so he had a few precious seconds to simply observe her. Her honey-colored curls were pinned firmly atop her head, unlike the day they had built the snowman and they had teased about her neck. Her hands moved quite a bit as she spoke to the other woman, expressive and alive, just like their owner.

The older lady tending the counter—Jacob vaguely recognized her as a Mrs. Shaw, the proprietress—stepped forward to greet them.

"Mr. Hammond," she exclaimed. "Miss Hammond. What a pleasure."

Jacob managed a nod, watching Nell in the corner. She still had not noticed them.

Alice took a steadying breath and spoke in a quiet voice. "I've come for my fitting. Miss Addington said the dress was ready."

Jacob gave Alice an encouraging nod. She offered a weak smile.

"Oh." Mrs. Shaw's face tightened. "Yes, I believe so." She turned away. "Miss Addington, Miss Hammond has arrived for her fitting."

Nell at last noticed them; her mouth parted, and she very nearly dropped the fashion plate she was holding. Her eyes flicked to Alice but were drawn back to Jacob's, likely because he was staring at her unabashedly.

"Mr. Hammond," she stammered. "Miss Hammond." She cleared her throat and set down the fashion plate. "I will be with you shortly."

Mrs. Shaw joined her and the other customer, presumably to step in. Nell spoke with them for another minute before turning and coming to join him and Alice. He grinned, and she blushed furiously. Perhaps it was wrong to enjoy her blush so much, but he could not seem to care.

"Whatever are you doing here?" she asked. "When you did not respond to my note, I feared something was wrong."

Alice straightened her shoulders. "I thought to brave town for once, and we meant to surprise you."

Jacob raised an eyebrow. "Clearly we are not adept at surprises if we caused you undue worry. I am sorry; we ought to have told you we were coming."

"You needn't apologize. I am glad to see you both." She turned to Alice. "The fitting should not take terribly long, so you needn't fear. And I am anticipating only a few alterations after this fitting, so it should be finished in time for the dinner tonight."

"Thank you," Alice said softly.

Nell waved another seamstress over, instructing her to take Alice back to the fitting room. When Alice had vanished into the back room, Nell turned to Jacob.

"And how did you convince her to come?" she asked suspiciously, though not without humor.

He gave a short laugh. She knew Alice so well. "In truth, it was not terribly difficult. I think she has begun to realize that staying at Oakhurst forever is not as tempting a future as she'd once imagined. I owe that to you."

"And how is that?"

He smiled. "You've helped her realize there is a world outside the estate and that she ought to be a part of it."

She shook her head. "I am certain she already knew that. She simply needed a reminder."

"I am grateful all the same." He tried to ensure Nell knew how much he meant his words. "Truly."

She did not look away, her gaze caught in his. His heart was bounding, skipping in his chest.

"Miss Addington!" Mrs. Shaw's sharp voice called across the room. "Miss Hammond is waiting."

Nell tore her eyes from his. "Excuse me," she stammered. She stepped away, but he caught her arm, not caring in the least what Mrs. Shaw—or anyone else, for that matter—thought.

"I meant to ask the other night at tea," he said. "I don't think I ever had an answer from you. Will you come to the dinner tonight?" he asked. "Please say you will."

She nodded, leaning forward for the briefest of moments. "Of course I will." And then she hurried away, disappearing into the back room. Jacob could only grin foolishly after her.

When he stepped onto the street a minute later, it was with a lift to his heart and a bounce to his step. Such was his distraction that he did not notice Miss Fowler until he had nearly walked right past her.

"Mr. Hammond," she called, claiming his attention. "How good to see you. Whatever are you doing here? Surely you are not in need of a new gown."

She gave a coquettish smile, as if her jest had been rather hilarious.

"No, no," he said. "I simply brought Alice for a fitting. Miss Addington is finishing her dress for dinner tonight."

"Indeed? Cutting it rather fine, isn't she?"

He raised an eyebrow. "I think she has done a remarkable job with the time given her. I only hope it does not delay her own arrival to the party."

Her mouth dropped. "Miss Addington is coming tonight?"

"Yes, of course."

Something dark appeared in Miss Fowler's expression, but it was gone in the next instant. "How wonderful," she said brightly. "I am very much looking forward to it."

Her voice was not quite right—a bit too high and false—but Jacob did not have the patience for her games. "I shall see you this evening, then. Good afternoon, Miss Fowler."

And he strode away, his mind already returning to the warmth in Nell's eyes and his anticipation for that night.

CHAPTER NINE

Nell gave a sigh of relief as she snipped the last thread from the red silk dress. She'd finished, and with a few hours to spare. She carefully wrapped Alice's dress in paper and tied it with a knot. She would deliver it herself, arriving early for the party in order to do so.

Well, that and to see Jacob. Because her fleeting conversation with him that morning had not been nearly enough. The thought of spending the whole evening with him made her toes curl in anticipation. Though she would miss spending the night with her family, they had not made one word of complaint when she'd explained her invitation a few nights before. In fact, after exchanging knowing smiles, Mama had volunteered to do her hair and Diana had fetched her new blue shawl, insisting that Nell borrow it for the party.

Which she ought to be preparing for right now. If she ran home, she would have just enough time to change before walking to Oakhurst. Well, assuming Jacob did not send the coach for her again. Which she was certain he would. Such details did not easily escape Jacob Hammond.

Voices sounded from the front of the shop. Nell frowned. Who on earth would be coming in so late on the afternoon of Christmas Eve? All of the other seamstresses had already gone home to spend the evening with their families.

"Nell!"

She sighed at the sound of Mrs. Shaw's voice. Heavens, did that woman know how to speak softly?

"Coming," she called. She tugged on the knot on her parcel once more, ensuring it was secure, and then carried it to the front room. Oh, she knew Alice would simply love the dress. She grinned in anticipation of seeing the girl's face when she put the gown on.

But her grin faded as she stepped into the front of the shop. Mrs. Shaw stood beside Miss Fowler, of all people. She was dressed in a lovely pelisse, deep green with a pleated waistline. That had been Nell's work of early September.

"Yes, Mrs. Shaw?" Nell's voice was hesitant. Something felt very odd about this.

Mrs. Shaw frowned. "You'll be staying late tonight, Nell. Miss Fowler has ripped her dress and must have it for Christmas tomorrow."

Nell's heart dropped into her stomach, twisting and aching inside her. "Tonight? But it is Christmas Eve."

"I am very well aware," she said sharply. "But considering how behind you have been on your work, you should be glad I am not dismissing you altogether."

Nell bit her tongue against the unfairness. She was only behind because of the snowstorm trapping her at Oakhurst, not because of any fault on her part. But Mrs. Shaw's face was hard, unyielding.

Miss Fowler stood watching her, her expression all innocence. "I am terribly sorry to spoil your evening," she said with false sincerity. "But I had my heart set on this gown for tomorrow." She handed Nell a bundle of fabric. "I know it shall take you but a minute to fix the tear. You have such a talent for this."

The only talent Nell had at the moment was not throwing Miss Fowler's gown back into her face. She was not a fool; she knew precisely what game Miss Fowler was playing. Nell had seen her and Jacob speaking outside the shop when he'd brought Alice to her fitting that morning. The horrid woman had flirted without restraint, though Jacob had seemed indifferent. But it was completely obvious now that Miss Fowler was determined to cause Nell to miss the dinner party at Oakhurst, all so she might have Jacob to herself.

Nell turned back to Mrs. Shaw. "I need to deliver this dress to Miss Hammond. I'm afraid I don't have the time to—"

"You'll have time for whatever I assign you." Mrs. Shaw's eyes narrowed. "I shall find someone else to deliver the gown."

"Oh, I should be glad to," Miss Fowler said brightly, as if just thinking of it. "I am heading to Oakhurst shortly, in fact. It would be no problem, I assure you."

Miss Fowler's plan worked perfectly. Nell was forced to hand over Alice's dress and could only watch with pain arching through her heart as the conniving minx left the shop, not glancing back even once.

"Tonight," Mrs. Shaw said, tugging on her gloves. "You'll finish that repair tonight, or you'll not have a position in the morning. Lock up when you are finished."

And she left without another word, the darkening evening swallowing the woman up.

* * *

Jacob would have been embarrassed by how obviously he was watching for Nell, but he could not quite bring himself to care. The Alfords had already arrived, and they exchanged amused glances every time he crossed to the window overlooking the front drive. Alice was still upstairs, waiting for Nell to bring her newly fitted gown.

Jacob was filled with a strange energy, unable to keep still. When Mr. Jameson arrived with his wife and children, he greeted them enthusiastically. The vicar was taken aback by the warm welcome; Jacob was sure the man was as confused as could be considering he had yet to attend services since his return. Although, perhaps the time had come for him to reconsider his avoidance of the church and its cemetery. A cold gravestone had no power over him, no claim on his happiness. Not any longer.

Not to mention attending services would be another way to see Nell every week.

When he heard another coach arriving outside, he could not hold himself back any longer. He left the others conversing in the drawing room and stepped into the entry, hoping it was the coach he'd sent to Nell's home for her. But the woman handing her things to the footman was not Nell. Miss Fowler turned at his footsteps, flashing him a charming smile. Her father, a quiet sort of man, climbed the stairs behind her.

"Good evening, Mr. Hammond," she said.

Jacob barely registered her words as he craned his head around her. The Fowlers' coach was the only one in sight. He sighed. Nell was surely on her way. He simply needed to be patient.

"Good evening, Mr. Fowler, Miss Fowler," he said, focusing back on his two guests. "I am so glad you could come."

Mr. Fowler murmured a short thank-you before slipping into the parlor, no doubt to find the solitude of a quiet corner. Jacob could not help but sympathize with the fellow; social events did not seem quite his cup of tea. He turned back to Miss Fowler, who had made no move to join her father, but instead waited in expectation.

He cleared his throat. "You look well tonight."

It was barely a compliment, but she beamed as if he'd lavishly bestowed praise upon her. "Thank you, sir."

He noticed a package in her hands. "And what have you brought with you?"

"Oh, this is just Alice's dress. Shall I take it up to her?"

"Alice's dress?" he echoed. "But where is Miss Addington? She promised to bring it herself."

Miss Fowler shook her head. "Oh, did she not tell you? She asked me to deliver this because she is unable to come tonight. Something to do with unfinished work, I believe." She lowered her voice. "Mrs. Shaw seemed very put out with her. I daresay she has been found wanting."

Jacob took in the details of Miss Fowler's face. Her pretty features were shadowed in the candlelight, her chin jutting upward. And even though the woman had been nothing but polite and charming to him and Alice, he knew at that moment that he could not believe a word she said, for anyone who knew Nell at all would never speak a word against her.

"Indeed." His voice held a sharp edge. "Well, I should not like to keep you from the party. Please, let me take the dress up to Alice. I'll return shortly."

She furrowed her brow but could apparently think of no argument against him. "All right," she said finally. "But do hurry back. I admit I am anxious for this lovely evening you've planned."

He did not bother with a response, already starting up the stairs, taking two at a time as he neared the top. Something was not right with Nell, and he was determined to discover what it was.

He strode to Alice's bedroom and knocked. At her "Come," he entered, finding her seated before her vanity, wearing her dressing gown, with her hair in an elaborate twist. Her maid backed away.

Alice swiveled on her chair, staring at him. "Jacob, whatever are you doing up here?" Her eyes traveled to his hands holding the package. "Where is Nell?"

"That is exactly the question," he growled. "Miss Fowler delivered your dress with some ridiculous story about Nell being forced to work tonight."

"What?" She stood abruptly. "You must go find her immediately."

He gave a tight grin. "That is precisely what I hoped you would say." His grin faded. "But, Alice, are you sure? I do not wish to abandon you to host this party alone. This was meant to be ours together, a new tradition."

She hesitated at that, pressing a hand to her stomach. But then she shook her head. "I can manage Miss Fowler for an evening. You must worry only about finding Nell."

He exhaled, his determination returning with renewed force. "Thank you, Alice. You're a wonder of a sister. Have I told you that lately?"

"Not nearly enough," she said as she came to take the package from his hands. "Now, go on. Nell is waiting."

Jacob flew back down the stairs and out the front door without even a glance into the drawing room. He was being terribly rude in abandoning his own party, but the Alfords would understand and the Jamesons would surely forgive him in time. He hardly cared what Miss Fowler thought of him.

As he ordered his horse to be saddled, he had only one thought.

Nell.

CHAPTER TEN

THE CANDLELIGHT FLICKERED, SHEDDING ONLY the barest light on Nell's work. She bent over her stitching, straining her eyes to see her needle against the shadows. Blast this dress. Blast Miss Fowler. The tiny rip that she had claimed would take Nell "a minute" to fix was in actuality a tear across the back of the skirt that had taken the better part of the last three hours to mend. And she still had another small hole to fix on the other side. What on earth had Miss Fowler done to the poor gown? And all to keep Nell from the Hammonds' party.

The party. Oh, how Nell wished she were there instead of alone at the wretched shop. It was cold, the fire lit only with a few coals, and she could hear the faint sounds of wassailing up and down the streets around her. Surely Mama and Diana were wondering where she was. Or had they thought she had already gone to the party? Had Jacob's coach arrived at the house, only to find her missing?

"Blast it all," she muttered. And then her vision blurred with tears— hot, frustrated tears. She should be with her family, or she should be with Jacob and Alice and the Alfords, having a pleasant dinner.

She pressed a hand to her head, attempting to collect herself. Moaning and griping would do nothing to help her situation, and neither would crying.

She took a steadying breath. Perhaps if she hurried, she might be able to join her family for the last merriment of the night. She bent once again over the dress.

A knock at the front door made her jump and nearly lose her needle. She sat still for a moment. Had Mrs. Shaw returned to ensure she was working? She set down the dress and took up her candle, hurrying to the door. A shadowed figure stood outside, hidden by the darkness.

She set down the candle and unlatched the door, pulling it open. As the figure stepped inside, the light of the candle illuminating his face, her mouth dropped.

"Jacob?" She fell back a step.

He closed the door behind him, keeping out the chill of the evening. Not that she noticed any cold; she was far too focused on the fact that Jacob Hammond stood before her in the shop for the second time that day.

"Good evening, Nell," he said in that gentle baritone of his. "You seem to be running a bit late tonight."

"I—yes, I am, I-I had to—" Her voice was misbehaving, and she stopped to clear her throat. What was he doing here? Should he not be hosting his dinner, Oakhurst bursting with warmth and laughter? "I have some work to finish. Mrs. Shaw . . . well, she—" She sighed. "I am sorry, but I do not think I shall be able to attend your party."

Jacob gave a wry grin. "I had thought as much, from what Miss Fowler said."

"Oh," Nell said a bit dumbly. "She delivered the dress, then, I assume. Is Alice pleased?"

He shook his head. "I could not tell you. I left nearly as soon as Miss Fowler arrived."

He'd left his own party. Why? To come see her? The thought was ridiculous, and yet here he stood before her, watching her with a piercing intensity that left her middle soft as butter.

"Why are you here, Jacob?" Her voice was but a whisper.

He tugged off his gloves, his eyes dancing in the candlelight. "I could not bear the thought of you trapped in this drafty shop, working your fingers to the bone on Christmas Eve. Truly, I cannot bear the thought of you doing it any day."

She shook her head. "There's nothing to be done, I'm afraid. Mrs. Shaw was perfectly clear that I am to finish mending Miss Fowler's dress tonight, or—"

"Miss *Fowler's* dress?" He stared at her, his voice indignant. "That is the work you are doing?"

"Well, yes."

His jaw tightened. "How dare she. I knew she was meddling, but I never imagined *she* had caused you to miss the party."

Nell sighed and rubbed her arms, the chilly night air seeping in through the windows. Her fire in the back room hadn't been much, but it was better than nothing. "Jacob, it hardly matters. I still must finish my work, and you must host your dinner. Please, go and enjoy your evening." She forced a smile. "I'm certain I will be able to join my family before too long. You needn't worry about me."

He peered at her, his brow furrowed. "I'm afraid it is far too late for that, Nell. All I seem to do is worry about you."

Her breath caught in her lungs as he stepped closer. His eyes raked over her face, and she was only vaguely able to regret that she was likely a mess from working all day. His words stole the rest of her attention.

"I worry that you are not cared for," he said, raising a hand to cup her cheek. "I worry that you are not happy." His thumb traced her cheekbone, and she closed her eyes, her heart nearly pounding out of her chest. His voice softened even further. "And I worry most of all that you are not loved as you should be, Nell. Because you deserve love and happiness and so much more."

She blinked her eyes open and stared up at him. Was he truly saying these words to her?

He took her hands and pulled her to him, bending his lips to hers and kissing her softly, gently. Nell trembled—from the cold and from the pure elation that coursed through her entire body. Her hands escaped from his and slowly wound around his neck, her mind a tangled mess of disbelief and joy. He slipped his arms around her and drew her closer, his lips insistent, his warmth intoxicating. Her heartbeat sounded in her ears, demanding to be heard.

When Jacob at last pulled away, leaning his forehead against hers, she managed to gulp in a few breaths of air.

"That was certainly worth missing the party for," he said mischievously.

She gave a breathy laugh and shook her head. "You are shameless. And I find I do not care in the slightest." She slid her hands down to his chest, feeling the beat of his heart through his waistcoat.

He pulled her tighter, his eyes growing somber. "If you'll have me, Nell Addington, I'd like nothing more than to spend the rest of my life loving you."

Her vision blurred; she was crying, tears spilling onto her cheeks even as an uncontrollable smile spread over her face. He *loved* her. Jacob loved her. She could not speak, her voice tied in knots as it was, but she managed a nod. Yes, she would have him. Of course she would.

He kissed her again, sending a thrill of heat through her center. But she pulled back, needing to say the words that fought to escape her. "I love you, Jacob Hammond. I think I may have loved you since I was a girl, only I never realized what it was that I felt."

He swallowed hard and raised her hand to his lips. "Then, I am luckier than I could ever have imagined."

She shivered at his touch. "You are cold," he said, releasing her and shrugging off his coat. She protested, but he did not listen as he draped his coat around her. It smelled of pine and snow.

"Come," he said, taking her hand. "We'll go to your family, tell them the good news. And Alice will be waiting to hear from me."

"We will shock them entirely," she said with a laugh. "I'm still having trouble believing it. What if I wake tomorrow, sewing in hand, and discover this has all been some wonderful dream?"

He shook his head, his eyes fixed on hers. "You need not ever come back to this shop. You need never sew another stitch in your life if you don't wish it."

"Oh, but I am so very good at it," she said with a raised eyebrow.

He grinned. "I have no doubt. Perhaps you might put those skills to use for Alice's future nephews and nieces."

She coughed, and heat flooded her face. He laughed. "There is that lovely blush I am so fond of."

He kissed her again, and she found she did not care about her red face or her cold hands or her messy hair.

She cared not at all.

EPILOGUE

Seven years later

"What of this one, Papa?" Edmund's young voice carried through the snow-laden trees, and Jacob turned to find the lad standing beside a fallen tree, its slim branches splayed beneath a layer of frost.

"Oh, I think we can find one a bit bigger than that," Jacob said, tousling Edmund's cap. "This would hardly burn for a day or two, let alone until Twelfth Night."

Edmund nodded, squinting in concentration as he peered about the wooded area. For a boy of five, he had remarkable focus, something he had certainly inherited from his mother.

Jacob crouched beside him and pointed west, where the sun was just beginning to drop toward the horizon. "I saw a few logs that might be suitable just over there, past that stand of trees. Perhaps worth a look?"

The boy's blue eyes brightened, and he scurried away, his boots leaving small prints in the inch of snow that still clung to the ground. In truth, Jacob had already scouted the area the day before and discovered the perfect Yule log, thick and heavy. But he wanted Edmund to find it, as the boy had spoken of little else in the past week.

"You've found the largest log again, haven't you?" Nell made her way to him through the snow, little Louisa perched on her hip and the nursemaid following behind. Nell's lips tugged upward, betraying her amusement despite her admonishing words.

"What is the point of a Yule log if it is not the very biggest?" Jacob moved to her, taking Louisa and swinging her up toward the clouded sky. Her squealing giggles filled the air, joining the merry singing of the servants as they gathered greenery and pine boughs with which to decorate Oakhurst.

He settled the two-year-old in his arms, and her small arms came around his neck. "Are we there, Papa?"

"Soon, Louisa," he said, tugging on one of her honey-colored curls that fell down her back. "I have great faith in your brother."

Sure enough, Edmund gave a shout not a second later. "Here, Papa! This one is enormous!"

Jacob winked at Nell. "Enormous should do well enough, I think."

She sighed. "I suppose we may as well put these men and horses to good use, since we brought them all along."

"Now, that's the spirit." He kissed Louisa and handed her to the nursemaid following behind Nell, then took his wife's hand and pulled her forward.

She laughed. "I cannot say who is more enthusiastic—you or the children."

"You've had far more Christmases than I," he said. "It's only fair that I be allowed a larger share of enthusiasm."

"You and Alice both," she said. "I imagine Mr. Turner is quite overwhelmed by her zeal for the holiday."

"It was fortunate he married her in summer, then, or he might have changed his mind." He grinned cheekily at Nell, and she slapped his shoulder with another laugh. Her laugh touched every part of her face, lighting her eyes and forming adorable lines around her mouth. He could not resist tugging her into his arms, pressing a kiss to those lips he so loved.

"Jacob," she protested, pushing him back. "The servants."

"They hardly mind," he said. "And if there is any day a man can kiss his wife without a care, it should be Christmas Eve."

She tipped her head to one side as she fought her grin. "Well, I can hardly argue with that."

Jacob kissed her again before she could change her mind.

ABOUT THE AUTHOR

JOANNA BARKER WAS BORN AND raised in Northern California. She discovered her love for historical fiction after visiting England as an eleven-year-old and subsequently read every Jane Austen book she could get her hands on. After graduating from Brigham Young University with a degree in English, she worked as an acquisitions editor before devoting herself full-time to writing. She enjoys music, chocolate, and reading everything from romance to science fiction. She lives in Utah and is just a little crazy about her husband and two wild but lovable boys.